THE TERMINAL INCEPTION

THE BLACKWELL CHRONICLES BOOK 2

JAMES T. AND CYNTHIA A. RUNYON

WESTBOW
PRESS
A DIVISION OF THOMAS NELSON

WestBow Press books may be ordered through booksellers or by contacting:

WestBow Press
A Division of Thomas Nelson
1663 Liberty Drive
Bloomington, IN 47403
www.westbowpress.com
1-(866) 928-1240

Because of the dynamic nature of the Internet, any web addresses or links contained in this book may have changed since publication and may no longer be valid. The views expressed in this work are solely those of the author and do not necessarily reflect the views of the publisher, and the publisher hereby disclaims any responsibility for them.

Any people depicted in stock imagery provided by Thinkstock are models, and such images are being used for illustrative purposes only.

Certain stock imagery © Thinkstock.

ISBN: 978-1-4497-8951-0 (sc)
ISBN: 978-1-4497-8954-1 (e)

Library of Congress Control Number: 2013905515

Printed in the United States of America.

WestBow Press rev. date: 3/25/2013

To All Those Who have Blessed Us

To James and Holly Runyon for their commitment to this project and tireless encouragement in following the path the Lord has placed before us.

To our daughter Cherith for her input and ability to find the smallest of errors. You are our Word Princess.

PROLOGUE

TUESDAY MORNING, JULY 7, 1966

Climbing the dusty trail, Demetrio sensed the crimson sky peppered with gray clouds was a clear indication of the day he was about to experience. "Nonlo lasci prego piovere," he mumbled in Italian, begging the heavens not to rain. Following his ascent, Doug ran up from behind.

"What are you complaining about?"

Rough English sputtered from his lips, "I hope that no rain comes."

Doug's eyes darted toward the sky, "Well, Friend, a little rain might break the monotony," he laughed, slapping him on the chest and running ahead. "Come on, we're late."

In the distance, the gathering clouds rumbled with authority.

Cresting the summit, the portly Italian worked his way through the ruins toward the tent filled with a dozen or so other doctoral students receiving their assignments for the day. Looking outward from his elevated vantage point, he grumbled, "So che sta andando piovere ," he switched to English again, "I know it's going to rain. And soon. On us." He stepped down into the tented area.

"Rain will not be your only problem, Mr. Giancoli," the expedition leader spoke with his eyes still on his thick pad of assignments. "And yes, I said "mister." The word "doctor" may never work its way to the front of your names if Mr. Taylor and yourself cannot be in attendance at 7:00 sharp."

Snickering from fellow students filled the tent as Doug glanced over at Demetrio sheepishly. The Friar returned to his clipboard and then offered a wink to his tardy friend.

Friar Virgilio Canio Corbo had been the expedition leader at the Herodium for close to four years. For every student researcher, it was a true privilege to work for the man who had excavated everything from the Shepherd's field in Bethlehem to the Mount of Olives. However, along with the honor came the strict regimen of working under his supervision. Friar Corbo dominated time and used it as his weapon.

A firm breeze swirled through, pushing clouds into the last open patches of sky.

"Where was I?" the Friar called with just enough of an Italian accent to make him sound even more intelligent than his I.Q. already proved. "Yes, here I am. John and Mohammed, please spend your efforts in the Triclinium." His eyes lifted above his spectacles. "Excavate around the benches. We are trying to determine whether Herod had the benches built or the Jewish Zealots added them during the uprising in A.D. 66."

They quietly wrote down their orders and moved toward the edge of the gathering.

"Nicole, you will be paired up with Yehoshua. Work in the Miqveh."

Nicole's hand went up, "What are we to find? The ritual bath has been thoroughly excavated and researched," she replied with an air of confidence.

"Yes, Miss LeClaire, it is vital we discover whether that particularly important feature was added during the first or second Jewish occupation; either A.D. 66 or 132. That three to four generational difference will shed much light on many other areas within the site. Look for anything that will solve that puzzle. Are there any other questions?" he asked in such a way as to not expect any.

"No sir," came the meek response.

Thunder rolled off in the distance causing a shiver down Demetrio's spine. Something niggled at the back of his mind telling him this day would be anything but normal.

"I believe we have gone through the list except for Mr. Giancoli and Mr. Taylor." Cradling the clipboard with both arms to his chest, the professor looked up with a smile. "Gentlemen, I have special work for you. Please put forth your efforts in the first bathhouse; the mosaic there needs more cleaning."

Both men groaned while the other students tried to keep from smiling.

"It will be a slow process, so take small brushes and try not to dislodge any of the thousands of tiny little tiles."

Doug responded with a kindergartener's disappointment in his voice, "Yes sir."

"Well my friends, those are the assignments for the day. Next Friday is your final opportunity to turn in Chapter One of your dissertation. Many have already handed them to me, so I will be leaving for the Studium Biblicum Franciscanum in Jerusalem to begin my reading: a reading that I know will be, well, enlightening." The students collectively felt uneasy.

Looking at his watch, he continued, "Those who have not given them to me still have a little over a week to turn in a work that should be at least 40 pages in length. If there are any questions, I will be here for a few minutes. If not, please progress to your assignments and begin to uncover history. Thank you."

The students broke off in all directions, and Doug met up with Demetrio who was already plowing full steam ahead. "Dem, do you think he has it out for us?"

"I would think we are not his favorite students," he answered with a small smile.

The wind changed direction and dropped a few degrees in temperature.

"Yeah, I bet we aren't on his Christmas card list." Doug looked up toward the sky to see the clouds rolling like waves. "I haven't ever seen a morning like this. It's creeping me out."

"I hoped it would sprinkle just a bit to break the monotony, but I don't like the look of this." Demetrio responded.

"Yeah, this isn't normal. The sky is changing so quickly. There's something, uh, ominous about those clouds." Doug cleared his head with a shake. "I'll get the trowels if you'll get the brushes."

"As you say, 'that's a deal.'"

The men selected their equipment and started down the mountain.

"Can you believe that Herod built this fortress?" Doug asked trying not to think about the way the storm was drawing in about them. "He actually took the peak of that mountain over there," pointing off to a hill that appeared to have the top sliced away, "and put it on this mountain; just because he could. He built a multiple story fortress in the desert with dining rooms, porticos, and interior and exterior gardens. The earliest known domed room is here, and then he had that pool," he said gesturing off in the distance, "that makes the Olympic sized one at the community center look like a kiddie pool. Wow, what a guy."

"It is not hard to do things such as this, with thousands of Jewish people at your disposal," Demetrio rolled down and buttoned his sleeves. "These people knew that they, and most of their family, would be killed if they did not, how do I say, volunteer their efforts."

"Just a technicality." Doug smiled. "I say this place is amazing."

The sky began to darken and now clearly encircled the ancient mound on which they stood.

Having walked the mile to the bathhouse, they continued through the main entrance and stopped.

Demetrio moaned as he sat next to the large circle enclosing a geometric design. Staring at the mosaic, "It is certainly beautiful. But still, I would rather work at another location,"

"You said it. While we're cleaning an old mosaic, everyone else is digging up ancient pottery and jewelry. Who knows, they might find Herod himself. Josephus said he's buried here."

"Doug, I doubt they will find Herod today."

"Who knows? I tell you, I won't be late tomorrow," he joked picking up his brush.

Sweeping one of the large pomegranates located on the outer edge of the mosaic Demetrio responded with a grin, "I think that was Friar Corbo's idea."

The men worked at the mosaic, brushing and cleaning, using water when needed. Periodically, they would pull up some corroded debris with a trowel, but for the most part, the work was simply tedious.

The breeze grew more intense as they worked until they had to button their sleeves down over their arms for warmth.

Lightning streaked the sky above them, creating a thunderous boom loud enough to compel the men to drop their tools and cover their ears.

"Man, I think we need to go," Doug cried, raising his voice over the sudden noise of the increased wind speed.

Demetrio stared at the mosaic.

"Did you hear me? Let's work on this tomorrow!" He repeated out of frustration and anxiety.

"Doug, help me with this." Demetrio spoke through a momentary lull in the wind. He still looked at the trowel that had found rest in the middle of the montage.

"What is it?" he responded.

The Italian looked closely at the excavation tool and where it was located, "Qualcosa e differente."

Doug looked confused, "What'd you say?"

"I am sorry. I said something is different – not right."

"It looks fine to me," Doug answered not taking his eyes from the sky above.

"No, this portion is not like the rest of the mosaic." He brushed dirt from a section of the flooring, "It appears to have been repaired or possibly added at a different time."

Doug, pulling his attention from the sky to the floor, "Why would you say that?"

"Look," he pointed with the flashlight he'd pulled from his belt, "the grout is made of a different composition and has dissimilar brush markings."

"Yeah, I guess I can see that."

The men shivered as the temperature dropped a few more degrees.

"It looks like it was finished or added by someone who didn't have the same expertise as the other designers." Demetrio leaned against one of the walls behind him and thought for a moment.

Darkness enveloped them as gray clouds billowed over the mount.

"Doug, would you please hand me the larger trowel?" he asked as he returned to the 2000 year old picture.

"Dem, what are you going to do? If you mess up that art work, Corbo will have your hide and mine. Remember, he said we may never have the word doctor in front of our names."

"I remember," he replied not looking up. Tiny pelts of rain wet his hair, and he had to reach up a moment to push the thick black mop aside. He leaned back down to continue his work.

"Why are you still scraping? You never make a move without clearing it through the big man himself," Doug said pulling the small trowel from his partner's hand.

Looking up he shot a worried glance over his shoulder. "I need to find out what has happened here." He stuck his hand out, "May I have the larger tool?"

Doug slapped it into his waiting palm with a *thunk*.

Methodically he began to outline an area that formed a square in the center of the floor design. "Something happened here. We must know what or why." He looked up with a cocky smirk. "What is the word, fate?"

The Herodium had held the storm from their location long enough and now began making its presence known in earnest.

"Dem, let's get out of here. The weather's getting worse." He stood to look around and saw apparent sunlight farther down the mountain, "Hey, the weather's clear down there. How can that be?" Thoroughly freaked out he spoke quickly, "We can come back tomorrow. Maybe tell Corbo about your discovery."

"I cannot leave," he answered without looking up. "If you need to go, then you may go. I must uncover the truth here." He, gesturing up without removing his eyes from his task, "I think the skies are telling us to find it."

"The skies?" Eyebrows near his hairline Doug laughed nervously, "You're talking crazy, man. Let's go!"

"Almost loose." Demetrio had traced an exact square between rows of tiles in the center of the mosaic. Continuing his methodical dissection, the line progressed deeper and deeper.

"We are at the base of the floor slab," Demetrio said sinking over three inches of his trowel into the groove below the surface of the mosaic. Following the newly dug channel around all four corners, he continued, "This section has been removed and replaced at one time – long ago," he spoke confidently.

Lightning flickered like a strobe over their location with thunder following closely behind. But like Demetrio had spoken, the weather and the finding seemed entwined. The potential discovery at their fingertips held their attention.

Doug shouted above the noise, "So what's under it?"

"I do not know. Help me."

Both men stuck their trowels beneath the different corners of the mosaic slab but could not move the heavy flooring without bending the feeble utensils.

Doug brought out a real garden spade, "I brought this just in case."

Demetrio smiled. Such tools were not to be used by the students.

They placed the garden tool under one corner and broke the last of the connection that had helped to hold the slab in place for over 2000 years.

With Doug pressing down on the spade, Demetrio inserted his fingers under the chunk of flooring and began to pull. Slowly, the 30 pound section of mosaic came loose revealing an open vault approximately six inches deep and a little less than the size of its cover.

Placing the piece of hand-made mosaic to the side, both men huddled over the opening.

"Dem, we may be in trouble here," Doug said as lightning struck the side of the Herodium and lit a small fire on one of the few trees in the area.

The atmosphere around the two men grew black, and the wind blew at a constant 20 knots. Hail hit the tools at the edge of the mosaic with a pinging sound. The Herodium that had earlier repelled the atmospheric phenomenon now acted like a magnet that pulled all of its fury upon them.

"What's in there?" Doug tried to speak over the forces around him.

Demetrio bent over the vault and shined his light into the gap. Both men looked at each other, and then Doug pulled up a vellum covering that quickly fell to pieces in his hand. What would have normally been a tragedy and the loss of an artifact was immediately dismissed by the vision of the small rectangular device that had been entombed within the vault for thousands of years.

The men moved back and looked at each other once again. They'd expected a cash of coins, a small idol, or a tablet. This was no treasure.

"What is this, Doug?" Demetrio asked, quiet alarm growing in his voice.

Lightning struck a column outside the bathhouse and shook the ground.

"What on earth? I don't know. I've never seen anything like it," he shouted.

Demetrio bent over and slowly brought up the new discovery. The four inch square finding, roughly a quarter inch thick immediately blinked to life upon his warm touch. Both men jumped as Demetrio dropped it like a hot rock.

With the storm now at full strength and culminating on their position, both men huddled next to the wall where a partial roof protected them.

Doug picked up the device and looked at the small screen. "What is this thing?"

Rain now fell in buckets and lightning struck the ground on the outskirts of their position. The thunder warned them as if they'd opened Pandora's Box.

"I do not know," the Italian yelled as he bent over and looked at the display. "It says, 'For the eyes of Dr. Todd Myers.'"

Doug added, "I've never seen this kind of technology. How did this get under the mosaic?"

Hail sounded like bullets ricocheting off of the rock walls.

Staring at the discovery, Demetrio spoke under his breath as the raging storm blistered the Herodium with light and sound. "This is not from the past, but from the future. Who could have left this? Who is Dr. Todd Myers?"

"I have a feeling we'll both be old men before we know the answer to this riddle. We need to go. Let's get this to Friar Corbo." Drenched in rain, the two men turned simultaneously from the shelter into the tempest, illumined by a terrifying world they did not know existed.

"Honey, are you alright?" Sara whispered. "Hudson, wake up," knowing the risks of waking him too abruptly she lightly massaged his shoulder.

He mumbled something, but didn't awaken.

Getting nervous, she slid from the bed quietly, her light gown slipping over her slender frame as she tip-toed to his side.

"Hudson, Love. Wake up," her frown mirrored his unconscious one. Lifting her fingers to his cheek, she wondered for the hundredth time tonight what he had been through in the week he'd been gone.

The man shot up into a remarkably alert position and looked around the room, sending Sara unceremoniously back on her haunches.

"Where am I?" he barked uncertainly.

"You're at home with me." She spoke quietly. Her left knee was throbbing from the twist it had taken, but still she kneeled down beside him once again. "Everything's alright. Everyone is fine." Her hand came back to his cheek for the caress she knew would begin to calm him.

The Secret Service agent saw her long blonde hair and bright blue eyes in the morning light and relaxed. He stared at her for a moment, then pulled in a deep breath and exhaled the visions he'd been unable to dispel in his sleep.

She reached for a tissue from the night stand and wiped the sweat from his forehead. The reality of his dreams faded, and he hauled his legs over the side of the bed.

"Hudson, what were you dreaming?"

Hunched over, he felt the weight of the world on his back as he considered her question. Instead of answering, he focused on the pink silk pooled around her knees, lifting his eyes to see it draping her lovely legs. He drew another cleansing breath into his massive frame before feeling his strength begin to return.

"You were yelling this time - needing to stop something before the end of the world as we know it." She sat next to him on the bed. This time the worry seeped into her voice. "What happened last week?"

She knew better. He knew she did. "Sara, I… I can't tell you. Even if it were allowed, it's too incomprehensible to explain." She stood even as he spoke, and lifted his chin in both tender hands as if he were one of their children. He prepared himself.

"You just disappeared. Four days. The children prayed. I prayed. I prayed for your safety every moment of every day."

Tears filled her eyes without spilling. It made them look even bluer. He looked into her eyes for the first time since he'd returned, and smiled weakly, "Your prayers, they meant everything. God Himself got me through. I'll tell you about it soon enough. Some things I can share, it's just that, I can't yet."

Keeping secrets from her ranked as one of the most difficult tasks he went through as a CIA agent. But, while he didn't enjoy the secrets, her protection outranked his need to share his experiences. Besides, he liked her purity. He enjoyed that she only saw the world as beautiful and clean, never the true evil he found around every corner.

"Hudson, have I lost you again?" He looked up to see her smile knowingly and tried to grin in return.

"Aw. Ow," he grimaced gingerly. How could smiling hurt?

"Baby, what can I do to make some of this better?" she asked, snuggling next to him on the bed, and looking as innocent as ever. Her sweet question brought some ideas to his mind.

He leaned over to kiss her lightly and caress her bare shoulder.

"Children!" Sara shouted in his ear as she bolted upright. Finding air instead of what he was aiming for, he pitched forward onto the bed. Alone.

The room erupted with noise as their two children burst in.

"Mommy, look what the Easter bunny brought me," Amy giggled, holding a large basket of candy in one arm and a stuffed bunny named Cotton she'd just gotten for her fifth birthday under the other.

"Yeah, look at all of this," seven-year-old Michael added, evidently having worn his shirt backwards all night. "I won't need breakfast today, because I have all this candy."

"Wow, Buddy, that sounds great," Hudson tried to smile with the left side of his face in a way that didn't look like a grimace. He quickly noticed Sara's disbelieving glare.

"No one eats any candy until after lunch," She laughed as she took control of the situation.

Straining through the soreness, the agent got up and went over and pulled his children to him on the floor, "Do you know what day it is?" he asked looking at their bright eyes.

"Yeah, it's Easter," Amy yelled, grabbing a large chocolate bunny from her basket.

"That's right. This is the best day of the year," Hudson continued.

"The best day is Christmas because we get presents," Michael's guileless frown made his heart lighten.

"No, Easter is the best day. It's the day Christ rose from the grave." He lifted them to their feet in one motion and patted their bottoms toward the door, "Get your clothes on, we're going to church and celebrate!"

The children scooted off to their rooms in excitement while Sara looked at her husband.

"Hmmm. I've never seen you quite that excited over Easter." She'd know him too long to not see a difference today of all days.

"My love," he said, wrapping his arm around her waist, "I have a completely new understanding." He kissed her once again, lingering before taking a moment to look her over. "Now. Let's get dressed."

He released her and started toward the shower, "Oh and by the way, we'll have some new friends going with us to service."

Sara stared in stunned silence at her husband as he closed the bathroom door.

—

A buoyant smile lit Todd Myers' face as the automated front door slid open for him. Visiting hospitals had never been his favorite task. Ministry had required it of him for years, and he'd enjoyed bringing the light, grace and peace of God's Word into the darkened rooms and sometimes hearts of those in pain. But opening a patient's door often brought unwelcome surprises. He shook off the memories.

Today, he giddily entered the gift shop to pick up a balloon bouquet to add to the stash already in his arms. Hospitals had never made him feel like this before.

And, while every visit was different, he'd spent the last two nights here in this world class facility, and returning from his brief shopping trip gave him the feeling of coming home.

Balancing a dozen roses and a box of chocolates in one arm, and a large bag filled with clothes from a high-end ladies store on the other, he paid for the balloons and wrapped the attached ribbons around his fist for security.

He inhaled the fresh orange scent as he passed a janitor cleaning the floors, and sighed. Today was Easter. He couldn't stop from smiling.

Landscapes dotted the white washed walls of the corridors on the way to his destination, and Todd noticed many a rank and style of military uniform as he navigated Walter Reed National Military Medical Center.

He smiled at the Captain as he entered the elevator.

Six floors and a brief evasive chat about the reason for all his purchases, he exited with a spring in his step.

Loud Hebrew shouting coming from down the hall changed his spring to a sprint. Doctors and nurses from every corner of the floor were running toward the room with the noise.

"Oh, Aaliyah," he muttered under his now heaving breath. A balloon, caught in the breeze, slapped him in the face.

"*Ghadal, ghadal!*"

Todd pushed his way through the multitude of doctors and nurses.

"*Ghadal, ghadal!*"

"She's saying stop!" he yelled, finding Aaliyah standing on her bed preparing to hit a nurse with a bedpan. Her olive colored eyes were wide with fright and she was obviously about to cry.

"Dr. Myers, I have to give her this last shot," the frantic nurse spoke back at him. "I came in, turned on the television because she looked bored and lonely and then took out the shot. She started pointing at the TV as if she'd seen a ghost, and when she saw the needle, she went nuts."

"Yes, ma'am, I imagine neither one of them helped the situation." He tossed his bundles onto the chair, wrestled the balloons into submission behind it and pushed his way to Aaliyah's side.

"I've got to report this. I think she's having a nervous breakdown or something." The nurse herself looked close to tears. Todd shook his head and sighed.

Aaliyah's hand reached into his immediately, and he helped her sit down on the bed once again.

"She's fine now, just nervous. She comes from a very small village and hasn't seen much technology. The uh, last week has been really tough for her, and I probably shouldn't have left at all, but I'm here now," he stated.

Looking at the large crowd, he dismissed them with a waving motion, "It's alright now. She's fine. Nothing to see here," he chuckled. They hesitated. He put on his warmest smile, "Thank you for your concern and the situation is under control. Thank you everyone."

The crowd finally dispersed leaving the lone nurse with her last shot at the ready. Todd spoke quietly to the tiny woman who had caused all the commotion. After a minute or so, she slowly raised her arm and looked away.

"Nurse, I believe she's ready. Please make it quick," he begged.

She administered the shot and grumbled, "Well, I'm glad that's the last one. The doctor should be in a few minutes to give you her papers."

"Thank you."

Looking back at the beautiful fair skinned woman, he melted in her gaze.

"Tawd, no go gaen," she said in broken English, grabbing again for his hand.

Sitting on the side of the bed, he touched her cheek, "No Aaliyah, I won't go again."

He picked up the box of candy he'd hastily tossed on the chair and opened it. "Try this," he offered with a big smile.

Looking into the box, she picked a truffle from the middle and took a bite. Immediately she began talking excitedly.

"Aaliyah, slow down. My Hebrew is not as good as yours."

She continued to babble as she took another.

Todd laughed and showed her the roses and balloon bouquet. She gently felt the petals of the flowers before turning her wide eyes toward the balloons. She stared. Her mouth opened and then shut again.

"Balloon," he said pointing to the large Mylar sphere covered with the words, "Get Well Soon."

"Buhlooon."

"Good."

She tugged on the strings, watching the balloons bounce up and down. He turned to open the bag of clothes purchased for her. Pulling out and setting aside the pants and shirts, she focused in on a red dress.

Touching gently the silky looking material, she looked up at Todd. He felt his face warming.

"Yes, it's yours." He picked up the dress and mimicked putting it on. "You wear it."

She cocked her heard to the side, looking like she had no idea what to do next.

"Wow, this is going to be fun," he said with some concern, "we're going to need the nurse to come back and show you how to put it on. How are we going to explain this?" He rubbed the back of his neck for an instant before pressing the call button.

—

Hudson waited on the front steps of Abundant Life Church. The non-denominational congregation his family had attended for years probably occupied the face of a *Hallmark* card somewhere. Its red brick, stained glass, and large Corinthian columns finished with a tall spire pointing into the blue April sky.

It gave the presence of a beautiful country church that in reality sat in one of the larger suburbs of Washington. The cherry blossoms finished the look of perfection.

He'd always loved driving to church on Sundays, and rounding the corner to see the pristine building. Today, however, it could have been a dilapidated warehouse for all he was concerned. It wasn't the building who had cared for and ministered to his family last week. The church was its people. And these people meant so much more to him today.

Of course, they'd been there many times before. When Hudson was shot protecting a Congressman, the sweet people of Abundant Life watched after his family while he recovered. When an assignment forced Hudson to be gone for several weeks, the people always came to help Sara and the kids get through the lonely nights. So, the beautiful façade of the century old building represented the beauty within more than the years of upkeep.

As Hudson watched the parking lot, Sara entered the portico from the tall white doors behind him. "Honey, I've had everyone in that building asking about you. Your face is all scratched up, you're still limping and that bandage on your head is just drawing questions like flies. When I dropped the children off in Sunday School, Michael told his teacher that the beat up bad guy's a lot worse."

Hudson laughed then held his side, "It hurts to laugh," he squinted.

Sara moved closer and spoke quietly, "We should have discussed this earlier, but with it being Easter I forgot. What do I tell everyone this time?"

With a quirky grin he grunted, "Tell them I was a little slow taking out the trash last night, and you had to teach me a lesson."

Sara raised her five-foot-four-inch self to her full height of nearly hitting his chin, with her heels on, and held up a tightened fist, "You better not get yourself in this kind of situation again Mister, because I kind of like your body the way it is."

Hudson kissed her on top of her head with a smirk, "I'll do my best, baby."

Tires squealed and Hudson turned his head to observe a car entering the parking lot. It was a black sedan with plain wheels, a short antenna on the top and government plates. "That has to be them," he mumbled. "Come on honey, they're here!"

He reached for her hand and pulled her along behind him. "I've never seen you so excited to introduce me to your friends," Sara nearly ran into his backside as he stopped abruptly before crossing the parking lot. "These people must be very special to you."

"You have no idea. They both saved my life."

"What are their names?" she asked trying to keep up with her still limping husband.

"Todd and Aaliyah. Oh yeah…" Hudson stopped in the middle of the parking lot and took his wife's hands. With a funny look on his face he announced, "Aaliyah is from another country and doesn't speak very good English. Hardly any English at all. Maybe just a few words. Really probably zip, nadda, zilch."

Sara frowned at his oddly evasive speech.

"She will also be pretty overwhelmed, if I'm guessing right."

"Overwhelmed?" she squeaked in confusion.

"Yeah, pretty freaked out," the agent murmured.

Sara stared sideways at her husband. A moment later a white SUV pulled around them and rolled down the window. Dr. Tom Meadows, a local pediatrician poked his head out.

"Hudson, what happened to you?" he yelled.

"I fell out of bed," Hudson responded blandly. The pediatrician laughed at his quick retort.

"Well you may want to start sleeping on the floor," he parried then drove off to get out of the way of the black sedan waiting behind him.

Sara continued the conversation, "Hudson, don't worry about me. Aaliyah and I will get along just fine. Women have an implied sisterhood." She started again for the car leaving Hudson to wonder what on earth that meant.

With the agent trailing she asked one more question, "How long have you known Todd and Aaliyah?"

"It seems like millennia," he offered. "Hey, wait up!"

Aurius of Antioch, as he was known in the king's court, viewed the azure sky of northern Israel from his breakfast table. Looking over his shoulder, he allowed himself to watch his lovely Jewish concubine finish dressing. Given different circumstances he could see himself falling for the small beauty, but that was not why he was here.

His hand hovered over a bronze plate replete with pomegranates, melons, tzabar, dates, and various breads. He chose the last fig and popped it into his mouth, bursting its sweet, gooey flesh.

A gentle breeze floated in from the balcony. He walked out onto the uncovered space, ducking as always to clear the doorway with his six-foot two stature.

His vantage point from the Herodium offered a clear view of northern Israel. A glance to the right and the man took in the beauty of the fertile desert adjacent to the Dead Sea. *How could a body of water incapable of sustaining life grace the land with such splendor?*

Looking straight from his second floor living quarters in the main tower, Aurius saw Jerusalem. Its inhabitants would be scurrying about this morning after an entire twenty-four hours spent honoring the Sabbath. Irritation narrowed his eyes.

"Fifty-two days a year lost to such worthless worship. A waste of man hours," he muttered under his breath.

It irked him to see the devotion these Jews had for their God. *Nonetheless, I am determined not to be angry today,* he thought to himself.

With a brief look to the west he considered the Mediterranean Sea and all of the ships moored in the harbor of Caesarea Maritima.

Another irony, to see ships from the balcony of one's home in the desert. But how delightful to think of them bringing treasures from all over the known world to this little oasis. *When my mission is completed, I must vacation on the coast,* he thought as he turned from the view and retreated into the room.

"I'm sure the coast looks much different than when I visited last," he laughed aloud to his steward. The poor man looked at him blankly but smiled dutifully. His use of English made him even more a man of mystery among the staff.

"My, how the years have changed the landscape of the seaside." This time the steward only nodded a good morning to Keren, the lovely concubine, as she moved past him to sit in a blue and white woven chair.

"Good morning." She spoke demurely in Greek. She studied their morning breakfast tray, a delicate finger rested on her full lips. Taking the opportunity to look at her for a moment without her awareness, he tilted his head back and wondered at her unassuming sweetness. He only had a moment before she turned and caught him gazing.

"What is it, my Lord?" she asked innocently, touching her newly curled hair and gently patting at the tucks in her stola to be sure all was in place.

"Nothing at all, Love. Just enjoying the view." She blushed at the compliment and finished the bite of melon she had chosen. Plucking up a small roll, she came to him and kissed his cheek.

"I will see you this evening at the usual time, my Sweet," he called after her.

"Good bye, my Lord," her voice rang out lightly down the hallway as the steward closed the door behind her.

As Aurius removed his night clothes the servant gathered his daily wear and waited to help him dress. Aurius gazed in a polished copper mirror surrounded by a large wooden frame and pulled at his beard.

"I look forward to cutting this off," he muttered. At 54, he was considered fairly old for the time. But he had kept his athletic build strong and lean and the sun had blessed him with enough of a tan to add strength to his face. In all, his appearance allowed him to gain a higher level of distinction in this society.

But having always been clean shaven, the beard would not be missed when this charade was over.

The man stopped pulling at his unwanted facial hair and stared into the mirror. *I wonder.* He thought for a moment. *Is this all worth it? Today marks one year in this country. How can anything be the same after living as Aurius of Antioch?*

When offered this mission, he had taken it with enthusiasm. Knowing prison awaited him; helping out someone in the highest level of government was an easy choice. Righting a great wrong in his own life far outweighed the fact that he was likely being used by that man.

Nonetheless, I'm restoring a future that should have been. For her. He reminded himself. That his greatest desire and his superior's plans had happened to coincide seemed nothing short of miraculous at the time. Now he wondered. He didn't believe in miracles.

Aurius gazed at his warbled reflection in the first century mirror. How crude a thing to be so highly valued here. After a year, everything still seemed disconnected, so disjointed, yet all was going according to plan.

He suddenly realized that he'd never truly expected to be successful in his mission, imagining something to stop him before now. Today's work held the key, and nothing even remotely threatened to stop him.

Thinking back, Aurius remembered that one year ago today he'd been on his way to prison in a very different world than this. With no hope and no one to even worry about him, he'd briefly considered suicide. He had a gun in his desk, loaded as usual for security purposes. Sliding it from the drawer he'd gripped it between his fists, indecision gnawing at him.

When one of the men guarding him had been called away for a few moments, the other was on his cell phone in the corner hashing out details of motorcade transport and arrival times.

The moment before he pulled the trigger, the guard outside had crashed through the open door and barked orders for an emergency meeting with a higher up somewhere. So the gun was shoved back into the drawer and his shaking hands were hidden in his pockets as he followed the guard to the waiting vehicle.

After that Saturday evening meeting where they'd defined the objective of this mission, he'd been given until eight the next morning to be en-route. With less than 12 hours to plan a project that a Special Forces team would take weeks to work they offered him every available resource.

Obviously, the will of someone more important than himself had cleared the way for the well-equipped and detailed mission.

Knowledge of first century currency, clothing, and customs, research into the geography and geology of the time they stored in an iPad packed with several long-last batteries. They'd called in an expert in middle-eastern culture to give him some pointers on living in ancient Israel, and to help him know what to wear, how to look, how to carry himself and generally how to blend in. Fortunately the man also had several outfits of workable ancient styled clothing on hand.

He laughed at the demonstration he'd received at how to dress. Looking back, learning through trial and error had proved more effective.

Next, a numismatist came - now in the middle of the night - to explain the currency of the region and allowed him to "borrow" their collections of 1st century coins from the countries of Egypt, Israel, and Turkey. How could they know which coins were actually used at this time in history? Another miracle that they were all useful to him.

Someone suggested uncut or rough cut stones of varying degrees of preciousness just in case. Rubies, sapphires, emeralds, and diamonds arrived an hour later from one supplier, and some topaz, opals, pearls, and amethyst arrived from another. He hoped their rarity in the region would offer more options.

Several pounds of gold, silver and platinum completed his stash of wealth. Most of it arrived as small, unmarked one ounce bars. He remembered looking at the bundle, as if to read the real amount of protection it offered. Lifting the large sack he'd hoped he could carry the heavy satchel through the desert.

Sheep skin bladders from a local Amish dealer arrived and were filled with three liters of water. Raisin cakes, dates and some hard flat bread concealed a small dagger at the bottom of another large leather bag. Aside from the water strapped to his back, most of the equipment hid under his voluminous clothing, with the precious items on a leather strap across his chest and the leather bag of fruit, clothing and the dagger hanging on his belt. After only twenty hours his preparation ended.

Aurius' blue eyes came into focus in the so-called mirror, and a smile grew on his face.

"Yes. It's still worth it," he smiled.

"In a year I've risen to the top, and in the next few days, it'll all be over. My life will be as it once was." He grimaced. As it should have been." Turning from the mirror he walked across the mosaic floor to the servant who now waited at attention to put on his broad striped tunic.

He stood a moment to admire the color in the stripes, not because of the vibrancy of the hues, but for what it represented. The adornments meant wealth, power, and status in society. The stripes indicated his level of senator in the Roman world.

He took a moment to feel the border of the toga that would be placed over his tunic. The toga showed that he held a curule office with power to enforce public order. That honor could only be earned by election. He had never been elected to office, at least not in this century or country, and he certainly wasn't Roman.

Waving the servant on in his work, he decided to take today, of all days, to reminisce – as he was practically dressed - about how far he had come. In his previous life, importance and power had followed him as much as he'd worked for it. The positions had taken a good many years to attain.

This time around it had only required one year. One long year. This last year had required much harder work than anything he'd ever worked for in the past. Just one year ago had been his first day in ancient Israel as a man completely unprepared for the journey.

Arriving just east of the Dead Sea his mission officially began as he exited the sphere, temporarily leaving his pack and head dress in the cockpit. Everyone in modernity believed the area to be desolate and uninhabited at this time, so present day Jordan had proven to be a good spot for entry. At least its desolation allowed his landing to cause no disturbance. Only when he realized his position as a man left alone in the middle of a land that could barely sustain life did he rethink its qualification.

Having been raised in a wealthy home and spending the last 30 years in a leadership role - sending others in to do the work he now set out to do - made him ill-equipped for the task at hand. Indeed, logistically he should have been the last person sent on any mission. His qualification for this mission lay elsewhere. He'd wanted it, and they held prison over his head.

But stepping from the vehicle he wondered. The landscape filled him with terror. He turned and grabbed his head dress from the sphere, feeling the heat radiate from the sand even this early in the morning. Hand to his forehead he peered across the desert.

Squinting out the bright morning sun he could vaguely see the Dead Sea. Off to the left should be the city of Jerusalem. Still shading his eyes he turned in a slow circle and took a quick survey of the land, absent-mindedly patting where his shirt pocket should be with his right hand. Mentally he kicked himself for trying to fish out his Armani sunglasses.

Barren land lay all around him, but some trees in clusters drew his attention far off in the direction of Jerusalem. At least he hoped that was Jerusalem. Turning back toward the sphere he shrieked in shock as momentary blindness overcame him. The highly polished mother-of-pearl covering reflected the sun like a white mirror.

Blindly he grasped for the water bags still within the cockpit and straightened to remove himself from the interior before the two parts reunited with a bang, barely missing his right hand. Immediately, the vehicle disappeared.

He blinked. "Well, that was final, wasn't it?" Exhaling, he turned on his heels to begin the journey.

For a moment the world blurred into a sea of sand and light. Taking a deep breath, he positioned the head covering and fitted it over his eyes. It offered a surprising relief from the sun's glare. Scanning the horizon again, he set out on his mission, just hoping he would make it to civilization.

Thirty minutes later, worry nagged at him as he struggled for breath with each step. The air four hundred feet below sea level felt thick and heavy in his lungs causing him to labor his breathing. Tiny droplets of sweat that had beaded on his face and the back of his neck upon entering the ancient land morphed into rivulets streaming from every pore on his body.

He lifted his eyes to monitor his heading. It looked right to him, but his navigational skills faltered in this glaring light. Looks counted for 100% of his directional equipment, so he marched on.

Several hours later, his clothes dripped with sweat. Knees weak from the strain he fell onto them a moment and felt his worries grow into fears. He should have reached at least a town on the outskirts of the city by this time. He could see his destination, but it looked just as far as it had an hour ago.

His sleep-deprived mind struggled to reason through the situation. He thought for a moment until he came to the conclusion that slogging through hot sand takes much longer than jogging the pavement around the track at the gym. Fifteen miles at home would take about 2-3 hours with all this weight he carried. Here he had no point of reference.

Reaching for his water skin, another concern took precedence over the time and distance. His water supply had depleted faster than he'd anticipated due to his output of sweat.

Even though he was dressed like anyone living in the area at this time, the clothing on his unconditioned body became a detriment rather than benefit. He understood that the layers of cloth worn by those in the Middle East acted as insulation by either trapping or releasing heat and allowing the body's temperature to remain constant.

Still, air conditioning and only a couple thin layers of clothing had been his climate far too long to make the change in a day. For him, layers of cloth soaked with his sweat just added weight and heat making every step hotter and heavier.

Sighing, the exhausted man readjusted the fifteen pound pack on his back and the smaller one under his clothes and started to move again. Even his expertly made authentic sandals had rubbed blisters everywhere they touched. The hot sand ground into the wounds, making each step seem unbearable. All dreams of success vanished along with his hope for survival.

Finally, after four and a half hours in the desert, the man dropped to his knees from heat exhaustion, unable to rise from the desert floor. In reality, he'd landed only yards from the well of a local town. If not for the children playing in the area, he never would have lived through the day.

Aurius sighed with the memory. *Another miracle*, he thought, yet he had no God to attribute it to. Funny he should be thinking of gods and miracles on today of all days. But he knew the only people to thank were simple, uneducated, unimportant people in a small village called Machaerus who found him there, piled in a heap.

The servant finished with his tunic and picked up the toga to be placed over it. Aurius looked at his hands.

"They are much tougher and stronger now," he said making a fist, "Much better prepared for the adventure ahead." The cool cloth slipped easily over his head and one shoulder.

"I will finish this work," he smiled. "The fates have willed it."

The manservant gestured for him to sit as he slid bright red sandals onto his feet, the final vestige of a man with his influence. Looking at his feet he realized how they had toughened also. The sandals that he despised such a short time ago were now desired above the expensive shoes he had once worn. In a funny way, they were an example of his ability to adapt and conquer.

The family in Machaerus had rescued him, and upon regaining his strength he had paid them well from his stash. They had provided him food, shelter and most importantly time.

He had one year to perform his tasks before anyone might come to stop his work. One year would have to be enough to change history. His rescue had been fortuitous. They'd offered him healing and kindness, and he'd gleaned language skills, cultural understanding and political knowledge.

The four months he stayed in Machaerus were a strong platform on which to work. That simple family had given him the time and the tools needed to complete his assignment.

With a wave of his hand he dismissed his servant and turned back to his breakfast table for a moment. Walking over to the tray of food he tore a final piece of bread and placed it in his mouth. The blue of the sky grew brighter by the minute, drawing Aurius back to the balcony once again.

"Today will be a beautiful day in Israel," Aurius commented as the cool dry air blew through his toga. Picking up a cup full of watered wine, he took a sip.

"Not a cloud in the sky. A perfect day to complete my work."

Watching an eagle glide to the east, the prophet's eyes stopped in the direction of the Dead Sea. Holding his gaze for what seemed an eternity; he finally broke the stare and stood straight.

"They're coming," he whispered. His mood broke with a grin, "I know they are."

Aurius of Antioch turned and headed for an anteroom just off of his main quarters. Pulling a wall hanging from its mount and a dagger from a table he started edging around a block in the wall. That the chunk of stone had been removed previously was obvious to anyone looking. The faux mortar fell like dried dirt.

Using a dagger like a crowbar, he carefully placed it into the sides and pried the block loose. When it was out far enough, he dropped his tools and pulled the mass free. Resting as he had left it approximately 4 months earlier, lay a bag containing his iPad.

Emptying the makeshift vault, the prophet quickly replaced the block and threw back up the cloth wall hanging showing the King hunting deer. Aurius laughed at the representation.

"Herod's girth is far broader than this picture depicts. Although the artist would probably have been killed if he'd made the king's portrait more…accurate," he said with a smirk.

Checking the contents and finding everything ready, he headed for the main bed chamber. Putting on wristlets, rings, and various other accoutrements he finally left the room and made one more stop at the balcony.

Looking off to the east and placing a chain around his neck given to him by the King, he relaxed.

"I know you're coming, but this time I make the rules."

Turning, he headed for the door to exit his chamber.

"Let's end this," he growled. The wooden door slammed behind him.

3 — SUNDAY MORNING, APRIL 19

Dr. Todd Myers rolled the black sedan over to the curb a little after 11:00, applying the brakes a bit too hard and nearly throwing his passenger into the windshield. He glanced in her direction briefly to see that the fragile beauty was unharmed; then dropped his head onto the steering wheel in exhaustion.

On the other side of the car Aaliyah sat stone-faced, wide-eyed and braced for battle. Todd closed his eyes and exhaled for the first time since leaving the hospital. He could still hear the small woman breathing like a locomotive. *It's a miracle she hasn't passed out from hyperventilation,* he mused.

One hand on the door grip and one on the door handle, she looked like a criminal about to make her escape. Chuckling to himself he imagined she'd have done that very thing had she figured out how to open the door. Thank heaven for child-proof locks which evidently came on the front passenger's side of this government vehicle. Of course, who wouldn't be terrified with the car hurtling through space at the breakneck speed of 35 MPH?

The glove box lay open on her lap, the contents spilled onto the floor. Her purse hung on her elbow and he noticed a Kleenex package hanging out of it. The nurse must have helped her fill the purse while he filled out exit papers. Todd took a moment to grimace at his own sad attempt to help Aaliyah with dressing like a modern-day American woman. To say he'd been clueless about sizes and styles and, well, dressing know-how, would be an understatement.

But right now every bit of his focus needed to be on the task at hand. Out of the corner of his eye Todd saw Hudson coming toward them with Sara, and he sprang from the car like a gymnast. Quickly rounding the front of the car he tried to wedge himself between his friend and the passenger door.

"Wow, how is everybody?" He ran his left hand through his light brown hair as his right jutted out to cover as much of Aaliyah's terrified face now plastered to the window as he could casually manage.

"Sure is great to see you! This must be your beautiful wife. What a beautiful day! Couldn't ask for a more beautiful Easter morning! Boy, I sure am saying beautiful a lot." His attempted smile looked more like a grimace.

Hudson stared at him a moment in an effort to figure out the reason for his friend's nervous behavior.

"Yeah, a beautiful day," he said cautiously. Gesturing to his wife, "This is my wife Sara. Sara this is Dr. Todd Myers. I owe him, well, a lot."

Sara looked him over as he spoke, curiosity about his strange behavior piquing her interest. Finally, eyebrows lifted just a tad, she extended her hand to him.

"It's nice to meet you. Thank you for helping to bring my husband back in one piece. Or at least close to one piece." His big bear hug nearly eclipsed her last word.

"Wow," he effused again. "Good to meet the woman who puts up with this guy. He talked quite a bit about you last week. It's good to put a face with all that I've heard." Hudson looked at him like he'd gone loony, while he kept Sara in his arms like an overgrown child leaving his parents for summer camp the first time.

Rocking a moment with her he managed to turn her away from the vehicle and gestured with his head toward the car window to Hudson whose eyes had started to narrow.

"She is not doing well," he mouthed over her shoulder.

Todd's frenzied speech and movements couldn't dull the roar that was rising from the front seat. He pulled away from Sara and turned back to Hudson.

"Her first car ride didn't go so well," he grunted.

"Oh what a beautiful building your church has," he spoke loudly trying to keep Sara's attention off the sudden burst of foreign language working its way through the darkly tinted windows of the automobile.

"What am I hearing?" Sara tried to work her way around.

"Oh, nothing important, Honey," Hudson replied trying to figure out what to do with the terrified and irate woman in the front seat. The whole idea of having brought her back from where they'd been was so utterly unexplainable. And Aaliyah's behavior was not making this any easier. Opening the door a small amount, the agent made a shushing sound and spoke words of quiet reassurance. Todd opened the back door behind her and attempted the same words in Hebrew.

"Everything is fine. It's alright," they both shushed and consoled. Hudson patted her on the arm like one would a small child. Aaliyah glared at them and renewed her Hebrew tirade. The two men bumped their heads simultaneously, instinctively retreating from the furious woman.

The seminary professor worked his way back to the window. "Yes, these Hebrew women love coming to church. She has been practically screaming at me to get here so she can go to worship."

Sara lifted an eyebrow, obviously bemused by the strange behavior. "Um, you know, she doesn't sound happy to me. She sounds pretty frustrated," Sara smiled at the men patiently, still trying to see around Todd into the car.

Hudson unbuckled the passenger's seat belt, pushing the door open against Todd's five foot eleven inch athletic frame. Holding her hand he helped the young woman from the car.

Todd held his breath praying she wouldn't explode in front of everyone.

"Sara, this is my dear friend Aaliyah." Pointing to Sara, "Sara…, Sara."

The petite young woman stood straight as an arrow, hazel eyes narrowed. The loveliness of her olive skin in the simple red dress contrasted with the "fight or flight" syndrome evident in her stance. She fidgeted with her light shawl, not knowing how to hold herself in the unfamiliar clothing.

Nodding in understanding to her husband Sara offered a hug to the nervous woman, her mind wondering at the information and background details she wasn't privy to. *Must be interesting stuff to have an experienced agent and a knowledgeable professor stumped about what to do with such a small little lady.*

"It's so nice to meet you. Let me take you inside and introduce you to some of my friends. I'm *sure* these gentlemen have things to talk about."

Gently pulled by Sara, Aaliyah resisted until Todd assured her it would be alright with a few Hebrew words.

Both men watched the women as they walked away. "She's beautiful, Todd. She cleaned up very well."

"Yes she did," he replied with a smile. He feigned the wiping of sweat from his brow. "I didn't think we were going to make it here."

Hudson laughed.

"It was anything but funny for a while. She didn't want to ride in the wheel chair out of the hospital. She may only be a little taller than five feet, but she is strong. Wiry. She hopped out of that chair like a gazelle! They almost committed her for psychiatric observation."

They started toward the building, the agent offering another chuckle.

"She got into the car, well, uh, we, uh, got her into the car. But once we hit the on-ramp…I guess, when we started going faster than a burro, or water buffalo or something, she just went nuts. I had to slow the car way down on the highway. I'm amazed that I didn't get a ticket for driving like a geriatric."

Hudson laughed out loud and clapped his hands. "Oh, I love it. What a story."

"I can travel the world, thwart history, reverse evil men's plots, but I can't control a tiny little woman from a third world country. Or something like that anyway."

The ladies had entered the building, and the men were walking the steps across the portico. Hudson put his arm around the professor giving him a hug as he pulled open the large door to the building, "Todd, you are starting to understand what every married man learns through much pain and sorrow. You can't control a woman."

The door closed behind them.

—

Ten minutes before the service, the halls of the small church were filling with people leaving Sunday School. Todd and Hudson entered the vestibule to find Dr. Thomas Patrick standing in his usual place, greeting people as they entered the sanctuary.

"Todd," Hudson pointed, "I want to introduce you to my Pastor."

Hudson tried to make his way through the congestion toward the Pastor when he was stopped by Charlie and Betty Corten.

Charlie smacked Hudson soundly on the back wrenching a grimace out of the Secret Service Agent. The poor man immediately regretted his action.

"Hudson, what have you been through? When you asked us to take your family home last week, you looked great. Have you been in an accident of some kind?"

Todd smiled wondering how his friend was going to get out of the question.

"Yes, I would say so," Hudson responded elusively, "Charlie, it's great to see you. You were so kind to take care of my family in my absence. I owe you."

Betty interrupted giving Hudson a hug. "You don't owe us anything. That is what friends are for."

The agent continued his forward movement until he reached the goal. In his early 60's, Dr. Patrick was the perfect image of a Pastor. He was wise and had a thorough grasp of the scripture. In his presence many had been moved to share their lives with him. Problems, blessings, and even life stories, he listened quietly and gave Biblical answers that meant something. Nothing trite, nothing irresponsible ever escaped his lips.

With warmth and true caring he turned and looked his friend over a moment, "Hudson what has happened to you? And you, my friend, seem to be pretty scratched up as well," he motioned to the professor.

"Dr. Patrick, I want to introduce you to a friend of mine, Dr. Todd Myers." The gentlemen shook hands. "He's a professor at Southern seminary teaching…"

Todd jumped in after the obvious pause, "I teach Ancient Studies specializing in Ancient Languages and Archaeology."

"How fascinating. What brings you into town? You're a long way from Louisville."

"Well, we worked on a project together last week, and we still have a few loose ends to tie up." Todd wanted to run his finger under his collar. He wasn't used to evading questions.

"Well, sir, it is a privilege to meet you. Please, be kind in your correction if I say anything inaccurate this morning."

Dr. Myers laughed. "I know I'll be blessed by your sermon, Sir."

The Pastor was ready to greet the next person in line when Hudson stopped for one last thought. "Pastor, I really need to come in and talk with you in the near future."

"Sure, Hudson, anytime."

Todd watched him trying to form a sentence, "I, uh, really think, uh, that, some things I have learned recently might offer this church, and all churches, uh, a stronger story to tell."

"Well, I uh. I look forward to hearing what you have to say," the Pastor replied, taken aback by Hudson's statement.

Leaving the Pastor they walked into the traditional sanctuary. The building formed the typical rectangle with a balcony at the back and a pulpit in the front. Behind the pulpit, three rows of chairs housed a small choir of no more than 25. Flanking the choral group to the left was a black baby grand piano and on the right an electronic organ.

There on the left in the 5th pew from the front were Sara and Aaliyah. It was obvious through Sara's hand gestures and bright smile she was introducing Aaliyah to another of her friends. The small Hebrew woman fidgeted, quietly scanning the room for Todd. When she saw him she immediately left the small group and ran back toward him.

When all heads turned to follow the young woman in red, Hudson knew that Sara would be in damage mode, trying to smooth over with the older couple the breach of protocol by the Hebrew female. The agent knew his wife was quite up to the task.

Aaliyah walked the last few steps with the men. "Hey, Honey, did you get the kids into children's church?" Hudson smiled taking his seat.

"Oh yes, they love their class."

Todd sat next to Hudson while Aaliyah was on the far side.

Sara whispered to her husband, "You will need to tell me what is going on here."

"What do you mean, honey," he said putting his arm around his wife, hoping to divert the obvious questions he knew were coming.

"You know what I mean, Hudson Jonathan Blackwell."

Using all three names was a technique she only reserved for the children when they were in trouble.

"It's as if she's never been in a church before…or even a building. She was mesmerized by the large screen up front showing announcements. She felt the pews, carpet, walls, doors, my dress. She's freezing as if she's never experienced air conditioning."

The professor overheard the conversation and placed his jacket around Aaliyah.

"She'll hardly look anyone in the eyes, as if she doesn't feel she's of the right social class to be here. Aaliyah is a beautiful lady and looks to have such an innocent heart - almost naïve." Sara stopped for a second. "I know you haven't been to Africa in the last week, but I would swear you picked her up out of some pre-industrial village and plopped her right in the middle of one of the most powerful cities in the world."

Mumbling, Hudson responded as the light grew dimmer in the worship center, "Sweetie, that would be crazy, right? Oh, look the service is beginning."

Sara raised an eyebrow at Hudson's obvious off-put. "We'll talk about this later."

Todd whispered in Hudson's other ear, "I don't see you getting out of this one."

Sara offered Todd a look with her bright blue eyes, indicating that she knew he was somehow in on whatever was going on.

Cowering from her stare, he pushed back in his seat and looked forward.

Abundant Life Church was very traditional in its approach and everyone seemed to enjoy it. During each of the elements of the service, Aaliyah eyes focused steadily on the front. The piano and organ thrilled her soul during the prelude. She loved hearing everyone sing and especially enjoyed the music by the choir, which was obvious by her mumbling of

Hebrew words and the spontaneous clapping of her hands — something that was not done much in this small church. She seemed enthralled when the lights changed, or a new PowerPoint slide went up. By the time the Pastor began his sermon, it was evident that she had already been part of a life-changing experience.

"Good morning, everyone, on this most important of the Lord's days," Dr. Patrick said as he placed his Bible on the pulpit and opened it toward the back. "We will be in several books of the Bible this morning," the Pastor walked to the side of the pulpit and looked out at the people. "This is Easter Sunday morning, the day when we celebrate the resurrection of Jesus. It is through this resurrection that we have life, the possibility of eternity with God the Father.

This morning I am going to take a different approach to an Easter sermon. I want to trace through Jesus' life to show the miraculous ways God protected his Son, and therefore, why He has the ability to protect us and care for all of our needs. Here is a brief overview.

Let's think for a second about Mary. What if Joseph had rejected her; taken her before the priests for having a child out of wedlock? The story would clearly have turned out much differently. Or think about Herod, and how he tried to kill Jesus by slaying all of the baby boys in the region. If God hadn't have sent an angel to Joseph in a dream, how would the story have ended?

Has anyone heard of the transitive property in geometry? I see a few hands out there. This property simply states that if A equals B and B equals C, then A equals C. It seems very simple, but it took centuries to understand, and I believe it can apply to our sermon today.

It is my argument on this Easter morning, that if God can miraculously protect His Son who was to come and offer His life on our behalf, then He can protect us.

Please open your Bibles to Matthew 1. We are going back to the beginning and will spend our time tracing the life of Jesus to learn about His protective Father." He returned to the pulpit and paused a moment to let the buzzing of page turns to subside before he began to read.

Hudson felt a buzzing in his own coat pocket while Todd looked at his waist. Even though both men had their devices muted, half of the church looked over at the pair with "silent" devices.

The agent was the first to get his phone from his pocket and look at the number, and the professor did the same. With both their phones in front of them, each man noticed they were receiving calls from the same number.

Looking to the women next to them and making a quick apology they left together, rather awkwardly, through an exit in front leading to a hall adjacent to the sanctuary. Todd was the first to answer the call.

"Hello, this is Dr. Todd Myers."

"This is Hudson, who am I speaking with?"

"You need me to come where?"

"I am at church, Sundays are my day off. Get someone else on the case."

"I am an archaeologist, but this doesn't sound like my area of…"

"So you found something. What has that got to do with me?"

"That has to be some kind of mistake."

"It said what…that is not possible."

"No way. Fine, I'll be there."

Hudson took control knowing they were speaking to different people about the same problem. "We will be there in 20 minutes. I want all personnel on lock down and all equipment with a triple guard. Do you understand?" He jabbed his finger at the screen as Todd finished his call.

The professor looked at his friend, "What happened? I mean, how could anything like this have happened?"

"We need to go. My wife is not going to like this." He peeked into the sanctuary and caught his wife's eye, then closed the door knowing she would bring Aaliyah along with her.

Within seconds both ladies came through the door.

Eyes filled with a weary sadness, Hudson looked at Sara.

"You have to go, don't you?" Sara asked. "It's important isn't it?"

"Very much so," he said as if knowing what he was about to get into.

Giving him a big hug she reached up and kissed his lips, "Go. I'll do the Easter egg hunt with the kids."

"I'm so sorry. I'll make it up to you and the kids. I promise. I love you."

Todd was trying to explain the same situation to Aaliyah, but it was obvious that leaving her would cause a scene. "Hudson what do I do?"

"We need to go. She's our problem. We'll find a place to park her when we get there. Church is no location for drama – especially on Easter."

Turning and walking down the hallway, Hudson looked back to find his wife on her knees in front of a chair praying. He knew that if what he thought had happened did happen, they would need all of the prayers they could gather.

4 — SUNDAY MORNING, APRIL 19

Aurius was highly prized by the King. Many an hour he spent in the man's presence, yet he had never been invited into his private chamber. His sigh resonated against the stone walls as he descended the staircase from his quarters on the second floor of the main tower.

To his right, the steps that led to the last two floors stretched from the landing below. The floor above his own remained open for the many dignitaries Herod entertained. Even some generals had enjoyed a night or two, along with the usual heads of foreign countries and a few of his concubines who occupied the space permanently for guests' amusement.

Aurius had heard many a story from the third floor, and more than he cared to hear through the limestone walls. Nonetheless, an invitation to the place had never been offered him. But that was about to change.

At least he hoped it would after today's meeting with the great ruler.

Herod himself resided above it all, on the uppermost floor where he allowed only the elite to enter. A heated bath, sauna, temple room and many other amenities were rumored to fit the spacious residence overhead.

Aurius ducked under the ceiling just above the turn in the stairs and began his descent past the first level which housed the head of security for the fortress. This level alone offered him freedom of movement with its domed ceilings and many pillars lining the heightened walls. He entered the great hall, marveling again at the privilege of seeing this place as it was intended to look.

These domes were the first of their kind, but the room itself he considered the gaudiest of all with the floor paved with white and black mosaics, and the walls covered in frescoes of many colors and designs. Indeed, it was a sight to see.

Shading his eyes he stepped into the bright daylight of the central courtyard and wound his way quickly through the hot and cold bath houses, saunas, and several mini-temples to various gods. Unless he wanted to scale a mountain this was the only out.

Roman guards lined the exit but made no eye contact as he continued to the main gate. Aurius sauntered as casually as possible past them all, looking as if he were merely out on a stroll. His focus, however, remained on the chariot he needed to procure for the short trip downhill to the pool and central pavilion some 400 feet below.

Commanding the waiting servant to bring a chariot, Aurius of Antioch looked down toward his destination. The earliness of the hour allowed for only a few gardeners puttering amongst the various flowers forced to bloom in this desert region. This oasis in the wilderness was a testament to Herod's ability and he marveled at all he had accomplished in this primitive time. Even the pool below him would dwarf four Olympic sized pools. Hundreds could easily swim at once, but the twenty-five he'd counted in the pool at the King's birthday party were the most he had ever seen bathing.

"To the Central Pavilion," Aurius commanded the servant who had just returned. He opened the door as Aurius stepped into the seated chariot drawn by two horses and helped the prophet into position. The servant walked to the side of the team of horses guiding them slowly down the steep grade to the base of the mountain.

Acres of wheat, hay, and safflower covered the countryside. The lush vegetation in the area always surprised Aurius. Rows of beans, chickpeas, and various legumes could be seen surrounding crops such as melons, and berries. Even the breeze from the coast carried the smell of citrus from the orchards of Shamouti oranges, lemons, kumquats, and limes.

This land did not produce naturally as did the lush and green Northern Israel. Here it should be desolate, but the countless hours of forced labor of the Jewish people produced this lovely landscape. They dotted the entire hillside, digging, tilling, pruning and planting. Farther to the left several others hung from the side of the tower, fixing mortar joints, painting or adding more garish additions to the already extravagant dwelling... all employed by the great King Herod.

Even his guide walked the half mile up and down the hill dozens of times a day for residents and guests of the king. Aurius of Antioch might have been one of these workers if not for luck.

"Luck," he mused, *"had very little to do with it."* Returning to that place in recent memory gave him pause. He had achieved so much in such a short time.

Four months he had labored in Machaerus, finally grasping a good part of the language and customs. But in spite of his ability to at last blend in culturally, his newly tanned skin and white beard did little to cover the fact that he was not a Jew. His easy and confident manner, developed from years of playing in the political arena, gave him an air of defiance in this ancient era of submission and servitude.

Aurius stretched his left arm, draping it over the back rest of the small chariot, and let a small chortle escape. His height had brought him attention. At 6'2" he towered over most men. Whether his height or manner, something about him had alerted a centurion passing through Machaerus, and he was arrested and jailed for subversion.

At the time he'd been terrified, but now he realized how well-placed that fear had been. Having met Herod personally, he now understood the old saying that it was better to be a pig than Herod's son. The man's paranoia drove him to kill time and again. His own family, generals, consultants, servants, not to mention the many Jews and anyone remotely suspected of treason suffered because of his mental illness.

Thus Aurius, the arrogant white-bearded giant received a quick trial and conviction and sat awaiting his execution for three days. The awareness of his situation seeped into his bones. All his work and plans had no hope of completion.

His desperate mind summoned a time when he'd attended Sunday School with his grandparents as a child. A story about a man named Paul who'd been arrested. In the story he remembered how Paul freed himself from death simply by stating he was a Roman citizen and thus required a hearing before the Emperor.

So Aurius did the same. In the best Greek he could muster, he detailed that he was a Roman citizen, and therefore wanted a hearing before the Emperor. Immediately, activity and anxious words flew between guards and the centurion just entering the room. He was told to sit and not speak until the matter could be attended to.

Looking back at that moment, Aurius wondered at the convenience of the thing. Why that story should come to mind. How the centurion walked in right as he requested the hearing. He paused in his memories. So many things should have gone wrong, and yet all had resolved in his favor – up until this moment. He shook off the feeling of Providence for the third time in a day and resumed the memories leading up to this minute.

Knowing that his next hearing would be before the man he had come to find, Aurius had sat on the filthy stone bench. Formulating his thoughts and plan of action quickly took precedence over shrinking from the putridity of the place. There he had taken stock of his skills and advantages and coordinated them with his ultimate purpose and come up with a strategy he knew could be successful.

If not, he'd rot in this cell until his citizenship could be disproven and his death sentence finally carried out. Just minutes after completing his blueprint for success, seven soldiers arrived to escort him into the great hall.

Aurius caught a glimpse of the ruling Roman King over Israel. The man before him was terrifying in his presence. Short and robust, the king appeared close to 80 years of age, complete with gray hair and a long beard hanging over his regal clothes. None of this inspired the physical reaction he experienced, just the complete terror of whether his words might free him or impose his execution.

Remembering his first entry into Herod's presence always brought him some measure of pride. He had moved gracefully past the massive columns and seats full of spectators with all the self-importance he could muster. He carried himself like an emperor, head high and nose in the air. Once past the fifth set of columns he was able to view the entire front of the room. Up a few steps from the floor, Herod the Great sat in the center flanked by three high magistrates on either side. The King's chair rose above the others, but all were over-sized to the extreme with the center being the grandest. All had attendants flurrying around attempting to meet their every need.

Twenty feet before the throne, the entourage stopped and left him alone. For a moment he thought he might faint. Unlocking his knees, he breathed deeply and relaxed.

"Good King Herod!" came a loud voice reading from a parchment, "You have before you one who has been tried by the court of Jerusalem and found to be guilty of subversion and treason." Fire lamps burned ominously all around the dark windowless room as the audience grew silent. "He has claimed his right as a Roman citizen to receive this hearing before the King. The judgment is now yours to render." The announcer bowed, and procured his position to the right of the throne.

The King picked up one last grape from a tray held by a young female slave and waved her off. Looking up condescendingly from under his bushy eyebrows he spoke, "You do not look like a Roman to me."

Knowing his Greek was limited, he chose his words carefully. "I am a proud member of Roman society."

"You do not sound like a Roman. You do not look like a Roman either, therefore you must be an enemy of me and of Rome."

Aurius took the first risk imposed by his plan and interrupted the King, "My name is Aurius of Antioch and I am a prophet." The name had rolled off his lips just as he had intended it to. A moment before he'd almost used his given name.

"A prophet," the King sat up a bit straighter.

"Yes my King, a prophet," he tried not shake. "I have spent many years in the East studying the stars. I have come to show you what I have learned."

Herod cocked his head and peered down on the man. "A prophet. A seer. What have you learned that would make me think you are any other than a treasonous liar?"

Years before when his daughter was young, he had entertained her with simple magic tricks like pulling a coin from her ear. He was never good at it, but his daughter loved it and wanted to see it again and again. Standing as tall as possible, the prophet quietly pulled his hand from his tunic. Secretly palming the *Bic* lighter he always kept tucked in his robe, he waved his hands around and after pulling one hand from another and making large motions; he lit the lighter making it look like fire was coming from his hand and causing the entire room to gasp.

Being a magician, or at least pulling it off this time, he drew everyone's attention to his other hand while he returned the lighter to his tunic. Roman soldiers were looking for large items when placing criminals in jail, not tiny vials in one's undergarment.

The King jumped to his feet while the other magistrates began whispering among themselves "You are a magician!"

He tried not to contradict the King's accurate assessment outright "No sir, I am a prophet." Staying focused he looked the king in the eye-something no one did-and spoke with authority, "Have there been lights in the skies?"

Laughing, the King grumbled dismissively, "There are always lights in the skies. Too many to count." The room broke out in mocking laughter to support the King.

"I believe the King knows of the one I speak. Is there a light in the sky that your astronomers cannot explain? One shining down on your kingdom?"

At this, Herod left his platform and made his way gingerly down the few stairs to the floor. He came face to face with the prisoner. The room fell silent.

Herod whispered, "Who are you, and why are you here?"

Aurius repeated the question "Is there a light in the sky that your astronomers cannot explain?"

"I know the light." The King spoke now with quiet eagerness.

Aurius the Prophet felt more confidence at the King's momentary weakness than he had since beginning this mission. "I have studied it."

"What information do you have?" The King continued.

Being genuine and clear, the tall man looked down at the Monarch and said, "I know that it brings peril to you and your nation."

The King's eyes grew wide as with a fear that had suddenly become apparent.

"Given the opportunity, I would consider it an honor to work in your court and prepare you for this storm on the horizon. May I say, Sir, that I have studied all over the east to ensure *your* kingdom remains strong? I am no subversive. I am at your will," he finished by lowering his head and bowing slightly.

Herod looked the man over before returning to his chair. He stood focused on his new prophet for several seconds before sitting.

"This man will be immediately released into my custody and shall be given the position entitled, 'Prophet of the King.' He will use his training and abilities to benefit the empire." Still looking shaken by the private conversation, Herod observed again the man before him, "As I have said, so let it be done." The King immediately left the room, ending the day of court before noon.

Following the King with his eyes, Aurius knew peace for the first time in months. Everything was on course. He had gotten himself out of the worst possible situation. It was indeed a monumental occasion, and things had gone splendidly ever since. He shrugged off the haze of remembering and breathed in deeply the warm air.

"We must be at the base of the mountain," he mumbled as the Central Pavilion came into view in the distance.

"Direct to the bathhouse," he barked at the driver and gripped his cloth bag tighter.

Passing the large pool encircled by over 80 columns, the chariot slowed in front of the Lower Bathhouse. The driver helped him step down, took his orders to be back in an hour and left as he had come. Aurius proceeded into the large building.

After searching the anterior rooms, he knew he was alone and would be left that way for quite a while. He walked across the open expanse filled with pools of differing temperatures. Beside a large potted plant in the corner, he bent down and dug just under the dirt surface. After finding a few tools and the elements to make mortar that he had left days earlier, he went over to one of the most notable spots in the room—a large mosaic of geometric designs, pomegranates and apricots.

If a prophet had special knowledge from the divine, then Aurius of Antioch would fulfill half of the requirements. For he chose this spot because he knew it would be one of the few places left unscathed millennia in the future.

The man stripped bare and began to cut at the intricate flooring. Using special tools he edged out a shape from the center of the mosaic. With shovels he pulled up the square and laid it to the side. After digging a deeper hole below it approximately six inches farther down, he pulled over the sack he had been carrying and opened it.

Extracting a glossy tablet of sorts approximately four inches square, the man touched the front glass causing it to come to life with a dull white glow. Sitting down, the prophet allowed his fingers to run over the screen until he was content with the outcome and tapped the glass covering again forcing it to black.

Anytime within the last six months, Aurius could have buried the package, but waited until his one year anniversary to celebrate the culmination of his plan. The tall man chuckled at the irony.

Speaking in English, "Yep, it's amazing knowing that by planting this today, I'll hasten the visitors tomorrow. They have no idea what they're getting into. Everything is in play and can't be stopped."

Pulling out a highly oiled vellum wrap, the man now covered in dirt positioned the tablet in the makeshift vault, replaced the block and did his best to recreate the mortar. After half an hour, the floor was immaculate and looking like it had before. Locating the tools back in the planter, the man jumped in the hot bath.

Finishing a quick wash he redressed, grabbed his bag and left the bathhouse. Once outside, he looked off to the east and smiled.

"Gentlemen, the bait is set. The question is, "Will you be able to hang on once you bite the hook?"

Seeing the chariot waiting at the edge of the building, Aurius of Antioch stepped up and spoke in Greek, "To Jerusalem, I have important information for the King."

The horses were up to speed quickly, and the vehicle left dust in its wake.

5 — SUNDAY, LATE MORNING, APRIL 19

The lack of traffic on Easter Sunday made the ride into Washington smooth and easy. What would normally have taken over an hour due to congestion lasted approximately twenty-five minutes. Of course, Hudson's disregard for the speed limit helped to shorten the time.

In the back seat, Todd felt Aaliyah grip his arm with ferocity at every turn, burying her head in his shoulder to hide her eyes. The professor stroked her hair gently, knowing her unaccustomed eyes couldn't watch the visions blurring past her window at break neck speeds. Remarkably, except for a few squeaks, she remained quiet for the entire trip.

He tucked her hand around his arm and tried to smile at her. His attitude and Hudson's had reverted to their earlier focused concern, and she sensed it. Nevertheless, she bit her lip to remain quiet.

Holding the delicate young woman helped to calm him. His admiration for Aaliyah grew with each passing minute. He could not imagine the strength it took to be uprooted into a new world and not crack under the pressure. He placed his hand around her head as it was tucked into his shoulder and gave her a gentle hug. She gripped him more firmly.

Hudson continued on in silence driving the car to its limits. With every mile, he grew angrier. *We've taken care of this*, his mind repeated. *It can't be true.* The agent regretted the day he was called to head this special project. It had turned into a nightmare for him, his family, his new-found friend and possibly the world itself. He'd thought the technology could be used for good. So many opportunities were available to better humanity through this thing, but he hadn't realized the extent of the collateral damage when its intentions were used for personal gain. *Lord, please don't let this be happening again.*

The borrowed black sedan turned down 17th street, and after a few quick turns, finally reached its destination. Driving up in front of the large building and leaving the car was something never done being that it was across from the White House. Hudson didn't care. He was called out of church on Easter and taken away from his family on the most important holiday of the year. *They can park the car!*

Leaving the keys in the vehicle, they walked up the steps to the structure Mark Twain called "the ugliest building in America," and Harry Truman titled, "The greatest monstrosity in America." The Old Executive Office

Building was originally the State, War, and Navy Building. Its impressive size and foreboding appearance were patterned after France's architecture of the Second Empire, and was one of the few examples in America of the short lived style.

Rounding the first landing, Hudson was met by running armed gunmen. Credentials at the ready, he simply lifted into their view the hand holding them and passed as they parted to allow him and his two guests access. Prepared for their arrival, the security did not ask for any information but escorted them like dignitaries.

The presence of snipers on the roof and other personnel moving secretively about informed the agent of the high alert status of their mission. Several men moved in to walk the group into the building, others were branching out to secure the street. Even the White House had their guns focused his direction.

What have we gotten ourselves into? Hudson wondered.

Flowing with adrenaline now, Hudson no longer limped but stood straight and tall. His joints didn't ache, and he felt like he could run a marathon - something he just might have to do.

Walking through the front doors, Hudson looked the part of a top government official. Dressed in his best Easter garb, a navy blue suit with red tie, he engendered respect and confirmed his image as the man in charge. The agent saluted the men in full military dress standing as sentinels at the front door and continued walking. Todd and Aaliyah followed behind as quickly as possible with Aaliyah pulling herself deeper into the professor with each step. Hudson almost told him to just pick her up and carry her. She looked terrified.

The agent looked at each doorway they passed, noting that the Office Building was the site of signings for the peace treaty for the Spanish-American war, the Treaty of Versailles and the United Nation's Declaration in 1942. Due to the fact that Hudson had the highest of security level clearances, he knew the CIA and NSA had several secret offices hidden in the bowels of this great building. Since they were all being escorted, it looked like the professor and Aaliyah had the same clearance. He sighed at the long debriefing that surely would follow this event.

Stopping at the second set of elevators, Hudson pushed the down arrow.

"Are you ready for this?" he asked looking at Todd.

"No. But what else can I do? Can this be true? Are we going to have to go back?"

"I pray to God the answer is no." Hudson shut his eyes only a moment before the elevator doors separated.

They all filed in as the agent pushed the button that would take them to the bowels of the building. Following a twenty- second silent ride, the gates opened to a cacophony of sounds. Security exited left and right, and the three in the elevator were stunned at the busyness before them.

The basement had evolved into a war room one hundred feet long and sixty feet wide with recessed and hanging fluorescent lights. Long glass walls showed five smaller rooms on each side. In the center of the expanse sat a table over thirty feet long.

The three left the elevator to find two more full dress military soldiers standing at the guard. Showing his credentials as a matter of habit, the men allowed his group into the space, nodding at the several hundred people running in all directions, hands filled with papers and talking on cell phones.

Stopping just outside of the elevator, a tall man in high dress uniform with four stars on his shoulder walked across the room and extended his hand. "Agent Blackwell, I am…"

"Yes sir, we haven't met, but you are General Shaffer of the Joint Chiefs," Hudson replied. "This is Dr. Todd Myers, and Aaliyah… uh, just Aaliyah."

General Patrick Shaffer shook Todd's hand and looked at the woman before speaking to Agent Blackwell once again. His graying hair, barrel chest and shorter stature made him seem friendlier than his status as leader of the United States Military. "Yes, I was brought up to date on your, uh, colleagues this morning."

Turning back toward Aaliyah, a smile lit his sincere steel blue eyes. "Honey, I bet you're terrified." Aaliyah just blinked at him and clutched Todd a bit tighter.

Everyone who knew the general fully believed him to be fair yet firm. A reprimand from this man – who had led the Special Forces, orchestrated several wars and liberated multiple countries – was well-earned. The General escorted the guests to the center of the table. The room grew silent, and people stopped their calls to find a place to prepare for the action ahead.

Speaking to the group as a whole he placed his fingertips in front of him on the table, "Everyone, this is Agent Hudson Blackwell, Dr. Todd Myers, and Aaliyah. I want you to treat them with the same respect and help that you would give me." The room understood the gentle introduction to be a directive.

He and another man at the table pulled out three seats, "Friends would you please sit down here." The guests took a seat.

"May we get you anything to drink?" the General offered.

Hudson spoke up, "No thank you General. We have had a really hard week. We were looking forward to spending time with our families and thanking our God on this important day." He looked directly at the General. "So why are we here?"

Sitting on the edge of the same side of the table as the three, the General began to speak. "I have been apprised of your recent mission." He gestured around the room, "Everyone has been brought up on your mission. Until yesterday, none of us knew of the project, the events of last week, or the way you might have saved the world."

Hudson did not change his stare.

"We have every branch of government represented here, and all of us have trouble believing that what you went through actually happened."

Todd chimed in, "Sir we don't believe it ourselves. I guess if it weren't for Aaliyah…"

"Yes, Dr. Myers, I guess Aaliyah is a concrete example of the mission."

Todd loosened his tie and unbuttoned his top button and checked to ensure that his olive-skinned appendage was warm enough with his coat on.

Hudson brought the conversation back around. "General, we were scheduled for a debriefing starting tomorrow. Everything we know will be told to everyone's satisfaction. I apologize for the secretive nature of the work, but the events that occurred were due to criminal activity and possibly a leak regarding the project, and not because of the assignment itself. All the horror should be behind us now."

He stood to walk around the table. "Hudson, I wish that were true."

"What do you mean?" he said responding while Todd narrowed his focus.

The General stopped at a small table that housed a mini vault. After punching in the digits he had programmed, the door opened. He retrieved a small sack.

Walking back to the table he placed the sack in front of them.

All three looked at it. Aaliyah pulled back a bit feeling the apprehension associated with the secret contents.

"What's in the sack?" Todd asked.

"Well, let's open it," General Shaffer said while pulling a device from its cover. After placing it on the table, he folded his hands and monitored their expressions.

Hudson spoke first, "It looks like a computer think pad of sorts."

"Yeah, I have one kind of like that, but mine isn't that small. Maybe it's a newer version?"

"You're right Dr. Myers, it is a newer version. One that hasn't been released yet. Only a few are in the hands of the public, and those were given to heads of industry and several leaders here in Washington."

"Why are we here to look at a new version of a computer device?"

He looked up, "What's interesting is where we found it."

"Okay," Hudson said, ready for the next big revelation.

The room quieted with even less movement.

"We found it in Israel." The General was waiting for the shoe to drop.

"Does the company have a production facility over there?" Todd questioned.

"No sir, Dr. Myers. Only 25 of these have been given out, and none have taken a trip across the ocean. No, we found this at the Herodium. Do you know where that is?"

"Of course," Todd jumped in. "I've visited that location many times."

"Well, then you know of the lower bathhouse."

"Yes, a great example of one of Herod's building projects."

"You should also know about the…" pulling a sheet from the table and reading from it, "the pomegranate and apricot mosaic contained within the room."

"Yes, it's the only mosaic left nearly intact at the sight."

Frustrated, Hudson jumped in, "I'm tired, and I really don't want an archaeology lesson."

"I understand, Agent Blackwell. We found the tablet there."

Hudson's voice sounded weary, "So, someone took one of these over to Israel and left it while sightseeing."

"We didn't find it in the room. We found it under the room."

Both men spoke at once, "Under the room?"

"We found this item in the dead center of the pomegranate mosaic about 8 inches down."

"Someone has to be wrong. That area has been well-documented. Thousands of pictures have been taken of the mosaic. It'll be easy to trace when someone dug up the area and placed it there. Because this tablet is so new, it would have to have been in the last few weeks."

"Yes, logic would agree with you Dr. Myers. However this wasn't found in the last few weeks, it was discovered in 1966, and has been in a vault until this morning."

"What? 1966?" Todd jumped forward.

"Not possible," the agent barked. "Even if it were, what does this mean for us?"

"Dr. Myers, would you please take the tablet and read from it?" Pointing at the black device, "Please pick it up."

Slowly, the professor reached across the table and pulled the device closer. Tapping the front glass, the machine came to life. After reading the opening screen, he pushed it away and stared at it.

"Gentlemen, this is the newest design of personal computer coming out of Silicon Valley. It has several new factors. The first is that there are no moving parts, buttons, switches, etc. The next is that it is totally enclosed in a glass-type, impenetrable case. This thing will take some level of gunfire, and still do your taxes. The last and most important feature is that it's driven by light, and the heat coming from human touch. No batteries necessary. If what we think has happened, did, then this would be the perfect way to send a message. It could last indefinitely."

Hudson looked at his friend. "What does it say?"

Before Todd could speak, the elevator opened with a small entourage led by the President. All military personnel stood at attention, and all other employees backed away.

"Mr. President," spoke General Shaffer.

"Good morning, General, I believe you have some information that could be of national security."

"Sir, we are trying to work it out. We wanted to get as much information possible before we bothered you on this holiday."

"Thank you General, but the country comes before my personal enjoyment."

"Yes sir."

"Is this the device I've heard about?" he picked it up, and read the opening page.

"I believe we have a rogue agent. Hudson, what do you think?"

"Sir, I haven't read it yet."

Picking it up, the President flippantly tossed it to the Secret Service Agent. Hudson touched the screen.

The beginning of the message said to deliver it to Dr. Todd Myers on this month and date. It was the contents of the next few lines that put fear in the hardened government representative.

Todd, you beat me. You took away all hope I had of restoring my past and correcting a universal injustice. You won the battle, but I will win the war. If you have received this tablet, then I am very close to completing what you interrupted the first time.

Understand that I will finish this, and if you decide to come back, I will be prepared. You will need more than a battered agent and an uneducated commoner to stop me. I have unlimited resources and the ear of a King to ensure my desire. All of heaven will not help you.

Aurius of Antioch

Hudson placed the tablet on the table and looked up at the President. "Sir, we have more than a rogue agent here. This is a man with a personal vendetta. He's out for vengeance."

The room fell silent at the agent's assessment. General Shaffer was not a man to be kept in the dark. "Who is this man, and why is he out for vengeance?"

The professor had remained quiet for the last few moments, not believing what he saw was occurring – or had occurred.

Turning her face toward Todd, Aaliyah said the first words she had uttered in hours. "Ma karah. Ma karah?"

"What's she asking?" Hudson questioned.

"She wants to know what's happened. What do I tell her?"

"Just tell her everything is going to be fine. There's no need for her to worry."

After relaying the message in broken Hebrew, Todd smiled weakly.

His persuasion obviously lacked enthusiasm as evidenced by her raised eyebrow. Todd just lifted her hands to his chest and smiled a little more broadly.

The General cleared his throat. "Dr. Myers, what have you done, and why is he after you?"

"Sir," Hudson raised his hand like a stop sign, "what clearance level does the room have?'

"The President and I have a level-five clearance. Most everyone else has level three and below."

"Sir, the mission we just finished requires level five clearances. The project concept mandates level-three clearances if your department is allowed to know. However, we are not to divulge information to anyone but those directly linked to the mission, and then they must have a level five clearance. I suggest we empty the room."

The chamber fell deadly silent awaiting the outcome of this unusual confrontation.

The President nodded, "Everyone out now!"

It took several minutes for the space to empty due to the intentionally narrow exit options. When everyone under clearance had removed themselves, including the military guarding the elevator and the security watching the President, Hudson stood.

After removing his jacket, loosening his tie and rolling up his sleeves, he backed against a wall and folded his arms. Waiting until the professor

45

finished pouring Aaliyah and himself a glass of water, he spoke, "Todd, make sure I don't forget anything."

"Except for Aaliyah, I've tried to force it from my mind," he nervously joked into his water cup.

"I wish I could," Hudson spoke looking at his two friends.

"Mr. President, General Shaffer, gentlemen, you may want to sit for this."

The men pulled up seats directly across the table as Hudson glanced at the linoleum floor and walked to the far end of the room. After several seconds, he turned and began to speak with clarity. "Around three years ago I was asked by the now late Dr. Keith to help guide a project for him. It involved time travel."

Surprisingly, the information had no effect on the room.

"You see, he was going to use one of the lesser understood variables in Einstein's Law of Relativity to make a tear in the fabric of…"

The General interrupted him with a tight smile, "Hudson, please get on to the pertinent information. I'm not in the mood for a Physics lesson."

"I'm sorry General. I guess I wasn't in the mood for a History lesson earlier either. Let's see." He thought a moment before proceeding. "Last week's mission actually began when Dr. Keith was murdered.

Mr. President, everyone believes the Doctor's death to have been a suicide, but it didn't make sense to me. Why would a man about to make world history kill himself?"

The President shrugged, "There have been crazier stories out there."

"Yes sir, but Dr. Keith wasn't one of them. Seeing his life's work come to fruition gave him a huge reason to live, and he had no reasons to want to die.

The genius behind this project would never have killed himself while awaiting the practical application of his theories. No. The man who killed Dr. Keith took the focal point of the project - the time-vehicle - and entered the past."

"How did he get access to the machine?" the general barked. "What happened to security?"

"Yes sir, he had help from the inside."

"The inside? Who was it?" Shaffer demanded.

"Please, just give me a few minutes. I'm getting to that."

The President brought the conversation back on target, "How did you know how to find the vehicle?"

"Yes Mr. President, this is a difficult concept. But to make it quick and easy…" Taking a coffee cup from the table, he held it high. "Let's say this is our vehicle." He set it down and stood two black binders in front of it, "We need to get to the other side of this barrier. Because the machine is bending space time, it can go through this notebook to its location, and then adjust time to its final date." He made a gap in the book ends and pushed the cup between them.

"The real problem is that the vehicle has to go to a place known to be vacant in present time as well as the past time it is set to arrive in. Otherwise, it will materialize into a mountain or the wall of a building or something. It will not affect the machine or its occupants but will definitely make a mess and be difficult for the people of the time to explain.

So, to answer your question, when the vehicle goes back in time, it essentially takes up space in every time up to the present. Once it comes to rest, the onboard beacon starts sending out a signal. This time we very quickly traced it to a location underneath the Temple Mount in Israel."

Taking a cup from the tube next to the cooler, Hudson filled it with water and took a long drink.

"Following several meetings, we decided that, because I was the only one who knew how to drive the thing, I had to pilot it back in time to arrest the thief and the man I believe killed Dr. Keith. Around this time, I was sent to Kentucky to meet with Todd," gesturing to his friend.

"He had led many trips to Israel, understood the culture and the language and was one of the few to ever go in the underground tunnels where the vehicle was located. We had to have his knowledge."

Todd gave a half wave with his free hand. The other gently patted Aaliyah's shoulder.

"Yes," the General grunted at the professor, "But how did someone with no background on the case or military training get into that machine to travel back in time with you?"

"He got himself shot," Hudson answered flatly.

The professor jumped in, "Hey, I didn't want to get shot. I was trying to get you to the tunnels."

"Yeah, buddy, I know, but you did get yourself shot," he replied with a smile.

"Yeah, well I feel better now," he grinned at Aaliyah and moved his previously wounded arm around.

"Professor Myers intended to get me into the underground cavern housing the vehicle then leave. From there, I would navigate the machine, and he would make his way back to the states. But because of his injury, he nearly lost consciousness. We continued to take fire. I couldn't leave him there unprotected. So I strapped him into the machine and left with him hoping I could figure something out on the other side."

Finally Hudson sat and put down his cup. "I didn't see anything else I could do."

With a smirk Todd chimed in, "I'm kind of glad he made the decision he did."

"Obviously, Hudson, it all worked out for the good. Continue," said the President.

The General looked less generous with the breach of protocol.

"Well, we had the vehicle return to its last time stamp and retraced our steps back out of the tunnels under the Mount, and by this time the good Doctor had lost a great deal of blood. We were in a strange land in a strange time and the person who knew anything about the language, people, culture and lay of the land was practically unconscious.

The Lord provided and, well, we fell into Aaliyah's house."

The woman straightened up at the mention of her name. Both leaders looked her way.

The General responded, "And how did she get here in our time?"

"General, I will get there soon enough," he said while standing and starting to pace.

"Through Aaliyah's kindness and provision, we were clothed, fed and taken care of. I don't believe Todd would have made it if it weren't for her expert care."

Todd put his arm around Aaliyah and gave her a kiss on the cheek. She cuddled in closer, having no idea what she'd done to earn it.

"Over the next few days while Todd was recovering, I was scouting out the land looking for our killer."

Shaffer jumped in again. "How did you know where to find him?" Shaffer queried.

"I knew his target." Sitting on the edge of the table, he took a breath. "You see, before he left in the time machine, I happened to interrupt his departure, causing him to leave the instructions for his mission."

"So, tell the General who he was after," the President said nonchalantly.

"His mission was to kill...well, to kill Jesus Christ."

"He was sent back to kill God?" The General slapped the table with a disbelieving shout.

Aaliyah pulled back from the table, but Todd held her tight.

"Yes, I would say he was trying to kill God. But because someone as visible as Jesus would always have a following, I easily tracked him down. From there, I just laid low until I could find the target. And just as I expected, he surveyed his mark before making a move on him. I spotted him in the crowd, and then it was a run until the end."

"So you did get this maniac?" General Shaffer asked waiting to hear the rest of the story.

Looking over at Todd, "I wouldn't say *we* got him, more like God's providence did."

"What do you mean?" asked the President.

Professor Myers pulled himself from Aaliyah's side and stood, "God is in control. Even with all of our technology, we can't stop His plan."

Rolling his eyes, the President countered, "We don't need a Sunday School lesson, Dr. Myers, just the facts please."

"I consider this a fact. It's what this whole day is about. Easter. God's Son was going to die on a cross on our behalf and rise three days later. If God's got it planned, it *will* happen. No one can stop that. Not even a mercenary."

Hudson smiled in agreement, "It ends up that Roman soldiers apprehended him at the time of Jesus' arrest." He paused a moment. "He was crucified alongside Jesus. We did everything possible to get him out of there, but we couldn't."

"One more time, how did she get back here?" The General asked, pointing at Aaliyah. Her eyebrows lifted at his gesture.

Todd responded, "In an attempt to slow Hudson and me down, the assassin rigged up a good old first century trap. He knew that we were taken in by Aaliyah, so he rigged a snare to ensure we were either slowed down or emotionally affected by the outcome. By this time I had grown to love our benefactor, and when we found her in a pit with puff adders, we had to spend precious time getting her out while he tried to finish his project."

"She got bit," Hudson went on to say. "We killed many of the snakes, but one got her. She was on death's door when we decided to bring her back here. She had been too kind to us to leave her there to die. And just as my friend has said, he simply couldn't leave her. I'm just getting to know the professor, but he tends to be pretty determined when he gets an idea.

We pulled her back through the tunnels to the vehicle. Falling debris from the earthquake knocked me out..."

"Earthquake?" they asked in unison.

"Yes earthquake." Todd answered. "You really need to read the gospels. Anyway, I dragged Hudson and Aaliyah into the vehicle, tied them in, gave myself a quick tutorial of the machine and picked a final location that would engender the quickest response."

"Yeah, they landed it right in my office. The Oval Office." The General looked over at the President.

"Yes, I'm sorry about that, but everything came out alright," Todd beamed, walking over and hugging his first-century jewel.

The buzz of the fluorescent lights filled the silence. Finally, the General responded. "So how does all of this relate to Aurius of Antioch?"

"The assassin was just a pawn in this whole thing. A mercenary doing the will of the people who paid him." Picking up the tablet from the table, he spoke, "The man who wrote this letter is the man who sent the original assassin. I'd say he's gone back to complete what we stopped last week."

"And from what appears here, he'll be ready if anyone decides to stop him," Todd said.

"So, who is it we're looking for?" the General shot up angrily.

Hudson looked uncertainly at the General, "It can only be one person, but that person is supposed to be in jail." Looking at the President, "It has to…"

Holding up a hand, "Hudson please stop right there. General, I'm initiating Executive Privilege and sealing this information right now. I regret doing this, but please leave the room."

Out of obvious frustration, "Mr. President, the military should know what's happening here."

"I will bring you and the military into this case when I believe it to be necessary."

The General stared at the President for several tense seconds, before he complied and left the room.

Once he was out of the area the President stood, paced a moment then spoke, "Men, I know you've been to hell and back within the last week but your country needs you again."

The agent and professor looked at each other with a dread in their eyes. Slowly turning back to the President, they remained silent.

"He never went to jail," he said rather flatly.

Both men reacted with a barrage of questions.

He halted them. "I didn't send him to jail. I couldn't."

Sitting on the edge of the table with his arms crossed, "He was too high a ranking Senator to just disappear into some forgotten cell. Conspiracy junkies would have had a field day, there would have been congressional hearings, and eventually the mess in my office would have gotten out."

He stood again, "No, I was going to allow him to rest under the watchful care of professionals, and then try to restore him back to his position.

I'm sorry that I changed my mind after our last conversation but there wasn't anything I could do. We can't let the world know about this technology."

Reluctance crossed his face. "Then, last night I got a report that he was nowhere to be found. I have half of Maryland searching for him."

"Where's the vehicle?" Hudson asked.

"It's just where you left it, right in my office," the President answered.

Hudson looked over at Todd and then back to the President, "I have a feeling you're going to wish you locked him up."

The leader responded, "If we get him back, believe me, I will personally dig a hole and bury him in it. Let's get to the White House."

Aurius of Antioch had yet to grow accustomed to carriage transportation. The hour it took to travel from the Herodium dragged on. Long legs like his needed the comfort of a stretch limo. He closed his eyes and allowed the longing for the silence provided by the vehicle's enclosed interior, the air conditioning and listening to Caruso sing "La Donna e Mobile" on the stereo system to drone out the wearisome clip clop, clip clop of the team of horses. He figured the monotony would make most anyone in modern times crazy after a year, let alone someone with the refined tastes and privileged upbringing of Aurius.

The ride from the Herodium into Jerusalem seemed an eternity. The spring day brought cool temperatures and bright blue skies, yet it still took an hour to cross the barren expanse that is Israel.

His head fell back against the primitive headrest. Educated in an Ivy League school, he held a law degree, had served in politics over twenty years, and owned a mansion in one of the most elite areas of Washington D.C. Still he could put up with the clip clop, clip clop, the dust, the bugs, the smell, the whims of a schizophrenic tyrant King and the loneliness for a few more days to correct the injustice that haunted him.

Looking out the window to the west while passing Lower Jerusalem, the man knew it could be worse. When his carriage, or rather the King's carriage he was riding in, passed - everyone moved out of the way. Most didn't own an animal they could ride and in Lower Jerusalem owning a goat raised a person's status to "wealthy."

Those eyeing him as he drove by would never in their lives be afforded the opportunity to ride in a vehicle such as the one he was sprawled in, let alone own one. He watched the one room dwellings made of clay and thatch most not having a closeable door - he knew it could be much worse.

Making their way through the Kidron Valley, the vehicle turned and paralleled the Eastern wall of the Temple Mount. Having made the trek dozens of times, Aurius was still amazed at the size of the limestone blocks forming the massive wall around the temple complex. Each block weighing tons was placed with precision. Even in his time this technology was beyond possible.

Passing the central entrance that would eventually be the Golden gate, the passenger laughed to himself. "Centuries from now the Muslims will close this entrance off to ensure the Messiah doesn't have a way into the Temple. What foolishness. There is no Messiah nor will there ever be." The driver looked at him a moment, questions in his eyes at the foreign tongue Aurius used. Priests entered the Temple gate as the vehicle ambled on.

Rounding the northeast corner, Aurius saw his destination; the massive Antonia Fortress. The walled structure with four towers sat on the northwest corner of the Temple compound. Each tower rose fifty feet in the air and each was built to help guard Herod's palace just to the south. Evidently, Herod had named the last three towers: Phasael after his brother, Hippicus after a friend, and Mariamne after his favorite wife.

Aurius paused. Last week Herod had Mariamne killed, fearing she might take his throne. He slowly shook his head. The man was truly insane.

"I have to get myself out of this country. If he finds out I'm using him, he will do much worse than just kill me," the prophet muttered the words in English, before the vehicle stopped at a large staircase directly adjacent to the fortress.

Mainly a military outpost, considerable political business also happened within its 15 foot walls. Aurius of Antioch gingerly descended from the carriage and looked up the long set of steps.

He straightened his clothing and stood tall, inhaling to boost his confidence. In a few moments he would meet with the King. This time would not be to share some magic trick or play on the King's paranoia by stating another of his family or leaders may be after his throne. He winced at those unavoidable moments.

No, today would be life changing. The entire mission centered on this moment in time. If any day mattered in his crazy world, it was this one. The carriage rolled off behind him as Aurius began his ascent toward destiny.

—

The President escorted the three time travelers to the White House through underground tunnels. Hudson knew that most high profile buildings in Washington provided access to the President's residence through these underground caverns.

Initially designed as raw tunnels to allow the leader of the free world a mode of escape in case of an attack, the barren rock now displayed a plush passageway housing personal rail cars for dignitaries to travel throughout the city without fighting traffic.

Because of the tunnels continued importance, the Secret Service patrols them physically and has listening devices planted throughout, ironically, to ensure privacy. Even the cities sanitation department needs special clearance to clean the sewer system when a blockage occurs within a mile of the White House.

Entering the most famous house on earth through the gymnasium, they continued on by way of a back staircase through several checks until they reached the Oval Office. The President walked in ahead of them all and sat casually behind the Lincoln desk. He smiled and nodded toward the root of their problem.

There, before them, was the time machine - a vehicle with so much promise. So far, only destruction and personal pain had been produced by the billion dollar project. The apparatus looked like a giant pearl cut in half with the top portion suspended telescopically from the lower half. When placed together, the machine was about seven feet in diameter. The base, consisting of four tubes, shot straight up into the mother of pearl exterior of the lower half, supporting it, but making it appear delicate and unstable.

Hudson quickly walked over to the vehicle, and after stepping on a pad attached to the leg, worked himself into the cockpit. Placing his hand on a square on the right side of the black panel, the glass cockpit came to life.

The dash consisted of four main areas. The left two quadrants were time specific while the right two were delegated to location. The right side of each half was blinking, showing the agent that its last jump was to the year 5 B.C. with a specific coordinate indicating the hours, minutes, and seconds of its last location. Just to the right of the seconds number was a negative figure in meters. It had been below sea level.

Todd looked over the rim of the vehicle.

Pulling up a holographic visual representation of the globe, Hudson was quickly able to see where the machine had last been. Asking the professor he said, "What do you think of that?" pointing to the graphic display.

"What time is he in?" Todd asked and Hudson responded by pointing to the number blinking on the dash.

With his hands running through his hair, the Ph.D. backed away from the machine and sat on a thick leather chair across from Aaliyah. He knew she wanted to comfort him by the way her arms lifted and fell twice. Nevertheless, she left him alone to think. With his elbows on his knees, he stared at the floor, "It looks like he's going to try again."

Hudson pushed around on the dash for a while longer before he worked his way out of the cockpit, "I'd say you're right." He sat in another of the seats usually occupied by world leaders. "Todd, the problem is he's locked us out of the year five."

The President stood up and walked around the desk sitting on the front edge. "What do you mean he's locked us out of the year five?"

"Just that, we can't go back to 5 B.C. and apprehend him."

Speaking with caution, "Why can't we?"

Hudson responding with regret, "Someone has locked that year out. The sphere has encryption in it to keep people from stealing it. My body signature is one of these safeguards. Only those whose palm print is recognized can even access the workings of the vehicle. However, each area of the sphere can be locked down as well."

Everyone in the room looked at him.

"Let's say, I don't want anyone ever landing the machine in the Oval Office again, I'd put a pass code on those coordinates ensuring it never happens."

The President affirmed the idea, "Let's do that," he smirked.

"The code can be anything up to 25 digits long. It could take months to crack. This was a failsafe plan to ensure the machine only went where we wanted it to. We never could have guessed that someone on the inside would misuse it."

"Well, what can we do?" the professor questioned.

"Because of our limited understanding of time travel, we are dependent upon the orientation of the earth. Therefore, we can only jump into the past on the exact day we leave.

Today is April 19th, therefore we can't go back into the past to December 25th or June 6th, only April 19th. We can go to any year in the past as long as it is April 19th."

"Any year but year five. Is that right?" asked the President.

"Yes sir," answering reluctantly. "It looks like our friend wanted some time to work his plan. By locking us out of his year, he has essentially been there 365 days even though he left just this morning.

"Mr. President, you didn't see or feel anything in the White House today?" Pointing to the sphere, "It gives quite a kick when it jumps."

Quickly answering, "No Hudson, I left early this morning for breakfast at the Capitol. And because it's Easter, we are on a minimal staff. No one should be inside this end of the building today."

"That seems pretty convenient," Todd responded. "So what are our options?"

Hudson stood up and looked at a picture of Lincoln hanging on the wall, "Well we can't go back before he gets there because we'd be waiting a year for him." He turned and looked at the men across the room, "All we can do is return a year later. Sadly enough he's going to know exactly when we'll be there, and it sounds like he'll be ready."

"Yeah, I think you're right," the professor answered. "But," he stood and paced the plush carpet containing the seal of the President of the United States.

"What are you thinking, buddy?"

"He hasn't been able to get anything done yet. The timeline hasn't changed. Everything is as it was," he gestured around.

"Okay, so…," the President reacted.

"So, we know exactly what he wants to do, and if I'm right, he's waiting for one miraculous event to occur, which hasn't yet." With a big smile the Ph.D. continued, "There's still time to stop him."

Hudson stood with his arms folded against a wall, "You know friend, *time* has never really been a problem for us."

The men looked at each other.

Aaliyah felt secure for the first time in hours.

—

At the top of the steep, encased stairway to the Antonia Fortress, Aurius entered the mammoth opening to the fortification. Passing several soldiers in full gear holding shields, he was amazed at the level of activity within the building. The King's presence garnered attention from all staff and military. All possible entrances into the facility were manned. No one would kill the King today.

Feeling the solidity of the twenty ton blocks about him, the prophet marveled at Herod's ability to build. This level of precision and scale with such a large medium required vast knowledge, architectural skill and planning. Looking around he saw perfect lines, ninety degree angles, domed ceilings and decoration on the level of some of the palaces in Europe built twenty centuries later. And in just about seventy-five years it would all come crashing down under Emperor Titus.

Aurius walked on toward the tower called Mariamne and ascended its grand staircase to the second floor. There he saw two guards at attention in front of doors made from Cedars of Lebanon; the largest trees on the continent. The opening impressed him at 15 feet tall. *At least I don't have to duck around here*, he smiled to himself. Once again, he noted the reason for the great scale was not necessity but a display of Herod's grandeur.

The prophet had grown to like the crazy little man. Herod had been kind and gracious toward him, sparing his life and giving him a beautiful place to stay – beautiful for first century Israel anyway – he'd provided him with food, clothing, and any luxury Aurius might desire. Herod certainly treated his prophet better than his own children, many of whom he had killed. Although, as Herod's seer, he didn't need to read the future to understand that in an instant everything could change.

He had witnessed the mass executions and crucifixions numbering now in the thousands. The prophet had seen the sport of killing another man or a captured animal. He had observed soldiers abducting women and children to work on a project for the King. The debauchery at dinner parties, the murdering of friends, relatives and his own blood out of desire to keep his position - a position that death would eventually take -could not be forced from Aurius' mind.

No, Aurius was on borrowed time and he knew it. The minute he became unimportant or stopped producing, he would be returned to the place he was plucked from, and this time without the hope of a stay of execution.

So far, in the six months Aurius had resided within the King's court, he had performed simple but astounding tricks. With the knowledge encased in the second computer pad, easy science experiments were simple to come up with using materials he found around him. He'd learned to use earth forces and elements to produce a result. He once drew water into a glass using fire. He sprinkled basic elements over a flame to affect its color. Once, when he was really behind the ball, he simply folded a piece of dried vellum into a makeshift plane and the King threw it around the room for an hour. Each test was basic 5th grade material, but to those in the first century these proved his magical powers and allowed him to rise to the top as quickly as he had.

The army profited from his wisdom as he helped them fine tune ideas for crossbows, trebuchets, and catapults. Aurius helped in the designing of longer lasting vehicles, and other minor ideas which he knew were being invented in nearby regions already, or historically were developed about that time.

He lifted an eyebrow at how many 5th grade experiments involved rubber bands, plastic flexible tubing, springs, wires, batteries and simple chemicals that can't be bought or created in the first century. Aurius had run out of tricks, and he knew it.

As for his prophecy, he merely told the man things he already knew were going to happen. Each day he researched who the King had killed and why, then used the information to his advantage – fueling the King's trust in him. Aurius reminded himself that he never aided in someone's death that wasn't already going to be killed. Still, there weren't many of Herod's family, leaders, or commanders left to implicate with some baseless accusation.

Thus the next few minutes had become do-or-die for the prophet. Looking through a large open window in the tower, he glanced off to the east. And seeing the Dead Sea, he was once again reminded of the visitors that would be coming. They were coming to end his mission, his purpose and reason for living.

He spoke quietly in English, "You will not succeed this time." The soldiers looked at him questioningly. "You'd be wise to stay in your own millenium."

The prophet began to turn back, but the view of the Dead Sea grabbed him once again and he stopped. Quietly and with determination he spoke, "You will be coming, if not tonight, then tomorrow morning. I'm ready."

Gripped with this knowledge, Aurius turned toward the door, straightened himself, plastered a smile and spoke aloud, "There's no turning back now."

The soldiers looked at each other and then back at the mysterious prophet whom they considered to be a magician. They didn't question his peculiarities.

In the best Greek Aurius of Antioch could muster, "Epitrepste mou na perasoon." *Let me pass!*

Time ticked by on the mantle clock for a full minute before the President started to speak, "So when do you leave?"

The reluctant agents looked at each other before turning back at the President. Hudson spoke first, "Sir, I'll go back. I'm the leader on the project, and I'll be the one to catch him before he destroys the timeline."

The President nodded.

"But, he's staying here," he spoke, pointing at the professor.

Todd jumped up in protest, "Not a chance! You need me. I speak the language and know the customs. If something comes up, I'm better trained to get us out of it."

"Todd, I'm not taking you back. I'm still in charge of this project. That's the end of it," Already standing, he began to pace the presidential seal pattern in the rug beneath his feet. "I can't take a civilian on another project like this. You weren't supposed to go last time." He paused for effect, "And you got shot."

"Yeah, well, except for this huge scar, I'm fine. Thank you." He touched his bicep to find the large shiny crater on his arm, "And what did you cauterize the bullet wound with, an anvil? I've never seen a scar on a burn patient as bad as the one you left on me."

"I saved you didn't I?"

Todd continued, "I may have made it - without the scar…I'm going!"

"It can't happen."

The President stood up and took charge of the situation. "Men, I believe you are both specifically suited for the task." Looking at the agent he began, "Hudson you are a well-trained operative with knowledge on how to infiltrate a dangerous situation and complete the mission." Gesturing toward the professor, "And Todd, as you stated, no one will know the language and the culture like you will."

The President stopped. "No one will know it better than you, except for Aaliyah," looking over at the young woman who had been quiet for the last 20 minutes.

The men glanced at each other. Todd spoke first, "We can't take her back there. We just took her away from that place. Talk about a civilian, and totally innocent."

Hudson took up where Todd left off. "Yes sir, she isn't strong, can't use weapons, and we can hardly communicate with her."

"Madoo hoo cal anod motacal ly?" asked Aaliyah.

The men became quiet as Todd tried to calm her concern. Speaking to both men, Todd explained, "She wants to know why everyone's looking at her."

The President interjected, "Ask her if she wants to go. You men have told me how that little woman took you in, fed you, healed you, protected you, fought snakes and essentially was willing to die for you. That sounds pretty strong to me."

He let it sink in, "I believe she would be perfect for the mission. Her understated presence would draw less attention to you."

Walking back toward the Lincoln desk, he changed from a suggestion to a command, "Guys, she's vital and must go. I feel the mission will not be possible without her." He stopped and folded his arms.

Todd was aghast, "You can't truly think that adding her to the equation will make the mission more viable. I won't take her."

Hudson affirmed, "Yes, there's no way that would help any of us."

The President sat in his chair, "Men this is not negotiable. You are the only option we have for this assignment. Life as we know it, the country as we know it is at stake. Our very identity and sovereignty are in jeopardy. There is no option here. I couldn't think of a better person to get you around in first century Israel than someone from there."

"She's from a time some 30 years later. This is the reign of Herod, a different ruler than when she was there," Todd said out of frustration.

Hudson sat in a chair.

"Gentlemen ask her what she wants to do."

They looked at the leader.

He continued more methodically and directly, "Ask her if she would rather stay here by herself in some hospital somewhere or be with you in her homeland."

The men were beginning to see that they were being manipulated and she was the pawn.

Pulling out a cigar from a drawer and lighting it he added, "You see, she doesn't speak the language, has no concept of 21st century life. She isn't accustomed to our food, clothing, housing, or lifestyle. I bet she can barely use a fork, and a bathroom is most likely a terrifying concept for her."

Wisps of cigar smoke curled around his head, "Because of her situation, she would have to go into a facility accustomed to people with her type of…, her type of problem, until you get back."

Speaking first, "What type of problem does she have and what type of facility would that be?" Hudson asked eyes furrowed.

He drew in the smoke before letting it out in a puff, "A mental institution. Some type of psych ward. It's an awful set of circumstances, but what else could we do? She would be terrified without you and could hurt herself and possibly others around her. They might have to sedate her."

Standing and beginning to pace the room while holding the cigar, "My real concern is that they would believe her to truly be insane."

Both men knew where this was going and looked at one another. Each recognized the growing rage mirrored in the other's eyes.

"I have a lot of pull, but not necessarily with the psychiatric community. She could very easily be institutionalized until she understands reality like we do. However, that would be difficult since she doesn't come from our reality."

Todd walked over and sat on the edge of the chair Aaliyah was sitting in. "You cannot mean what you're saying," his voice sounded weakened.

Hudson looked on with vacant eyes.

The room was beginning to lose its crisp splendor due to the cigar smoke and the sudden feeling of pervasive evil. "Professor, I mean everything I'm saying. Sadly enough, I would not be able to protect her once you leave." Lowering his voice, "So as I have said, ask her what she would like to do."

Speaking slowly with concern, "Mr. President, that isn't a fair question. She would leave with me no matter the outcome or destination."

"Then you already know your answer," the President spoke through a waxy smile.

Hudson took over the tense situation, "Sir, may we have a few minutes to work through our options?"

"I'm going to review today's schedule, and will be back in several minutes. Please feel free to make yourselves comfortable."

He left through a small curved door in the middle of the oval room, and the men took chairs next to Aaliyah.

"Hudson, something's wrong here. My spirit doesn't feel right about him."

"I know. I feel the same way. I have a gut sense that somehow he's winning here. What his motivation would be for sending us all, I can't guess. But yes, something's not right."

Todd thought for a second before whispering, "You know, if he is somehow linked to this, we're the only people on earth – at this time – with the ability to stop what's happening."

"The thought had crossed my mind. It's obvious the tablet was never supposed to be sent. Because it was, he lost control of the situation."

Hudson interjected, "Yeah, other governmental agencies got involved that may never have known about the sphere, time travel or the man in the past."

"This has definitely put a crimp on any plan he may have had. Somehow, it looks like Aurius and the President have the same intent…"

"But with different aims," the professor finished. "There's no way that the President is out for vengeance. That wouldn't make any sense."

"No, it wouldn't."

"So what do we do?" asked Todd, knowing their time was short.

"There isn't much we can do, it looks like the President wants us all to go we'll just need a plan to ensure we don't fall into the trap that's obviously been set. One that will remove all three of us from the equation."

"What plan would that be? The cards seem to be stacked against us."

"Todd, you're right, but I have a feeling God's going to work out the hands."

With a big smile, "He tends to be in control no matter what we do." He stood and grabbed his friend's hands, "Let's pray God will guide our steps."

"That's the best plan we could come up with," Hudson replied feeling much stronger and more confident.

The group circled up and prayed for God's provision and guidance. Even though the young woman had no understanding of English, the universal need for God's intervention crossed cultural and even time lines. She knew Jesus and prayed for the men in her own way.

Flipping a switch and turning off the recording equipment to the Oval Office, the President stood and pulled a few more puffs from his cigar. Yes, the man he sent into the past made the mission personal and brought other agencies needlessly into the work. And yes, those in the other room had a concern about his involvement. But not all was lost.

If his man in the past could fulfill the mission, none of this would matter. Everything was still on track. Taking one last puff, he tapped the cigar in a waiting ashtray, and reentered the Oval Office.

Aurius entered the cavernous space lined with banners from countries governed by Rome and stopped. To his surprise, the King was encircled by military commanders and senators in a heated debate over a new building project to take place on the coast. Standing next to a large window and looking over the drawings resting on a table, Herod noticed his prophet at attention next to the door.

Separating the mass of people before him, the King walked toward Aurius. He sounded magnanimous, "My dear prophet, what brings you to Jerusalem?"

Not wanting his information discussed before the delegation and refuted out right, Aurius did his best to fall back and regroup for a later time. Bowing and throwing his hands far to the side, "My King, I was not aware that you would be in such deep negotiations. I will return at a later time to discuss my visions with you," he replied backing toward the door.

"Do not be ridiculous," the old man said as he headed for his large chair positioned against one wall of the room. "You have earned the King's ear." He grew louder, "Is not that right everyone? Aurius has become even more important than my generals because he is able to see things before they happen. Those trained to protect me cannot even see a threat within my own household," he gestured to the crowd.

Looking over at his military commanders Herod continued, "Gentlemen, why is it that you cannot seem to see a threat within my palace or, even more importantly, within my family when there is one?"

The men were growing uncomfortable with the line of questioning. Cyprianus, a tall, athletic man and also the top military leader in the room spoke up, "Good King, we had no idea that Antipater would try to overthrow your government. Your oldest son had always followed your wishes and until Aurius implicated him, there was no reason to have suspicion. We still have found nothing to his claims."

Herod started to scream. "So you are saying I killed my son for nothing. Is that what you believe has happened? Do you want me killed Cyprianus? Do you desire my death? Should I just lie down and allow you to run me through with your dagger?"

Cyprianus bowed with his head to the floor, "Of course not, good King. I am given the task of protecting you. I take that seriously."

Herod sat down, "Then listen when someone with Aurius' abilities speaks of threats to my life!"

"Yes good King." The look he gave Aurius showed his sincere hatred. Backing away, the general kept his eyes focused on the prophet.

Aurius knew that within the room, he had no friends but the King. Throwing out the name of Antipater allowed the King's attention to be diverted from Aurius' past to the treachery of his sons. The prophet knew that history said that he would be implicated, and who is to say someone else would not have made the suggestion if he had not.

Cyprianus had thoroughly searched Antipater's background and found nothing, therefore when the King asked for his son's head, Cyprianus was made to look like an incompetent. History was clear the King would die within the next few months and once he was out, it was a sure bet that Aurius would be next to die, most likely at the hands of Cyprianus.

Aurius tried to look away from the dead stare given by the highly decorated and armored general.

"So, back to why you are here," Herod redirected his attention. "My loyal subject, Aurius of Antioch, what is so important that you would come to Jerusalem? You have my attention."

Sitting back the King remained quiet as the entourage took their chairs or stood around the room. Cyprianus did not move from his position.

Extremely nervous as he was, his thoughts jumbled for a moment, yet he stood instead in quiet confidence. Finally, taking the center of the room directly in front of the King, Aurius began. "My King, I fear for your life."

The room began to mumble and several generals spoke out.

"Everyone quiet," The King commanded. "What do you know?"

"Great King, for several nights I have received a vision." Knowing that prophets seemed to see everything in a vision and were highly regarded for their mode of information, Aurius thought it wise to continue the mystique.

"Yes, what have you seen?" Herod asked moving to the edge of his seat.

Starting to pace the floor as he moved his hands above his head. "I saw what seemed to be a trident as the god Neptune would wield. Yet, the three teeth were not sharp but dull." Letting that sink in he stopped.

After what seemed like an eternity he continued. "The handle which would usually be dull on the end was sharpened to a point."

The room was enrapt with attention, whereas Cyprianus' steel blue eyes had not moved from their stare of him.

"Aurius, what does it mean?"

He returned to the center of the room, "The three prongs represent three threats to your kingdom, for at the sharp end of the handle, only one man stood."

Herod was about to come out of his chair.

"The man with the reverse trident pointed at his heart was holding a kingdom in one hand and eternity in the other." Aurius didn't know what holding eternity meant but it sounded very big. "That one man was you, King Herod."

Backing away, Aurius dramatically fell to his knees.

The King stood up as the room erupted. Walking over to his prophet, the King pulled him up from his feigned exhaustion. "Everyone remain quiet. Please find this man a drink."

Walking the seer over to a chair next to his, Herod allowed him a second to regain his thoughts. After the faux prophet took a large drink, the King continued, "Aurius, in the short time I have known you, your sole desire has been for my protection."

Cyprianus tilted his head forward at the verbal jab.

"Perchance, did you see what the threats are?"

Taking another drink and shaking for affect, Aurius stood and walked back to the center of the room. "Herod, three threats shall come against you. All are focused on ending your reign, yet one is more nefarious than the others."

Knowing he had the room in his hands, except possibly for Cyprianus, he started to speak and move with strength. "The first threat is in the form of a delegation from the east. They shall come seeking a King but will not seek you. They will hunt for one who was born and will eventually remove you from your throne." Looking the King in the eyes he continued, "When they come I would allow them to continue their search, for they will lead you to your competitor.

The second threat will be mercenaries trying to stop your humble servant," Aurius said bowing. He stood back up, "Dark forces know of my ability to protect you and will try to remove me, so that this imposter tyrant king can grow and thrive. This threat will appear in the desert just east of Machaerus."

Sounding humble, "Sir, I am your meager servant, and if I must die for you, then let it be."

Herod stood to speak to Cyprianus, "Aurius shall have protection both day and night. At no time will he be with less than a unit of 12 men looking out for his welfare. Is that understood?"

Quietly, Cyprianus spoke, "Yes, King Herod," the look he offered Aurius proved he knew him to be a charlatan.

Aurius returned the look with a smile. "I believe the mercenaries will arrive tonight. May I lead an expedition to apprehend them?"

"Yes. Let it be so, and when you have them bring them before me."

"Of course."

Walking to the center of the room he lifted his voice, "My prophet, tell me of this last tooth for I believe it to be the greatest threat."

With wide eyes, the seer continued. "Good King, the last tooth has far reaching consequences. He begins as a child. If this Jewish child is allowed to grow to a man, he will have a name that is even greater than yours. His abilities will be heralded in scrolls and parchment for millennia. His existence will show you to be a small and tyrannical king. He must be stopped. You must use whatever power is in your control to remove this threat, or you good King will die, never to be remembered for your greatness."

With the final words, Herod walked back to his seat in a trance as the rest of the room remained totally silent. Every official in the space was taken with the thought of a child king.

Following several tense minutes, the king stood and began to speak. "Aurius, I have no way to thank you for what you have done for me. Believe me; I will repay you for the love and care you have given me."

"I am only your servant."

He spoke to the senators within the room, "Have you heard of a child king?" All shook their heads.

To the military leaders, "Have you heard of any competition to my throne?" Several responding with an emphatic no.

Cyprianus said, "We have no proof that what this man says is true. We..., I have heard of no threat. We know of no child king. This is ludicrous. If there is a child king there would have to be a grown king somewhere and we know nothing of that."

Herod quickly went into a rage, "You knew nothing of Antipater, and yet he was after my throne."

"Sir, we found nothing that would have given any indication of his motives."

"This is the same situation! You have obviously missed something; something life threatening."

Yelling at the people in the room he stood, "I want everyone examined. Every political leader and their families, ever military leader, even my own family scrutinized."

Beginning to walk back to his seat as the people in the room settled in with the knowledge of what the king's edicts meant for their lives, he stopped and turned back toward Aurius, "Prophet, you are highly prized in my kingdom. You will be rewarded for your loyalty."

"Allowing me to lead the military expedition that will apprehend one of the threats on your kingdom is reward enough."

With a smile of satisfaction, Aurius of Antioch exited through the large doors leaving turmoil in the room behind him as he began his descent down the cold limestone stairs.

Upon reentering the Oval Office, the President stopped and feigned respect for the silent prayer being offered up before him. Normally, the man would never have slowed his pace into a room which was rightly his. But he needed those three with their heads bowed to return to the past. It was vital for the sake of his mission that they disappear from existence in the current time.

President Hayden Christopher Langley knew how to play the game. He'd been in politics for a very long time. No, worshipping a higher power did not suit him. Security was the real god worshipped by Americans. People were sheep, following whoever offered to take the best care of them. He smirked silently. But he did know how to look the part.

His sneer morphed into a mask of concern.

He cleared his throat, "Time is not on our side, gentlemen. What's your answer?"

The small prayer chain quickly broke up, and Hudson stood. "We'll all go back," he released a heavy breath, "There isn't much of a choice."

Langley walked over and patted him on the back, "My friend, there is always a choice."

Todd wanted to retort but thought it better not to. "When do we leave?"

Looking at a 19th century grandfather clock in the corner, the President responded, "It's around 10:45, I say noon is a nice round number. That will give me an hour to get everything ready for your trip."

"Noon!" Todd barked. "We can't leave in an hour. Give us a day."

"I'm sorry, but we don't have that luxury. As you said earlier, the timeline hasn't changed yet. Who's to say that two hours from now he won't have completed his mission? It will be much more difficult to restore a timeline than to stop someone from destroying it. No, I'm afraid it has to be in an hour. The quicker you're in that vehicle and out of here, the better it is for everyone."

Behind him, Aaliyah began to pray again. She had to know the man in front of her was like a king forcing her Todd and friend Hudson into something they desperately didn't want to do. She prayed aloud for God's protection on the men, not knowing that she would be going with them.

Hudson stuck a hand out in front of him, effectively stopping the professor from saying anything else. His eyes looked across the room and found Langley's full of victory.

"Noon it is," he forced the dare from his thoughts.

"Are we imprisoned here or can we make a few stops before we leave? I'd like to see my wife before I go."

President Langley cocked his head in thought. "Hudson I'm not your warden. We're all working for the same end." Shaking his head he slammed his fist on his desk. "It's vital that we stop this madman before our world is unrecognizable." He paused again for effect.

"So, no, you're not locked here, we'll have drivers available for each of you. Please just be back and prepared to leave at noon."

Immediately, the group dispersed. The President disappeared into a side door, Hudson went down to the motor pool and Todd grabbed Aaliyah's hand and headed down the back steps and into the Rose Garden.

Even though it was still early in the year, Aaliyah was mesmerized by the beauty of the rose bushes. The professor loved her curiosity with all things new. Her 29 years of life in a harsh country and travel through time had not diminished her innocent view on the world. Having never seen anything with the radiance or fragrance of the world renowned garden, it was hard for Todd to pull her away from the multitude of colors toward the many other things he wanted to show her before they left.

Exiting the garden through a gatehouse, the pair walked the few blocks toward the Washington Monument. Aaliyah was accustomed to large limestone buildings but had never seen an obelisk due to their origins in Egypt, and stared at it until she was able to touch it and look up at the way it pierced the sky. Because it was Easter morning, the Mall was nearly empty allowing the couple a private view of the monuments without the bustle of the crowds.

Sitting on a row of granite benches, Todd looked at his foreign beauty with the large green eyes. How was he going to tell her that having just rescued her from an oppressive, dictatorial government, they were about to go right back into it yet in a more dangerous time? The professor didn't have the words and just looked off toward the Lincoln Memorial.

Aaliyah did her best English, "Tawd? Tawd, okay?"

He smiled at her attempt. "Very good, Aaliyah. Yes, I'm okay." Knowing she was cold, he buttoned his jacket she was still wearing.

She smiled.

Beginning to speak in Hebrew, "Aaliyah, do you see that building down there? The one with the columns?"

Responding in English, "Yayus, Tawd."

Pulling her tight and pointing, "That building is dedicated to a very famous man. His name is Abraham Lincoln."

"Avrahim Lican."

"Yes, Abraham Lincoln. Before his time, many within this country," making a large gesture, "believed that it was right to keep people as possessions. Make them do what you want them to do."

"Avad."

"Yes, a slave. People were taken from their families from all over the world and forced to do other people's work. It was kind of like your country. You were forced to do the work of the Romans."

Aaliyah's countenance changed.

Pointing, "That building is dedicated to a man who practically gave his life to stop that oppressive treatment. He was killed by someone who didn't want slavery abolished."

She stared intently at the building circled by white clouds flying over head.

Redirecting her attention the opposite direction, he showed her the Capitol building. Its alabaster color and columns gleamed against the bright blue sky.

"Our representatives meet in that building."

Not understanding representatives, Todd further explained. "In your country, leaders rule over you. In America, we elect or get to say who we would like to make our laws and give our country direction. Each person in this country is equal with no one lording over us."

Aaliyah responded in her native tongue, "No slavery, and no King?"

"No slavery and no King. Everyone is equal. In that building they make laws that are designed to help Americans and not hurt them. Many times they get it wrong but they do their best to help the country with what they do."

Standing, Todd took Aaliyah by the hand and started to walk around the monument. Pointing to the World War II monument with all of the flags and reflecting pools he continued, "That monument represents a great war the entire world was in. America was able to remove bad leaders and restore those countries back to strength. We could have taken them under our rule but that is not what we are about."

Looking at the obelisk, "This monument is dedicated to our first and probably greatest leader. A humble, God fearing man who helped us break away from another country so we could govern ourselves and not have a ruler over us. His name was George Washington. Once this country became independent through a great war, he could have very easily become King yet he would not take that role because he wanted this great nation to remain free from the possibility of tyrant leaders."

Stopping in the direction of the White House, Todd took Aaliyah's face in his hands and looked into her eyes. "Love, this country began with the idea of religious freedom. We wanted to worship Jesus Christ freely without rules or restrictions."

"Jaysus. I luv Jaysus."

"I know you do and so do I. But right now, someone is trying to erase everything this country is about. This person doesn't like Jesus and wants him removed from our history."

Trying to find the right words, "In a very short time I'm going to have to go and try to stop him. I'll be returning to your country where Hudson and I will attempt to bring him back."

With an immediate response and determination in her eyes, "I go... too." Continuing in her native tongue, "I love Jesus and will give my life for him. Todd, this is my country and you cannot return without me. The Lord told me as I was praying in that building," pointing toward the White House, "that I was needed to do his work. I am not sure why he would need me but I cannot ignore his call. I will be leaving with you."

Her statement was very matter of fact and in the short time Todd had known her, he knew when she meant business. The Lord had paved the way for her involvement without having to break the news of the President's ultimatum.

—

Hudson directed one driver to pick up his wife and appropriated another one for him. After a short phone call he settled into the back of the vehicle and began to pray. Twenty minutes later, his wife walked into the National Gallery of Art. Her form filled out the polka-dotted spring dress perfectly, from the wide neckline to knee-length hem. The agent found her image far more beautiful than any of the Monet's or Renoir's that graced the building.

"Hi, Honey," he said as she sat next to him on the bench.

"I didn't know you liked 16th century oil on panel," she said looking at the pictures in front of them. "You're more of a Rembrandt or Raphael kind of guy."

"Yeah, usually. Today, all of the nativities in here got my attention. How was the ride over?"

"Well, it isn't every day that the White House limousine picks you up."

He smiled, "No, that was probably a first, wasn't it?" He changed the subject. "Do you think that's what it looked like?"

"What looked like?" she clarified.

"Do you think any of these panels represent the way it looked when Christ was born?"

Sara scanned the room, "No, I would guess not. I'm fairly certain Mary and Joseph weren't wearing 16th century Italian clothing and owned a castle." She smiled at her own humor, and was rewarded with a laugh from her preoccupied husband.

"Hudson, why are we here?" she asked, looking at him as he stared at the wall.

Turning his head toward her, he grabbed her hand, "I have to go again."

"When?"

"In an hour."

Sara's eyes began to moisten.

"Honey, it's going to be alright," His arms wrapped around her slim shoulders and held on for dear life. "I shouldn't be gone but a few days at best."

"Hudson, you're not physically back to 100 percent yet, and whatever you went through may take years for you to mentally grasp." After a pause, she lifted her hand to his face, "And yet, I feel this is where you're supposed to be, and that the Lord will bring you back to me." She looked over intently, and her bright blue eyes sparkled.

"You know, I bet it was much more rustic than that."

"Pardon?" she laughed through the tears beginning to slip down her face.

"The nativity," he said, staring again at the panels. "I bet it was barren and primitive. God would have had to shed his heavenly garb for the most basic of what earth offered to fully represent man. I bet, except for the beauty of the Savior, the rest was pretty unappealing and not worth painting."

"Probably so," she responded wondering about the deep thoughts she rarely heard from her husband.

Hudson stood, "Honey, I have to go."

She grabbed his neck and standing on her tip toes whispered a prayer in his ear.

Hudson kissed her longingly before they walked out to the limousine waiting at the curb.

—

Everyone met back at the White House before noon where they were escorted up to the Oval Office.

"Did you get everything in order?" the President asked.

Neither Todd nor Hudson liked the way that sounded, and their expressions proved it.

"We had a quiet lull before the storm." The professor amped up his mental prayers.

Hudson winked at Todd then added, "We're ready. What do you have for us to take?"

"Everything is loaded into these bags," pointing to the coffee table. "Clothing, basic food and water for a few days, monetary goods to barter with, a few knives. The basics for a mission like this. I hope this will be an in and out process, and that you won't be there more than a couple days."

Todd jumped in, "We hope that too."

After looking through the bag Hudson threw one to Todd and the other to Aaliyah. "Let's get dressed."

Aaliyah was shown a bathroom to change in while the men just stripped down right in the Oval Office. Within a couple minutes everyone was back and dressed. The men were in Roman garb and had dark, plainly-colored tunics with an off white colored toga. Aaliyah was rather nervous because she was also dressed Roman with a white tunic and magenta colored toga. Having been set up to be married to Todd she wore a golden colored stola.

Aaliyah started speaking a mile a minute to Todd.

Hudson asked, "What's she talking about?" as he strapped on a knife under his toga.

"She's not Roman," Todd responded. "She knows that her Greek has an accent and that she'll be easily spotted.

Hudson, if she's picked up they'll charge her with crimes against Rome. Insurrection, treason, stuff like that. It would mean the death penalty."

Looking at the President, "Why have they made her Roman?" Hudson asked.

"It was all that we could come up with on such short notice. Don't worry, if you do your job right, she'll be safe," he waved off any further arguments as he pulled a cigar from a box on his desk.

Todd and Hudson just looked at him. They were being set up. And they could do nothing about it, but pray. Each acknowledged the thought with a quick nod of determination.

Stuffing the last of the contents from the bag into secret pockets sewn inside his garment, Todd looked over at his partner. "Well, are we ready?"

"I don't know if the answer to that could ever be yes, but let's go anyway."

Getting in first, Todd took the far seat with Aaliyah following close behind. He grinned at Aaliyah the moment she realized the only available seat was sitting on his lap. And he didn't seem to mind. Hudson came in last, securing his belt.

"Mr. President, if I were you I'd leave the room before this things goes." Hudson spoke quietly to the man he wanted to hurt.

Waving a hand, he moved toward the exit, "Sounds good to me. I look forward to this being behind us in the next couple days. The country and I owe each of you big for this. God speed." The President left through the curved door in the wall.

Hudson palmed the right panel, and the vehicle came to life. The interior lighting blinked on as did the readouts on the dash. After several quick touches, the four telescopic shafts within the cockpit began to slowly drop the upper half of the pearlescent sphere in place. A loud clamp indicated the locking mechanism had kicked in.

Aaliyah's heart was thumping so solidly Todd could feel it coursing against his chest through her back. For a few moments the cockpit was totally silent. After turning off the cabin lights, the sphere was completely dark except for the dash lights in front of them. All colors of light-emitting diodes blinked and illuminated the small craft in which they were encased.

Hudson looked at the quadrants on the dash. Checking each of the areas, he made a few changes. The vehicle had originally returned to the year five, yet because they were locked out of that time, he would return them a year later. He programmed four B.C. into the computer.

Also seeing the GPS coordinates, the agent made a deviation. Not a large one, but one that would allow them enough time to exit the vehicle if an army regiment were waiting for them to arrive. He changed the seconds on the position to land them one mile north of the original destination.

"I hope that'll give us enough time," Hudson said aloud.

"Buddy, God's going before us in this fight, it's going to be alright. All you can do is your best."

This time Hudson knew what he was up against, "I don't think my best is going to be good enough."

The agent checked every area of the sphere one more time. "Is everyone ready?"

Todd held Aaliyah firmly as she closed her eyes. "Let's do this!"

Smiling, Hudson touched the blinking green light on the screen and pressed his head into the headrest in the seat.

"Ten, nine, eight."

The machine began to hum.

"Seven, six, five," the computer counted down.

A smell started to form in the air that reminded its occupants of ozone.

"Four, three, two."

The laser below came to life and a reddish-yellow aura was reflected out of the four tubes at the base of the machine.

"One."

Todd could see a blue glow from within the sphere caused by the intense electrical power whirling around his body. He felt his form tingle.

"Zero."

The Oval Office filled with light from the millions of tendrils covering the sphere. One could almost walk on the electricity that engulfed the room.

When the occupants thought they couldn't take the high pitched sound emanating from within the vehicle and the pressure formed within the room any longer, the vehicle exploded into history leaving the room as it was before.

Feeling the pressure wave through the residence, the President knew they had returned to the 1st century. Pulling out a gold plated lighter from his pocket, he lit the cigar in his hand. With a smile, he glanced at the fountain in front of the White House encircled with impatiens and begonias.

"It's going to be a beautiful day."

The President took a long draw, headed down the hallway and returned to his activities without another thought about the three who had headed 2000 years into the past.

Aurius stood on the highest point in Jerusalem before the impressive cedar doors of the stronghold called the Tower of David. He'd read about it, of course, but had never been so close to what is now called the Citadel. The massive defensive structure dominated the only point in Jerusalem higher than the Temple Mount.

He wasn't looking forward to interacting with the military. Ruled by a paranoid king they were a suspicious and shrewd lot with the weaponry, know-how and muscles to eliminate any threat. Walking into this place to grab himself a few men to help him take out his competition wouldn't be easy. Even with direct – albeit undocumented – approval from Herod.

The gate moved toward him, opening halfway and revealing three guards in the entry, all imposingly armed. Aurius swallowed involuntarily, his breath suddenly caught in his throat. The heavily armored soldier on the right barked out a request for identification that nearly sent him back down the steps behind him. Instead, he lifted his chin in feigned arrogance and held his signet ring aloft. With a curt nod, the commander on the left directed the others to open wide the gate and permit him access to the world of the first century military.

As a phony prophet who was currently manipulating the King, entering this building had never crossed his mind as a viable option. The Pentagon of its time overflowed with military leaders who could smell a fraud a mile away, and Aurius was definitely a fraud; a fake with few options.

Once inside, Aurius saw what appeared at first glance to be chaos; a large open square with connected tunnels running off in different directions. The prophet didn't have to practice divination to recognize that the tunnels separated the training ground into segments. A soldier on horseback led the way for others down one tunnel. At the entrance of another, two men engaged in sword play slashing at one another while young, obviously new recruits watched and were quizzed. A wooden beam in the third tunnel absorbed the hits and misses of arrowheads as marksmen-in-training learned their skill. But, Aurius was being led toward the furthest tunnel, known fondly as the lion's den.

Following the centurion down the passageway, their progress stopped at a large room filled with tables full of high ranking military leaders doing everything from drinking, playing cards and sharing war stories to looking over maps for future conquests. Upon Aurius of Antioch's unexpected entrance, the room of heavily equipped men fell silent.

A soldier named Thorius who had been sharpening his dagger walked up and met the intruder with it still unsheathed.

"Who might you be?" he asked turning the blade in his hand.

Knowing these men had rarely, if ever, seen him since he worked directly with the King, the prophet put on his most confident air, "I am Aurius of Antioch. As prophet to King Herod I require one of you, along with a small regiment, to come with me."

The room erupted with laughter, grumblings, and general disregard for the stuffy old man.

A Praefectus Castrorum in the back yelled, "One of us is to come with you and take our soldiers? What orders do you have? Has Herod given you an edict?"

Standing tall, "I just left the King and he said I am to be given your full cooperation."

"Where is it written? Where is his seal?" laughed a Pilus Prior taking off his breastplate.

"The King has had no time to have the paperwork written, however, you see the seal of Herod on my signet ring." He again lifted his fist for all to see. "You are to come immediately."

"I say you are not the King, a Senator, a Prophet or any other position of note in this kingdom. Your accent is foreign and your manner deceptive. I believe we have some form of trickery in our midst." Thorius was grandstanding for his comrades, and Aurius could see through all his bravado. It didn't slow his pulse, however, from reacting to the man's unknowingly keen insight. Or the fear that grew every time he turned that wicked-looking knife of his.

The pseudo prophet now stood toe to toe with the man as he continued, "I believe you are a threat to King Herod. You know what happens to one who stands between Herod and his throne, yes?"

Aurius faked a sneer, "Move aside or have your own head handed to you, you overgrown goat." When the brute forced his dagger under his throat, Aurius knew he had overplayed his hand

His threats no longer idle, Thorius continued, "Who are you to threaten me? If I slit your delicate throat here and now, no one would bat an eye. They would simply remove your carcass to the dung heap. Is not that right gentlemen?" The group nodded good-naturedly in agreement. "You would just disappear and would never be seen again. What now do you have to say?"

"Well, I *personally* would say that the King would be terribly disappointed," Cyprianus interrupted as the men in the room stood at attention. "Yes, Thorius, I would say that even though we Romans are exempt from crucifixion, our good King might make an exception for you if you even put a scratch on his all-knowing prophet."

Sitting in front of Aurius on the edge of a table he gestured to the others, "Please men, at ease." The room returned to its previous state.

Cyprianus turned to Aurius and looked at him, eyes unblinking.

Thorius backed away and bowed, "Sir, forgive my hasty reaction. How could I know he spoke the truth? He reeks of insolence, Sir. Nonetheless, I would consider it an honor to take my men and aid this, uh, man, in his task."

"Thorius, I believe that would be praiseworthy on your part, but we do not yet know what our dear prophet has in mind." His eyes continued to bore holes in the poor man, "Aurius of Antioch, why do you need the services of the military?"

Feeling uncomfortable in the room and knowing Cyprianus was more of an enemy than a friend, "As I told the King, men are coming to interrupt my work. It is my job to ensure his welfare and if I am removed, I cannot foresee threats that may be aimed at cutting his reign short."

Standing and pacing, "So someone is trying to kill you. How do they know of your work?"

"My prophecy is known throughout the east. There are several entities who would have me removed in order to defeat the king."

Cyprianus continued, "How do you know they are coming?"

"A vision." It was getting harder to lie. He felt the sweat forming droplets beneath his armpits.

"You saw this threat in a vision?" His disbelief echoed in the poorly-held snickers around the room. Soldiers had little respect for those who claimed to have visions in order to obtain power. They secured power with military might. Anything less disgusted them. Aurius knew this, but stood his ground all the same. As of this moment, it was all he had.

"A great vision within a dream, as I saw other visions that have protected the King."

"Is this the same method for which you implicated the King's son?"

Knowing where this line of reasoning was going, "Yes and no. I had a vision of Antipater killing his father while I was fully awake," he feared his attempts to be convincing were failing miserably.

Cyprianus stopped his pacing and raised his voice, "There was no proof that Antipater had ever done anything against his father. No proof!"

"The King believed what I had to say and made the necessary adjustments."

His tone now was deceptively quiet, "The King murdered his own son. Your influence has left this kingdom in a shambles! Scores of innocent people have been investigated or killed because of your so-called visions." The words echoed off of the dark limestone walls. "No one is safe while you are here."

Chilled at his words, Aurius grabbed at his last chance at composure. Making a fist, he once again held high his signet ring and its granted powers to Cyprianus. "You will do as I say or I will report you to the King. I would hate for him to investigate you as well. I imagine your family would also be rather upset."

Trying to regain his composure, Cyprianus shut his eyes as the room fell silent, "How many men are coming to kill you?"

"Some."

"How many exactly is some?"

"Two. Two men are coming. I need no more than six soldiers to apprehend them."

Cyprianus stood and walked to the back of the room. After a quick drink from a barrel he finally spoke, "Thorius, get your best fifty men and have them ready within the hour."

Aurius interrupted, "I only need half a dozen."

Patting a soldier on the back, he smiled, "My good Dritus, I want you to get your best fifty men as well and be ready to leave with Thorius." The soldier stood at attention and saluted in acceptance before leaving in a hurry.

"Men, I will be leading this expedition personally," he commented as he walked quickly to a spot in front of Aurius, "Our dear prophet is highly prized by the King and we need to ensure his protection as well as the defeat of anyone who may seek his life."

Aurius began fumbling for words, "But this is excessive. Six men are all I need."

"It can never be excessive if it means your protection," Cyprianus said getting nose to nose with the prophet. Speaking where only Aurius could hear he made his position plain, "My friend, I do not begin to know your game, but if you send us on a wild dog hunt for your own gain, I will be sure to tell the King of your inaccuracy in prophecy and will delight myself in gutting you in his presence."

Backing away and continuing a stare, "Prepare this fortification. An invading force is coming against the King by way of his prophet," he said raising his voice. "I want this facility on lockdown and all men at their posts." Accelerating from the room through the tunnel, Cyprianus could be heard yelling, "The King will not be threatened on my watch!"

Aurius knew that if he were wrong about the traveler's timeline, he would most likely not see the completion of his mission. The room became a frenzy of activity as the knot in his stomach tightened.

—

Within 30 minutes, the multitude of soldiers and equipment left the Citadel and raced full speed to the area Aurius had described. Never had the prophet seen such an exit from Jerusalem. Every type of compliment available made its way in the forward march. A few small siege machines highlighted the mass exodus from the compound.

Obviously, Cyprianus was going to involve as many men and resources as possible to make a spectacle of Aurius.

The General led them on horseback while Aurius trailed close behind in a chariot. The prophet had never been in a vehicle of this type at this speed and wasn't sure the wooden axels could take the incessant beating.

The remaining men and equipment followed after. Seeing the long line of soldiers marching six abreast was beyond description. Many Hollywood movies had tried to describe the vision, but all had come up short. Even at a quick trot, the men stayed in formation without missing a step, chewing the dust billowing off those in front.

The entire organization incomprehensibly included more than one hundred fighting men, carts carrying food, water and supplies, medical personnel and a few others like the cooks and their cart of supplies.

Roman equestrians were sent ahead to way points to ensure fresh horses, and water was prepared for the men so they could continue their forward trek. Following brief stops in Jericho and Machaerus, the small army made its way the last fifteen miles to the spot Aurius had entered the country exactly one year before.

The farther the regiment traveled from the Dead Sea, the more desolate the countryside became. When Cyprianus arrived at the final hill, he stopped and waited for Aurius to catch up to him.

The prophet pulled up alongside the general and Cyprianus spoke without looking at him, "Is this the place where your threats are to arrive?" His voice was condescending and hostile.

The temperature was well over one hundred degrees in the blazing sun, and the desert to the east seemed to have no end. Desolation. The word came to mind regarding the many small mountains and rocky outcroppings, without a single living thing to be seen.

Aurius knew that, at best, his guests had yet to arrive. This knowledge was something that pleased yet worried him. "Yes this is where they are to be."

"Then we dig in and prepare," Cyprianus responded, turning his horse to gallop back to the leaders of the fighting men.

Aurius stepped from his vehicle and walked ahead. It was just a short time ago that he had arrived in the time machine, and could still make out the imprint in the dirt where it came to rest. Bending down and picking up some compacted ground, he let it fall between his fingers.

Rising again, he turned and scanned the horizon and whispered, "Are you coming?"

Up to this point, everything in his plan had moved along perfectly. If God existed, Aurius would have attributed many miracles to Him by now. He hadn't been killed by one of the many ways an illegal immigrant with plans on manipulating the kingdom could have met his demise. It was almost laughable that he still lived, much less that he had the ear of the King and could command regiments like the one arriving now and taking its fortified position just west of him.

But no, Aurius knew there was no God who cared. For He surely wouldn't have taken his wife and daughter from him. A loving and caring God would never have allowed stray bullets from a gang initiation to tear through an inner city mission and kill his two beautiful ladies. The sweet mother and daughter now only in his dreams had been two innocent people giving their time freely on behalf of their God. They knew their only reward would be telling of God's love and mercy to yet another lost and wayward soul.

No. A good God would never allow that to happen. As a mere mortal, he would give his all to stop evil from hurting his family. Why wouldn't an all-powerful God? Aurius would have given his life to save his wife and daughter.

He heard every day here "There is no god but Caesar." He was beginning to agree. At least Caesar had the power over life and death, something the impotent god his wife and daughter followed evidently did not.

Aurius' purpose in conducting his part of this plan was to bring his wife and daughter back. Nevertheless, he felt justified in knowing that the byproduct of his work would be to eliminate the message of one whom the world turned into a God, yet was not.

Taking a deep breath, the prophet walked back to his carriage with determination. He would squash the reputation of this God and have his wife and daughter back even if it meant that he would give his life to fulfill the mission. The goal was worth the sacrifice.

Cyprianus gripped the saddle with his powerful thighs in order to lift himself up for a better view of the man twenty yards ahead of him. He watched him a moment through hate-filled eyes. This so called prophet had belittled him in front of the King; the Roman soldier looked forward to settling the score.

Upon pushing activation on the panel of the sphere, everything began to change. The reluctant travelers watched as the solid outer shell of the orb became opaque altering their view to become somewhat like looking through a foggy window. The Oval Office instantaneously disappeared and everything around them turned to a hazy mixture of brown and black.

It was understood very early in the calculation phase that if the sphere were returning in time and relocating its position, the first thing it would do would be to find its new site by the most direct path available - a straight line. So, for instance, if it were moving across town, it would simply move horizontally through whatever was in its way.

However, if the sphere were going to another location on the globe, the scientists deduced that the vehicle would still choose the shortest path between the points. Thus, with it traveling half way across the world, the direction of the space and time change occurred directly through the outer mantle of the earth.

The view outside the vehicle proved to be a blur of strata altered to allow their trek through space as the vehicle attempted to find its position from the Oval Office to waypoints just east of Jerusalem.

Once the vehicle found its new location, by design it would then begin its ascent into history. The science showed that it would take about one second per every hundred years to return into the past. If it were translocating, that would add additional time.

Heat radiated warmed the air. Vibrations buzzed through their clothing, intermittent bursts of ear-piercing sound and the sheer terror of not knowing where they would end up or *if* they would end up, made the twenty-five second expedition through the earth and time an eternity for the travelers.

Upon coming to rest, the passengers were violently thrown forward in the cabin of the machine, bringing them back to a modicum of reality after trying to do everything possible to dull their senses from the overload of the ride. Hudson and Todd were hanging from their safety straps while Aaliyah was thrown forward and now rested against the upper section of the sphere.

After a pre-programmed amount of time, the canopy on the steaming vehicle opened, releasing Aaliyah to the hard rocky ground below. All proximity lighting immediately came on. Not that it was needed due to the sun's position being straight overhead. The remaining occupants reactively closed their eyes allowing their pupils to adjust to the intense illumination. After several seconds Hudson was able to see the dark panel before him. Matching the programmed time and location to those presently blinking on the other side of the cockpit, the agent confirmed that they had arrived at the place they were looking for.

The professor released his straps. Holding the safety belt with one hand, he worked his way out of the precariously placed sphere and ran over to Aaliyah. Picking her up, she said, "Ani vadoor gamoor." *I am fine.*

"How is she?" Hudson barked at him without looking, trying to check the systems on the machine that offered the only way back to their time.

Aaliyah rose as Todd looked her over. "I think she's okay. She has a bump on her head and a few scrapes from the fall, but says she's going to be alright."

"Good," Hudson turned their direction for a visual corroboration.

"Hey, buddy you better get out here and look at this." The professor's voice was nervous.

Hudson worked his way from the vehicle, falling to the ground just as Aaliyah had. After wiping off the few cuts the hard rocks added to his already bruised and beaten body, he saw what both of his passengers were already staring at.

"Oh, no," he mumbled sounding defeated.

The sphere was wedged precariously between two large boulders and listing about 30 degrees forward. One of the struts was crushed under the weight of the vehicle while several others were bent.

Todd spoke, "Is it going to be alright?"

Mist rose from the outer hull as the ice formed during reentry began to steam in the intense heat. Within a minute, the outer covering was dry again and glistening in the sun.

"Huh," Hudson muttered, climbing on a boulder behind the vehicle. "The good thing is that you really can't hurt the sphere. See the way it melted the rock around it? The outer shell is diamond coated - designed to protect itself from the insane variations in surroundings during travel. We could land this thing inside of a mountain and it would form a perfectly spherical cavity around itself. Just like this. Someone in the future is going to have a heyday explaining how these boulders melted with perfectly curved arcs in them."

Aaliyah put her hands on the newly smoothed stone.

Coming back around to the front Hudson looked underneath, "What worries me is this."

The only part of the machine not contained directly within the sphere was the high-intensity laser cannon. The cannon completed the operation of the apparatus by opening a temporal hole. Fueled by Uranium 235, the activated sapphire laser could, given the opportunity, punch a hole in the moon and keep going. Currently, it was engulfed in a red steam.

"That doesn't look good," Todd mumbled.

Beginning to sweat, Hudson rose from the ground, "As I said, the sphere portion of the vehicle is covered in melted diamond. Pretty hard stuff, but they couldn't cover the peripherals with it. That thing with the red fog is the laser that allows everything to happen. Without it we don't go anywhere."

Hudson precariously climbed back into the cockpit and pushed a few quadrants on the dash. After scanning through menus and sub-menus he found the information he searched for. The values for the laser quickly validated his fear. Working his way back to the ground with his friends sitting in the shade of a rock, Hudson broke the news.

"The laser has evidently cracked its sapphire lens."

"What does that mean - it's "cracked" its sapphire lens?" Todd sarcastically added air quotes for the word cracked.

"Just that, the laser won't work. And without the laser, we can't leave." After a pause, "looks like we'll need to find one," the agent said matter-of-factly.

Aaliyah knew nothing about technology. But she understood their lifeboat was sinking.

Todd became irate, "How can this happen? I mean with technology this advanced, all it takes is a bump and the machine locks the driver in the past? What kind of designing is that? My undergrad degree is in engineering, and with just a Bachelor's degree I would've done a better job than that! You had to have had scores of Ph.D.'s on this project!" He threw his arms in the air.

"We aren't supposed to just be jumping all over the world with it," just as upset, Hudson said through the small hand cloth he'd just pulled out of his burlap bag. "Every jump we make is to be checked and rechecked before we go. It was never designed to just put in a coordinate and make a trip into the desert. All locations are scouted out before we ever leave, to ensure this doesn't happen."

"Oh God, what are we to do?" Todd asked his Lord, feeling defeated and looking to the heavens. He sat down on a rock and stared off into the distance.

Seeing the men's reaction, Aaliyah spoke quietly. "Hatpaleel, hatpaleel!"

"What's she saying?" Hudson asked looking under once again.

Todd broke his gaze and watched at the woman who seemed comfortable in the desert. She was right, and he should know better. He sighed wearily.

Aaliyah yelled this time, "Hatpaleel, hatpaleel!" Without formal education and having a first century world view, the woman's wisdom came forth. She knew their only option was the Lord and they must rely on Him to get them out of their present plight.

Holding Aaliyah's hand, Todd responded, "Good idea." He called out to Hudson who still wiped around the bottom of the machine, "Pray. She's telling us to pray."

Trying to edge his way out, he finally rose from the ground and spoke quietly, "I don't think anything else will help. The future's in God's hands now."

In the center of the desert, with temperatures well over 100 degrees, the three reluctant travelers grabbed hands and asked the Lord for His guidance in solving a problem they knew they couldn't. For several minutes each person opened their heart to God in heaven, they ended the time feeling stronger and more encouraged - even though nothing had changed. They looked up and dropped their hands.

Hudson spoke first, "Well, until the Lord tells us how to fix that machine without any tools or equipment, our first priority is to complete the mission. If God allows us to get home that'll just be icing on the cake."

"Let's pray he does," Todd retorted.

"Amen."

Going over to the sphere, Todd pulled their provisions from under the seats and gave each person their bag while Hudson climbed up the short cliff behind the machine and looked off in the distance.

"Do you see that over there?" he said pointing to the south.

Aaliyah and Todd walked up alongside the agent and found the sight before them.

"Haetsva haroomi!" Aaliyah said several times with many other words that were too fast to be understood. She ran down trying to get behind a large outcropping and pulling at her clothing.

The professor followed, doing his best to calm her obvious fear. After a short conversation the professor yelled up at Hudson. "It looks like the Roman army is doing maneuvers in the desert. Aaliyah doesn't remember seeing such a large group at one time without going to war against some other country."

The terrified woman looked in all directions trying to find a way out of her position. Knowing she was clearly dressed as a Roman added to her fear of the people who had enslaved her nation.

"It's going to be alright. Just relax. I'll protect you," Todd said trying to sound strong, as if he weren't also nervous. He pulled a water jug from his sack and gave it to Aaliyah.

Continuing his information to Hudson, "She says that several times when they were looking for certain people they would raid villages in large groups. It isn't normal that they just work in the desert without a reason."

Aaliyah shook the canister and gave it back.

"Yeah, they're looking for someone alright, they're looking for us," the agent mumbled.

"What did you say?" Todd asked investigating at the empty water canister.

Coming down from the rock face, "I said they're looking for us."

The professor's face went white. "You sure they're looking for us?"

"That's the only explanation. They're setting up in the area where we were supposed to land. If we hadn't have changed our landing site, we'd be arrested right now."

"We've got another problem."

"What's that?" Hudson asked not really needing another dilemma.

Shaking an empty water canister, "These jugs have no water. It looks like no one went out of their way to fill them. We don't have any water for the three of us to make it to the nearest city. At these temperatures," judging the heat, "we'll be stopped in our tracks in a matter of hours." With a slight laugh, "Just think, at least we won't have to worry about a trial and long excruciating crucifixion."

"Great," Hudson said sarcastically. "It sounds like things are looking up," he tried to laugh. Sitting on a rock feeling defeated, "Todd, we aren't supposed to make it back. You know that, don't you?"

"I thought I heard the cards stacking against us." He smiled wanly at his own joke.

No water, a broken vehicle, the entire Roman army just a mile south looking for us," Hudson counted off on his hand, "in a tough world with a crazy man trying to alter the future and everything we know. I don't know if things could get much worse."

Todd jumped in trying to lighten the situation, "But I think we've been through harder."

"What would that be?"

Laughing, "Just last week! Please tell me you remember. That was no cake walk, and God got us through it."

Hudson smiled as he stared at the ground.

Sounding encouraging Todd continued, "I'm an eagle scout. I've had a little desert training - but nothing like this."

Hudson stared at their female companion and knew they were in her hands. "Aaliyah is our only hope."

She looked up.

He continued, "She's lived here all her life. She'll know where to find food, make fire, find water, and shelter…"

Todd also looked over at the woman who was becoming uncomfortable with all of the staring. "If there is any hope, it's in her skills."

"Who would have guessed we would be relying on a five foot, one hundred pound woman for our safety? Talk to her and tell her the mess we're in."

It took several minutes for the professor to truly convey the concepts. He was trained in ancient languages but knew that 21st century knowledge of the 1st century was limited. However, she was quickly picking up English as he was gaining a better mastery of her vocabulary and syntax.

Aaliyah understood the need for water, food, and shelter all too well. She smiled brightly and spoke, "Ow kay."

Hudson smirked, "Did she just say okay?"

"Ow kay, me hep."

Todd translated needlessly, "I think she's going to help."

Pulling Todd by the arm, she walked him back up to the top of the rocky ridge. Pointing in several directions, and speaking slow Hebrew, Aramaic or Greek so he could understand her in at least one of the languages. Todd came back down after several minutes and relayed the information to his friend.

Feeling like the temperature had raised ten degrees in the last few minutes, Hudson walked over to the professor. "What did she say?"

"She hasn't been in this area before, but has a good knowledge of this type of terrain. Aaliyah showed me several areas where she thought we could find water. There also seems to be a few rocky valleys where she thinks we can make shelter for the night."

Feeling invigorated and patting him on the shoulder, "Well, it looks like we're back in business. You know, we just might make it out of here."

"I never really had a doubt. I was just hoping it wasn't in leg irons or something like that. Should I get our stuff?"

"Yeah, let's get ready to move," Hudson responded with a new purpose in his step.

"What are we going to do with this thing?" he said pointing at the sphere.

"We have to hope no one steals it in the next few days. It will only open with my palm print so I'm not worried about someone getting into it."

Todd brought the conversation to a point, "What will a 1st century person think if they found this?"

"I'm hoping no one comes by here in the next few days. There isn't much I can do about it with it being broken and all."

He smiled. "Should I tell Aaliyah to lead us to the water and shelter?"

Hudson looked Todd in the eyes, "Yes, but we have an errand to run first."

Hudson and his entourage were getting thirsty. With the sun and heat at its apex, they would need water and nourishment very soon, but they also needed to get a closer view of the activity before finding all necessary provisions.

They had spent two hours trekking through the wilderness east of Israel. Sheer 1000 foot drops, hard rocky ground, little if any vegetation, and a few small Ibex climbing the dusty precipices now defined their reality along with a small Roman army just waiting patiently in the heat for something to happen.

Trained in reconnaissance, Hudson was accustomed to tracking and surveying the enemy. And, normally, the secret service agent would have been worried about having these two novices as his sidekicks. But somewhere along the way he realized how much of a help rather than a detriment they might be.

Todd was a black belt in Tae Kwon Do and, as he had recently learned, an Eagle Scout. His muscular frame belonged on a personal trainer instead of a professor in the hallowed halls of academia, and his high intellect made him quick to observe what was happening around them.

Aaliyah turned out to be the best at ducking them out of the way at the first sign of trouble, be it the Roman soldiers or wild animals they encountered. Many times after leaving the sphere, she spotted a legionnaire scouting about for threats to the main army's position. Under her guidance, the travelers doubled back, climbed into one of the many caves, or hid behind a rock feature.

After walking what had to have been close to three miles of valley floors to cover the one mile to the army encampment, they were finally able to view the action without becoming part of it. Aaliyah climbed up the backside of a large outcropping and signaled. Creeping up next to her they both fell flat on their stomachs in order to look down at the fortified Roman position.

"They're dug in," Hudson mumbled.

"I'd say so. They're in basic flanking patterns." He directed Hudson's attention to where he pointed, "At the front, they have manipular formations. See the three lines broken into segments? Each line is offset to ensure that none of the breaks become a weakness."

He focused toward the back, "They even have echelon patterns on either side. See the way each side comes off at an angle like when geese fly south for the winter? One man is just to the side of the other."

Perplexed, Hudson angled a glance at him. "How do you know so much about Roman warfare?"

Todd smirked, "Just because I'm a seminary professor doesn't mean I don't like gladiator movies."

They both chuckled.

"You're an enigma to me, you know that?" Hudson responded.

"Yeah, and I like it that way. And, okay, I've done some research about this era, being so interwoven Biblically, as it is."

Aaliyah had seen all she wanted and inched her way from the edge.

"If there is anything good here, it's that they're all focused one direction; to the east."

"Yeah, there's a weakness in the back. They're expecting all of the action to come from one way," the professor continued.

Hudson pointed toward the front of the formation, "Do you see that circular area there about 100 yards east and directly in front of the forward-facing line?"

Somewhat perplexed, "What is that?"

Answering the question, "That's evidently where he landed last time. He's expecting us to pop up right there."

"It would've been easy work for them if we just could have helped the process by landing right there," Todd chuckled.

"I'm not here to help them out," Hudson responded seriously.

In the back center, behind all of the expendable troops, several tents stood. "He has to be in one of those," the agent thought aloud, wiping his brow.

"It doesn't sound like a good idea to just knock on his tent and see if he would like to go home with us. He's going to be really well protected."

A small rock fell from the cliff, just under their position shattering one hundred feet below. The men instinctively pulled back to the same spot Aaliyah had discovered several minutes earlier hoping not to be seen.

Hudson tried to reassure them, "I don't think they saw us."

"No, but it doesn't mean they won't come and investigate. The Roman army wasn't the best in the world at this time for nothing. They'll be sending some legionnaires to check this spot out."

Aaliyah looked at them wide-eyed, "Wee gow. Gow, gow!"

Hudson agreed, "We need to go now!"

—

Cyprianus tore another piece of meat from the collective plate in the officer's tent and looked at the mass of men standing at attention in the sun with disgust.

"Why are we here?" Dritus asked, sharpening his dagger. "No army in its right mind would try to conquer from the east." Without looking up he continued, "There are a thousand miles of desert out there. The only people trained to live out here are the nomads."

"And they would never start a war from the east," Thorius laughed while finishing the statement. He poured more wine into his glass and drank it down without a breath. "We have brought our men into the driest and hottest spot on earth on the whim of a so-called prophet, and we are supposed to protect his life - and not the King's. I do not like it Cyprianus. I have been trained to protect Rome and its provinces, and would give my life for my King. But not for him," he spat.

"Relax gentlemen, just a little while longer," Cyprianus said calmly.

Dritus jumped up, "You do not believe someone is really coming? That there is some kind of truth to his lunacy." More of an accusation than a question, he sheathed his dagger and waited for the response.

Thorius watched the leader.

Cyprianus looked around at the men who were waiting in the sun. The young leader of thirty years was just as dedicated to his King as Thorius or Dritus, if not more. He had killed many in the name of Roman expansion. Had decimated villages at the whim of a King. Had been in more hand-to-hand combat than men twice his age and had the scars covering his body to show for it. Even when he disagreed with the orders, he completed them to the best of his ability. Nonetheless, he didn't like his men suffering.

His pent-up breath released. As a general, he knew that a few foolhardy missions would make his men second guess his leadership, no matter where the orders came from - and he needed his men fresh. His combat troops surpassed all others in the region and he planned on keeping them that way. Looking over at Aurius, his anger grew.

"No my good Dritus, I do not believe anyone is coming to kill him. However, the longer we are here, the more rope we give him to hang himself with," Cyprianus focused his gaze at Aurius.

Dritus and Thorius looked at each other and smiled. Payback would be sweet.

—

Aurius of Antioch sat in his tent knowing all of his cards were on the table. He also knew that if he lost, it would mean his life. He refused the food or drink offered by the servants. He had gambled and lost.

Looking out over the countryside, the prophet watched the desert full of men. Hundreds of them it appeared, with weapons, machines, wagons, and supplies - all waiting in the sun. Five hours had passed and still they waited – at the orders of the three leaders resting in the tent adjacent to his.

As Aurius looked over at the officer's tent he saw Cyprianus watching him intently as the other two carried on, smiling and laughing. They were mocking him. Probably constructing his end together with some new form of crucifixion that took longer and was more painful. Only the worst form of punishment would suffice for a prophet who wasn't prophetic, and right now, Aurius had no more "prophecy" left to tell. The opposition had to be out there. He had planned it perfectly. There would be no way they could allow him to finish his plan. His guests would be coming.

His eyes grew wide, "What if they changed the landing site?" Aurius mumbled to himself in English. He lifted himself from the cushions and started to pace the tent. "They would have known that I'd be expecting them. I sent them an invitation. If I know they're coming, then I'd find a way to confront them when they got here."

Aurius stopped pacing and looked off in the distance. He yelled, "How foolish! What was I thinking?"

Cyprianus turned again toward the prophet, not understanding the foreign tongue he jabbered as he entered his tent. Shifting his weight from the tent stake, he moved to enter Aurius tent.

"What are you saying my dear prophet?" the general gave a slight bow before taking a drink from a chalice he had carried over.

"The heat must be getting to me," Aurius responded in Greek knowing the bow was an insult.

"Yes, it is getting to everyone," he said condescendingly. "I am sure my men will be mumbling in unknown tongues after a few more hours in this sun." With a smile, he nodded in the direction of the men waiting in the heat. "Aurius of Antioch, we have been in the desert now for over five hours. Would you be able to summon the spirits to determine when this threat will come? Or should the men prepare for dinner?" He bowed insolently yet again, "I would not want them to start their meal if this threat to your life comes in the next few minutes. It would be much more efficient for the men if they could plan their next rest around the small war we are to wage on your behalf."

The prophet felt very vulnerable and out of his element. "Cyprianus we must send out scouts in all directions."

Standing straight, "And why would that be?"

"Because I… uh, have just become aware that… that this location has been compromised," he tried to keep his own uncertainty from his voice.

Walking forward, "Why would this position be compromised? Did you not see this spot in your dreams, or a vision, or in a pattern in your beard? However you prophets work, you were very certain that we would find your enemies here. Were you not?"

Seeing the general closing the gap between them, "My visions are not always precise. They sometimes change with the stars."

Cyprianus stood toe to toe with the prophet, "You were very certain about this spot," he jabbed his finger toward the ground. "Of the countless places on this earth, you took us exactly here. A place in the desert no one in their right mind would come to. You were very confident five hours ago. What has happened? Have you had another vision?"

"General, we must send out scouts. They must go north, east, and south."

"Did your newest vision come up with those directions?" His glare could melt a weaker man quicker than the heat. Aurius focused on what he needed to say next.

Even though Aurius had close to 30 years of age on the young man staring him down, and had wrestled and wrangled with diplomats, congressmen, senators, and even world leaders, he felt intimidated and very small. They could kill him quickly and leave him in this large desert to never be found.

Summoning up his courage he enunciated clearly, "You are to follow my lead. The King has given me total control of this mission, and I am telling you to send scouts out to the north, east, and south."

Without breaking his glare the younger man breathed in slowly before answering, "Aurius, if that is your name. I do not trust you and never have. Somehow, you have fooled the King, but you do not fool me. I have known men like you all my life. You have your own agenda at play. I will eventually see through your plan but because I have not yet, you are still alive. I will give you a few more hours before I kill you and tell the King you fell in a hole and broke your neck, or were bitten by a viper of some kind. Throwing you from a cliff would be easiest. I could take your body back without many questions."

The prophet tried to hold his ground as his stomach churned.

Turning and looking at the soldiers to the north, "No, to my weakness, I have not seen through your plan yet, but I will. My real fear is that the King is in danger while his best soldiers are waiting in the desert. It would be extremely unfortunate for you if anything happened to him while we were out here."

Snapping back to look at Aurius, "So no, I will not be sending men in any direction. Not north, east, south, up or down. They will stay here for several more hours and if nothing happens, you will be the men's meal tonight. Do you understand what I am saying?"

"You have been very clear."

"Good," he said with a smile. "You might want to check the rock formations or look at the stars for a vision to get you out of this. That is what I would do - if I were you." Cyprianus turned and started to walk from the tent as a pile of rocks fell from an outcropping a quarter of a mile to the north east.

"What was that?" he yelled to Dritus and Thorius.

The men instinctively stood when the rocks fell and responded to their leader.

Thorius spoke first, "I do not know. I see no animals over there."

Dritus continued, "Nor do I. None of our men are on that cliff. What would you have us do?"

Cyprianus looked off at the rocky mountain in frustration. He knew from the many years of warfare under his belt and the teaching he had given to a multitude of recruits that the best place to be was on the high ground. Something he had overlooked in this mission because he had believed it to be a wild goose chase. The general's recent words were coming back to haunt him.

Glancing at Aurius who now had a look of superiority on his face, Cyprianus knew the rocks must have fallen as a result of an outside force. And if he lost men on this mission, it would be because he didn't do his best planning, and therefore would be held responsible. He shook his head in irritation. He had been certain, so certain, the man was lying.

Starting to bark off orders, "Take twenty-five of your best trackers and divide them up to cover those four different ridges," he pointed to areas around the encampment. "I want four men to scout that outcropping. If someone was there, I want to know."

"Yes sir," both officers spoke as they ran off in different directions to spread the word.

Cyprianus did not look back at the prophet, but found his horse and jumped on its back. He rode up and down the line looking for weaknesses in their position and ranks. If this threat did happen to be real, he was determined to make up for his lack of judgment.

Aurius sat back in a chair and smiled, "So you are here." He laughed. "Servant," he said barking at a young man outside of the tent, "Bring me wine!"

Having taken the easiest path possible onto the cliff, Hudson knew the Roman army would do the same, so the way they entered could not be the way they would leave. The agent was beating himself up for not allowing an exit strategy; he should have thought more about the possibility of getting trapped on the ledge. Yet, at this point there was nothing else that could be done; they would be leaving down a sheer rock face on the back side. The descent would be difficult for climbers in contemporary gear let alone those in faux 1st century garb.

Hudson and Todd ran along the cliff looking for the easiest way down.

"This might be a possibility," gestured the professor, "it looks like there are enough hand holds to get us down."

"I don't think so; see down there," pointing, "that drop looks too high for Aaliyah. What about over here?"

"Nope, there is ten feet of sheer face."

While the men were discussing an exit strategy, Aaliyah was brushing at the ground with a branch from a small bush.

"What's she doing?" asked Hudson half looking back.

"The leaders down there will be sending their best trackers. Aaliyah is literally covering our tracks. She's lived in this world long enough to know the tricks."

After sufficiently rubbing out as many marks as possible, she looked over the edge of the cliff and started down. She gestured and spoke up to the men above her, "Tis waye."

"Her English is coming along," smiled Todd.

"I hope she knows what she's doing, because we're out of time."

Following the young woman closely now Todd beamed back at him, "Hudson, this is her world. If anyone can get us out, it'll be Aaliyah."

It took almost an hour to make it to the dry river bed below. The work was slow and tedious with several jumps to parallel rocks. The young woman's abilities far surpassed the men's as she led the way down, making perfect choices for hand and foot holds.

Aaliyah's decisions on when to move parallel and when to go back up to find a better descent forced them to trust her instincts instead of trying to protect her. Finally, they allowed her to just lead. Their female guide was a natural in this land and had been trained to survive by simply surviving.

Trying to exist in the first century at the bottom of the socio-economic ladder required one to have skills - and she had them beyond any twenty-first century outdoorsman.

At the dry river bed below, Todd was out of breath and growing thirstier by the second, "If we don't get water, we're not going to make it much longer."

"I agree," Hudson said bent over with his hands at his waist.

"Aaliyah, we need to find water," Todd said using his hands to imitate drinking.

"Vatah? Yes, vatah!" Aaliyah understood the term and immediately started walking.

Having just climbed down the side of a cliff, she had plenty of energy and looked as if she could easily go back up. Heading toward a bend in the dry riverbed next to the edge of the rock face, she found a small clump of bushes. With the sun offering just a few more hours of light, the heat was still strong and could be seen radiating like a mirage before them. She pressed on leaving the men in her wake.

"We better follow her," Hudson said starting to move.

"I don't know if I can."

"It's either that or death."

Todd grinned, "Well if you put it that way." He got up.

The men met up with Aaliyah who was digging at the edge of a bush.

"This river has to have been dry for a thousand years," Hudson muttered as he helped in the digging.

"Yeah, but often in the desert, water flows under the ground. People have died standing two feet above the life giving substance." Todd moved rocks away to help in the work.

After five minutes of digging and using rocks for shovels, the young woman yelled, "Vatah, vatah," upon seeing the dirt darken and become moist.

They were sweating profusely in the sun, but the farther they dug, the moister the dirt got. After forming a hole several feet across and two feet deep, a small puddle formed in the bottom large enough to fill their canisters.

Aaliyah tore a piece of cloth from her tunic and wrapped it around the top of the bottle. It worked as a partial filter and was good at keeping the large particles out. The water was brown but drinkable and had never tasted better to the dehydrated time travelers.

"It's going to be dark in a couple hours and we need to find a place to stay the night and possibly something to eat. Can Aaliyah help us?" Hudson asked as he took another satisfying gulp.

After downing another liter each, they filled their bottles and set off toward the northwest. Todd grabbed some of the sticks from around the base of the tree, placed them in his tunic and ran up from behind.

As they followed the valley between the cliffs, Aaliyah stopped by several plants and picked the flowers from them. Offering them to the men and receiving blank stares, she tore off a petal and stuck it in her mouth. "La'uhcole. La'uhcole!" She ate another scarlet colored petal.

"She wants us to eat. I usually like ranch on my salad but I guess you can't have everything." He placed one in his mouth. "It's not great, but it might keep us alive."

Hudson looked at his friend who seemed to have survived the vivid-colored flower and placed one in his own mouth.

Aaliyah removed every flower she could find and placed them in her makeshift pockets while talking a mile a minute to Todd. She refused to move forward until she had every red bloom. A few more of the flowers appeared as they traveled and she picked every one quickly before continuing on again.

Todd spoke after a long silence, "It seems that the Persians call this Thuliban, as best as I can decipher. It is where we get our word turban and for flowers, the word tulip. They kind of look like hats if you turn them upside down," he put one over his head.

Aaliyah glanced behind and giggled at him. Hudson lifted an eyebrow.

"Anyway, she says they're edible and lucky for us, about to go out of season. So we need to count this as a blessing."

"God is going to provide for us. I know he will."

Forty-five minutes later, Hudson observed what seemed to be a large cave about sixty feet up a cliff to the east. "Let's go over there."

Making the short climb alone, he found a large cavernous opening facing the direction of the Roman army. That bit of information was disconcerting to the secret service agent, yet his fears were assuaged when he saw its depth. They would need a fire to fend off the deep chill of the desert. Being seen remained the obvious concern.

The desert in Israel would easily get down into the 30's at night under the clear dry skies. None of the travelers were wearing anything more than 1st century summer clothing, so hypothermia lurked in his mind as a likely outcome if they didn't have a good solid fire.

Finding his way back down he looked at Todd and Aaliyah, "Let's stay here tonight. We need a fire as a first priority. It'll be dark within the hour and then we'll need shelter from the real cold."

"I'm already on it boss," pulling the sticks from his tunic. "I didn't spend years becoming an eagle scout for nothing. It's going to save our lives tonight." He started up the cliff grabbing anything that would burn along the way.

"Mazavone," Aaliyah uttered the word clearly, then launched into a long flowing explanation even Todd couldn't understand. After a moment of slower conversing, Todd walked back to Hudson.

"She seems to think we can catch some food."

"Foowud, yez, foowud." She seemed very proud of her English as the put on a big smile.

"Okay, Todd, you get the fire going, and we will go catch some game."

Todd continued up the rocky face while the other two headed off along the ridge. The professor would have loved to have had a match or lighter. Some steel wool and a battery, some flint or even a pair of glasses to use as a magnifying glass would have helped. Nope, all he had was sticks. "Looks like we're going old school," he spoke to no one in particular.

All of his training, and he didn't have the most basic of survival equipment. His troop leader was probably rolling around in his grave right now, if he had passed on which Todd thought about for a second and wasn't sure. "I need to give him a call when I get back, if I get back." He got back to work.

Having made fire quite a few times with just sticks, he knew his best chance was with the bow-drill method. He tore some cloth from his tunic and started making the drill.

A quarter of a mile away Aaliyah put a hand out behind her telling Hudson to stop and remain quiet. She took off her sandals and climbed 20 feet up the face to a small rocky outcropping. Moving as slowly and quietly as possible, she looked over the rocks and came back down.

Whispering, "Sahkeen."

Hudson put his hands in the air, "I don't know what you need."

"Sahkeen, sahkeen," she pointed at his dagger.

"Oh, knife, sure, here it is."

After handing her the knife, she slowly worked her way to the place she was before and then in an instant started slashing at the other side of the rock. The agent saw several small animals run out. A couple bolted right up the cliff face where others seemed to run out and fall. Evidently, they hadn't made it through the onslaught of the knife attack. Getting over to the small animals as quickly as possible, he wrung their necks and put them out of their misery. Not something he'd received training for, but it worked none the less.

The furry creatures looked to be 18-20 inches long and resembled a rabbit with no ears. Hudson had never seen anything like them but wasn't going to look a gift horse in the mouth, hungry as he knew they all were.

Aaliyah pulled the three remaining animals from the small hole in the rock and held them out at arms-length.

Hudson golf-clapped for her as she came back down with the largest grin he had ever seen her wear.

"Hyrax," she whispered.

"Hyrax is it? Great job!"

She smiled as they walked back to the illuminated cave.

After making the short climb up the cliff, they found Todd sitting against the back wall warming his hands.

"If I knew making fire would have been that easy, I'd have stayed here and let you go hunting," the agent said jokingly.

"Easy. Did you say easy? I've been here for half an hour trying to make that thing work. On TV it takes a couple minutes. Obviously, they do a lot of editing for time! Look at these blisters." He showed Hudson a bloody spot on each hand.

Laughing, "Do you want me to fix those for you?" Pulling his knife out and sticking it in the fire, "I can cauterize those for you. It won't take but a second."

Hiding his hands, "Forget it. If you want to do to my hands what you did to my shoulder." His attitude changed, shifted to the dramatic side of him. "My dream was always to be a shoulder model, and now because of this scar the size of Montana, that will never happen."

"Oh. Well, you're alive aren't you?"

The men laughed quietly.

"You should see what your lady did." He said, pulling the animals from a bag as Aaliyah got in close next to the professor.

"Did she catch these?" Todd couldn't believe it.

"She says they are hyrax and there seems to be some good meat on these little guys."

"Great work, Aaliyah. Thank you," Todd said to the petite woman as he pulled her over and gave her a kiss on the cheek. "We wouldn't make it without you."

She blinked her acknowledgment of his words. She understood little of his language, but everything from his eyes. "Let's get these things prepared," he said, pulling out his knife.

Todd and Aaliyah began preparing the meat. Each had a knife and started talking back and forth. There were several gaps in the conversation as the professor went from Hebrew to Greek to Aramaic, trying to find a word that was understandable. When he found one she knew, she would then teach him the word in Hebrew. Often the small woman would say something in English sparking a 'good job', or 'great work' out of the consummate teacher.

As Hudson walked toward the entrance and looked out over the vast and rugged expanse, he couldn't help but think that the two were perfectly comfortable in this desolate wilderness. He had no doubt that, given the circumstances, they would survive fairly well in the desert and be content doing it.

They were comfortable together and had a deep connection. It was funny to think that it took a time machine and a trip 2000 years into the past for the Lord to bring the right person for his friend. A woman who would love, honor and cherish him until his last breath. Yet, in the crazy world they were living in, it made sense. He sighed, uncomfortable with his own thoughts. He missed his family.

Taking in the beauty of the desert, the brightness of the radiant star overhead, and the bright white of the moon against the dark blue skies, he couldn't help but think of his Sara. She would love the view he was seeing, relish the conversation around the campfire or just sit next to him, taking in the experience with the man she loved.

Hudson never really liked the song "Somewhere Out There," but at this time it seemed appropriate. Could his love be looking up at the same moon that he was? He knew that it didn't make sense. She sat comfortably in their home over 2000 years into the future. Her great, great, great, great grandfather wasn't even born yet.

Still, the notion that she was there with him gave him strength to make it through the night. The thought that she was putting his Michael and Amy to bed and reading them a book gave him security. No. They were fine. His work would help to protect them from a world that could possibly be devoid of hope and a future.

"Lord, I will do my best to follow your plan, please be with my darlings tonight, and let them know that I love them," he whispered with his eyes closed and his hands raised.

Turning toward the two who were laughing and putting the meat on a skewer, he relaxed, "How can I help?"

"Come on over, Buddy, dinner will be ready soon," Todd smiled knowing the agent felt like the odd man out.

"Dinnuh, redee," Aaliyah said with a smile.

"So, what did you think was going on when Aaliyah was hacking at the rock? I'll bet you thought she was fighting a bear. She told me the whole story." Todd laughed.

Hudson smiling, "I didn't know what she was doing. The way she was slashing with my knife," he made a psycho type slasher motion, "she could have come up with a gory Big Foot or something. I was pretty nervous."

They laughed a while over the day's experiences. Everyone knew in the back of their minds the storm was coming - one that would change each of their lives forever. But for now, they enjoyed the company and the adventure. They ate together and became close friends. A connection they would need when the sun rose.

The assembly at the Antonia Fortress concluded late into the evening. Herod immediately ordered a carriage be brought to carry him to the Jewish Temple. While Aurius had indeed eased his fears and offered him expert directions time and again, his concern over this new Jewish king had escalated in his warped mind. For years, he had vigilantly guarded his kingship, removing every threat to his powers, even killing his own family when necessary. To hear that a Jewish child had been born - within his own territory, no less – to one day become King of the Jews. A child who could rally the Hebrew people against their Roman King - this was more than he could take.

Exiting the Fortress by way of The Porch, he noted how quiet it was at the end of the day. His footsteps echoed across the stone floor beneath him. Six blocks of open-air marketplace stretched downward from the Antonia Fortress, right in the center stood the Jewish Temple: the highest place of worship for the Hebrew people.

His expression morphed from thoughtfulness to a hard annoyance. Herod tolerated the Temple, even though he essentially built it for the Jews. Its majestic surface sparkled with a covering of solid white granite. Four large columns supported the overhang protecting the gold-plated entrance. More elaborate goldsmithing decorated the area above the enormous doors. Disgust for the waste curled his lip.

The Romans had great success in conquering other countries due, in part, to their ability to allow the nations to retain their basic religions. This syncretism tended to ease civil unrest in the occupied nations and Israel was no different. Even though the aging King would rather use that gold to decorate one of his palaces, he knew the building helped to keep the people at bay. So he cursed under his breath at the structure and continued past it toward the Royal Stoa.

The King's face twisted knowing this is one of the few areas within Israel where he had no power. He knew he could find the Chief Priest, the Pharisees and the Sadducees within the depths of the colonnade. These men held control of the Jewish religion, and - even though they could not put people to death - they could do just about anything they wanted to the Jewish people. The King smirked at the thought of what the men within the grand columns had done in the name of God. For all intents and purposes, they were not much different than he.

Having only been under the roof of this open air colonnade a few times Herod felt uncomfortable – a rare feeling for the King. He had little control over anything occurring within these walls including the activities of the guards, the temple rules, their dress, and even the language they spoke. No, with the Jews he simply tried to stay away.

But tonight he needed answers. And he was willing to wake the entire nation of Israel to find them. He would not be stopped by a few religious leaders.

The King's guards were halted by security for the Chief Priest. "Let me pass," Herod demanded.

The guard appeared unaffected. "It is late," he spoke, "the Chief Priest has retired for the evening."

"He will want to see me," the King replied.

"Good King, the Chief Priest is in contemplation and never sees anyone the day after the Sabbath. As he is the highest officer of our worship, you have no right to disturb him," the other guard interjected.

"It is a matter of utmost importance. He will see me." Herod stood his ground.

A furrow formed in the Jewish guard's brow. Forced entry by Rome into the Temple was unheard of. "I am sorry, we cannot interrupt him," the disconcerted Jewish guard finally spoke.

"You will bring me to him!" Herod shouted. *I have no time for this insolence*, he thought.

Herod's head guard ordered the contingent of six behind him to take a more protective stance while more Jewish guards made their way to the area.

"Sir, you must come back in the morning. You have no right to be here."

The King lost control of his well-guarded temper, "I have every right to be here. I own this land and can run it as I see fit! Where is he?" Herod spat.

The Roman guards were now surrounded by no less than a priestly security force of twenty. They were definitely outgunned on this encounter and everyone knew it including the King.

"I will not leave until I speak to him. It is about a Jewish King."

"A Jewish King," one guard repeated somewhat shaken.

One guard leaned over and whispered to his neighbor who cocked his head and turned toward the group of additional men coming to their aid. After a few moments of Hebrew chattering, Herod recognized the word most often spoken was 'Messiah.'

The King continued with the thought. "Yes, I am here about the Messiah." He didn't really know what that inferred, but he knew the Jews often mentioned the coming of the Messiah, and if it offered an audience with the Chief Priest, he would use it to his benefit.

The Priest's guards looked at each other with concern when one spoke, "Let me speak with the Chief Priest." the higher ranking soldier turned on his heel and left.

The word Messiah worked like magic to gain him an audience. He gritted his teeth – an audience with one of his own subjects. Full access to anyone in his kingdom should be at his whim. Inhaling slowly, he calmed his nerves and decided to make the best of the situation. He had won this small battle and looked forward to winning the war. He would have his payback. The King smiled.

After what seemed an eternity, the Chief Priest came out in all of his regalia and greeted the King. "King Herod, I apologize for my guards. I regret they kept you waiting so long." He bowed before him. "You know we are your loyal subjects and are at your service."

Herod accepted his unspoken apology yet knew there was no friendship in his words. The Jewish people did not love the Romans any more than he loved the Jews. The man now nodding toward him in a show of deference was their leader. Herod knew the man hated him. How could he not? Nonetheless, he accepted the self-aggrandizement to the extent it would give him answers.

"Joazar Ben Boethus, my good friend. How pleasant it is to see you," the King waxed a smile for the religious leader.

"My King, we are blessed to enjoy your company this eve," the Priest returned the smile. "Please come in out of the night to my humble dwelling," he moved the guards out of the way and escorted the King through the large double doors at the rear.

To call the place humble was a gross understatement. Behind the twenty-foot doors, were rooms leading off in all directions. The King could see dining and entertaining rooms. One room overflowed with neatly bound scrolls and desks, and another housed what appeared to be the bedroom. The multiple hallways led to other areas that the King could not see. This humble dwelling almost rivaled his palace. Almost.

Extravagant mosaics graced the floor and tapestries covered the walls. Each of the oil lamps gleamed with gold-plating as well as other various objects hanging from the walls and ceiling.

After himself, the Chief Priest was probably the wealthiest person in the nation. So even though most every golden item within the room held a place in the worship of the Lord Most High, the King saw only the gold and the wealth. To the king, gold equaled power.

Sitting at a long table covered with bowls of fruit, Herod spoke, "Joazar, I have been negligent in thanking you for your help."

Feeling important, "What help would that be, my King?"

"Why, your help with the census. We could have never conducted it within this region without your support. Your *encouragement* allowed Rome to better know how many we have within this great country."

Sitting across from the King and tilting his head a moment, "Consider it my privilege. I whole-heartedly support our King and want to keep this country strong both for God," he said pointing up, "and the Romans," he finished, gesturing toward Herod.

For many years now, the Chief Priest had been nothing more than a religious figure head doing the bidding of the Roman government. Everyone in the room knew it, and, as long as Herod could manipulate the man in that position, he would allow him the freedom to lead the people and the benefits that came with it.

"My friend, I thank you for your loyalty and will reward you for it. Tonight, however, I need some information that only you can offer."

"Anything," he replied, leaning in toward the bushy bearded ruler.

"I have been told by my prophet that a king is to be born in Israel."

"You are the King," the priest responded. "Are congratulations in order? Is there to be another royal birth?"

"No. That is what bothers me. I have been told this king will be Jewish."

The Priest removed his heavy cloak and paced the room. "A Jewish king in a Roman province? Not possible!" He wasn't convincing.

The King stood, "What is it that you know?"

"Nothing my King. You are the only King and shall remain so." He looked away.

"Dishonesty does not become you. I have lived a long life because I can tell when people are lying. What do you know?"

The Priest paced the floor before backing against the wall. The hoary bearded old man shifted in his seat. He felt insecure for the first time in a while. "There have been mumblings about a Messiah for centuries."

"Explain this Messiah. Why have I not been told about another king?" Herod was losing his patience.

Joazar walked forward to try to calm the slightly unstable leader, "They are just mumblings, Sir, nothing more." Stepping back he began to put it together, "The Jewish people have always wanted a Jewish King." He let this slip first knowing he could resolve the matter quickly. "However a delegation from the east came through a few days ago looking for the same King you speak of."

"What delegation?" Herod sat up and listened.

"A caravan of close to fifty men. The leaders looked to be astronomers. Whatever they were, they have been watching the star that is resting above us right now."

"Yes, I have seen it in the night sky, and my prophet told me of this delegation. What did they ask you?"

Sitting in front of the King, "They asked me just what you have. They wanted to know where the Jewish King would be. They evidently want to honor him with extravagant gifts."

"Gifts," he mumbled out of frustration. "What did you tell them?"

"Just what I told you, I know nothing of a Jewish King. You are my only King."

"Where are they now?"

"I do not know. They left several nights ago, and I haven't seen them since," fingering his goblet on the table. "They said they would not leave the area until they found this King, so I believe them to still be in Jerusalem."

The King stood again and walked to a large fireplace glowing with the embers of a recent burn. "Again, I ask: tell me about your Messiah."

"Our Messiah. Why would you want to know about our Messiah?"

"I asked a simple question, and I want a simple answer. If this Jewish King is your Messiah, then I need to know more about what your teachings say about him." Turning he pointed in the face of the thin religious leader, "Tell me all you know of the prophecies regarding a Messiah."

Backing away Joazar replied, "May I call for a few scholars to come and help with your questions?"

Herod waved him off, "Yes, of course. Do it quickly."

The Chief Priest scurried off down a hallway and returned within five minutes with three other men. "Good King, these are lead priests and teachers of the law. Between us we should be able to answer any questions you might have."

"Thank you, gentlemen, for coming." They looked meekly at him. "I will ask the same question. Tell me of the prophecies about your Messiah."

The men laid their scrolls on the table and stood at attention.

After looking at one another, the one dressed in a long dark toga spoke first, "The Messiah will be born of a virgin. The book of Isaiah is very clear."

The King smirked, "A virgin. How is that going happen?"

The religious leaders were wide-eyed and without answers.

"Can anyone tell me where I can find this virgin? That would make my life much easier."

They shook their heads.

"Then this information is of absolutely no help to me. What else do you know?"

Another man spoke, "The book of Genesis says he will come from the tribe of Judah."

"That could possibly be thousands of people, am I right?"

They agreed.

"What else?"

One dressed in priestly garb spoke, "The book of Jeremiah says he will be a descendant of King David."

"Nice information, but could still be one of thousands."

They began to rattle off information in rounds. "Great kings will pay homage and tribute to him. That is seen in the book of Psalms."

Herod wiped his face, his blood beginning to boil, but he listened as they continued.

"He will be rejected."

"He will be killed."

"He will be mocked and spat upon."

Herod smiled cruelly, thinking how he would enjoy fulfilling those prophecies.

"He will heal the blind and deaf."

"He will ascend to heaven and stand at the right hand of God."

The King had heard enough. "None of this helps me. Give me concrete information." He thought for a second. "Do your scriptures say where he will be born?"

"Yes," one man said. "In the book of Micah it states, "But you, O Bethlehem Ephrathah, you are a small village, yet a ruler will come from you, one whose beginning is from a great past."

The Chief Priest spoke, "The Messiah is to come from Bethlehem."

Herod stood, "Bethlehem?"

They nodded their heads in agreement.

The King of Israel started for the door as the other men looked at each other in confusion.

Joazar Ben Boethus, the Chief Priest of Israel asked, "Good King, what do you plan on doing with this information?"

The King turned and faced the religious leaders. After thinking for a second, he smiled and dropped his head, "I plan on finding him and giving him his due." The ruler's words were strict and resolute before turning again toward the exit. After one of his guards opened the massive doors, Herod left into the dark night.

Descending a large set of stairs on the southwest side of the Temple complex called the Robinson Arch, he found a carriage awaiting him. A guard opened the door and asked the King where he would like to go.

"Take me to the Citadel as quickly as possible. We have an insurrection to stop."

The guards looked at each other before taking their positions around the vehicle. The King reclined in the back with a contented grin on his face as the carriage sped through the quiet streets of Jerusalem.

15 — SUNDAY EVENING, APRIL 19

The large group of Roman trackers made it to the ridge and divided themselves into five companies. The first division stayed at the bottom and searched the front of the small rocky peak. Rough stones comprised most of the geological formation which appeared to be around two hundred feet high. High enough to be a good position to view the Roman army encamped before it.

The second division went to the western side and the third to the eastern side. The fourth marched toward the back side, and the last company scaled the face of the hill to the top. The trained scouts knew how to find the most insignificant remains of evidence that humans had been there. If someone *had* been there, they could follow them like hounds.

The dry barren conditions made tracking difficult; the blowing wind rendered it nearly impossible. No shoe prints in soft ground, padded down grass, or broken twigs on trees along the path. After over an hour of investigation, and with the sun descending quickly in the west, the regiment made their way back to their commander.

Dritus patiently awaited them on horseback, and upon receiving the information, rode back to Cyprianus for further instructions.

"Sir, my men have thoroughly searched the mountain and believe that two if not three people were there fairly recently."

Aurius was listening as Cyprianus heard the news. "Three," he said in confusion, "who would be the third?" the prophet mumbled to himself.

Cyprianus looked over at Aurius in frustration, angry at a civilian's necessary involvement in military planning. "Two or three? Which is it?" He responded to the soldier.

He answered quickly, "I believe my men have found evidence of three."

Cyprianus listened intently with his arms crossed as the man continued.

"Most of the tracks were well rubbed out. The wipe marks were clear enough, but that made it difficult to see any noticeable indentions in the dirt. However, there were several places where different shoe impressions were left. There is a running bet among the men that it is two men and a woman."

"A woman?" yelled Aurius.

The seasoned soldiers looked over at his outburst before continuing.

"We found a spot where they dug for water behind the barrier and left a few tracks. One set was very small. They seem to be well-trained and look like they have the skills to make it in this terrain for a while." Dritus stopped and waited for instructions.

Aurius turned from the men and looked out at the countryside that was in the last few minutes of daylight. "Why would you have brought her? It doesn't make sense. Why bring her back to this place and put her in danger?" He rested his arm on a pole holding up his tent.

Cyprianus walked up behind the prophet. "What do you know?"

Aurius turned from his stance, awakened by the question. "I know just what you know."

The seasoned general had been in the dark long enough. "What do you know?" Anger colored his voice and his cheeks flushed, "You have been leading us on this wild goose chase long enough. You may have the King fooled, but I am not so gullible," he said as he pulled his sword from its sheath and placed it at Aurius' neck, "You will tell me what you know or you will be the first casualty of this war."

Dritus looked on with part satisfaction and part dismay. Thorius heard the commotion and worked his way toward the tent.

Putting his hands on the general's arm, "All I know is they are coming to get me."

"Who is coming to get you?" The sword was making an indention on his neck.

Pulling away as much as possible, "Two men are coming after me. One is specially trained in covert work. The other is well educated. They are a mixed pair, but efficient enough in completing their mission." He paused in anguish. "I *cannot* be taken."

The sword lowered from Aurius throat, "Who would this woman be?"

"She is just a local peasant woman. I have no idea why they would bring her."

Hand to his neck, his voice came out scratchy, "You have to catch them. They cannot stop my work."

Cyprianus had taken all the phony little prophet he could muster. Coming back around his fist landed in the man's stomach, "What is this work you keep referring to?"

Aurius fell to the ground gasping. After a few seconds he was able to get enough air to answer the question. "It is a personal job that will benefit the King when completed."

"So this never was about the King," the general spat.

Becoming terribly afraid, "Cyprianus, you must believe me, I have the King's welfare before mine. If I complete this task, he will benefit."

"You keep talking of a task. Stop being so cryptic and tell me what you plan on doing!" He grabbed him from the ground and held him in a headlock.

Barely able to breathe, he managed to squeeze out a few small words, "I must kill a Jewish infant."

Cyprianus loosened the lock and kicked him in the back forcing him to the ground. "We are out here in the desert, so that you can kill…a child?"

"I know it makes little sense to you who do not know the future." His voice broke, "But that is…what I must do." Aurius knew he had lost the war. His eyes pressed tight with the thought of failure.

The general looked at him for several seconds, his disgust obvious. Without removing his gaze from the man he spoke to his commander, "Dritus, give your scouts an hour's worth of rest, and then send them to find those who were on the mountain."

"But Cyprianus, wouldn't the morning be a better time to follow the tracks?" he answered nervous about the odd request.

"It is going to be fairly cool tonight and a fire should be easy enough to spot. Do as I said." His tone made it clear that there would be no disagreement with his commands.

"Yes sir." Dritus bent at the waist in a backward retreat and headed for his men.

"Thorius," he continued watching Aurius as the man worked himself up from the ground.

"Yes, General." The soldier stood at attention.

Speaking to Aurius, "You have forced me into positions that have required me to do despicable things for the King because of false visions. You have used your trickery to make the King jump at your every whim. You have brought hundreds of my men into the desert to hunt people looking to kill you."

Aurius began to back away.

Cyprianus hand slashed the air like a knife, "It all ends now. I will not allow you another opportunity before my King. Your false magic is over." Aurius did not resist the forceful push from the shorter man, "I will catch those wandering in the desert and will take them back to Herod as a validation of your vision in order for him to save face. However, you will not be there to reap the benefits. Your mission is finished!" His right fist caught Aurius in the face, felling him to the ground. The prophet tasted blood in his mouth.

Immediately changing his focus to Thorius, who had a look of astonishment, he ordered, "Take him into custody until I determine what to do with him. The men may need some target practice later."

"Yes sir!" The soldier quickly grabbed Aurius, unnecessarily forcing compliance at the end of his blade.

Cyprianus focused his attention to the north. Soon enough he would have his spies and be back in Jerusalem with one less thorn in his side.

—

Herod entered the Citadel to little fanfare. The building was normally slow in the evenings with most men preparing for the night or on guard at the various outposts across the city, however this night the building was like a graveyard.

Busting through the front doors, only a security guard knew he was there and because he was at his post, could not leave to announce the King's surprise arrival.

"Where is everyone?" Herod asked to his guards who were also surprised at the empty chamber.

"I do not know sir," one said looking at the other.

Walking back to the guard at the door, he called, "Where is Cyprianus?"

Nervously the guard answered, "He and many of his men are catching insurrectionists."

"How many of his men?" the King asked out of frustration.

"Sir, well over one hundred. Dritus and Thorius took their regiments along with those specially selected by the General."

"What insurrectionists?" Herod was growing impatient.

"Yes sir, a man under your direction came through earlier this afternoon saying your life was in danger. I believe he is your prophet. When Cyprianus heard you were in peril, he used all avenues possible to ensure your safety."

"Very good. I am glad to hear my good General takes my well-being seriously." Walking back into the large chamber and looking down several of the tunnels shooting off in different directions he shouted aloud, "Who else is here?" His words alone echoed back at him.

"Sir, I am the highest ranking officer here," the young man replied with false humility.

The King's mouth dropped. Marching back he stepped into the personal space of a young man no older than seventeen, "You are telling me that a new recruit is the highest officer in this bastion designed to protect the entire city of Jerusalem?"

With a shake in his voice the young man now spoke with obvious sincerity, "Sir, every position within the city is manned to your specifications. Your people are well protected, however, with the information we received this afternoon, every additional recruit was needed."

The King backed away before he took his wrath out on the boy. Never had this fortification been so empty. Never had he needed soldiers more than now, and yet had no access to any except the inexperienced child before him. He had no choice but to send him on this mission.

"Do you know how to ride?" he asked somewhat condescendingly.

"Yes, of course. I have been well trained, Sir," he responded with pride.

Looking to one of his soldiers he held his hand out, "Hand me the document."

The warrior grasped the edict written by the King in the carriage ride over. Concerned the seal might still be wet, he gently handed it to the impatient ruler.

The parchment was rolled and tied with a string, and on the outside was the royal seal. "Do you know where to find Cyprianus?"

"Yes. He is east of Machairus."

"You will take this to him this instant." He extended the document toward the young recruit.

"Sir, I cannot leave. I am the only man protecting this building."

Herod's voice rose with determination, "You will leave immediately and take this to him."

"Punishments are harsh if you leave your post," he feared for his future.

"I am the King," he screamed violently, "You will find a horse and take this to Cyprianus! You will not stop, drink, eat, or relieve yourself until this parchment is in his hands. This building can protect itself. Do you understand?"

"Uh, yes, uh, I understand." The poor chap tried not to show his fear and received the document with a forward bend, "I will get this to the general." He felt the vellum in his hands.

Speaking quietly yet determined, "You will do as I have instructed or your will have more to fear than the punishment for dereliction of duty."

The young man stood at attention as the King left through the large doors, entered his carriage and rode off into the dark night.

—

It took an hour and a half and three horses to get the young man to the military encampment. After showing his credentials to two different sentries, he was directed to the general's tent, which was also heavily guarded.

Standing at attention, the young man tried to act brave.

The general came through a flap on the tent with a scowl on his face, "Why have I been awakened?" He growled.

Tired and shaken he lifted the scroll, "Sir, I do not want to bother you, but this was given to me by the King." He thrust the document toward Cyprianus. "He said it is vital that you have it."

Snatching the parchment, he broke the seal and untied the string. After a minute he looked up at the young man, "Be gone."

He bowed quickly and hurried off toward the mess tent.

Cyprianus glanced down at his half toga, bare chest and legs and shrugged. Normally, a general would never be seen in front of the men without full dress, nonetheless this ranked on the highest of importance. He quickly put on a pair of sandals and left for the area that housed Aurius.

A jail of sorts was erected for the one and only prisoner. What looked to be four poles driven into the rough dirt were surrounded by rope and a guard at each corner. Aurius lay asleep on a mat in the middle of the open square.

Picking up a bucket of water sitting outside of the square with his free hand, he stepped between the layers of rope, entered the ring and threw the liquid on the unsuspecting prisoner.

Just as Aurius came to a sitting position from the rocky ground, Cyprianus landed a blow to his face, forcing him back to the dirt.

"Do you know what I am forced to do?" the general yelled full voice.

Trying to get back up from the blow, the man struck him again showing every striated muscle in his chest and arms.

Aurius once again felt the ground, this time tasting blood as well.

"I asked you, do you know what I have to do?"

Lamps were being lit throughout the camp.

"No, no, what are you talking about?" He tried to protect himself from another strike.

Grabbing him by whatever fabric he could find, the prophet was pulled from the ground and pushed into the rope taking down one of the corner poles.

Aurius backed away as Cyprianus marched forward with a scroll in his hand.

The general kicked the man in the side as he tried to make it to his feet.

A terrified Aurius saw soldiers starting to gather around the action.

Unrolling the document Cyprianus continued his methodical pursuit, "This is an edict from the King," he spoke quietly, dragging Aurius along the ground as he read.

"What does it say?" His tone was pleading.

Making it to his feet, the poor prophet tried to keep up with the quick pace of the general.

Most of the camp was awake and watching the activity going on in the middle of the camp.

Throwing Aurius down over a pile of rocks, "This is my next mission - one that is to start within twenty-four hours."

He yelled at a soldier behind him, "Bring me some stakes and rope!"

The prophet's heart sank. The paper somehow meant his death. "Whatever it is, I can work it out. Let me get with the King and solve this."

Laughing, he looked down at the older man, "No, I will solve this." Wadding the parchment up and throwing it at him his voice turned docile once again. "Do you remember telling me you wanted kill a Jewish baby?"

"Yes," he replied nervously.

"Don't worry, your mission will be completed. However, it will not just be one baby. I get the honor of killing all Jewish babies under the age of three."

"You have forced me into this!" he spat. "Your advice to the King has required me to kill many who were innocent. But I have NEVER killed a child. I have NEVER heard of such an order and my legacy will be that of annihilating thousands of babies in Israel."

"Cyprianus, I am sorry. This is my fight, not yours."

"Enough, I have heard enough out of you." The general turned and grabbed a spear from a soldier standing by.

"Sir, here are the stakes and rope," a young recruit said.

Aurius' eyes grew wide.

"You will no longer be advising the King."

"No!" Aurius yelled but it was too late. The general swung around striking the former prophet in the head with the borrowed spear, causing him to fall to the ground in a heap.

The thorn in Cyprianus' side would not be bothering him again.

A frigid gust of air seeped into Aaliyah's covering. The rocky cave was beginning to grow cold. She turned quietly so as not to awaken the men and found the fire had burned down to its embers, quickly becoming nothing but a warm memory. Knowing how difficult starting the source had been, more wood was now a priority. Deciding to allow her friends a few more hours of rest before they were on the run again, she silently picked her way around their sleeping forms until the mouth of the cave yawned before her.

She stepped outside gingerly in the darkness and found herself gazing at the most beautiful starry night. Eyes uplifted she prayed for a silent moment, praising her God and Creator for evidence of his work around her.

Drawing a deep breath she refocused and headed down the dark pathway to search for the much-needed fuel to add to the dying fire. This task was nothing new to her. As a child, keeping the fire burning in one of the many fire places had been one of her responsibilities. Filling it with wood had been the greatest challenge, but one she had grown accustomed to. During her short arranged marriage, maintaining the home and hearth fell to her as well, as it did to all the women she knew.

It did make her wonder, however, at the new feeling of contentment growing in her heart. Gathering fire wood never appealed to her as it did now. Now she did it to keep warm the man who loved her. Never had she offered that warmth to someone she truly cared for. Love changes things. To help the man who had rescued her from being an outcast without a protector in a male-dominated world - felt like such a gift. She would do anything to help Todd and Hudson as they had helped her.

In the week that she had known the men; her world had changed for the better. Hudson was one of the most honorable people she had ever encountered. In a world where men never spoke to women except to draw favors, the agent showed himself to want nothing from her. He merely cared for her well-being. He had strong, caring eyes. He would never take advantage of her and if need be would die to protect her. She could see it in his eyes. Her green eyes sparkled in the moonlight at the thought of his chivalrous manner.

At the thought of Todd, however, she blushed in the dim light.

She was enamored with the wiry, funny, intelligent man who made her smile. When she nursed him back to health she was amazed at his physique. She had known men to have large shoulders from throwing a hammer all day, or some men whose legs were strong and tight because they pulled wagons full of equipment where horses couldn't. However, her Todd was strong and well-built from head-to-toe, and yet gentle. He could hold her in such a way that filled her with a new and wonderful feeling of security. She knew nothing could get through him to her. He also made her laugh, something she hadn't done for a long time before their arrival.

Even though she was terrified in the hospital room, she giggled at the thought of him entering the space with the floating things and his jaw dropping to the floor seeing her yelling on the bed. She knew he hadn't had much experience with women and especially those from her time and place.

She picked up a few sticks and continued picking her way down the ridge line. She would go to the ends of the earth for her Todd. Be those ends a foreign place with large machines that move you around, or just back to where she started; a land where she had no hope and a knot in her stomach.

Aaliyah's fear crept into her throat for a moment before she swallowed it down again. A stick caught at her skirt from the ledge beside her, and she snatched up with a vengeance. Being returned to the abandonment and loneliness of the past terrified her. She stopped a moment and breathed deeply of the cold night air. *Perfect love casts out fear,* she reminded herself.

So, fearless she could be. Her eyes popped open as the moon came out from behind a cloud, and she suddenly became scared in the clear night. The moon was no longer a friend and the temperature seemed to drop a few degrees around her.

She took a deep breath and backed against a large rock. Before moving in the direction of the cave she looked up toward the sky and focused on a star brighter than she had ever seen and prayed that God would hear her. She prayed that her Todd was real and loved her the way she loved him. Reaching her hand out toward the luminary, and closing her eyes, she asked for God's protection. She prayed that the Jesus she had learned to trust would allow her something she never thought possible - true love. Aaliyah desired a love from a man that wanted nothing in return other than the joy in his wife's eyes.

Continuing her prayer, she raised her other hand and asked for children. She begged for security and long life in the arms of her Todd. The young woman had never asked for anything such as this before, yet everything seemed new. She had seen the Savior. He had sent two men to rescue her and she had fallen in love with one.

She smiled and her fear left. Love drove out all fear. Hudson and Todd were real and not a dream, and if they could come through time, surely a small woman in a big world could find happiness.

With tears running down her face, she opened her eyes to the star which shined even brighter than it had just a few minutes earlier. The huge moon glowed in the sapphire sky, and the world around her seemed happier.

She picked up the sticks she had dropped before her prayer and continued without fear around the next corner. When her arms were almost full, she found a few last sticks, completing her load.

Turning to head back toward her home for the night, two giant arms reached around her face, smothering her involuntary scream. A hand cut off her breath. Heavily weighted backwards she felt herself pressed into the solid pillar of human muscle behind her. The hand released only a moment, and before she could catch her breath, a mass of oily cloth filled her open mouth. Arms wrenched behind her and feet lifted from the ground, she was bound and held in the largest man's arms before her ankles felt the circle of ropes tighten around them as well.

She knew these men did not care to protect her and would kill her without remorse after doing things Todd and Hudson would never do. Terror welled up in her soul and spilled suddenly into silent but uncontrollable sobbing. The man hoisted her onto his massive shoulders and carried her off toward the darkened camp.

—

Several hours later, Todd stretched his arm out to where Aaliyah had been laying. In just a week, he had gone from happy and single to being incomplete without her. Every hour, like clockwork, he had stretched out to feel her warmth and let her know that she wasn't alone.

In the dark cave with the fire completely out, he wondered if she had moved deeper into the cave. Eyes still closed in lethargy he inched himself over a little further in her direction. Still not finding her form, he groped about in the dark for a few moments more. He bolted upright and turned his eyes toward the entrance of the cave. Except for the light from the moon bouncing off the cave's interior, there was no illumination to see by.

"Aaliyah," Todd whispered. "Aaliyah."

No answer.

"Aaliyah," he called a bit louder. "Aaliyah."

Hudson sat up at the noise. "Where is she?"

Todd stood to search the cave in the dim light.

"What happened?" Hudson asked, stretching a kink out of his neck.

"Aaliyah, she's not here," fear tinged his voice.

Finally grasping the situation by the terror in Todd's speech, Hudson gathered his tired thoughts and moved quickly to the edge of the cave.

"Where is she? Hudson, she's gonna be alright isn't she?"

"Let's not lose faith yet. Have you looked outside?"

"Not yet," he said running for the entrance.

Hudson held out an arm to keep him from leaving too quickly. "Todd, listen to me," he looked him in the eyes, "most likely everything's fine, she may have needed to relieve herself or something. But if it isn't. Well, we can't go and get ourselves taken hostage. Let's take this slowly and carefully." He pulled the man back into the cave.

Continuing, "She could also be out getting wood. We need to watch for the bad guys." Looking outside, "I don't see her. So I want us to head in different directions for five minutes and then work our way back to the cave. Do you hear me?"

Todd looked dazed.

"Did you hear me? You head five minutes to the north, and I will head five minutes to the south. Stay along the edge of this cliff face. If she's out there she wouldn't have gone any farther than that. She is smart and knows this land well."

"Yeah, got it. Five minutes north." Todd spoke through his anxiety.

"Listen, if there are bad guys out there, they will kill you as well as look at you." He grabbed Todd's tunic and shook him a bit, taking on the tone of a drill sergeant. "Todd, get on task. I need you focused and at your best." The agent's intensity awakened the professor to the world they were in.

"Hudson, we have to find her. We have to. She's relying on us. I love her…"

"We'll find her," his response was matter of fact and assuring. "Five minutes, no more."

"Got it."

They left the cave in opposite directions and prayed for the Lord's protection for their friend – an innocent woman dragged through time because of this mission, a mission too difficult to possibly complete.

—

By the time the soldiers arrived, much of the camp had left. Thorius and Dritus had taken their men and returned to Jerusalem. Cyprianus was to be the last to leave since this was his mission in the first place. He had decided that, when the scouts made it back, whether they had found anything or not, he would call for an end to this task along with the man who pulled the King's strings to make it happen.

The last party arrived tired, hungry and well into the night. Dropping Aaliyah on the ground at the General's tent, they announced their presence.

Cyprianus met them through one of the flaps.

Looking down at the woman, he was surprised at their find. "What is this?" he asked.

The leader of the troop answered, "Sir, we found this woman walking by herself about a mile north of here."

"She was by herself?" he asked, curious his soldiers didn't find men with her.

"Yes, we found her gathering wood in the dark."

"You were told there were most likely two men with her."

Aaliyah listened – contented that they hadn't yet found her friends.

"In this area of Israel, the wind and dry terrain prevent evidence from being discovered in the daylight. At night, it is nearly impossible. We did our best, Sir," the soldier said trying to justify coming back with only the woman. "It is by sheer luck that we found her," pointing to the woman tied on the ground. "In some of those ravines where the moonlight is blocked, it is black as pitch. We cannot see any caves and I do not want to jeopardize these highly trained men by slipping in the dark. It was my decision to stay to the valley floor and not climb the cliffs at night." He backed away, bowed his head and slapped his chest. "Sir, we will be ready to leave at daybreak and are certain to find the others that were with her."

Having lost all desire to catch anyone who might be trying to kill Aurius, Cyprianus forgave the soldier instead of breaking out his usual reprimand with possible demotion. "No Angelus, you have done well. Rest your men, for we will be leaving for Jerusalem within the hour."

"Sir, we know we can find the men given the chance," explained the well-intentioned soldier, concerned that he has let his commander down.

"You have done well. We will be leaving shortly." Angelus bowed out and caught up with his troops.

Looking her over, the general pulled the young woman from the ground and escorted her into his tent, eyeing the guards a moment before lowering the flap. For their part, the general's guards knew better than to question his motives with a prisoner -especially one as beautiful as this one. Looking at each other they smiled and went back to attention.

After untying the ropes causing her wrists and ankles to become raw, the general offered her a chair and a glass of wine. She rubbed her most sore areas but backed as far into her seat as possible, and taking the glass from the man, only drank after he did.

Laughingly he smiled at her, "I am not going to poison you," he said, noticing her reluctance to drink. "If I wanted to kill you, I would have already done it."

She took another small sip, yet kept her eyes on the large man.

Pulling up another chair from the tent and sitting across from her, he looked into her green eyes, "So what is your name?"

She remained quiet.

"I asked a simple question. What is your name?" His query was direct.

Meekly she answered, "Aaliyah."

"Aaliyah, that is a Jewish name, yet you are dressed Roman." Rising, he grabbed a lit oil lamp from a table and placed it next to her face. "You don't look Jewish, at least not completely so."

Speaking her best Greek, "I am Roman."

"No, you aren't. You speak Greek but have a Jewish accent. There is something about you. Something I cannot place. You almost look familiar."

"We have not met," she responded flatly.

"I know that we have not met, because I would remember someone as beautiful as you. However, our paths would never intermingle because I do not spend time with, well, treasonous criminals." His gaze persisted to rake over her with both interest and disgust.

She continued to look at him with fear of what he could do.

He placed the lamp back on the table and continued his questioning, "So why would a nice 'Roman' girl like you be roaming the desert at night? Did you get lost?"

"No, I was not lost," her voice was steady.

"No, you probably were not." Sitting again he asked, "So where are the men that were with you?"

"I will not tell you where they are." Her eyes were piercing and honest.

With a smile he nodded, "That would be too easy, would it not?" The long day now took its effect as he became more direct, "Do you know I could have the guards outside make your life very unpleasant?"

"Yes, I know."

"Do you also know that I could make you disappear where all they might find are your bones centuries from now?"

She did not answer.

"I know you are very well aware of how I can hurt or help you. Right now I have what looks like a Jewish woman dressed up as a Roman. That is definitely against the law. For all I know, you could have murdered one of our citizens and taken her identity."

"That did not happen," her eyes grew large.

"Yes, but I cannot prove you did not, and neither can you. All I know is that I was sent into the desert to find two men who were sent to kill a so-called prophet of the King."

"We are not going to kill him, just stop him."

He stopped at her rebuttal and looked at her again, "You look so familiar." He suddenly realized what he had heard, "What are you to stop him from doing?"

"We are to stop him from killing," she paused, thinking, "freedom?"

Cyprianus wondered at her answer for a second then started to pace. "Aaliyah, it is obvious you are not in charge of this mission you speak of. Somehow you were dragged into it, but, sadly enough, you are the one in front of me now.

Here is what is going to happen. You are my justification for the last twelve hours. The King wants someone's head, and because you are all I have, it will have to be yours."

Her eyes pressed tight, she tried to pray but found no thoughts. Aaliyah began to shake involuntarily.

Cyprianus poured himself another drink, "I will take you back and allow the King's guards to draw out whatever information you may have. If you are able to resist their interrogation, we already have several things against you. Impersonating a Roman citizen is the least of your problems, and that usually warrants the death penalty. It just gets worse from there. The King believes people are trying to kill him, so if you are connected to that, he will definitely make an example of you as he is so fond of doing.

At no point do I see you making it out of this looking as lovely as you do now."

Tears ran down her face as she finally began to pray aloud in Hebrew.

"You seem to be well educated. To speak fluent Greek and Hebrew would require some type of connection to the palace. Do you read Greek and Hebrew?"

"Yes," she answered quietly.

"You are quite an enigma. I would love to know your background, but honestly I have had a long day and need some rest. There are plenty of other mysteries that need my attention.

Guards," he barked as the men entered the tent. "Please take our guest and prepare her for transportation back to Jerusalem."

"Yes, sir," the men answered together.

"Gentlemen, if she is hurt in any way, you can know for certain you will be the next eunuchs added to the queen's guard. Is that understood?"

They nodded as one lifted her from her seat gently but by her upper arms.

"Aaliyah, it has been a pleasure," Cyprianus nodded with sincerity. "Understand, my dear, you will need a miracle to make it out of the fate ahead of you."

The woman felt small compared to the large soldiers dragging her away, yet in her heart she knew that her faith was great. It was a gift from God. She felt herself smiling weakly, not knowing if the Lord would remove her from the dark future ahead, but trusting He would be right by her side as she went through it.

Pebbles scattered under Todd's feet, bouncing and rolling over the edge of the cliff on which he ran. Blood trickled down one of his shins and gray-purple bruises were swelling along his left rib cage. He'd fallen more times than he could remember over the small boulders lying haphazardly along the path he followed. Not that he really cognitively registered any of this. His mind, his body and his heart all ached for Aaliyah's return. Images of her, captured by Roman soldiers, flashed through his mind every time he turned a corner and found no trace of her.

It tormented him, pushing him forward until a jag in the trail beneath him grabbed the loose thong of his sandal, throwing him face first in the sand. This time he stayed down against the cold rocky ground and let the tears fall - not because of the pain now penetrating his left ankle, but from helplessness and deep loss.

He wasn't accustomed to being out of control, and he knew his emotions were clouding his thoughts. Highly educated and accomplished, focus, determination and self-control had been his modus operandi since he was a teenager. With them he had excelled in every activity he'd undertaken. Now thirty-six, he had two Master's degrees, a Doctorate, his pilot's license, his black belt in Tae Kwon Do and he'd been skydiving enough lately to believe he'd mastered that as well. Staying on a task was what he did best. But, at the moment, he couldn't even see his next step.

He'd lost her. Failed to protect her. Had literally fallen asleep on the job.

After wiping the remaining tears on his garment, Todd lifted himself back up and called her name. "Aaliyah, Aaliyah." His own safety no longer a concern, he shouted louder. "Aaliyah, Aaliyah, where are you?"

Once again he picked up his pace only to be smacked in the face by a root protruding from the overhang and being knocked backwards to the ground. Lying on his back, he looked up through half-lidded, moist eyes at the stars above him. One star really, was all he could see, and it seemed to be pulsating, growing brighter by the minute. He stared at it, now hoping that she could see it too. "God please protect her. Lord, please miraculously shield her from all of the evil coming against her. Allow her to know that you love her, and that I will do everything to find her." The dirt grew dark from the tears falling beneath him.

Eyes closing out the brightness of the star luminating from the heavens, he continued his conversation with God, "Lord, I feel so inadequate. I'm so weak. I don't know why you would choose me for something this big. Oh God! My heart is broken, why are we here? Why at this time? This night of all nights? Where is she? Show me what to do. Don't let me miss anything in your plan." The words and emotions poured like a river from him. A deep-seeded hope within his soul grew in spite of the loneliness, grief and weariness.

Suddenly, he was no longer alone. Sitting up he called, "Hudson, is that you? Hudson, are you there?" No one answered, but he could feel another presence - as if he was surrounded by an army, but there was no one around.

Pressure waves drilled through the air. His ears picked up the faint sound of sonic booms, but they weren't menacing and destructive. The sound was beautiful. He saw what appeared to be asteroid-like spots of light shooting through the air. Although, the light wasn't as defined, more like ribbons of illumination so fast as to almost be indiscernible; he was watching, and he saw them. The sky almost glistened with the shafts of light.

Todd got up from the ground and stood tall. He felt a power and strength because of the light. It was a feeling he'd never experienced before, yet hoped it would never end. He dropped his arms behind him and raised his face to the sky. Even with his eyes closed, he could see the light. The emanations were not just a visual experience but part of his soul. The streaks came from all directions; some behind, some in front, some straight down and all were culminating over an area about 20 miles before him as he looked out over the desert plain.

The thought came to him as he breathed in the feeling of peace. Before he started his trek back to Hudson, he smiled. "Thank you God. You are here. And you are sovereign. I trust you, with everything. With Aaliyah." He turned and ran as fast as he could back to the front of the cave where his friend waited.

—

Hudson truly believed he would find the lost woman around each turn. The agent was very good at reading people and knew that Aaliyah would never try to leave or defect back to her old life.

When he fell through her door carrying an almost dead Todd, he quickly realized that she was just as misplaced as they were. Yes, they were lost in her world and out of time almost 2000 years, but she was also without direction in the same world: a woman without family, friends, or a future. There would be no way she would just leave to try to reestablish a life that never was. No, she was out looking for wood to restart the fire that took so much time to get going.

Approximately a quarter of a mile from the cave, Hudson stopped when he found a pile of wood. Backing into a crevice within a rock formation, he looked the area over and then worked his way back to the pile that was obviously out of place.

Bending down, the agent could see plenty of tracks. In the moonlight he viewed footprints working their way toward his present position. Looking the other way, he identified what would obviously be a group of people stopping at the pile of wood.

Standing, his heart sank. Aaliyah had an armful of wood when she encountered an opposing force, most likely Roman soldiers, and they now had her. What would he do? How could he find her and then remove her from whatever jail they had her in? And that was saying they hadn't killed her already.

Disillusionment swept over him.

Looking at the pile of sticks he prayed aloud, "God, what am I to do? I didn't want to bring her. What purpose is she in your plan? How are you glorified by her being taken captive? She is totally innocent in all of this."

The agent closed his eyes and inhaled a deep breath when he heard a faint sound. Cocking his head, he heard it again and simultaneously felt a pressure change around him.

His eyes opened wide and his body went into alert mode. Throwing himself to the ground behind a large rock formation, he peeked out and saw what seemed to be an ocean of light in the sky. The rays emanated out like waves, yet the agent couldn't determine their origin. Squinting to the heavens, he could faintly see that the waves were formed from streaks flying through the heavens. They were culminating over a ridge that was blocking his view.

Standing from his hiding place, he breathed deeply. Even the air seemed to be charged. Hudson was invigorated and renewed with a fresh determination. Every ache, pain and bruise that had been making itself known since his night in the cave was silenced. He felt like he could run a marathon.

"Thank you, Lord," he said out loud as he turned from the pile of sticks and headed back to tell his buddy the difficult news. Even though the next couple days would be the run of his life, he had hope now. The Lord had blessed him somehow. And with that special touch, he knew he wouldn't stop until the mission was over and Aaliyah was back in their protection. He turned on his heel with a full measure of confidence in his stride.

—

Aaliyah shivered as she lay tied in the back of a cart. She wasn't dressed to be in the desert at night, and her lean body offered her no warmth or extra protection. Kicking hay up around her form was all she could do to stay warm, and still she shook uncontrollably in the forty degree air.

After her encounter with Cyprianus, she had been taken by soldiers and tied to a post still remaining from a tent that had been removed hours before. She couldn't break free and wouldn't have tried, being surrounded by horsemen and marksmen trained with the bow and arrow. Besides, as the only female in the camp, every eye rested on her every move. No avenue of escape presented itself, and so she'd waited calmly, getting what rest was possible. Cyprianus' decree that she not be touched indeed was a blessing.

After twenty minutes tied to the pole, the camp made ready to move out. Two men transferred her to the back of an ox cart, tied her to the gate and forced her to walk. Aaliyah kept up well for the first few miles, but after falling a handful of times and unable to regain her footing, they finally threw her into the hay-filled cart and started off again.

She did what she could to just stay still, but eventually the shivering started and got uncontrollable after half an hour.

Lying on her side, covered in hay, she praised God. Through chattering teeth and in Hebrew, she proclaimed God's greatness and holiness. She sang songs of old and quoted as many sacred scriptures as she could remember. The woman thanked an apparently absent God for his protection even though her position couldn't be more precarious.

In mid-song when her body couldn't hurt more from the violent shaking, and her words were almost indiscernible, she saw something out of the corner of her eye. She went back to her song.

When the lights began to fill the sky, she rolled herself to a sitting position in the cart. "What is that?" she shouted.

"Silence woman," a large soldier on horseback yelled.

"Do you see that?" she asked again.

"See what?"

"That," she pointed upward, "the lights in the sky."

Another soldier jumped in, "I see nothing. Remain quiet!"

Pulsating sounds filled her ears while she sensed the air moving around her. "Do you hear that, or feel that?" She was becoming more emboldened.

The first soldier beat the side of the cart with his spear. "I am tired and do not want to hear from you."

The woman, who could barely move just a few minutes earlier, sat up straight as an arrow. "It is everywhere. They are everywhere. It is so beautiful."

"She is going crazy," one soldier said to the other after looking at where she was pointing. "Do you want me to deal with her?"

"No, the general was clear. Let her be."

"But what is she seeing? She seemed so normal just an hour ago. I generally hear this from prisoners who have been worked over in the dungeon for several days."

"She may well get her working over when she gets to Jerusalem."

Her eyes were wide trying to take in the heavenly spectacle. The more she saw, the less she shivered. The wind pulsating around her actually warmed her frail body that was on the edge of hypothermia. The deep sound accompanying the light was almost musical and matched with the song she was singing a few seconds earlier, so she continued where she left off.

Aaliyah was no longer cold. She did not shake or ache. All fear that had accompanied her imprisonment had subsided, and she sang to her God.

The young woman, in the hands of a merciless, godless regime, sang loud and strong, gaining strength with each note. Tears ran down her face as she looked to the heavens trying not to miss a moment of what the skies were doing before her.

The soldiers just watched the crazy woman in the cart. They found themselves looking up as they walked alongside the cart, hoping to hear or feel what she kept describing.

She would try to stand over and over again, hoping to raise her hands to the skies yet the length of the rope and the uneven terrain always forced her back to the bed of the cart. Eventually, the soldiers grew tired of yelling for her to remain quiet and just let her make the noise. Over time, several found themselves humming along with her singing. They thought it a catchy tune; she knew it to be praise to an ever-present and loving God.

—

Even though the men were only supposed to go five minutes out before turning back, it was close to thirty minutes before Todd arrived back at the cave to find Hudson standing there without Aaliyah.

He took a breath before he spoke, "So you didn't find her," the professor spoke, already knowing the answer.

"No, I'm pretty sure the Romans have her," Hudson answered with regret.

Todd held strong.

"To the south, I found a pile of sticks and a lot of foot marks in the dirt." Hudson looked at the ground.

"Why would she go out by herself? She knew that people were looking for us. How could she take such a risk?"

"You need to understand that crazy as it seems, she is the most trained to live in this environment. If it weren't her, it would have been one of us that got captured." He continued after a break, "From what I know of this time, they will be much more patient with a woman than a man."

Todd jumped in, "Yeah, they won't crucify her as quickly as they would us, if that's a good thing."

"Well, right now, that's all we've got. Get your stuff. If the Romans have her, she'll be held at the main camp site." Looking up he smiled, "What do you think of the fireworks display," gesturing toward the activity that hadn't let up since it began.

Gazing toward the sky Todd answered, "I think it means there is hope in the air." Dropping his gaze and putting on a determined face, "You know that from here on out, we're going into the lion's den. There will be no turning back."

The sun was now breaking over the eastern sky.

As daylight grew, Todd could make out the concern on his friend's face. Worry lines filled in from the dust of the area made the young man look much older. He knew that the weight of the world was on a man that never wanted the responsibility he was given. He was about to break the mood with a quick retort when Hudson spoke.

"Yeah, I know what we're in," gesturing to the lights which didn't disappear with the oncoming day, "But I think there's an army on our side bigger than that of the Romans. Let's go."

They started to walk to the south when Hudson halted their progress, "And by the way, the lion's den stuff is a bit over the top."

Todd laughed.

"I mean you can say we're going to encounter some opposition or we have a fight ahead of us, but lion's den? Who makes it out of a lion's den? It sounds totally hopeless. You know, I'd hope we would have a chance here. Unless your middle name is Daniel and you have something you'd like to tell me."

Sarcastically, "Well, I'm sorry if I got you nervous with the lion's den stuff. What about the term snake pit? Is that better?"

"I guess it depends on what kind of snakes are in the pit. Garden snakes are different than rattlers. I have a good chance of making it out of a pit with garden snakes - not as good with their poisonous cousins. I'm not sure if you have the bigger idea here." A smile broke Hudson's face.

"You are sure limiting my tools for the English language. If I can't use metaphor, what do I have?"

The men quipped back and forth lightening their mood. With the sun rising, it took less than 30 minutes before they were back in the area of the Roman encampment. Even though they didn't see a soul, they were diligent to stay out of the open. Concerned that their overnight hideaway would be manned with a military presence, they walked a mile to the south so they could get a look from a similar rock face surrounding the original landing location. Once they worked their way up the back side and found a spot to look down on the soldiers without being seen, they crawled out toward the edge and got their first look since leaving twelve hours earlier.

"They're gone," Todd yelled out.

Scanning the perimeter again, "It looks like they left."

The sun was rising fast causing a stark line to move along the valley below. The shadow was halfway across the valley surrounded by cliffs when they saw something.

Hudson spoke first, "What's that?"

Todd squinted. "I'm not sure. It looks like a person. A man."

They waited another ten minutes until the entire basin was illuminated and they were certain no soldiers were waiting in the rocks for an ambush.

"Let's get down there and see what they left us," Hudson said as he stood up and found a path down the front of the cliff.

It took fifteen minutes for the two to cross the distance to the center of the vacant encampment, and when they arrived, they found a man tied to stakes at four corners, severely beaten and probably suffering from exposure, considering his lack of clothing. His wrists and ankles were bloody from pulling at the ropes, and he was wearing what was left of a tunic that was wrapped at his waist.

Hudson and Todd stood between the man and the sun causing a strong shadow to form over his wounded upper body. With the intense light out of his eyes, he slowly turned his head and looked up at the men standing over him. Obviously he had the early stages of hypothermia due to the lack of shaking and lethargic movements.

After several seconds, he smiled. Showing blood stained teeth and speaking in a weak and raspy voice in perfect English, he said, "Professor Myers, Agent Blackwell, good to see you." He coughed, "You are right on time."

Todd spoke first, "I'm sorry Senator Hughes, but I can't really say it's good to see you."

Hudson continued, "Yeah, and from the looks of it, I'd say we're late."

"So what do we do with him?" Todd looked over at Hudson blankly.

"Yeah, that's a good question," the agent answered. They both stared at the wayward Senator they had come so far to apprehend. "So John, what do we do with you?" The man didn't move, but his eyes pinched shut against the new light of day.

John was facing the East, and as the sun rose, overhead light and warmth began filling the valley.

"It's obvious that you ticked someone off in the military." Hudson continued, "I guess we could leave you here and let the elements get to you." He glanced at Todd, "Are there any wild animals out here?"

"Well, the book of Isaiah talks about hyenas, jackals and owls. Even though I doubt we would find many this far out into the open."

Hudson glanced over at the Senator, "I guess it looks like sunburn during the day and icy cold at night are going to be your biggest problem. It could take days before that catches up with you though," he smiled at Todd, "I'd almost rather the wild dogs…"

"No, hyenas, not wild dogs."

"I'm sorry, hyenas. I think I'd rather they just end it quickly than suffer for days in the desert."

"Yeah, give me a good jackal any day. That's the best way to go."

Irritated with their careless attitude, the battered prisoner spoke with determination, "Untie these ropes and you won't have any trouble out of me."

Hudson dropped to his knees and pulled a knife from his waistband. Gripping it tightly, he pressed the blade against the man's taut chest until it made an indention.

Senator Hughes lifted his head and forced his eyes down to see how serious the agent might be.

"Senator," his voice was deceptively calm, "We have several problems right now. First, one of our team is missing - most likely apprehended by the army that left you here. Second, the time machine is out of order for the time being, and, at the moment, I really have no idea how we're going to fix it."

Hearing this news for the first time, Todd's gaze skimmed over to his friend with concern.

"Finally, we have you. And if you really want to know, I see you as the least of our problems. You, we can just leave here to die. Otherwise you are just one more mouth to feed. Leaving you here would simplify our plan."

Todd laid his left hand over Hudson's knife hand to calm him.

Breaking the uneasy silence, the Senator spoke in a strained voice, "Hudson, free me and I will give you no trouble. As you can see, I have burned my bridges in this time. And, I think I can help you with your missing team member. Was it a woman?"

Jumping in, Todd sounded anxious, "Yes, do you know where she is?"

Trying to look over at Todd, he had to close his eyes because of the sun's strong morning rays. The professor moved to offer shade.

"I know they found a woman last night and took her back toward Jerusalem."

"Oh, no," both sets of shoulders drooped at the news.

Hudson looked up at his friend feeling the impossibility of their situation.

"All is not lost. I think I can get you to her."

Hudson sheathed his weapon and rose from the ground, "Somehow you talked your way into pulling an army out into the desert to wait for us. But whatever set them against you has removed any credibility you might have had. They obviously left you for dead and will finish the job if you show up alive."

"Hudson, do not underestimate me. Even though I may never have the King's ear again..."

"You had the King's ear? Were you in the inner court?" Todd interjected out of astonishment.

"Yes, I was a prophet for the King," his attempted laugh turned into a cough.

"How in the world did you make that happen? You've only been here for a year if I understand the physics of time travel."

"Yes, Dr. Myers, it wasn't easy, but the King has been carrying out edicts based on my suggestions."

Hudson glared at him now, "So you deliberately changed the timeline?" Looking at his friend he shook his head and started to pace, "We may have a mess in our time."

"Agent Blackwell, I didn't change anything."

"What does that mean?"

"I brought a loaded computer, looked up Herod, found out what he did, when he did it, and just told him to do those things."

The professor began to think, "So when Herod raided areas of the kingdom…"

"I encouraged him to do what he was going to do already."

"Or kill family members."

Senator Hughes was quiet.

"What about killing every child in the city of Bethlehem?"

Speaking resolutely, "I only encouraged him to do what he was going to do already."

The professor paced to the south a few feet, causing sun to shine in the man's eyes. "Hudson, what if Herod was never going to do any of the things the Senator suggested?"

"What do you mean?"

"I mean, what if the timeline was written on our end because of the actions he brought about on this end?" pointing to the Senator. "Let's say, Herod wasn't going to kill his son, Antipater, but because the senator suggested it, he did. Or even worse, what if Herod would have never sent soldiers to Bethlehem but because of the information given by his prophet, he does, which means it is written as hard fact.

What if everything written in our history books about Herod's last year of life was brought on by John going into the past and suggesting ideas that may never have come about on their own?"

Everyone grew silent.

Senator Hughes became nervous, "Gentlemen, I only helped him with things I read about before I came into this time. You have no worries with regard to the timeline for Herod."

The agent spoke abruptly, "We don't have time for this. What should we do with him?"

Turning back, they looked at their new problem who was about to start a sunburn in the already rising heat, "We can't leave him here."

Going back to his knees in front of their prisoner, Hudson's voice grew dark, "You said you could get us to her."

The Senator responded quickly, understanding his situation, "Yes, I know how to get us access to where I believe they will be keeping the woman."

The professor grew frustrated, "How can you do this? There's bound to be a reward for someone turning in an enemy of the state, and you are definitely not a friend."

"Let me up, and I'll help you."

Hudson looked over at Todd and nodded in agreement. Bending down, he cut the ropes from the beaten and weary man. Once free to be Senator John Hughes again, he attempted to move the limbs that had been overextended for close to four hours.

"Get up," Hudson growled, "we need to find Aaliyah."

—

The Roman detachment carrying the female prisoner arrived in Jerusalem just after daybreak. The young woman had watched the skies all night and was encouraged to know that the display, although dimmed by the morning sun, was still visible throughout the heavens. She had pointed all night at the celestial show, but none of the men escorting her to Jerusalem could see it.

Many times a pressure wave knocked her back onto the hay, and the sounds would grow beautifully clear as the visions of light came close to her position. She wondered if insanity had overcome her. Remembering the events of the past ten days would have confirmed that theory had she not seen and lived them.

Who would believe that two men from the future fell through her front door? How could she explain that they came through time to stop someone from killing the Messiah? How impossible that she was taken 2000 years into the future to then be thrust even farther into the past. But how glad she was that she now knew and loved a man named Todd who had brought her with him to both protect her and stop another madman. If all that had happened did not make her a lunatic, then the beautiful sights she had witnessed all night must certainly be as real and true as the jolting of the cart beneath her.

As they entered the city, the detachment was intercepted by several soldiers in full dress garb. She knew by the color of their uniforms and the quality of their horses that they were the King's Guard.

She overheard the arriving soldiers speak to Cyprianus.

"Sir, your men said you apprehended a prisoner. You are to take her to the Herodium," the soldier said to the general.

"That is not going to happen. She is threatened with plotting an attack on the King. That puts her crime within our jurisdiction. Therefore, I will take her to the Citadel where we can question her properly. Once we have our information, we will release her to you, and she can be tried in court."

The other equestrian spoke, "Sir we have strict orders from the King to have any prisoners taken directly to the Herodium. He spoke to us personally." His powerful horse wrestled to remain still after its run to intercept the soldiers.

"Why would he care about this small woman?" he replied, attempting to hide his growing frustration.

"He believes the prisoner may be part of the coming uprising in Bethlehem. Because the information we have is conjecture, he wants to personally interview anyone you bring back to see where to find this Jewish King."

Cyprianus yelled, "She does not know anything about that. In fact, I doubt she even wants to kill the King," he gestured toward the small woman staring at the empty sky.

"That is not ours to determine. We are ordered to escort your men and the prisoner to the Herodium where she will be held."

Knowing there was nothing else he could say, Cyprianus directed most of his men to the Citadel. Ordering two soldiers to stay with him, he personally led Aaliyah to her future.

Speaking to the royal guards he gestured, "Lead the way."

The men nodded as they turned their steeds toward the King's palace southeast of Jerusalem.

Cyprianus knew that any of his soldiers could escort the 100 pound woman without him. He was not needed for this task. Yet somehow, he hoped to get out of his next assignment. Maybe, if enough time elapsed, the King would rescind his order and come to his senses. There was still a possibility he would not have to execute children. He shivered involuntarily. What a dark cloud that would bring over the country he had grown to love.

Having been born to Roman parents in Antioch, he had pledged his allegiance to the Empire, and attended military school at a young age, learning to fight and understand strategy. He had set himself apart by defending his country throughout the world, so when he was offered the highest military position in Israel, he gratefully accepted it.

So far, the leadership role had amounted to fighting and winning small skirmishes around Israel with the occasional unpleasant order from the King. But he had pledged himself to follow Herod's commands without question, and so he did. Yet, he had never, ever intentionally killed a child. Such a dishonorable, worthless, and evil order he could not obey.

There were campaigns where innocents had been killed when they fell into harm's way – such was the sad cost of battle. But in all of his years as a military leader, had he never known of an army being sent into a city to just kill the children.

And his orders had been clear: Kill boys in the city of Bethlehem under the age of three.

How could he explain his actions to his wife and children? He had a boy in that age range, a smiling, excited, and innocent boy. This child had done nothing evil against the world except see it through expectant and joy-filled eyes.

The General's gaze stayed to the ground as he headed out of the city, not because of the rising sun, but because of the terrible deed on his shoulders. His mind thought of his wife Livana, a beautiful and vibrant Jewish woman. How could he explain himself to her?

Although not a crime for a Roman soldier to marry a woman from the country he was serving in, it was known that marriage could not get in the way of any orders given by the King. As a military commander, he might be required to execute instructions against the spouse's country or even family.

Yet in the seven years he had been with his wife, he had grown to love her family. Yes they were religious zealots, but they truly believed in their God, and the highly focused and loyal military man loved that about them. Nothing could shake their faith in the idea that their God was real, and that He was sending the Messiah to save them.

Cyprianus himself was not religious and never really went in for the idea of the Roman gods. The stories behind Hercules, Mercury, or Diana were interesting, but he never put any stock in their saving power; predominantly because he saw no change in the life of the people worshiping them. Worshippers confused about life before offering sacrifices and praise to the idols felt just as alone after.

Anyway, the Roman gods were selfish and self-serving. Even if he did believe they were up in the sky living some wild life apart from the earth, why would he want to worship gods that were more dysfunctional than the people he worked with each day. The concept baffled the determined leader.

Livana and her family were special, even inspiring. Their lives revolved around the worship and service of their God Jehovah. Their rituals, eating practices, even daily activities all revolved around their love of God. Regardless of his own belief, he respected their worship.

On the horizon about five miles out he saw their destination and his heart sank. Why couldn't it be twenty-five miles out? If he had more time, perhaps he could find a way to shuttle the orders to another commander, or find something more pressing to do for the military.

He looked to the sky in despair, "Jupiter, if you are there, get me out of this," he mumbled quietly, but knew his prayer went no farther than the distance his voice could carry the sound. The General, who had never questioned an order before, was now placed in a position of wondering how he could fulfill it.

"Someone, somewhere, get me out of this," he whispered. "If there is a God, show yourself to me. If I ever needed you, it is now." He looked back to the ground and continued the trek. "Livana, please forgive me."

—

It took a little more than an hour for them to arrive at the stronghold. The King's retreat sent shivers down the back of the hungry and thirsty woman. To her it resembled a volcano, a flat-topped mountain providing the surface for the evil abode of Herod.

Being poor and living with the laborers in Jerusalem, she had heard the many stories of the difficult and dangerous projects Herod had her people working on. She knew how many of God's chosen had died building the fortress before her. Friends and relatives of her parents had lost their lives on the fanciful whims of this tyrant King who had died a year after Aaliyah had been born.

The imposing presence of the man-made mountain also forced her to face the reality that she may not make it out of the palace once inside. She took several deep breaths as the caravan ascended the steep road to the top. Looking toward Jerusalem she imprinted the picture to memory hoping to remember again the city where her Lord would be coming back.

At least the heavenly activity had not diminished as the day had worn on. In fact, more heavenly apparitions sparkled now than the night before. There was hope, and God knew of her plight.

The soldiers had long since ignored the ramblings of the prisoner who seemed too calm and joyful to understand her certain death sentence. So when she spoke out again, they just continued their march without looking up. However, Cyprianus heard her words and had taken to heart everything she had said throughout the night.

With a smile on her face and trying to stand and raise her hands once again, "Lord, I trust you, and all I have is yours."

They entered the large domed portico, and the sky disappeared from view.

When the military entourage stopped within the portico, Aaliyah's eyes grew wide as they tried to adjust to the light and take in the scale of the palace. She had never been inside this fortress that had loomed large on the horizon.

The soldiers stood at attention behind the wooden cart as Cyprianus walked to the back and untied the ropes attached to the woman's bruised and blistered wrists. Gingerly she touched the sores, feeling pain once again after the long unusual journey. She felt the General's eyes boring holes into her. He stood there motionless and Aaliyah looked at him intently, and for an instant, saw the man behind the armor.

Having been up for close to 24 hours, it was obvious the man's demeanor was affected by his lack of sleep, but what she saw there would not be cured by a good night's rest. His eyes glanced away as he attended to the rope he held, but still she felt the sadness and regret she knew weighted him down. He was lost - as if he were a young boy apart from his parents trying to find his way home.

Obviously bound by loyalty and duty, the General picked up a pair of wrist irons.

The prisoner watched his posture and manner. He moved slowly, with no enthusiasm. Clearly he did not want to leave her in this place - the fortress he knew would be her final destination. He looked away again and took in a deep breath.

Aaliyah never removed her eyes from him as new understanding dawned. Though she was the one being held, he was the true prisoner. She had hope and a future. He had nothing to hope in.

No, she knew her outlook was grim, but she served a mighty God who would not forget her and had already proven to walk with her in the direst of circumstances. The highly trained and respected general had none of this. His King was a tyrant who killed his own children to protect himself. For this powerful warrior, nothing offered hope, and she could see the longing behind his eyes. Only God could calm his troubled soul.

Lord, show yourself to him, she prayed silently as she watched him.

Closing his eyes and exhaling, he looked back at her. With a sincere smile, she tried to reassure him, "General, do not worry about me. I will be fine and am well protected. Shackle me if need be."

His piercing blue eyes grew hazy and moist. He dropped the irons to the ground, grasped her hand and helped her step down from the cart. The many slaves walking around tried to ignore the breach in protocol, but one woman stopped and could not help but admire the lady's grace and poise under such a horrible situation.

—

Being a Jewish slave in the King's palace meant that Keren had seen many things that were beyond description. Many ill-fated prisoners were dragged either screaming or unconscious down below the rocky floor. But here was a girl, really a woman in Roman garb, lifting her hand to the General to be escorted to the dungeon as if she were attending a grand party in his company. Under such obvious duress she was calm and composed.

The green eyed woman could not help but stare. How could this prisoner's gentle spirit so subdue the hardened soldiers around her that the General himself was helping her from her transport? An ox cart, no less.

Cyprianus looked to the ground and gestured onward indicating the direction for Aaliyah to walk. Straightening her outer garment and looking forward, the woman moved ahead with sophistication.

The soldiers fell in line to follow until Cyprianus put his hand up, "Stay here, I can manage the prisoner." They held their ground and turned to attend to the oxen.

Finding her curiosity piqued at this new arrival, Keren moved silently behind them through the cold limestone tunnel. The oil-filled sconces only lighted the most direct path; the shadowed corners provided a safe enough route in. Going out would be less simple.

As the two in front of her turned to enter the detention area, Keren emerged from the shadows just enough to get a look at the woman's face before she rounded the corner. What she saw took her aback.

Keren stood there blinking as if someone had shoved her from the darkness into the new light of day. Her heart pounded in her chest, and she realized she needed to take a breath. She could swear that she knew the woman, yet how that was possible she knew not. And the women she knew shared her world. She had no partial acquaintances.

But somehow a bond existed between them, a connection, something she could not explain. This kinship worked its way to the most inner part of her being. There were many people she would like to have known, many she admired, but never had someone captivated her so completely. Disconcerted, her eyes closed as she breathed to still her heart. Oddly, she was wildly excited and filled with peace simultaneously.

Finally, hands pressed to her stomach, she drew herself up and turned to head back up to the entrance and back to her original purpose for the day. But in her heart she knew that, even if it meant disciplinary action, she would see the woman again. It had to be soon. More than likely her execution had already been scheduled.

—

Aaliyah continued through the tunnels. In spite of it being a holding area, it was elaborately decorated. The young woman took in the lavish mosaics and hanging tapestries. They showed various conquests of Herod, a King conquering animals, people and countries - most she knew to be false.

A few more turns and another hundred feet and they had arrived at the few prison cells within the facility. These detention centers were used infrequently for things like the occasional family member thought to be planning a coup on the throne.

The large rooms secured with heavy iron gates were presently empty and usually stayed that way. When Herod was informed the army apprehended someone in the desert, he insisted they house them where he could personally question them. Aaliyah expected a visit from the King.

Cyprianus opened the gate and allowed the gentle prisoner to walk through it. Closing the entry with a loud reverberating clang, the man held onto the bars and watched as she took a seat along the wall and then looked back at him with a faint smile.

The General spoke in quiet tones, "I will choose a guard that I can trust. You will not be harmed beyond what the King may have for you."

With wide eyes Aaliyah replied, "Thank you."

"You will be wise to answer your interrogators as quickly and honestly as you can. They will extend the time with you if they think you are holding anything back."

"I will be totally honest."

"Yes, I believe that you will." He hesitated for a second before continuing, "Did you really see lights in the sky last night?"

Rising and walking over to the bars, she placed a hand on his, "Oh, yes, I did, and even though I cannot see them now, I still hear them. Something earth changing is happening. A great event has occurred!" she answered with excitement.

Wanting to believe her he tilted his head, "What? What has happened?"

"I do not know, but God is orchestrating it."

His lips pressed together out of desperation, "I wish I could see it. I would love to believe that a God exists who is a better man than I." His hands fell from the bars.

At that he turned from the cell and started back through the tunnel. Before she lost the military commander from view, she yelled one last statement, "There is a Leader greater than Herod, Lord Sabaoth is his name. God Almighty. The leader of the Armies of Heaven. He will give you purpose!"

The soldier stopped, looked back, then turned down a tunnel and left her view.

—

Todd and Hudson gave the Senator some water and looked him over. After determining nothing was broken and that most of his gashes had stopped bleeding, they started their trek out of the desert following visible tracks the army made just hours before.

Within a half of a mile, they found Aurius' outer garment unceremoniously thrown in a ditch along the path. Aurius gestured towards it, "That's mine."

Todd walked over and picked up the cloth, "Are you certain?" he asked Senator Hughes.

"Yes."

"It doesn't look like you are well-liked among the people. Cloth like this is expensive and the soldiers could have given this to their wives to use any number of ways."

Grabbing the outer mantle in his hands, "They could not have used this cloth because it is only owned by the elite. There would have been no way for them to explain how they came into possession of it."

Hudson jumped into the conversation as the Senator began meticulously wrapping the garment to cover his beaten and now sunburned body. "I think it's more than a possession problem. I think they're making a statement."

The Senator looked up.

"They obviously have turned their backs on you. To the extent they won't even take this expensive cloth and use it as pillow stuffing."

Everyone walked forward in exasperation.

After ten minutes of only hearing foot falls in the dirt, Todd spoke up again.

"So John, what were you thinking?" Stopping his march and turning to look at the man who had disrupted his life in such a great way.

"What do you mean?" he answered not looking him in the eye.

"You know what I mean. Did you not learn from the first time?"

Hudson remained silent wanting to hear the answer.

John Hughes continued to look off in the distance.

"Look at me," he yelled, "did you not get it the first time?"

"What did I not get? Tell me."

"You sent Clark, or whatever his name was, back to the past the first time to try and kill Jesus and he failed. And yet you tried again."

He stared at him with his piercing blue eyes.

"You had everything a man could ask for. Wealth, prestige, power. You had a privileged life coming from the best schools. Twenty years in the Senate, and you were the head of the Senate Intelligence Committee." His ranting led to pacing before the man he accused. "You led this project. You had the ability to change the world for the better.

This kind of technology could remove a Hitler or stop a Pearl Harbor attack. We could evacuate people before Tsunamis or earthquakes occurred. Who knows, you could have stopped the Stock Market crash of 29 or kept Islamic terrorists from taking down the World Trade Centers. So much potential, and you ruined it."

Todd planted his feet before the Senator and struck the pose of an angry parent with a rebellious teen.

"So much potential. All that power to do good, but all I wanted – all I ever hoped for – was to have my wife and daughter, home again with me." Tears pooled and spilled now as he spoke, running in rivulets down his beaten face. "All of history in my hands, and I can't bring back my beautiful wife Stephanie or daughter Katherine."

The professor, seeing the pain in the man's eyes, unfolded his arms and listened.

"Do you know what it's like to lose everything? What about you agent, have you lost your family? The people you love?" looking Hudson in the eyes. "No you haven't. You don't know what it's like to put on a smile for the world, while you're dying inside. I would have given everything, including my position and wealth to just seem them again, to feel the hope and the future with them in it. That's all I wanted." His voice trailed off and he stopped a moment to regain his composure.

"So no Professor, I didn't learn my lesson. My whole world died when they went on a mission trip to tell about - Him," he pointed to the sky, "and he turned his back on them. He could have protected or defended them, but he didn't. So yes, I am trying, once again, to remove him from history. I couldn't kill Jesus as an adult, so I'm going to try to do it again at his birth. If he's out of the picture, then Stephanie or Katherine won't be on some fool mission trip when they get caught in the middle of a gang initiation. With Jesus out of the way, my world is restored!"

Hudson spoke out of frustration, "Why didn't you just go and kill the gunman? That seems a lot simpler than this."

"Your Jesus wanted my family removed so I was just trying to level the field."

"But what about everyone else? Jesus changed the entire world, not just your family. What about the hope Jesus brings?" Todd pointed out.

"I have no hope," he replied flatly as he continued the walk.

Todd ran up behind him, "If you don't believe in his Deity and gift of salvation, you must see how Christianity, really following Christ, has changed the world completely for the better. Just following Jesus moral code elevates society to a higher respect for life."

"Many religions offer a high moral code. If someone wants to aimlessly follow the teachings of someone else, there are plenty of self-help groups and dozens of other religions that teach respect and love for your fellow man. They don't need Jesus for that."

The agent jumped into the conversation, "Senator, you seem to forget that most of those religion's views on humanity stem from the teachings of Christ. Without Jesus, society breaks down."

"I will take that chance. A solid government will offer the stability for a society."

He continued, "John, I know that you've grieved and will continue to feel loss. I don't have any idea of what you are going through. Without my family I'd be broken, at least for a time. But I know that I can trust my God, and that he will give me the ability to get through it. The sad thing is that you will never understand this until you let go of your anger and give your life to him."

"That will not happen," he retorted with hate in his voice.

"So that brings me to this." He grabbed the man by the back of the toga and pulled him to a stop. "You will not kill Jesus. I will ensure that."

Senator Hughes just stared blankly at him.

"You will not have an opportunity to get near Him because at the first sign of trouble, I'll remove you from the equation. Do you understand?"

"Here is what I understand agent, if I've done my job correctly, I won't have to kill Jesus because that will happen without me."

Todd interjected, "What do you mean?"

"As we speak, Herod is sending troops into Bethlehem to kill all of the boy babies," the senator said matter-of-factly.

The professor thought for a second and started to pace. Thinking out loud, "We know this happened because it's written in several of the gospels in the Bible. But Hudson, what if he started it early?"

"What do you mean?" the agent asked.

"We know that Herod sends troops in to kill the boys in Bethlehem, but what if John starts the process before it historically occurred? Is Jesus in more peril because of the events of the last few days?"

Obviously frustrated with the time paradox, "Todd, we can't stop an army, but I can stop this one man, and that's all I can worry about. God the Father will do the rest. As long as he stays away from Jesus, I'll be content." Looking at the Senator, "We need to find our team member and then get home."

"Agent, you rescued me from the desert, and I gave you my word I would help. I will do so. However until Jesus is dead, my mission is not complete."

"You get us to Aaliyah, and your mission is complete. Let's head out." Hudson pointed forward.

The professor followed the Senator. "Where are we heading?"

Senator Hughes said, "Machairus. There are people there who will get us some supplies."

"John, what do you think about the sky?" Hudson asked looking at the activity above.

"What about the sky?"

Todd spoke, "All of the streaks going through the sky. Don't you see them?" pointing up.

The Senator looked up. "I don't know what you're talking about. It's a cloudless blue sky."

"Do you hear or feel anything?" Hudson asked.

"I feel how much my body hurts."

Todd jumped in, "Are you experiencing anything out of the ordinary?" moving his arms around.

"Why do you keep asking that?"

Hudson looked over at Todd, "Why isn't he experiencing it?" The Senator walked ahead.

"I've got an idea, but give me some time to work it out," Todd mumbled while looking to the heavens.

The sounds of playing children accompanied the squawk of hens and distant male voices deep in conversation as the three men walked into the little town of Machaerus. Although the sun's position directly overhead indicated it was around noon, their cramping muscles and growling stomachs told them otherwise. But after stumbling over the ruts carved out by the army all morning, the bucolic farm setting of the village was a welcome sight.

They walked right through the middle of town rather than take time to case the area and find back streets to the place John was leading them to. Had their situation been ideal, they would have watched the village along with its main roads for a day or so to ensure no one was waiting to apprehend them. As it was, everyone in town stopped what they were doing to watch them parade through the main street.

Todd felt the empty bag at his waist once again to ensure that he was, indeed, out of water. At this point, thirst would seem to trump shelter. But Hudson had the lead on this mission, and though they'd not had nearly enough water for their journey and hadn't eaten for over a day, finding the place to stay ranked first. In spite of the attention they were receiving, Senator Hughes led them directly to the rustic rock home of the family that had taken him in close to a year earlier.

When the children in the courtyard saw their old friend, they ran inside and brought their mother out to meet the men waiting at the gate. She immediately bent down and whispered to her son as she pointed off in the distance. It was obvious to the agent that boy was to go find his father; a reality that did not make Hudson feel secure in his present situation.

Standing behind the Senator, Todd and Hudson watched the body language of the woman. Ringing her hands a moment, she released them suddenly and, gluing on a smile, wiped her fingers on her skirt before coming within ten feet of the gate.

Five minutes later, John had still not been allowed into her home, and Hudson wondered how great an idea it was to follow the man here. The poor woman kept nodding and smiling as she continued to look behind her, as if waiting for the cavalry to come.

"Senator, let's go, this isn't right," Hudson said as he saw eyes peeking through the cloth-covered windows around them.

"No, it's alright," he replied. "It isn't proper for a man to be in a house with a woman. I'm sure that's why she's so nervous."

The professor jumped in, "I'm with Hudson, there's more here than just etiquette. She clearly does not want us here."

John was wearing his own fake smile by now, "We'll get some lunch and then leave, but we have nowhere else to go," he said, trying to make it appear as if here were merely asking the time of day.

Hudson knew their options were slim. They had to get water and eat soon, and if they couldn't get it here, they would have to commandeer it somewhere else. An action he knew could have dire consequences.

"Just make it quick. The whole town's watching us," Hudson answered flatly.

After several more minutes and the promise of gold - an offer that turned the head of the professor listening in - they were allowed through the gate. Yet, with each step the woman took toward the house, her head clearly craned in another direction looking for something or someone to arrive.

Once inside, John and Todd sat on the floor as Hudson kept an eye on the street through the cloth covered door. Activity had picked up once they left the courtyard and the agent knew it would not be long until they had visitors.

With the many fields filled with grain and fenced areas with goats and sheep surrounding their location, the city of Machaerus was clearly a rural community. The inhabitants of the town made their living from the land and were most likely a minimal threat at best. Yet, even the most passive man might become a risk, given the right farm implement and a few of his best friends.

Hudson didn't have to possess the education of the professor to know that most towns of any size in the first century would have some sort of military contingency attached to them. And that's what made him the most nervous.

He knew all too well how easy it was to underestimate the people of this time. Far from the backward farmers he'd assumed them to be before last week, he now knew were very clever at solving problems. No, they could launch rocks from catapults with amazing accuracy. Their archers were deadly at over hundred feet, and they had runners, equestrians and carrier pigeons that could easily get a message to reinforcements within a matter of hours.

He also knew the Roman armies' propensity for death and destruction and actually felt less comfortable than he would in the worst part of any major city in America.

Seeing the men outside running suddenly in different directions Hudson spoke up, "Guys, we need to get going. We're in danger." He dropped the curtain and walked back into the room.

The woman of the house was putting bread and fruit on the table as the little girl stood at her leg behind her. Having tried to get the child to speak with him like she used to but to no avail, John's excitement about coming back to an old-fashioned homecoming was waning.

"You know normally, they would wash our feet and take our outer garments so we could be more comfortable," Todd said to the Senator.

Finally seeing the state of affairs John agreed, "I know. You're right that something's wrong. I hoped it might be only propriety as I spent six months with this family. They taught me the language and showed me kindness while I worked my way into the palace. I paid them well and we had a good relationship."

"All I can think is that the army came through last night telling of what happened to you," Hudson said while pacing. "Either they said you died which is why everyone is surprised and cautious to see you, or more likely, they said you were an enemy of Rome and that if you were ever seen, they should be notified."

The professor spoke up, "Usually they offer some kind of reward to motivate the commoners." He looked the Senator right in the eyes, "So I guess the question is, how good were you to them? Good enough they would protect you like family or good enough that an extra goat or sheep would motivate them to talk?"

Silence filled the next few minutes as the men took a few bites of bread and drunk their fill of cloudy water. The Senator looked into his cup and saw his dark reflection. The image looking back was not one he was proud of. For when he was arrested for subversion and was taken before the King to be tried, the family was scrutinized by the military.

He received a speedy trial at which he was able to become the King's prophet and gain all of the prestige and prominence that came with it. However, the family living in the humble house around him were examined and questioned for some time. Fortunately, they knew only that he had walked in from the East and collapsed at the edge of their town, but it took weeks before they were believed. Soldiers had come almost daily, inquiring among the villagers of the family's character and roughing up not a few decent folks.

After John became Aurius the Prophet, the family was freed and allowed to return to their lives. Yet, he never helped them in any way once he attained his lofty position in the palace. He never sent monetary provisions for the poor family, and at no point did he try to influence the King on their behalf. More importantly, he never came back to say thank you to a gracious household in a culture where hospitality and gratitude were highly valued.

John lowered his cup and looked over at the little girl staring at him from behind her mother's legs. He now understood why she would not talk with him, and he could not blame her. In his determination to bring back his own family, he had hurt hers. His heart sank.

Shouting outside broke the stillness in the tiny room. The woman ran to the door and looked from the curtain covering the opening. Hudson went to a window while Todd and the Senator stood flush against an inner wall.

"Hudson, that's a Roman soldier speaking, he asked if she had foreigners in her house," Todd whispered.

The woman yelled through the curtain while looking back into the room several times.

"She's saying that no one's here."

"I have no idea what she's saying, and even I don't believe her. I don't think she'd make a good actress," Hudson replied.

The woman and her daughter left the room and entered the courtyard.

Hudson dropped below the window with his back against the wall. Looking to the men next to him, "She ran out."

"We're in a mess," Todd mumbled.

"Yep. I see three soldiers heavily armed on horses. What are they saying?" looking at the Senator.

"Proerchonti apo tah spiti," yelled a soldier.

He answered calmly, "They want us to come out."

The clanging of metal from outside the house meant the soldiers were dismounting from their horses.

The Senator began to stand, "Let me go out. The soldiers will take me to Herod, and I will work everything out. He trusts me. I have done so well by him in the past."

Todd lifted an eyebrow, "Yeah, you've really been a great influence. Having his son killed, sending him on wild goose chases and forcing him to kill all of the babies in Bethlehem. Maybe he's wisely rethinking your great influence."

"You're not going anywhere," Hudson pulled him back down. "There's not a chance we're letting you out of our sight."

"We only have another minute or so before they come in," the professor said looking at the back entrance.

"What is there we can protect ourselves with?" Hudson asked crawling toward the back room of the house.

The professor picked up a broom and twirled it to check its balance. "I'll be fine with this. My third degree black was in ancient weapons."

"That's great for you, but I don't have martial arts training. The only training I've had on a broom was sweeping the floor when I was nine," the Senator said sarcastically.

Looking through the house, the agent found a pot of hot stew – fresh from the fire, clay bowls, iron knife-like objects and various wooden spoon-looking utensils.

"*Playsiadzoumay!*" a soldier said, pulling his sword from its sheath.

"He said something like 'We're coming in to kill you,' right?" Hudson grunted, pulling some things toward the front door.

"I didn't know you spoke Greek," Todd said with a smirk. He took the other side of the door. "I think you need to work on your syntax, but you got the gist."

Hudson just looked at him. He was in his element. The years of hand to hand martial arts training evidently gave him confidence in this situation. Hudson, however, was far more comfortable with some sort of 21st century weapon. Of which he had none. The Romans had the advantage and he felt ill-equipped.

He composed himself a moment before barking at the Senator, "Stay there." Hudson threw him a knife he'd found in the kitchen. "Use that if it comes down to it."

The Senator picked up the weapon and backed into a wall under a window. Having security attached to him most of his life, using a weapon for his own defense had never really entered his mind. He rolled the knife around in his hands using several different holds before he felt comfortable with the archaic blade.

Once again a warrior outside called to them, "*Playsiadzoumay!*"

The soldiers now stood on the other side of the cloth door.

The men glanced at each other with wide eyes and all simultaneously took a deep breath.

A sword pushed alongside the fabric covering the door and moved it over, forcing light into the room. Hudson and Todd backed themselves as far against the edges of the opening as they could, hoping not to be seen. Todd held tightly to his broom and Hudson pulled the pot of hot soup from the floor.

After opening the cloth and seeing the Senator sitting on the floor across the room, a soldier entered slowly. He was a smaller man, compared to the three in the room, but because of the plates of armor covering most of his body, it would take more effort to subdue the aggressor.

The soldier swore obvious obscenities as his eyes adjusted to the light. Once inside the room and with the men at this back, Hudson threw the pot of steaming liquid, forcing the man to shriek and pull at his armor. The second soldier ran in with his sword forward and Todd quickly thrust the broom handle into the side opening between his front and back upper plates just under his arm. Feeling that he had broken one of the man's ribs, he then pushed the broom father between the armor and then forward opening up the protection like a tin can. The second soldier fell to the floor, writhing in pain while the first was beginning to recover from the shock of the hot liquid.

Hudson jumped him from behind, and they fell to the floor. The professor, now with access to the other man's chest area, gave him a strong punch to the stomach and stood as he bent into fetal position to gasp for air.

Hearing the commotion inside, the third soldier ran in through the back door and went right for the Senator. Todd saw the direction of his travel and pulled the broom from the floor. Running over to protect his prisoner, he methodically beat at the last and largest soldier behind the knees and redirected the arbitrary thrusts of the sword while pinpointing areas of the man that were not protected.

At first the methodical blows from Todd just enraged the soldier more, but after a dozen strikes in the same spot behind his knees and under his arm, eventually he backed off in his attack, hoping to stop the steady onslaught from the broom handle.

Hudson, still grappling on the floor with the first soldier, remembered his days in High School and College as a state wrestling champion, the moves came back quickly and he was able to gain advantage by taking position over his back and putting the man in a headlock. Normally, he would stop the hold when the man tapped out, but now knew he had to take him to full unconsciousness.

Pulling tighter and tighter around his opponent's neck, he felt the man writhe and wiggle until his body drooped in defeat. Hudson held him for several more seconds to ensure he would be out for a while. He then jumped to his feet to help his friend with the last enemy.

Picking up the pot that held the stew earlier, Hudson tried to work his way behind the man that was thrusting blindly at Todd who was beating him black and blue with a small stick. They were all over the room knocking over tables and running into walls. The professor continued to agitate his opponent. Working their way back toward the wall, Todd fell over the man Hudson had taken down just seconds earlier, and the soldier saw his chance.

Running forward with his sword ready to eliminate the professor who had become a thorn in his side, the Senator stuck out his leg, forcing the soldier to the ground. Hudson ran up from behind and crashed the pot into the soldier's now helmet-less skull. He dropped to his feet and fell forward onto his fellow soldier.

Hudson lowered himself to feel for a pulse, "He's just out. He should recover."

Breathing heavy and seeing the man hurting in the corner, Todd smiled. "That one will be alright. I think I broke a rib or two, but he'll make it to plunder more villages in the future. I'm glad I went through those years of classes. I never thought I would use my knowledge against Roman soldiers, but it helped nonetheless."

"We don't have much time, that one will be getting up pretty quickly," he said pointing to the soldier he'd forced unconscious with a headlock.

The Senator stood and looked at the carnage in the room, "Now what do we do?"

Hudson remarked, "You need to get us to where they have Aaliyah."

"They are going to have her at the Herodium. Herod will want to interview her personally. That may work to our advantage. There will be fewer military personnel around since it isn't a normal detention center, although they will be better trained."

The men got quiet for a second.

The Senator thought out loud, "Because everything has happened within the last 24 hours, the information of my demise may not have made it to the palace. I still might be able to get in there as before. Cyprianus may be in no hurry to explain himself to the King." He looked the men in the eyes, "It would be normal for me to have several sentries assigned to me."

"Are you saying we need to take their uniforms?" Todd asked incredulously.

"I think we're about to head into the lion's den."

Todd reacted, "I thought you said we couldn't use metaphors like that. Something about them being too dramatic."

"It seems to work now," Hudson smiled, "Which uniform do you want?"

"I'll take the one without the soup on it."

The Senator watched the arbitrary banter and wondered how these men could have ever caught up with him.

"Let's get dressed," Hudson said, standing and starting to pull at the taller man's uniform.

Five minutes later the travelers were dressed as Roman soldiers while the other men took their Roman garb. With them gagged and tied, the faux soldiers threw the three men over the backs of their respective horses. As the town looked on, the travelers mounted the horses. Hoping the average person would not remember how many soldiers went in; they tried to assume their identities. With the meanest and lowest voice possible Todd yelled, "Zaytow tah Basileah Hroday."

The horses started down the street. Hudson yelled, "What'd you say back there?"

"Something like, 'Long live Herod and Rome.' It sounded official."

The Senator spoke up, "Those villagers may believe you're a soldier, but it will take more than a few words to validate you at the palace." He raced off ahead of the men.

Todd and Hudson looked at each other then kicked the horses forcing them to follow. A trail of dust was left in their wake.

Keren's heart pounded as she worked her way down the back staircase to the main kitchen. Warmth and the smell of roasting meat contrasted with the cold and hard limestone steps beneath her sandals. In a way it mirrored the emotions opposing one another in her mind. Recognition and fear, camaraderie and uncertainty warred to first place.

In all, nothing soothed the vacuum she felt after seeing the prisoner brought in a few hours earlier. She knew something had to be done about her. *But what?* She wondered again. No matter what she did, she could not get her out of her head.

Continuing into the welcome light of the main food storage area, the young woman closed her eyes a moment, trying to invent a reason to see the prisoner. A young man bearing a large tray of water pitchers nearly missed seeing her enter and sloshed water onto his well-ordered tray, shooting her a look of irritation as she passed.

Although labeled from her birth as a servant to the king, slavery seemed a more appropriate term. The only ending to her "servant hood" was death or dismissal. Nonetheless, her current responsibilities kept her in the comfort of the tower, and thus, she had more freedom than most and authority over some within the palace. Her status, however, did not yield any respect. Disgust distorted the features of the other Jewish slaves when she came into their presence.

Sighing, she continued on her way. Having received this sort of reaction for years never dulled the pain of rejection, and many times she had questioned her own decisions. But in the end, she knew there was nothing she could have done to change her path —besides kill herself. No, her choices were made for her the day she was conceived.

Her mother had headed up the mountain each morning to clean the palace floors for the King. Her father worked in his stables, caring for the horses. Because so many Jews worked at the fortress, a small town was built on the southern side allowing these indentured staff to come and go as needed, while offering somewhat of a normal life for them. Conscripted to working, they still were well-fed and did not want for many things.

Being a child raised in the slave village, Keren knew nothing of the world around her. Her family went to the Temple, but paid a higher sin tax due to their affiliation with the Romans. Freedom was never a notion discussed within her family, and she totally expected that her future would involve working in the fortress looming large before her each day.

Some of Keren's earliest memories were watching her mother speak often before the Lord in heaven, thanking Him that she only had simple, rounded Jewish features. Keren realized much later the reason for her prayers. Because the woman's mother was plain in appearance, she was never required to do more than cleaning.

As Keren grew, her mother sent her to work in the fields, a position no one wanted, especially when there were palace positions available. The hot, dry toil of threshing wheat or picking vegetables took its toll and aged a person quickly, yet she smiled and never pressed her mother on why she would not allow her a glamorous position such as cook or seamstress.

Her answer came one day when a Senator was escorted around the palace and saw the young woman working in the fields. He stopped the carriage and just watched her work for what seemed like hours. She knew her skin was lighter than that of most Jews, even with the tan she had developed in the fields, and she stood inches over the women around her. Keren's long lean figure, hair with auburn streaks and green eyes made her appear exotic and very desirable to the older Roman leader.

Returning immediately to the palace, he asked Herod for the right to take her to his home and promised to pay handsomely for the opportunity. Herod, no one's fool when it came to recognizing value, knew his friend's excitement meant the woman he wanted likely was a woman Herod himself would enjoy. He never lost the opportunity to gain a hidden treasure, and rejected the Senator's request, bringing her immediately into the palace.

Initially, the idea of moving from the fields into the fortress was a dream come true, until she discovered she was to be groomed for a position as a concubine. She now understood why her mother had been so harsh and determined to keep her out in the fields – always refusing for her the palace jobs. Keren was a stunning young woman, and her mother knew the King's lust was never satisfied. At the first opportunity, the King would want to add her to his ever-increasing stable of desirable women.

Realizing her only way out of the nightmare would be to take her own life, she did her best to smile during the day and cry most nights. Her God had placed her in that position for a reason, and even though her own people would reject her, she had a purpose in the palace, and would do her best with what she was given.

For the first few months, pampering and training occupied her time. Oil massages and perfume treatments made the days more bearable. The best food graced her table and she received training in the etiquette of a person appearing before the King. The other ladies seemed to enjoy their place and understood it to be better than working in the fields or the kitchen. Keren could only dream of those fates that had been taken away.

Since a Jewish home could not interact with prostitutes, her family was forced to reject her. So Keren lost not only the respect of her mother and father, something she held dear, but also their company. Even though she had yet to go before the King, her mother would not look up at her as they passed in the halls. Her father would stop his movements when he saw her, but continued his work a moment later. Sadness lined his face, reflecting the pain in his heart. The temple priests forced his rejection of her.

Loneliness weighed upon her lovely shoulders. Four months into Keren's stay her name came up for entry to the King. Dressed in a royal silk by her handlers, given jewelry, makeup and the most fragrant of spices, she was escorted down the long hallway. Her legs could barely carry her because of the shaking, and her stomach turned within. She prayed over and over again that she would be rejected and escorted from the palace. The most basic of flaws would cause a young woman to move from the highest place in the kingdom to a scullery maid in the kitchen. That fate was preferable to what she knew awaited her.

Her matron opened the large door to the cold stone room, and she entered quietly. The King sat in a large chair hunched over more food than one man could eat in a week. The door slammed behind her.

Walking a few feet farther into the room lit dimly by oil lamps, the older man pulled what appeared to be part of a goat leg from his mouth, took a drink from a large gold goblet and said, "Disrobe."

She stood there motionless for several seconds not believing this moment had come. Keren had been raised a proper Jewish woman and never believed she would truly be put through such disgrace.

It was just a few seconds later she heard him speak again. "I said, disrobe."

Knowing her life was at stake, Keren, quickly and awkwardly removed her covering until she stood before him, cold and shaking only wearing the jewelry on her wrists and neck.

She tried not to cry before the grotesquely heavy man, but tears fell from her cheeks anyway. With all her being she prayed she would be rejected. *Please Lord allow me to be flawed. God, do not let him keep me.*

"Turn around," he grunted through a mouth full of fruit.

The young woman turned trying not to cover herself with her arms.

"Stand straight, and look at me," he said with force.

Taking her eyes from the floor, she forced herself to look at the man she presently loathed. With all of the strength she could muster, she made eye contact with the person who had separated her from her family.

With a grin and taking another bite from the goat leg he pronounced her judgment, "You will do. We will meet another day." With that, he waved a hand in dismissal. She picked up her garment, wrapped it as quickly around herself as possible and rushed for the door, leaving the man to make love to his dinner as he was when she had arrived ten minutes earlier.

Now as Keren reached the base of the staircase, the memory seemed distant and sad. She turned right and moved lightly down a long hallway toward the main kitchen. The woman had always thought about that short time before the King. He had indeed called her back another time, and every few months after that. Hideous memories, all of them, but that first ten minutes had changed her life. There her heart had calloused, toward men, the world, and God himself. No longer was the world the beautiful creation she had thought it was, and no longer did she find joy in knowing her Creator. He had turned his back on her that day.

But the questions never ceased. Why would he allow one of his own to be abused for the pleasure of another? No, God did not love her, and so her worship of him became unimportant.

Keren remained in Herod's collection of women for nine years before her life changed forever. A mysterious man with an odd accent had found his way into the palace last year. Aurius, as he was called, was tall, refined, educated, and had an air of distinction about him — a quality she had not sensed from many men in Herod's court. Ten months ago, the women were once again called before the King, but this time the prophet stood with him.

Having never been summoned in a group before, Keren was nervous as to the reason. It became very clear when the King looked at the man and told him to choose. Herod was proud of the gift he was giving, and with a large smile said he could select one woman from his lot to be his own. Most of the women present had been in the harem for at least five years, so she imagined Herod's generosity had limits.

The man was taken aback and so were the women, but Keren stood tall and looked Aurius right in the eyes. To belong to this man would certainly be better than rotting in Herod's harem. As the other women fidgeted and whispered among themselves, the Jewish beauty stood with grace and poise. Naturally tall, her back was rigid and upright causing her to stand three to four inches over the women around her. And so Aurius chose Keren without much hesitation, causing a contentment to settle within her for the first time since arriving in her position.

Immediately, the Jewish woman's things were moved into a room adjacent to the guest's living quarters. She would miss some of the ladies in the King's harem, but this felt right. While her position had not truly changed, God had heard her cry for rescue from Herod. She understood no more than that, but that was enough.

The first few weeks with Aurius brought many conversations and awkwardness for both of them. He was not what she had grown accustomed to, being a woman in a position to meet physical needs. Instead of demanding impersonal actions, he talked to her. Aurius and Keren conversed most of that first night. He spoke little of himself, but asked many questions of her, appearing genuinely interested in her answers. He learned about her family, understood how she became employed to the King and her unhappiness in that role. In a moment of shy honesty she also revealed that in that lineup of women, she had chosen him before he chose her.

Without being told, she perceived that he had loved someone so deeply in the past that his present allowed for nothing but friendship. She understood their relationship to be platonic and looked forward to the long talks and walks through the gardens.

After weeks filled with evenings of enjoying one another's company, Keren grew to admire and understand this man without a past. Love, she could not fathom after being used and unappreciated by a man for so long. But Aurius' unexpected kindness lit a tiny flame of hope in her heart where she prayed love might grow once again.

One night, his eyes smiling into hers, he lifted her hand to his. He held her hand again the next evening, and soon every time they walked, his arm rested lightly on her lower back or elbow. One night in the middle of summer, three months after meeting the man, Keren came in to eat a late snack with Aurius and found him looking over the balcony. Upon arriving at his side she found tears on his cheeks and knew he had been crying.

Wrapping her arms around him she tried to fill the hole he obviously had in his heart. She just sat there with him for hours, holding him and wiping his tears. Not a word was said but that night their knowledge of one another changed entirely. No longer were they merely friends. Companionship turned to love.

A secret remained, she knew, that he would not share, one that had caused him much pain. But his healing showed in his love for her, and having never been either loved or understood, this brought Keren much joy.

If it was possible for an aging prophet and a past-her-prime concubine to look like an old married couple, they would have. They grew much closer over the next few months, and the days flew by. She rejoiced in her new life and hoped he would continue to love her as he did. Her only worry stemmed from such quick approval he had been given by the King. Quick approval often meant faster disapproval – something she had seen many times with the fickle, senile and unpredictable Monarch.

Even today she wondered at his disappearance. Entering the kitchen she pulled some fruit from a basket and placed it on a tray she found beneath the long center table. In the short time they had been together, he had never left without telling her, and yet he had been gone for more than twenty-four hours without a single word. No one within the palace knew of his whereabouts, and no one had heard anything about him. It was very disconcerting for a woman who had spent so many years in the palace and knew most of its dark secrets.

Trying to get her focus back on her reason for being in the kitchen, she pulled some bread from the shelf above and added it to the fruit. Finding a cup, she poured some wine and placed it on the weathered worn table.

Speaking quietly to avoid attracting attention she muttered to herself, "Why am I doing this?"

Keren knew there would be no reason for her to be in the holding area. She had never been there before, and her only duties now concerned Aurius.

"What is it about this woman that I must know?" She asked herself louder this time, her voice echoing in the cavernous empty room "There have been plenty of prisoners brought here. What is it about this one that won't leave my mind?"

The Jewish woman paced the room, her thoughts filling the air along with the fading smell of lunch. Was it the confidence exuded by the young woman that intrigued her? Never had she seen anyone, let alone a woman in a man's society, carry herself with such grace under pressure. Keren wanted that strength, not that she could ever attain it.

Was it that Aurius had mysteriously disappeared? The woman's arrival was not expected by anyone at the palace, and she was obviously not the usual type of person brought to the fortress. Did a connection exist between her arrival and Aurius' departure? It seemed far-fetched, but every minute her protector was away, she became more insecure and frightened.

She far preferred death over the life she had known in the harem. And now she had the confidence to commit such an act rather than once again wait to be used by the King at a moment's notice.

She wondered if this dangerous game she was about to play was because of the unexplainable connection she felt to the young woman. Something warm and comfortable about her eyes. She seemed so familiar. Keren had only felt this bond with her mother and father, and though she had no sisters, she imagined she might feel this way toward one if she did. But the feeling made no sense in connection to the prisoner. They had never met before, of that Keren was certain, and yet they were destined to be together. She knew this just as well. Their futures intertwined in some way.

So if the woman only had a few days left before they took her life, the Jewish concubine had better make the most of the time.

Straightening her outer garment and pulling a large shawl over her head, she picked up the tray containing the wine-filled glass and left the kitchen. Turning right, she walked down the cold, dimly lit tunnel toward the holding area. Keren, a Jewish concubine in the Roman King's court was determined to find the answers her life and her God had yet to offer.

22 — MONDAY, AFTERNOON, APRIL 20

Arms laden with sustenance for the prisoner and bribery for the inevitable guard, Keren moved slowly down the long damp tunnels, making occasional turns as they appeared. She never enjoyed walking into the bowels of the mountain, and indeed had done it only a handful of times. The temperature dropped incrementally with every step, sending a chill up her spine. She wished her hands were free so she might pull her garment tightly around her thin frame.

As she traveled, the tunnels grew darker and because of their location, the walls were no longer lined with oil lamps but torches. Keren's eyes would grow accustomed to the light of a torch and then she would move into a dim section just to arrive at another torch.

The floor and walls of the passageway were no longer covered in mosaics or banners but remained rough stone at this end of the palace. The uneven cobbles under her feet yielded painful bruises on her exposed toes due to her delicate sandals unintended for such rough terrain. The occasional sensation made her re-evaluate her reasons for risking so much to see this woman. Yet with each bump she encountered, she continued forward knowing the young woman would offer answers to questions she had yet to ask herself.

Turning another corner, she saw that the new passageway abruptly ended. Standing there in front of one last large opening, a soldier stood at attention. Not wearing a helmet or breastplate, he seemed perhaps more approachable than a Roman officer, although his physique and location in the fortress proved his qualification for duty and likely a bad attitude about bending the rules.

Keren put on her best sultry smile and confident presence and headed straight for the military man. Knowing there was no way to back out of her plan now, she lowered the shawl over her head.

The soldier looked her direction sternly, "What brings you to the dungeon?"

"I was sent to bring the prisoner some food this evening," she smiled, hoping he might just let her through. He crossed his arms over a massive chest and quirked an eyebrow. *Well, so much for letting me pass easily,* she though ruefully.

The soldier was in his early twenties and extremely strong by the look of his muscular build. She set her tray on the floor and moved closer, walking as temptingly as possible.

Reaching up to touch his shoulder in a companionable way she lifted her large eyes to him pleadingly. "Please, sir, you know the poor thing must eat. Can't you see how small she is?" Her hand lowered to his bulging bicep and she smiled again.

He tried to remain at attention but it was obvious he enjoyed the physical tension.

"I was not told of any food for the prisoner," he spoke firmly, but she could see by his averting his eyes that he was losing the fight.

He looked down at the lovely woman smelling of jasmine and tried not to smile.

"Sir, from what I was told, she hasn't eaten in some time. How can they question her properly if she begins the interrogation weak and hungry?" Lowering her head, she stepped to move in front of him now.

After a moment, he answered with a shake in his voice, "This is not normal procedure."

"Yes, I know," she sighed, "Starve them, bleed them, I understand. But you can see this prisoner is not your common criminal." She pressed a delicate hand to his tunic covered chest, and leaned her head back to look into his eyes again. "The information she offers could bring down an entire plot against Herod. We must ensure she is strong enough to be interrogated."

He inhaled the beginnings of his surrender as her other hand reached up to brush his cheek, "Now you don't want to be the reason that enemy of the state doesn't tell the King everything she knows. Do you?" her eyes played with him teasingly.

Clearing his throat and seeing his out, he gave up, "Uh, of course not. My allegiance is to Herod."

"I always knew it was." Removing the cup of wine from the tray, she offered it to him and allowed his hand to linger over hers for a moment before he took it. She bent intentionally to gather two apples and arrange the rest of the things on the tray, then lifted straight from the waist and, hands full, turned towards him.

"Now let me give some of this food to her, and I will be out of your way."

Noting a chair fifteen feet towards the entrance of the tunnel, she held out the tray for him to take.

"Would you mind taking this over there for me? You can rest for a few minutes and enjoy because you have been so diligent and attentive for so long. Just a short break."

"I cannot leave my post." He struggled anew with the idea.

She opened her lips a moment before she spoke, "You aren't leaving your post. There is only one way in and one way out of this tunnel, and two small unarmed women could never overtake you," Her sultry smile again appeared to disarm him.

"Very good, but I will need to check you for weapons."

Really, must I have to do this again? She shrank from him inwardly, but plastered her face with the same fake smile, and lifted the tray as high as she could and jutted out one hip, "I was hoping you would."

He grinned and began to work his hands over her body. Hating the groping, she told herself again how desperate she was to see the woman in the cell ten feet behind the soldier. He completed his task thoroughly, and she lowered the tray.

"Find anything?"

"There appear to be no weapons anywhere at all on your person," he leered.

"Well, enjoy your break. It is our little secret, yes?" She turned her body in the direction of the cell before she let her head follow and walked seductively away, rolling her eyes for good measure.

She heard him breathe out heavily before his footsteps faded down the hall.

When out of his view, she re-covered her head with the shawl and drew her outer garment about her. The area was barely lit and had to be less than sixty degrees in temperature. Hesitating before the iron-gate, she was not sure how she would find the woman who had captivated her so completely just a few hours before.

Gripping the cold rough metal, she looked in and allowed her eyes to adjust to the dark scene. In the corner she found the small woman resting on a pile of hay. Her knees were pulled up to her chest and she was visibly shaking due to the hours in the cold. She appeared to be talking to herself, but her words sounded like a prayer.

Keren watched in silence for a while before interrupting, "I have something for you to eat," she spoke warmly.

Looking up, the prisoner replied, "Thank you."

"I brought you some delicious apples, hand-picked from the gardens below the fortress." Trying not to sound nervous she stopped talking hoping the prisoner would continue the conversation.

Aaliyah just stared in her direction. The tunnel was dark and the only light was a torch behind the visitor causing the woman with the head covering to be enveloped within a dark shadow. Aaliyah wondered at the familiar presence she felt.

Keren finally broke the silence, "What is your name?"

"I am Aaliyah."

"That is a lovely name. It means exalted."

Her voice rose quietly from the corner of the cell, "Yes, my mother hoped a better life for me than she was able to live. However, I do not think she would believe this to be better."

"I believe that every mother wants more for her child than she had," Keren replied as her voice trailed off.

"When do you expect the child?" Aaliyah asked.

"Um, I beg your pardon?" Keren stumbled on her words in surprise.

"You held your middle when you spoke the word *child*." Aaliyah stood, "When do expect it to be born?"

"Maybe in six months or so," she replied, touching her stomach gently again.

"You and your husband must be very excited," Aaliyah said, walking a few feet toward the gate.

"He doesn't know."

Aaliyah remained silent.

Keren continued, "I fear for what will happen when I am found out." She looked down.

"Does your husband not want a child? That is one of the greatest gifts God gives to man," Aaliyah probed.

After a short break Keren answered, "I am not married."

"Your position here in the palace does not offer the kind of life a woman might dream of."

"Do you know what I do?" Keren asked, feeling she had been laid bare.

"My mother was in your same position here at the palace."

Even though the prisoner could not see the visitor's face, she knew she was ashamed of her role within the fortification.

"Your apparel, confidence with the soldier, and ability to move into secure areas could only mean you are assigned to the King. But do not be ashamed, God loves you, and I understand what your life entails. It is not easy."

Starting to open up, Keren hesitated only an instant this time, "And I desperately want to keep this child. I also love his father."

"Is his father the King?"

"No, I was given away months ago as a good will gesture to a prophet for the King. At first, I saw it as my way out of the palace, but as I got to know the man I was to care for, I grew closer to him." With a quiver in her voice and raising her head she added quietly, "I have never met anyone like him. He is warm and gentle, and has a confidence as if he knows everything that is going to happen."

"Then why would he not want this child?" Aaliyah jumped in with excitement.

"I know he has some hidden secret."

"What would make you think that?"

"When you spend time with men, you get to know them." She looked down. "He has a secret, something dark, and he will not be bothered with anything else until it is behind him. There is an area in his heart he has locked off from me."

"You must trust God." Aaliyah touched her arm through the bars. "Eventually, you will have to tell him, so if you love him and believe he loves you, then trust him and pray God will work it out perfectly," Aaliyah answered with confidence and a smile.

"I wish it were that easy."

"It is. God will work things out completely in his time. He has a great plan for you."

"I would love to think that is true."

Enthusiastically she answered, "Oh, it is. He wants blessings for your life."

Not agreeing with the words, Keren shot back, "How can you say such things? Do you not see where you are? How is being in jail a blessing? If God wants such great things for me, why would he not want the same for you?

Our God has turned his back on us. He has blessed me," she spat sarcastically, "with a life designed to please others at my own expense and pain, and he has given you a death sentence."

Aaliyah had not heard those words applied to her situation and suddenly backed away from the door in silence.

Speaking softly again, she tried to reverse what she said, "I am sorry. We do not know your outcome. Really, we do not."

"No it is alright," she smiled, "If my God desires to take my life, I will gladly give it."

Keren was perplexed, "How can you have such a peace? From the first time I saw you, I was drawn to find out why you have this amazing grace under pressure. How could you have bewitched Cyprianus in such a way that he would gently escort you to prison? I have seen what he is capable of and have never seen him as kind and genuinely concerned about anyone – let alone a prisoner – as he was of you."

"I did not bewitch him," she said laughingly, "The man was just seeing Jesus Christ's actions in my own life."

"Christ – it means *Anointed One*. Who is Jesus?"

"He is the God the Son - the One sent from heaven to redeem us."

"The Temple Priests pay for our sins with an offering to God," Keren said confused.

Moving back toward the bars, "Not anymore. Jesus has come to complete that system. No longer do we need a priest to intercede for us. We can go directly to God because of the sacrifice of Jesus."

"What sacrifice?"

"Jesus came from heaven with the sole purpose of giving his life for us. You see, the priests surrender an animal on our behalf, but God offered himself by coming as a baby to become a man. As God the Son, he is the full and final sacrifice."

"He died for us?" she asked, confused.

"Yes, he gave his life on our behalf, but the greatest part is that he rose again from the grave three days later. He conquered sin, so that we can commune with God without a priest." Excitement edged her voice now, "Do you understand that we can have a personal relationship with God and spend eternity with him through the sacrifice of Jesus? The Messiah has come!"

"How do you know all of this? I have never heard such ideas."

Aaliyah smiled. New to her as well, she hoped her words fully explained the reason for this joy in her heart. The woman needed hope, and her voice seemed so familiar. Aaliyah moved closer to the bars, but still could not make out her face through the shawl and low light.

"I know this because I have seen him and have heard him teach."

The woman's voice lifted in anticipation, "How do I find this Jesus? How can I hear his words for myself?"

Aaliyah lowered her head, thinking through the conundrum of time travel and the fact that Jesus likely cooed as a baby somewhere in the nearby countryside. Raising her head, a glow of realization gave her words, "There are some things in life you must believe without seeing."

Keren backed a few steps away and sighed heavily. Believing without seeing she understood. No one had ever given her something she could see to believe in. God was there, but evidence of his care for her had never existed. Until Aurius came. She looked up at the girl inside once again.

Aaliyah grew thoughtful, "The heavens declare God's greatness and power." She lifted a finger toward the woman's middle, "That baby within you is an illustration of his blessings, and my life and peace through trials are examples of his ability to offer hope. God has saved me before. I believe he will again. But in the words of Queen Esther "If I perish, I perish."

You do not need to meet Jesus to know him. You can have the same joy that I have and will have no matter what my outcome from these present circumstances."

Keren walked back to the door and touched the small fingers Aaliyah had curled around a bar, "I will think about what you have said. I need this hope that your Jesus offers."

"He can bring joy to your life," she replied, putting her other hand on top of Keren's.

Keren reached for the apples in her pocket, "Here take these. You will need your strength."

"Thank you."

"Did you say your mother lived here at the palace? What is her name?"

Aaliyah responded with sadness in her voice, "You would not have known her. She jumped from the tower when I was a child. She did not have the peace that Jesus can offer."

Hearing the soldier moving toward them in the side hallway, Keren responded quickly, "I am very sorry."

"I am too. I would have given anything to have told her about Jesus."

Her visitor glanced behind her down the hallway.

"Are you going to tell him about the child?" Aaliyah questioned her quickly.

Nervous the guard may hear her; she replied in a loud whisper, "Yes, I will tell Aurius as soon as I see him. He has been gone for over a day, and I am growing worried about his welfare."

Her words dragged Aaliyah back into the real world, "Did you say his name was Aurius? He is a prophet for the King? Aurius of Antioch is the father?"

The woman paused in her retreat to answer her quickly, passing under a torch as she did so, "Yes."

Aaliyah called one last question. "What is your name?"

Pulling the shawl from her head and lowering it around her neck in anticipation of greeting the soldier she answered flatly, "I am Keren."

Shock and joy rocked Aaliyah backward away from the bars. The woman's wide eyes, high cheek bones, milky complexion and warm smile filled her with peace as she looked into the face she had seen a thousand times. The woman who had cared for her, protected and taught her, and loved her beyond words looked into her eyes and smiled gently before turning to hurry so she could deal with the guard out of the view of the girl in the small prison cell.

Aaliyah froze as the woman turned the corner and left her view. "Oh, Mother," she whispered as a happy tear slipped down one cheek.

The rocky chariot ride from the Herodium felt very long. Cyprianus had been up for well over 36 hours, and every rock the wheels chanced upon or turn the horses took a bit too quickly caused the Roman General that much more discomfort.

Being hungry and tired was par for the course for the average Roman soldier, so the General had been in this position many times before. Other military leaders often sent their men into a skirmish while they stayed behind, but Cyprianus could not.

He was determined to make his men great through suffering, and himself great suffering with them. He refused to ask them to work any harder than he did, so if they didn't sleep, he didn't sleep. If his men couldn't eat, he wouldn't eat. It was his code and he had raised great leaders by following it. No, Cyprianus was not new to being tired. This fatigue that weighted his head and shoulders didn't come from lack of sleep or hunger but from what he was assigned to do.

With the chariot making its way to the dusty outskirts of Jerusalem, Cyprianus scanned the horizon seeing lamps being lit within the houses. The sun fell quickly from the sky, and the soft glow of oil lamps illuminated the town well enough for the driver to easily make his way through the narrow dirt-covered streets of the ancient city. They passed a small boy chasing a disobedient dog in the deepening twilight, and his thoughts turned to the work ahead.

How could he kill the children of his wife's people for nothing more than the meanderings of a false prophet?

The General had been part of many actions he was not proud of. It is impossible to rise to the upper echelon of the military without carrying out nasty tasks, and children had been killed in battle under his command. But never had he been asked to kill children in front of their mothers, leaving them behind to grieve their slaughtered infant. The thought made his stomach turn.

Arriving in front of his modest clay brick home, the driver walked back and opened the door, allowing the military leader to drag himself from his seat and disembark the royal vehicle. The driver left quickly to the sound of horse hooves clicking on the ground and tires rolling over the uneven road.

Cyprianus opened the gate to the courtyard and saw his wife Livana bending down and tending to an olive tree she had planted just a week earlier. When she saw him, she rose and smiled, "Hello, my husband. I am glad to see you."

Her warm smile gave him a brief respite from the task ahead. "As I am glad to see you. Good evening, my wife."

"I have food ready for you, would you like to eat?" she moved to his side, brushing the dirt from her hands before she hugged him tightly.

Wrapping his arm around her shoulders they fell in step together, "Yes, I am very hungry."

Cyprianus lived in the middle of a Jewish settlement. He had the opportunity to own a home anywhere in Jerusalem, as long as it would allow him quick access to government buildings, but he chose to live where he knew his wife would be comfortable because he was away so often. Even though his house was of the same design and size as the others around, it was obviously much better kept.

Being a Roman General allowed him an income that the other families did not have so his courtyard was filled with flowering bushes and fruit trees. He had a full stable behind allowing the animals to live apart from the family and one of the large differences was he had a door.

Most Jewish people had cloth covering the main entrance to their homes, he had an official door, so as he opened it and they walked in, he smelled the heavenly aroma of the dinner Livana had been preparing.

Upon entering the dwelling she pulled over a bowl and towel and bent down toward his feet. Sitting, he allowed her to remove his sandals and she began to wash his feet. The tradition was very much a Jewish practice, but Cyprianus never minded. First, he saw it as the most basic of human hygiene. Many a solder had been removed from the fight because of an infection in their feet. He had even begun to insist upon his soldiers cleansing their feet upon a return from a mission for their own health.

The most important reason the Roman soldier allowed the activity was that he knew his wife performed it not out of obligation but because of her love for him. Humming a song, she removed all of the dirt from the previous day, padded him dry and said, "Much better."

Livana looked up with a smile, "Are you ready to eat?"

Filling a bowl from a large pot on the fire, she placed it before him on the foot high tabletop already covered with bread, figs and olives. Sitting on the mat prepared for him, he looked at the bowl and smiled. "I love your fish and vegetable soup."

"I knew you would come home very tired and would want something tasty," she smiled back.

"Please, sit with me tonight," Cyprianus said patting the ground beside him.

Nervously she lowers to her knees, closes her eyes and began to whisper, "Baruch atah Adonai, Eloheinu Melech Haolam…"

Cyprianus stopped her mid prayer, "Please say it out loud."

Looking up, Livana was confused. Her husband had never asked to hear her prayers before. Cyprianus was very good to her in comparison to many Roman men and their Jewish wives. He had never struck or demeaned her. However, it was clear throughout their marriage that he wanted nothing of her religion or God.

He asked again, "You may pray out loud."

She started aloud this time, "Baruch atah Adonai, Eloheinu Melech holam, hamotzi lechem min haaretz."

"What does it mean?" he asked genuinely.

"Why, my husband, do you want to…?"

"What does it mean?" he said kindly yet with enough focus to allow her to understand the importance.

"I was thanking God for the meal and his provision. It means, 'Blessed are You, O Lord, our God, King of the Universe who brings forth bread from the earth.'"

She sat on the ground, pulled a piece of bread and began the meal. Cyprianus took a bite from the soup, absent-mindedly staring at a candle before him.

"Are you feeling well? You do not seem to be yourself," asked Livana watching her partner gaze into the light.

"Why do you believe there is a God, Livana?" he asked without moving his gaze.

The small Jewish woman put down her bread and finished her bite.

Continuing his questions, "In this terrible world, how could there ever be a God, or if there is, why would you worship him?" Slowly moving his head and looking her in the eyes, "Why would you worship a God that allows such suffering?" he gestured around.

"What has happened over the last few days?" Livana asked very concerned. She had never heard her husband ask questions about her God.

"Livana, the question was clear," he said trying to ensure his line of reasoning is understood. Speaking quietly and out of frustration, "I see you and your people pray before meals. I see them live their lives to a code given by a God. I see them go to the temple and spend hours there worshiping their God. They give the best of their possessions in the form of animals or vegetables to the temple for their God and yet I never see this God do anything."

Speaking sweetly and softly, "You do not see him work because you are not looking for him to work."

"What does that mean?"

Respectfully, she explained, "The Roman people serve themselves; they do not have enough time to see the beauty of God around them. They put up shrines to everything conceivable without giving credit to the one true God."

Cyprianus watched his wife exude an intensity he hadn't seen before.

"Juno is the goddess of women and fertility that the Romans worship. But God spoke through Moses that, in the beginning, it was not good for man to be alone. He made a companion who could help him. And so it is today. When a woman serves Juno, she is worshipping the very thing created by God for her. You are worshiping the creation and not the Creator.

What about Minerva, the goddess of wisdom? Solomon, in his many proverbs, says that the fear of the Lord is the beginning of wisdom, not the worship of some man-made statue.

Or Neptune, the powerful god of the sea," she waved her hands in the air, being facetious and not a little carried away now. "The God of the universe made the sea and everything in it on the fifth day. He spoke it into existence and did not labor doing so.

Each of the Roman gods is fashioned after part of the creation. Even Jupiter, the master of the gods and the main god your people worship is nothing. They say he can hurl thunderbolts from his hand, but it says in God's word that in forming this land, we are so blessed to tend, that the Lord God made the sun and the moon, and the day and the night. He made the heavens and the light to govern the day and dark to outline the night."

Taking a drink of wine, Cyprianus responded, "I understand what you are saying and agree. My people spend too much time at the altar of false gods, yet how is your God any different? How do I know that your God is any more real than Jupiter or Venus, Vulcan or Diana?"

Livana stood and refilled Cyprianus' cup. "I would say the best example of God's existence is in the way he has provided for his people."

"What do you mean?" he asked, drinking soup from the bowl.

"God has exceedingly blessed the Jewish people."

Practically spitting the contents of his mouth, Cyprianus broke out in a laugh. "Are you telling me the way your people are treated is proof that your God lives?" He laughed again while Livana watched on. "From what I hear, the Jewish people – people of God – were enslaved by the Egyptians for hundreds of years. And if I am right, your main city of Jerusalem is now controlled by the Romans. Your people are forced to work on our projects, and if at any point Herod decides to occupy your temple, you will be out. I would say your God does not care much for his people if he in fact exists."

Livana had never heard her husband speak of religion. Knowing that something powerful must have happened in his life in the preceding hours, she secretly prayed that God would guide her words.

"Cyprianus, my people have always been well taken care of when they kept their eyes on his ways," she replied, pointing up. "The only times in history when we were not on the winning side of a battle were when we tried to win alone and without our God's guidance." Sitting back next to her husband, the soldier, with excitement, she continued, "Look to Abraham. God started this entire nation through his faith and obedience. Or Noah who was the only righteous man left. David killed a giant because of his steadfast belief, and Nehemiah built a wall because he knew God had directed him to do so. The Jewish people have fought many more battles than the Romans and won every one that God desired for us to fight. We only lose when we look to ourselves, like now.

God's people have become selfish once again. When we humble ourselves and pray, he will bless his people once again. He will bless us when he sees our hearts are turned toward him, but not until. Our God is like a father who has to discipline his errant son. It does not mean he loves us any less, just that correction is needed to keep us on the path that is best. That is where we are today."

Pulling her husband a piece of bread, she went on, "We have turned our backs on God many times, but he has never turned his back on us. He always provides for his people. We have food to eat and clothes to wear," she said, gesturing around her. "He gives us the basic necessities, and yet has promised to send One who will deliver us."

Cyprianus had turned his attention back to the food until Livana's last sentence. "What did you say?"

"I said we have everything we need."

His mind became clearly focused, "No, not that, after that. Something about sending someone to deliver you."

Somewhat shaken by his question she answered, "Yes, God is sending a Deliverer."

"What do you know about this Deliverer? Tell me what you know about his birth," Cyprianus insisted.

"His birth?" Excited about her husband's new curiosity, she spoke as quickly as possible. "Yes there are several prophecies about his birth. It is written that he will be born from a virgin woman. He will be a descendant of Abraham, Isaac and Jacob."

Cyprianus listened closely to every word.

Trying to remember what she was taught, she paused a moment, "He will also be a descendant of Jesse and David. He is to come from the tribe of Judah, and will shepherd his people. He will be born in Bethlehem and be worshipped by shepherds…"

"Did you say born in Bethlehem?" he nearly toppled the wine glass in front of him standing to his feet.

"Yes, I believe the text says, 'O Bethlehem Ephrathah, too little to be among the clans of Judah, from you One will go forth for Me to be ruler of Israel.' But it also says 'There will be a voice heard in Ramah, lamentation and bitter weeping. Rachel is weeping for her children.'"

Knowing the answer already, he asked it anyway, "What does it mean that Rachel will be weeping for her children?"

"When the Messiah comes, the rulers will do all they can to stop him. It is written that they will kill all of the baby boys in the city of Bethlehem to ensure he does not live," she paused, "It will be a very terrible time for all of us, this forcing the Messiah and his family to flee to Egypt."

At that, there was a rapping on the door. Cyprianus lowered his head.

"What happened my husband? Why all of the questions? Why the interest in my God?"

"Please answer the door, I have a mission tonight."

Looking a Cyprianus, she felt sick. She knew he was about to perform an extremely ugly task. With determination, "You are sick. Stay with me. Allow one of the other leaders to take this task."

"Please answer the door," his head remained low.

She slowly walked to the entrance and opened the wooden barrier. Standing there in full military gear was Dritus. Having a slight disgust for the Jewish people, he looked over the small woman and spoke directly with Cyprianus.

Standing to attention, "General, we must get organized to leave. I have your gear in the carriage. The soldiers are prepared and waiting for your leadership at the Citadel. I expect the task to go quickly. We will be back in our beds by early morning," he ended with a smile.

Pointing to the courtyard, he directed the man back to his vehicle, "Give me a moment."

"Yes sir," he quickly turned and left the doorway.

Cyprianus walked to where his wife stood watching him, and wrapped his arms around her, holding her close to his heart. "Thank you for talking with me. I pray that if your God exists, he will show himself to me tonight." He added under his breath, "Especially tonight." He looked into her eyes once again, "You know I will always love you."

"I do know. Husband, if you truly seek God's heart, you will find him," she kissed his cheek.

Cyprianus took in a deep breath, stood tall and regained the edge in his eyes. Exuding the essence of a Roman General he spoke his goodbye to Livana, "I will see you soon," and left through the door.

After watching him enter the carriage and seeing it quickly leave through the dark streets, the young woman closed the door and knelt where she stood. Livana would remain in fervent pray for her husband until he returned.

Several miles past Machaerus, Hudson and Todd grabbed the ankles and armpits of their unconscious passengers and laid them gently on their sides in a roadside ditch. They weren't concerned about their captives coming after them any time soon. It would be morning before the soldiers could determine their position from the general landscape and, hopefully, by then their tracks would be worn away by other traffic on this road.

Sore, hungry, tired and weary, the three men trekked on for several more hours to the south until they saw a large glowing edifice looming in the distance.

"Is that it?" Hudson yelled as he reigned in the horse to face his companions.

With the sun setting off to the west, lamps could be seen glowing in windows. The limestone walls of Herod's summer palace shimmered in the sunset, warming the landscape with an ominous reddish orange radiance.

"That's where we're going," the Senator replied, stopping beside him. "That's where you'll find Aaliyah."

"There it is just in the middle of nowhere, and she's in there," Hudson said with concern. "How'd he do that?"

With his horse panting beneath him, the professor pulled up alongside Hudson before he answered, "He just cut the top of that mountain off," pointing to the obviously shaved geography, "and put it on that flat area over there, giving him a nice place to build a palace with a view."

Totally baffled Hudson cocked his head as if he could figure out the man's motives by staring at the structure five miles before them, "Why would he want to create his own mountain?"

Todd laughed, "You know what they say about real estate: Location, location, location. I guess he didn't like the original one, and a mile to the east was just better." He curbed his light-hearted manner and spoke more seriously, "Hudson, how are we going to get her out of there? Any ideas?"

Getting off of his horse and walking out front, the agent looked over the area. It was a barren desert with the Dead Sea off in the distance to his left and Jerusalem miles to the right. He kicked the rocky and dusty soil, "I honestly have no idea. Yet, there must be a way. God hasn't called us here to abandon us. So, how *are* we ever going to get in there?" His blocking hand did nothing to stop the glare to his left as he squinted at the edifice, "It has a sheer limestone face. The structure itself is placed directly on top of a mountain that doesn't have a single tree on it. There's no way to even get close to the fortification, even if we could sneak in. And from what I can see here, there is only one entrance."

The other men had lowered themselves from their horses when the Senator finally spoke, "Yes, Hudson, there is only one way in, and it's heavily guarded."

They looked at him, waiting for the encouragement to come. It didn't. Their eyes swung back to the structure.

Todd spoke up, "Then how do we do it, Aurius of Antioch? How are we going to get into a palace meant to protect a paranoid king?"

Without taking his eyes from the fortress he crossed his arms and answered, "You will need to trust me."

Hudson's eyes grew with incredulity, "Trust you?" His patience left him as he yanked John toward him by the throat of his toga, "Trust you? How can we trust you? I should be at home right now with my wife, not in a foreign land watching history. You have put my life, Todd's life, Aaliyah's life and the timeline in jeopardy, and you expect us to trust you?"

Todd broke in and pulled the agent from the Senator, "Calm down, fella. It's going to be alright." He brushed out the Senator's toga, allowing Hudson a moment to breathe, before he turned back to him. "Hudson, we don't have any other possibility here. We must get my Aaliyah out of prison. Who knows what's happening to her in there," his voice broke with the sudden thought. "He said he'd get us to Aaliyah."

Turning to the Senator he smiled briefly before charging headlong into his middle and knocking him to the ground. Todd jerked him off the ground by his garment, just enough to bring the terrified man's eyes to his.

"You will get us to Aaliyah," he growled out. "You will, or I'll kill you myself. Please understand that, to me, this is not one of the games you've been playing with God. And I will not allow Aaliyah to suffer for your deranged agenda."

The strangling man attempted a breath to get air around the head lock, "I swear it. I told you I would get you to Aaliyah and I will."

Todd loosened his grip and got up from the ground, leaving the frightened Senator rubbing his neck. "I'll get you to your friend, Todd." He spoke with a rasp. "I can get you into the building and to Aaliyah. The military within the fortress are, as yet, required to listen to my commands."

Hudson was not convinced. "Do we trust him, Todd? What if he turns on us the first chance he gets?"

"There isn't anything else we can do. We have to trust him."

"I'll get you in," the Senator replied resolutely. "If you follow my lead, you'll see her tonight."

The sun hovered on the horizon fading the orange glow over the Herodium to a deep purple. All three men watched the change, mesmerized by the beauty and hesitant to begin the next move in their mission without a plan. A plan impossible to formulate.

Todd and Hudson looked up at the darkening sky, noticing that the contrast caused the ever-present streaks of light passing through the expanse above them to become more apparent. The Senator watched them in wonder, trying to see what they were looking at and finding nothing. Eyes toward the heavens, he could see peace fall on their faces. The fear there a moment ago had faded away, revealing only confidence in their future.

John knew what they were heading into, and he was resolute in his plans. But these men saw something in the heavens that filled them with trust. He'd heard the phrase 'A reliance on divine Providence,' and that described precisely what they appeared to have now.

Hudson and Todd enjoyed the moment of peace together. It was more than peace. This was the impression that their destiny laid ahead of them tonight. The reason they were here in this time would be revealed and God's purpose fulfilled tonight.

The men looked at one another and then back at Senator Hughes.

Hudson's dark brown eyes looked straight into the Senator's as he pointed to the palace, "Lead on."

The men mounted their horses and headed off into the night, illuminated by gold trails of light directing toward one location.

—

Aaliyah sat back in her cell disbelieving what she had seen. Could that woman who looked roughly her age be her mother? It didn't make sense. Although little had these last few weeks. Somehow all of this fit into her Lord's plan. Her mind raced. Thinking back and conjuring up the dark memories of the past, she tried to make sense of what was happening now.

The sordid details of her mother's life at the palace had been known to her from childhood. As a teenager, her mother had been taken into the King's court as a concubine, forcing her Jewish parents to turn their backs on her. To Aaliyah's knowledge they never even spoke to her again.

The cold moist walls grew darker and more frigid as the memories stirred in her mind. With her focus on the lone torch burning in the hallway, she allowed the thoughts she had tried to forget to rumble through her.

Even though her mother was a concubine for the King, Aaliyah had never lived in the palace. Her home for as long as she could remember had been in Jerusalem. As a baby, a family had taken her in and given her all she needed to survive. They were not her parents and never pretended to be. They cared for her as a duty – one they were paid well for.

As a young child, of course she had not questioned the decision. Her mother had provided for her care and even spent much time with her throughout her childhood. Aaliyah had simply accepted it for what it was. With a smile, Aaliyah remembered some of the songs her mother would sing or exaggerated stories she would tell about Kings and rulers and palaces. She would could for an afternoon, tuck her in bed at sundown. Then in the morning, she was gone again. Her smile fell at the memory.

No, she had never questioned her mother's choice, but now she wondered. *Why did my mother not raise me in the palace?* She focused on the flickering flame of the torch on the tunnel wall as she sorted through the recesses of her mind.

Several seconds passed and she stood and started pacing.

Wrapping her arms around herself she began to realize why her mother sent her off to live with others. Aaliyah was not Herod's child, yet Keren was Herod's concubine. Her mother had often told her about her real father with pride, but as an infant born of another man in Herod's palace, Aaliyah would have been killed. Suddenly it came to her clearly.

She gave me away to save me. Tears pricked at her eyes at the realization. *She gave me away, but found a way to stay a part of my life. She so easily could have let me die – or be sent away. Now I see the effort she put forth in seeing to my welfare. What a sacrifice.*

Remembering the things of the past, Aaliyah realized her mother had hoped her child would have a better future than her own. Sitting back down with her back against the cold stone wall she allowed that realization to settle back in.

Keren certainly had worked to keep Aaliyah away from the palace. She must have feared a similar fate might happen to her daughter, and so took great pain to remove that possibility from her young life.

Because her mother visited so often, the young Aaliyah knew which days to expect her and looked forward to their meeting. She would draw her pictures in the sand or pick flowers in anticipation of their encounter. As she grew older, she had much to share with her mother at every visit. Until the day she did not come.

Believing it to be one of the few times her mother could not get into the city, Aaliyah waited until the next day, and then the next day, and then the next. Sometime later she learned that her mother had jumped from the wall surrounding the palace, cutting off her life and any future conversations with her daughter. Some scandal surrounded the act, but Aaliyah had been either too young or too wounded to understand.

Her caretakers had always been good to her and cared for her as well as possible, but a young woman without provision and needing so much love was not something they were able to offer. Her life would change.

Aaliyah thought of her mother only occasionally from that time on, choosing to remember her sweet face and beautiful warm voice. Now that she had seen her again, every memory overwhelmed her heart and mind like a flood.

Aaliyah pulled her knees up to her chest and thought about the question she had never dared to ask. *Why had she killed herself?* She supposed facing her own death in this cell made it easier to imagine these things now.

The query made her sick to her stomach. Such an act must have been brought on by deep and uncontrollable pain. Obviously Herod had not loved her and this awareness would have isolated her sweet and caring mother.

Also, as a member of the King's stable of choice women, there would have been some camaraderie among the ladies but also a great deal of infighting. With each woman clawing for the position of most desired, they might literally stab another in the back to get it, for with that position came power, wealth, and security. At least for a short time.

Aaliyah grew more sad thinking of her mother's life. "I'm so sorry you had to go through that," she said quietly hoping somehow the words could speak comfort. Her thoughts went back to the position her mother was in.

As a concubine, women did become too old to be desirable at some point. However, her mother was still young enough when she died that dismissal couldn't have been the problem.

Racking her mind for the answer, the young prisoner closed her eyes and prayed aloud, "Lord, please tell me what I don't know. Please give me an answer so I can encourage her if I ever see her again." Opening her eyes, a memory popped into her head as she methodically thought through the problem.

The woman, only moments ago told her how she had been given away to another man. Herod often decided to offer one possession or another to a dignitary or leader of this or that. Kings had done it for millennia, she imagined. These types of gifts were good will gestures, and were not optional for the woman being given.

Shuddering at the thought, Aaliyah rose from the cold bench and went over to the cell doors. She pondered about being given away. Only knowing her Todd for a week, she knew him to be honest and true, and would always protect her and her virtue from anyone who might try to take that away. The idea sparked a twinkle in her eyes. If Todd were alive, he would be coming to save her soon. She just knew it. And her Todd would *never* give her away.

Keren had been given away. Indeed she spoke the words not an hour before, but now confusion set in. Was Aurius the man to whom she was given? She racked her brain for the answer. She thought through everything her mother had ever said and remembered something. The words were barely there, but she could recollect her praying with her as a child and saying that she hoped she could find the love she once had.

"She once had, what does that mean?" Aaliyah said out loud not concerned if the soldier heard.

Could Aurius' disappearance, most likely brought on by her Todd, be where her mother's love went? Praying she or her man wasn't somehow the reason for her mother's suicide, she continued to think.

Her mother had spoken of her father as a great and powerful man. She said he was very tall and that he could…what could he do? She stopped her pacing to focus. Yes, he could see the future. It was now obvious that her mother's true love was Aurius.

The bits and pieces she remembered were starting to make a mosaic of Keren's life. Each piece individually had no purpose, but together they created a picture, and Aaliyah saw her mother's life in a way she had never seen it before.

Aaliyah walked over to the cell doors and held them tightly. The picture was complete, and it was one of despair. Her mother did not have parents, true friends, a love of her own, or her daughter.

Keren's one and only true love suddenly disappeared and she had no true future without the knowledge of Jesus. Her mother was totally devoid of hope, and chose to die, rather than live in this dark and horrible place.

Tears ran down Aaliyah's eyes as she felt for the woman who died decades past yet stood before her just hours earlier. Was she being given another chance? Could she offer her mother hope this time?

This time. She laughed aloud. The concept of time had never been given a thought before now. How could she save her mother who died some twenty years earlier? How could she have met a man who was from a time over two thousand years in the future, then travel thirty year before her own birth? None of these thoughts worked in her head, but they were in front of her just as the imaginary mosaic formed in her mind from the bits and pieces of her mother's life.

The Lord had something for her to do here. This was not the end of her life, of this she remained confident. Another opportunity to see her mother would present itself soon. It had to.

For a moment the silence comforted her. Just resting in the grace Christ had given her here in this forsaken cell was enough. A moment before she fell into sleep a realization struck her like a lightning bolt.

Why had she not seen it before? She had no siblings, or at least none that she knew. Thus, the baby Keren now carried might likely be her.

So far in the time Aaliyah had thought about her mother, she was only thinking about the person of her mother, she never brought herself into the picture. But, if the baby Keren carried now was Aaliyah, then everything that was already confusing would become surreal.

Could she place her hand on her mother's middle and feel herself moving? Keren must now be the same age as Aaliyah. To see your own mother at your same age is incomprehensible. Yet to make this more confusing, was her father the man Hudson and Todd came through time to apprehend?

Aaliyah went back to the corner of the cell but this time bent down, placing her knees on the cold hard ground. She knew she needed to pray and that her discussions with her God would help her to calm the crazy thoughts in her head and find out his will for her in this place within the dungeon.

"Oh Lord, God in heaven. Give me guidance," she began.

The young woman stayed on her knees seeking God's direction until deep into the night.

25 — MONDAY, LATE EVENING, APRIL 20

It was totally dark when the men arrived at the edge of the compound that was Herod's palace. The gold contrails streaking the sky were becoming more frequent, and Todd and Hudson had been enraptured with them since leaving Machaerus. What had initially looked like an asteroid field passing through the atmosphere, poured a steady light show all focused in one direction.

With the illumination came the sporadic sound attached with it. Men in the first century would not have known how to explain the noise, but Todd and Hudson had heard a few of these sounds in the twenty first century. They knew that what they were experiencing were sonic booms. Occasionally, one of the lights would come over their location close enough that they could hear the roar and feel the compression associated with it. It was an amazing thing and both men would track the lights as they passed by.

"What are you looking at?" the Senator asked stopping his horse mid gallop.

"You still don't see it?" the professor replied following suit.

"They're everywhere," pointing up with his hand, "lights and sounds all around us," Hudson responded.

"I don't know what you're talking about." The Senator was frustrated with their mind games and would be glad to separate himself from the men as soon as possible.

Hudson dismounted and stretched his legs. The professor did the same.

"Why can't he see them? Are we just delusional or is there a reason only we can see the greatest fireworks show on earth?"

With Todd looking up the ramp leading to the palace looming large before him he answered, "I have several theories I'm working through on that. Let's get to Aaliyah. If she can see it, then I know what's happening."

"I look forward to hearing what the Doctor comes up with on that." Hudson laughed and then looked toward the Senator, "Where is everyone?"

What would have normally been a massively protected fortification and would have had many checkpoints seemed to be devoid of real defense.

"You'd have thought we would have encountered a soldier by now," Todd wondered aloud.

The agent agreed, "I expected this place to be teeming with sentries."

"Believe me, they're here and could easily take you two misfits, so we aren't out of the woods yet, but I think many of them have been taken off for another, more important assignment."

Todd feigned indignation, "Did he call us misfits, Hudson? I'd say we were oddballs or eccentrics, possibly nonconformists or rebels, maybe even loners, but never misfits."

The agent chuckled but was then brought back to the words the Senator had just said, "What mission?"

With a smile, Hughes replied, "Nothing you need to worry about, just understand that because the military aren't as in large a number, it will be easier to get you to your partner."

"What mission are the military on?" Hudson became more frustrated, and glanced at Todd, "Do you know of anything that the military as a whole would be working on at this time in history?"

Racking his brain Todd began to think out loud. "They could be doing maneuvers, but with what our friend here took them through last night, it would be wise for them to rest up."

Pacing the ground and kicking up dust, "There aren't any wars taking place. Hudson, we're smack dab in the middle of the Pax Romana. Rome is at peace and doesn't do any real expansion or undergo any conquests for the next two hundred years. And Jerusalem doesn't come under attack for another fifty years or so.

In 4 B.C. there isn't anything I can remember about Herod needing the army. The next real information we have comes from the Bible and it says the army will go into Bethlehem to kill the Jewish babies under the age of two but that isn't for a couple years, I think."

Following another streak of light with his eyes Hudson thought out loud, "I don't know what it could…" Todd turned to see why he'd paused mid-sentence at the same time he heard the clanging sound of metal being pulled from its sheath. Hudson held the Roman sword attached to his uniform, directly at the Senator's throat.

"Tell me you haven't," Hudson growled.

John knew that a short retort could get him killed, so he remained silent.

"Hudson, what's going on?" Todd queried his high-strung friend.

Grabbing the Senator's toga with his free hand, Hudson pulled him from his horse, and, forcing him to the ground with a thud, pressed his knee to the man's chest, "I'll ask you once more. Tell me you didn't."

"Hudson, stop, you're going to kill him." Todd ran over to yank Hudson off their only hope into the palace. The Senator began to cough as the two comrades rolled away from him to the ground.

John rubbed his neck, "What has gotten into you? I told you I'd get you to Aaliyah, and I'm going to do that."

Hudson stood up and kicked Hughes once in the side. The man winced and then protected himself from more of the same.

The professor grabbed Hudson's arms and held him before he lost his mind and killed their ticket into the mountain fortress.

"Hudson, calm down! What is wrong with you?"

"What did he say he would do with the King?"

"What do you mean?"

"How did he become a prophet for the King?" Hudson asked again, angrier this time.

"I think he said that he researched information about the King, found out what he was going to do and then just encouraged him to do it. That way nothing in the future really changed, and he still looks like a prophet by agreeing with and encouraging the King to do the things he was already going to do. Pretty creative if you ask me. That is, if going into the past to change the future can really be that smart."

The Senator listened to the dialogue.

"Todd, I think one of the most important events in history is very quickly about to take place," he gestured to the star glowing, and the streaks crisscrossing the sky. "What if he sent the soldiers early?"

"Sent the soldiers early? Where?"

"What if he," he accused, jabbing his finger at the prisoner, "encouraged Herod to send the soldiers into Bethlehem tonight?"

"No, he can't do that. The soldiers aren't supposed to enter Bethlehem for quite a while. From our best guesses, Jesus may have been a toddler when the Wise Men came through and subsequently when the soldiers kill all of the babies under two in Bethlehem." Rubbing his forehead he looked at the man still lying on the desert floor, "That doesn't happen anytime soon."

The professor looked at the agent, "He couldn't have. Everything would be different. Babies that weren't supposed to die will be killed, and those that aren't born yet will live. That could change millions of events in the future." His mind started swirling, "It would also mean that Jesus' normal timeline would be altered. What would Mary and Joseph do? Would the birth story even be changed with thousands of military men besieging a town that isn't supposed to be overrun for two to three more years?"

Hudson once again grabbed the Senator with one hand and held his sword to his throat with the other, "Tell me you haven't encouraged Herod to move early."

A line of blood formed on John's neck as Hudson pushed harder, "Tell me!"

"Okay, okay, please stop." He tried to back away, "I did it. The soldiers are heading to Bethlehem tonight. All I did was to encourage him to do something he was already going to do."

Hudson threw him back to the ground, replaced his sword in its sheath and sat on a large rock facing the visual cacophony to the west. His partner sat next to him.

"Buddy, this can't happen. Everything's going to be messed up. Who knows what we've changed just by being here, but to kill babies who weren't supposed to be killed or not remove the ones that never were. Who knows what those ramifications might be?

What if some of those babies that are killed were future disciples? They'd be the right age. What if one of those babies is Paul or Peter?

Also, it's much easier for Joseph to move Mary and the toddler Jesus to Egypt than to try and move a mother who's going into labor. I know God has all of this worked out but, well, this is too much to take in. What are we to do?"

Thinking a second, "We're here now and must get Aaliyah out. Looking to the sky, I believe Jesus will be alright. How could we be men of faith and believe anything but that God's plan will be accomplished," Hudson said resolutely. "But as for us, in this time. We aren't supposed to be here. All we can do is our best, and trust our heavenly Father to guide us."

A concussive wave blew between them with a streak of light heading directly to the glow to the west. The event awakened them again to their reality.

"God will protect his Son, and his plan. He's given us the job of getting to and protecting Aaliyah," Todd said with a smile and standing again to his feet. "Let's go get her," he smiled, pulling Hudson up.

"Get on the horse," the agent ordered, "and get us to our partner."

All three men mounted their horses and Hudson asked, "How are we getting in?"

Hughes pointed forward, "Right through the front door."

"Well then, lead the way. Time's of the essence," Todd answered.

Starting up the mile long stone ramp toward the entrance of the palace, the only thing that could be heard was the clip-clop of horse hooves. As they passed the large pool, Todd thought of the many times he had been at that location in the future only to see its remnants, yet there it was in its full glory. The building before him wasn't even there except for a few remaining walls. It would be destroyed, ironically by the Romans in 71 A.D. due to the Bar Kokhba revolt.

Seeing the vineyards and orchards to the right and support village to the left, Hudson was amazed at the organization it took to ensure the King was well cared for. He refocused his attention as the Senator approached the stone arch entrance. If problems arose, they would occur here.

The soldiers standing at attention on either side thrust their spears forward causing the Senator to stop his gallop into the fortress.

"Who goes there?" one soldier said wearing the insignia of the King's personal guards.

The Senator sat high on his horse and spoke in clear Greek, "I am Aurius of Antioch with my personal guards, and I need to see your prisoner."

The soldiers looked at each other.

The other soldier spoke, "Aurius of Antioch, we were told you were dead. Cyprianus, just several hours ago said you were killed in an accident in the desert."

Shooting back, he exclaimed, "Do I look dead?" Getting off of his horse, he continued toward them, "Feel my garment soldier, do I look like a ghost to you?"

Taken aback they stammered, "No sir, you are not a ghost, but we were told you were dead."

"The stories of my death are greatly exaggerated. Now take me to the prisoner."

Nervously, the soldier on the right began, "Sir, no one is supposed to see the prisoner."

Todd and Hudson dismounted and stood at attention behind Aurius.

"Yes, sir," the other speaking up, "We have strict orders that only the King see her. He will question her personally tomorrow."

"You would not have that prisoner if it were for me."

Todd grimaced.

"I alerted the King of her threat, I organized the military to capture her, and it was under my orders that she be brought here, so I will see her and each of you will take me to her."

Todd and Hudson grew concerned at the escort of two military men.

"Sir, we cannot leave our post," the younger guard said.

"I am Aurius of Antioch. I am the King's personal prophet. I am a high ranking official within the Roman political system, and when I say you will escort me, you will escort me!" he said almost yelling.

The two soldiers in their young twenties looked at each other, and the higher ranking one finally conceded, "Yes sir, follow us."

"I will tell the King of your help to me."

The young men grinned at each other.

Walking through the main covered entry way, they turned and headed down a side tunnel and into the mountain itself. The temperature within the chamber dropped with each and every step and the torches grew farther apart causing the space to enforce the foreboding feeling it had earned.

With the clanging of the metal on their garb and the slapping of leather on the floor as they walked, Todd's heart sank. Concern for what his Aaliyah had been through gnawed at him. Was she cold and hungry? Had they tortured her? Would she ever forgive him for bringing her back to a place where she was put in such jeopardy? The real question bothering him became clear: Could he forgive himself for bringing her back?

The lead soldiers turned another corner, and at the end of the hall, a sentry stood at attention.

"Who goes there?" the young man said, not expecting any visitors.

Aurius walked forward between the soldiers and spoke with authority, "I am Aurius of Antioch. I am the King's prophet, and I desire to see the prisoner."

The young man stood his ground, "Sir, no one is to see the prisoner except the King."

"I am the voice of the King when he is not here, and I wish to see her."

The other lead soldier who had broken protocol spoke next, "Acanthas, let him through. He is responsible for catching this enemy of the state and will take responsibility for anything that happens to her."

"He is correct. Let me through," he said pushing past him as Todd and Hudson did the same.

"Yes sir," Acanthas said meekly.

Senator John Hughes turned the last hallway to find three cells. Once he reached the end, he saw a young woman kneeling and opened the mechanism to the center door.

"So, you are Aaliyah," he said with a smile.

She looked up slowly from her time of prayer.

Todd pressed around the Senator and into the cell.

"Tawd, Tawd," she yelled.

The professor put his finger to his lips and shushed her. Speaking in Hebrew, "Quiet."

She couldn't help but hug him when Hudson walked into the dark space after Todd.

The other soldiers were still around the corner discussing what was happening when they heard a cell door slam.

"Gentlemen, I told you I'd get you to your partner, and I've kept my word."

Hudson ran over to the prison door and shook it to find that it indeed held fast. "You can't do this."

"Yes, I can and I have," he spoke quietly. "I told you I'd complete my mission and presently thousands of soldiers are preparing to begin a small little scurmish in Bethlehem. I'm going to go there to ensure my work is done, and then my wife and child will be back with me, and everything will be returned to the way it should have been."

Todd ran to the door, "John you can't do this. Hurting a lot of innocent people won't stop the hurt you have inside. Only Christ can give you peace. Surely you know that by now. Think about what you are doing."

Through the bars he sneered, "I have thought about this for years and will have my redemption."

At that, Aurius of Antioch turned and approached the soldiers who were trying to understand why his guards were locked in the cell with the prisoner.

"Those men eluded Cyprianus in the dessert. They were the ones I sent him after. He failed. I used magic to lure them into the prison. I wish them to be left there for the night."

Their faces went blank.

"So do you understand me? They must remain locked up. They are the real threat to the King. You will receive a commendation when the King finds out how you have protected his life."

The man the travelers had come through time to find turned the corner and disappeared from their view. What was left in the dark space were three inexperienced soldiers unsure of what to do, two fake guards shaken by the experience, and a young woman simply happy to see the man she loved alive and well – and in her cell.

The Senator stalked from the prison feeling a renewed air of importance. Behind him he could hear the utter confusion he had left in his wake. Knowing that Hudson and Todd would receive execution for misrepresenting Roman soldiers caused him to pause a moment to reconsider his quick thinking.

With a single backward glance he turned a corner in the passageway, feeling a little regret. The 21st century men were only doing what he had originally sent them to do. True, the professor was a late addition to the cause, but still chosen by him for the initial project.

It was he, the great Senator Hughes who was the head of the governmental oversight on the project. He had allocated the money for the venture from the Congress and had worked hand in hand with the designer, Dr. Keith.

Initially, the Senator never thought the concept possible, but knew the technology gleaned from such a scientific work could benefit the United States in other advancements, as was seen with the space race of the 1960's. However, when the designer got closer and closer to actually perfecting time travel, his thoughts turned towards the greater good.

With a technology such as this, America would become the savior of the world. If something bad happened, going back to solve it, or at least forming a plan for the problem, would be simple. If a drought occurred, the citizens could be told to stockpile food. If a financial crisis loomed in the future, the government might essentially try different options until the right one solved it. Yet, the greatest advantage of the technology would allow the United States to gain strength in the world.

If a tsunami were about to hit a coast, the country affected could be warned, offering credibility and thanks to the good old USA. With foreknowledge of a future Hitler, the technology would allow that person to simply have an *accident* early in life causing him to be removed from the equation. When a country became dangerous and a threat to the safety of the American population or an ally of the United States was introduced, the project would allow for the problem to be stopped before it started.

To Senator John Hughes, anything was possible. Aside from truly considering the ramifications of such "adjustments" in the timelines, and if side-affects occurred, they would be weighed against the good of the change and decisions made from there.

However, when the project was approximately a year from completion, he went home one night, the night of the anniversary of his wife and daughter's death. The house, chosen by his wife and decorated through her efforts and those of their daughter, seemed so pointless now. As he passed through the long halls, noting the fine paintings, beautiful silverware, plush couches, and feminine color choices, he couldn't help but long for the women. He would have given his life for her. At that moment the idea came to him. No longer did it matter if the machine became a solution to a national problem. Its greater purpose, to him – its reason for existence – was now the restoration of his family.

At first, guilt weighed heavily on him. But the longer the idea steeped in his loneliness, the more possible it became to conduct this one mission.

Originally his plan centered on finding someone to go back into the past to stop the gang members who killed his family. A simple in and out procedure. Still, he stewed in his misery, growing angrier over the reason for their senseless deaths. They were simply following Christ in his work. Doing as he did. Offering their lives to serve others. The more he pondered the more vehement his anger grew toward the man so many had followed in humility and self-sacrifice.

Aurius turned the last corner before his way out and saw the light of the entry illuminating the arch ahead. He paused again, his thoughts on the families of the men he had left within the prison.

He spoke out loud as he rubbed his hand along the damp rock walls, "This is a war and they are the casualties of war." His voice echoed along the cobbled floor, "If their God wants them out, he can get them out!"

Aurius left the shadowy tunnels and entered the illumination of the main fortress.

—

The travelers glanced at each other in the dark cell, seeing the actual guards confused in the passageway before them.

"He set us up," Hudson quietly hissed under his breath.

"Yep, no honor among thieves," the professor scowled.

"Atah, vah, atah, vah," Aaliyah beamed in Hebrew.

Looking over her physical condition, he found himself relieved to see her looking so strong.

"Yeah, honey, I came, I came," he continued in Hebrew. "Are you alright? Did they hurt you?"

"The Lord protected me. I am very good, and you came for me! You really came for me! No one has ever come back for me before." She leaped into his arms, wrapping every limb around his armored body, nearly dragging him to the ground under her unexpected weight. Unaware of her impact she continued her welcome by kissing his face repeatedly and saying over and over. "You came for me! You came for me!"

"I wish we had more time for this, Sweetie, but we do not," he managed through her kisses and trying to regain his balance. Forty pounds of armor didn't seem so heavy until you were knocked off balance. He helped her back to the ground even as she kept up the happy reception.

Todd turned a beaming face in Hudson's direction and grinned sheepishly, "She's glad to see us."

In response, Hudson pulled his sword from its sheath, "Then why isn't she jumping on me and kissing me? I'm pretty sure she's a lot happier to see you."

"Yeah, maybe," he replied as she finally released her hold. Still grinning he pulled his sword also. "So, what's your plan?"

"Can you sound official?" Hudson said continuing to speak quietly.

"Listening to their conversation, it's obvious they have no idea what's happened. They aren't sure if they trust us or Aurius," Aaliyah came alongside him and tucked herself under his arm, still smiling up at him.

"I don't think you're going to ever get separated from her again," Hudson quirked.

"I hope not," the professor grinned in return before moving her to stand behind him. "Here goes."

Both men put their swords up.

In Greek, "As exo, as exo!" Todd barked as forcefully as possible.

The soldiers looked at the men behind the bars, still in confusion.

The lead soldier took control, "Why has the prophet put you in jail?"

Todd barked back, "Aurius is a liar. He has plans on killing the King."

The soldiers' mouths dropped.

Knowing the travelers uniforms indicated they were of a higher rank, Todd continued, "If you do not let us out, and immediately, your heads will be removed at the neck within the hour. Cyprianus failed in his attempt to execute him for treason. Now let us free so we can finish what we started."

"Why were you his guards when you got here?" another soldier asked.

Looking over at Hudson with concern for an instant, he refocused on the soldiers. "The King is unaware of his subversion. Aurius believed us in his service, as we led him to the cell where we told him he would find the spy who turned Cyprianus against him. Obviously, his divining powers saw through our attempt to lock him in this cell until the King might be informed of his treachery.

Now, release us immediately!" He walked toward the door, leaving Aaliyah in the shadows.

The young soldiers looked at each other, not knowing how to proceed.

"Now!" Todd yelled.

Hudson hit the wall with the butt of his sword for effect, causing the tunnel to echo with the metallic sound.

"Yes sir," the soldier in charge agreed. He jogged forward and unlocked the door, standing there until the men had exited.

Turning as he left the prison cell, Hudson grabbed the still confused soldier behind him and shoved him against the wall of the tunnel, knocking him unconscious. Todd took care of the one holding the door, and in a matter of moments, the two had pulled the shocked soldiers, half unconscious, bound and gagged into the back of Aaliyah's cell.

"We couldn't have them coming after us," Hudson mumbled out of breath.

Todd agreed.

Pulling the beaming Aaliyah from the cell, Hudson gestured to the opening and allowed her to exit in front of him where Todd prepared to lock the cell door on the guards. Slamming the door shut, he exhaled heavily, "Wow, that went well," he said with a smirk.

Aaliyah jumped back into the professor's arms, and again kissed him anywhere she could get to him.

Todd laughed, "Honey, I'm glad to see you too."

"Atah vah, atah vah," the jubilant woman bubbled as she snuggled against him, still kissing him all the while.

"Yeah, we came. We couldn't leave you," Todd nearly giggled himself at her reaction.

"You guys need to get a room," Hudson said jesting.

"If I were married, I would. You aren't a licensed minister are you?" Todd grinned. "Hey, I am. I wonder if it's legal to marry yourself?"

"Uh, no," the agent said flatly. "Is she ready to go? I mean is she physically able to go with us?"

"One hundred percent. We got here before the torture started, praise God."

"Well, let's go," the agent started down the hall.

"You know, we're pretty good at this time travel, infiltrating another culture, breaking into the castle and rescuing the damsel in distress stuff," the professor said as he pulled Aaliyah to his side.

Hudson remained serious, "Don't count your chickens before they're hatched. We need to find the Senator."

The three turned the corner and snuffed out the torch leaving the new prisoners in the dark.

—

Keren could not sleep after her encounter with the young woman in the prison levels below her residence. Never had she see a lady with such grace under pressure.

Rising from her bed, she loosely tied a garment around her body and left through the large door toward the main hallway.

What a beautiful name, she thought. *Aaliyah*. It meant exalted, and for Keren, she could see that the young woman about her age genuinely was. There was something about her that garnered an humble and gentle spirit.

The woman, beautiful in her own right, had seen many women throughout the years but none of them was gentle and none knew humility. The queens, concubines, and servants within the palace had been hardened by the years. Knowing they were just at the whim of a man who would never love or appreciate them caused those within the palace circles to be self-serving and back-stabbing. Keren had seen that in herself until she met Aurius.

Long ago giving up hope, she had resolved to be a marketable commodity and began living as such. However, the day she was given to Aurius, she knew her life had changed. He was a man who brought back her worth as a woman and fostered softness and gentleness within her. The prophet genuinely cared for her and wanted to know her thoughts and dreams. A tear came to her eye as she tried not to think of what might have happened to her love.

Focusing her thoughts on the prisoner below, she wondered if that little woman could have initiated a conspiracy to kill the King. The idea seemed so wrong with reference to the person she had met. Keren's head dropped to see the tiny bump her middle now made.

After several flights of cold limestone stairs she found the kitchen. Not really hungry, but knowing her room only held more questions and her bed a spot that should contain Aurius, she pulled some figs from a basket.

Movement from the main entrance adjacent to the kitchen caught her attention, and Keren left the figs on the table to walk toward the doorway. Glancing through the main opening her heart dropped before speeding up at the sight of Aurius exiting off the main hall.

Seeing his tall figure leaving by way of a side tunnel she called out as she ran his way, "Aurius!"

The Senator stopped suddenly, his attention broken from his thoughts. As if being removed from a trance, he smiled and went over to Keren, hugging her as she wrapped her arms around him.

"Aurius, I have been so scared. You have never left me before without warning," tears ran down her face as she buried it in his shoulder.

"I know my love, I know," continuing to hug her. "The last several days have been very busy, but everything should be back to normal very soon."

Looking up she saw his eyes and questioned him, "What is happening?"

Knowing that the soldiers may want answers quickly, he tried to appease the obviously shaken woman.

"If everything goes well tonight, the world will be made right, and I will be back in your arms before morning," he assured her, all the while speaking to his own concerns.

"What needs to be corrected? Everything is beautiful right now. Please don't leave me. I feel your mission is not right, and there are things I need to tell you," her head fell onto his shoulder. With one arm she held his neck and with the other the child inside her.

Placing a hand on her cheek he brought her face to his, "I will be back soon. Everything will be better."

The Senator knew that if his mission were accomplished, he would have never gone back into the past and met Keren because his wife and daughter would never have been killed. The thought made him a bit sad because he had grown to truly love the first century woman.

She filled the void that had so long been burning in his heart. Her love and concern for him was genuine and her spirit sweet; much like the combination of the two women he had lost so many years ago. His face grew cold and hard.

"My love, I must leave but will be back soon. I will see you in the morning."

He separated himself from her, kissing once more the beautiful woman who had been his comforter for the last six months. Turning toward the entrance, he found the horse he had left just a short time earlier. After mounting it, he gave one last look to Keren, knowing he would most likely never see her again.

With her standing in the center of the open space and the torches flickering, he could see tears falling from her eyes. Every part of the Jewish woman was beautiful, from her figure and face to her spirit and strength. He loved her, but he had other business of greater import and was fueled by a far more violent emotion.

He turned his face toward the ramp and left the facility. With a yell to his horse, he started toward Jerusalem, never planning to return.

Keren, having spent so much time with men in the past was able to read them like a book. She knew that Aurius loved her, but she also knew there was a place within him that she could not reach. A spot very dark and private; and one he would have to work through on his own.

With a reality that she would never see him again, and that she would be either forced to abort her baby or leave the palace as a defiled Jew, the woman fell to the ground. The weight of the world had fallen upon her and she cried out to God. "Jehovah, why would you leave me like this? My God, why do you forsake me?"

Trying to make out the words through uncontrolled sobs, "Oh, God, my God, please help me. Please redeem me."

Her face fell to the ground and the only thing that could be heard in the cavernous space was crying.

27 — TUESDAY, VERY EARLY MORNING, APRIL 21

Hudson breathed a sigh of relief as he navigated the tunnels leading to the main exit. The clapping of sandals followed closely behind him as Todd and Aaliyah fought to keep up. To leave Aaliyah's highly guarded cell with her in tow had been miraculously lucky. After being left there by Aurius it should have been their grave.

It's not like it came as a surprise anymore, but while Hudson was certain that God the Father would not allow God the Son to have his birth, life, and effect on history altered by one tormented man, he wasn't so sure that God wouldn't permit Todd or him to be hurt or even killed in this time far away from their homes. After all, man's sin had resulted in this evil timeline problem, just as man's sin caused all kinds of evil things to happen to innocent people.

But so far, God had sustained him and his partner in their work and obviously protected them on this mission. How else could he explain his ragtag team arriving safely in a time machine, landing in a first century desert, finding water and food, apprehending Senator John Hughes, finding and rescuing Aaliyah, and breaking free from the King's personal prison?

A brief smile crossed his face as he recalled an action movie he must have seen a while back. The hero took out hundreds of bad guys, arrested the evil villain, and rode out of town - shooting from his vehicle at the herd of goons trailing him in well-equipped hummers with guns a-blazing. Of course, the guy left the scene without a scratch. The tires didn't blow, the splintered glass didn't cut him, and the man wasn't shot or even slowed down. No way in the real world could that occur.

Todd banged into his back at his abrupt halt. Flattening himself against the wall of the long hall he pressed his hand backward into Todd's shoulder to indicate they do the same, as three soldiers passed through the corridor to their left.

Then again this doesn't exactly feel like the real world, he quirked to himself. *And God has given us the ability to beat the odds.*

As the soldier's footsteps descended into the adjacent corridor, Hudson's heart cried a quick "thank you" to his heavenly Father for getting them this far into the mission. *Lord, my God, I know you will keep Christ safe and His timeline secure, but I need your help with the rest of the variables. Show me how to apprehend this guy before he does any real damage. And please, bring all of us home safely. I need my family.*

Giving the go-ahead to the others, he turned the last corner to find the area brightened with the illumination of lamplight. He guessed that they were in the last few feet before they entered the grand arch to the main exit. He pulled in a cleansing breath and looked back at the professor.

"Are we there?" Todd whispered also out of breath. "We may not have much time before the guards get themselves out of the jail below."

"Yeah, I know," Hudson said wishing for a pair of tennis shoes as he tried to push the straps away from a blister on his ankle. "Let me look around the corner and see if everything's alright."

Peeking around the wall, he looked out into the rocky cavernous space to find it empty except for one woman sitting in the center crying. Seeing his horses still at the entrance he turned back toward his friends.

"Are you ready? How's Aaliyah? Is she ready for a ride?"

Pulling Aaliyah close, he relayed the questions to his love. After a quick kiss on the cheek and a hug, she smiled and nodded.

The agent said, "I'll take that as a yes."

Todd chortled, "Isn't love fun?"

"Yeah, the best," he answered vaguely, "But we still have work to do. Except for a woman in the room, the space appears to be empty. We just confidently walk toward the exit, get on the horses and go. Got it?"

"Sure, sounds easy enough, let's go."

Taking in a deep breath, the agent started through the doorway leading into the room. Portraying an air of confidence, he walked without hesitation toward the main entrance passing the crying woman in the process.

Todd stayed in step with him, slowing an instant to let his eyes adapt to the light glowing from a dozen lamps within the space. Aaliyah took up her position in the rear.

After passing the main gate, Hudson found his horse and mounted it, securing the bridle and adjusting the awkward armor. Todd grabbed the reigns of his own mount, then glanced behind to offer his hand to Aaliyah in order to help her mount the large animal. His outstretched hand found air, and he panicked.

A heartbeat later his eyes found Aaliyah kneeling beside the woman lying in a heap on the floor. Confused, the professor left the animal and ran back to her.

"Is everyone ready?" Hudson asked, prepared to lead his partners out into the night. The light above caught his attention. What should have been a black sky shimmered with apparent fire from the emanations amassing less than five miles off in the distance. "Look at the sky, Todd," he spoke with his eyes focused heavenward.

After receiving no response, he glanced back, "Hey Todd look at," he stopped mid-sentence with mouth agape, dismounted his horse, and ran back to find out what was happening. "We need to go, and now!" he whispered forcefully as he arrived at Todd's position on the floor. He could hear Aaliyah calmly assuring the woman on the flat surface next to her.

"I know. I don't know what's going on," Todd stammered. Aaliyah put the woman's head on her shoulder and continued to speak in soft tones.

"Aaliyah's saying it will be alright."

Obviously frustrated and looking around for an enemy to enter the space at any time, "What does that mean?"

"Give me a second."

"That's all you've got. There's no more time. We have to go."

Bending down, Todd whispered in Aaliyah's ear, "Hey sweetie, we need to go now!"

"We cannot leave Keren," she said flatly, still hugging the lady at her side. "We will not leave Keren." There was no more discussion.

"Who's Keren and why can't we leave her? Never mind that," the professor stopped what looked to be a long explanation forming in her eyes, "What I am saying is that she is not coming with us," trying to put his foot down.

"This is Keren, and she must come," arm around the woman, Aaliyah's face showed a new and almost desperate defiance.

Not understanding the reason behind her odd behavior, Todd's temper grew shorter by the moment, "We are already at a disadvantage. She will slow us down and might get us captured."

Her face did not change. He stood up trying to regain his composure.

"What did she say?" Hudson said quietly.

"She's not going without Keren."

"Who is Keren, and why won't she leave without her? I, uh. Todd, she has to leave her!" His left hand slid down his tired face while his right inadvertently reached for his sword. His next words came out quietly, "I've lost control."

"I know, I know, just give me a second." Bending down again, the professor tried to make sense of why this woman had become so important. "Aaliyah, who is she?"

"This is Aurius' mistress, and she is carrying his baby."

Todd bolted upright, feeling a strange mixture of irritation, amusement, and confusion. He passed on the information.

"I'll kill him when I see him." Hudson growled, looking Todd in the eyes, "How could he have done this?"

"I don't know, man," he answered shrugging.

Grunting his words out, Hudson whispered, "No matter, this isn't important tonight. At the moment it's not our problem." He closed his eyes in silent prayer once more before chopping out another command, "Get her up and let's go!"

Grabbing Aaliyah by the arm and trying to remove her forcefully, she yelled out, "No, Tawed, no. No leaf!" She hugged Keren more securely looking up at the travelers as if protecting her baby.

The men had not seen this side of Aaliyah and were taken aback.

Aaliyah continued, "She was a concubine for the King and given to Aurius. If she is bearing a child she will be forced to abort it or will be sent from the palace in shame." The woman in her arms cried out at the elaboration.

Hudson looked on, only distantly wondering what Aaliyah was saying. "Most likely she will be out on the streets."

Todd finally replied to her argument, "Aaliyah, we cannot be of help here. This is not part of our mission. I am sorry but we need to go."

"Todd, she is a banished Jew. She did not choose this life and it is your fault that Aurius came into her time. She has absolutely no where to go."

"I am sorry, but there is nothing we can do for her," he confirmed.

At Todd's words Aaliyah began to cry.

Turning, Todd relayed the information to Hudson.

"You know that's not our fault. We didn't start this whole thing, and what are we supposed to do with her? How can traveling around with us in the desert tonight actually help her situation?" Hudson spat.

Caressing Keren and speaking into her ear, Aaliyah slowly rose and walked over to a wall leaving the woman on the floor while Todd followed.

She began speaking with tears rolling down her cheeks, "Todd, she has to come with us. There is no other way."

"You know that is not possible. We are trying to catch a madman and get back to our time. You must let her stay here."

After a long pause, she grabbed Todd's hand and looked him in the eyes and whispered, "Todd, listen to me. She is my mother." She looked at Keren.

He dropped her hand in shock and spoke loudly and clearly in English, "Your what?" His eyes ran from one woman to the other trying to make sense of her statement.

"She is my mother, and the baby she is carrying is me."

Hudson knew something was wrong. Todd shouted and then started mumbling inarticulately to himself in the corner. He rushed over to find out what extra difficulty had been added to their mission.

"What's wrong?"

Todd looked into Hudson's eyes and blinked twice, "That woman over there is, she is, Aaliyah's mother."

"I beg your pardon? That's not possible." A "V" formed between his brows as he attempted to assimilate this new convoluted piece in the timeline. "How? How does she know, Todd? Ask her!"

Todd asked Aaliyah several more questions.

"Aaliyah, how do you know that, uh, this, um, that her baby is you?" he questioned, still totally perplexed.

"I just know. Keren is my mother, and she is carrying me," she said confidently.

Running his fingers through his hair he started to pace, *Oh Lord, help us to sort through this. And quickly!* He prayed.

Calming down, the professor answered Hudson, "It's possible. That woman is the right age, and from what I learned from Aaliyah before we came back, she has the right history." He stopped to let it sink in, "That woman named Keren is Aaliyah's mother." A goofy grin popped onto his face, whether from the stress or the insanity of the thing, he couldn't guess.

"And to make it even more fun, the baby she's carrying is Aaliyah," he grinned, giving his tummy a pat for good measure. "Hudson, we have to take her with us."

Both men stopped their movement to let the surreal concept sink it.

Todd continued very seriously, "If Keren stays here, she will most likely be executed because she was connected to Aurius who has now been found out to be a false prophet. If she is executed then Aaliyah will cease to exist, and will not help us in the future when we came back initially.

With this line of reasoning, I will most likely die, and you will not complete your first assignment," backing against a wall, he looked at Aaliyah. "Hudson, you know I plan on asking her to marry me if we ever get back, so I don't see any way around this."

Allowing the men to talk it through, Aaliyah lifted Keren gently from the floor and held her for a moment, "We will take you to Aurius. And everything will be fine."

Keren smiled into the kind woman's eyes, and breathed out a sigh of relief.

"What are the odds of this happening?" Hudson said, still confused.

"What? Hudson, everything we do is against the odds," he smiled, placing his hand on his shoulder.

"Does Keren know Aaliyah is her daughter?"

"No. Aaliyah didn't know how to broach that subject. Even though Aaliyah is still from this time generally, she has grown a lot in the last week. She's traveled through millennia and seen our world. She didn't think Keren would understand the idea."

"She can't tell her," Hudson shot back.

"I know, she won't," he spoke quietly, looking at the two women together. "I think Aaliyah is just happy to see her mom. She lost her once, and is going to ensure she doesn't lose her again."

Hudson started toward the horses and waved his arm gesturing for everyone to follow. Todd moved the two women along behind him and they entered the dark night. Aaliyah looked to the sky with tears of joy streaming down her face.

"It's getting brighter, Hudson," Todd said, gesturing to the firmament.

"Yeah, I think the event is about to take place."

"Aaliyah, ask Keren if she sees the activity in the sky."

Hudson mounted his horse and held his arm out for Keren to saddle up behind him.

"Keren, do you see the lights in the sky?" Aaliyah asked as she helped her mother onto the back of Hudson's steed.

"I see a bright star and many other stars," she answered weakly.

"But, do you see any lights moving in the sky?"

"N-no, I do not see any moving lights," she answered perplexed.

After relaying the information Todd spoke to Hudson, "Keren doesn't see the lights either." He got on his horse and pulled Aaliyah up behind him.

"Well, do you have an answer yet?" Hudson asked.

"Pretty close, just need a little more data."

"Oh, by the way, do you know the quickest way to Bethlehem?" Hudson smiled.

"The shortest distance between two points is a straight line. I'd just say just head to that tremendously bright area over there. Those millions of search lights make it pretty obvious where Bethlehem might be."

At that, Hudson kicked his horse and the four people fled out into the night, a night getting brighter by the minute.

—

The Senator left the Herodium full gallop, but stopped near an outcropping about a mile from the fortification to assess his situation. Remembering the Biblical account he had been told as a child, the soldiers were not able to kill the baby Jesus. Angels had warned Mary and Joseph, and obviously the soldiers had not been able to find him. Chances were that Aurius would not have any better luck.

Lowering himself from the animal, he took some water from a skin on the side of the horse and looked to the sky. Seeing the star, he knew that it had guided the wise men to Bethlehem. However they had been thousands of miles away and could easily follow it.

However, just as the wise men would need help from locals, he would need help. For now that he was within a few miles of the city, a large star overhead would not assist him in finding a manger within a small house or outbuilding. He needed more information.

Sitting on a rock, he laid back and looked at the sky. After several minutes of thinking through his options, he heard horses off in the distance. Quickly pulling his steed around the rock, he crouched down and watched for where the sound was coming from.

An instant later, he saw two horses carrying two riders each. "It can't be them," he spoke aloud.

Continuing to bend down he saw the horses pass by, and knew immediately it was Todd, Hudson, and Aaliyah. Strangely enough, the fourth person looked to be Keren.

After the horses had passed and left a trail of dust in the air, Aurius stood and watched them leave. "How did they get out and why would they bring Keren? Why would they bring her here?"

Trying not to have his thoughts emotionally clouded by the addition of Keren to the mix, and regaining focus, he smiled. "I don't have to find the baby Jesus, they will."

Getting back on his horse, he relaxed intentionally, "They will take me right to him where I can finally finish what I started."

He followed after the travelers with determination, using them as the bait to help him catch the game that would change his life.

Cyprianus rode slowly in the carriage toward the Citadel, using the opportunity to strengthen himself mentally for the repugnant work ahead. The soft deep blue of the sky did nothing to help his unenthusiastic efforts at zeal for the mission ordered by his King.

Looking through the open window he saw one bright star glowing to the south, dimming the effect of all the other constellations. He wondered about its purpose in the heavens tonight. Never a superstitious man, he had often mocked those beneath him who cursed the stars for their defeat in battle and thanked them for their victories. Still, tonight, the two things he could not explain seemed divinely connected: the bright star and the evil command of an irrational king.

He had heard the King's order clearly enough and understood it to a point. But even Herod's madness didn't usually go this far. Looking at the dark night sky, he saw nothing but gloom and dread on the horizon. The vivid light of the luminary would only serve to highlight the wretchedness his men would bring on this night. His eyes fell in shame and loss. What kind of man had he become?

God of Jewish wife, if You are there, save me from this wicked thing. I must serve my King, but this goes against all I want to be true. Please stop this mission. Help me.

Thinking of his wife's God reminded him of her earlier words over dinner. Could she be right that her God was sending a deliverer for the Jewish people? He had dismissed the idea at the time because of the illogical nature of the idea. The Jews had been ruled or held captive by one state or another for a thousand years. Why would her God suddenly decide to deliver his people?

His path turned from the countryside into a small Jewish town of tiny houses with lamps glowing in the windows. Of all the difficult times the Jewish people had encountered, this was one of virtual peace. The Romans had conquered them, but allowed them to maintain their own identity. As long as they paid their taxes and didn't cause trouble with the government, they were free to live their lives under the protection of Rome.

Pulling the edict from the King out of his satchel, he opened the seal once again to read the direct and urgent order issued earlier in the day. After reading it through thoroughly, he crumpled the parchment in his hands and dropped it unceremoniously back into his pack.

Many times had orders of the same nature come through the line of command. Execute this one or that one because they plan to subvert the King, the country of Rome or some other such thing. Eliminate this group of rebels organizing themselves in this area or that. These edicts came all for the sake of Rome, Israel or the King. Weariness weighted his shoulders. He wished his driver would just take him away from the city and be the explanation for why he couldn't fulfill his obligation yet the clip clop of the horse and roll of the wheels continued on.

A new thought stuck him. *Are we killing a potential King? Or is this about destroying the future Deliverer of the Jews?* The leader wondered to himself.

Cyprianus knew kings very well. He understood them to be selfish, egocentric, and maniacal. If the Jews were about to get a new king, they would be no better off than they were presently. But if their Deliver had just been born…

The driver turned the vehicle onto the road leading up to the Citadel. Cyprianus knew that a new king was not what the Jewish people or his wife needed. However, deliverance at the hand of their God, well, he reconsidered what his actions would be given that certain knowledge.

Never in his life had he wanted anything to do with gods or religion. The gods his people worshiped were just as dysfunctional as those who went to them for guidance, safety and prosperity. But a God who took the time, care and forethought to deliver his people might be the God Cyprianus could worship.

Deliverance, he understood. As the leader of the military for the region of Israel, he had been sent in to conquer other warring nations, and, on occasion, freed people from oppressive regimes. Cheers of gratitude from the newly rescued echoed in the chambers of his memory, and his heart swelled at the feeling it brought.

He thought of the children gathering around his horse, the mothers crying knowing their families could eat again, and the fathers shouting with appreciation and respect. It was a great feeling to deliver people from fear and hurt. Was this the same type of delivering Livana's God would do for her people?

Seeing the Citadel lit up with a thousand torches, the commander knew his ride would end very quickly, but the line of reasoning continued in his mind. *What did the Jewish people need to be delivered from?*

A true and good God would never send a king such as the ones he had known; the people would be no better off. What would a Deliverer look like? A Deliver worth his salt would have to save them from something other than the mild oppression they now encountered. He subconsciously nodded his head in confirmation of his own thoughts.

The Romans allowed the Jews to continue their traditions and worship. Other than the forced labor Herod had inflicted on a relatively small number of them, they did not need to be freed from Herod. He was nearing the complex where the dreaded night would begin, but he indulged himself a moment more in his contemplations; the vehicle rolling slowly on.

Remembering the hours of prayer his wife spent on bended knee and the weekly traditions and rituals her family practiced, Cyprianus mused that the best thing their God could do would be to deliver them from themselves.

The sacrifices and ritual never ended for Livana. Just as soon as she completed the work to be done in preparation for the Sabbath, she started it again a week later. Every year the sacrifice was offered to remove their sin and the transgressions of the entire nation, but each new day brought new concerns of cleansing and uncleanliness. It seemed like they never ended the effort to be rid of their unworthiness.

And for what? He wondered.

When the Romans went to the temple it was to appease the god or goddess with something concrete. When it was done, it was done until you wanted something else from the gods.

The carriage stopped and the driver lowered himself from the vehicle. Walking back, he opened the door and allowed Cyprianus to leave the last respite of a difficult night ahead. As he did so, he ended his ponderings with a final thought.

A real God would save them from themselves, from the never-ending ritual of proving their worth. Yes. A real God would personally free them from their uncleanness and offer them peace. And life spent with him eternally.

Pulling out a red cape, he removed the one he wore for travel and handed his pack to another servant and began his ascension up the stairs.

If there is a God, he will not permit me to murder his long-prophesied Deliverer. Then we shall all be saved.

Swirling the red cloth about his shoulders and fastening it into place he stood taller and regained the focus in his eyes. His stride stiffened, and by the time he made it to the top, he was the man he needed to be.

Entering the fortification, a young recruit saw his appearance and announced their leader's arrival. The room full of noise, business, and general military commotion silenced at his entrance.

Cyprianus stepped to the center of the large chamber and lifted his chin.

"Men," he faltered momentarily, unable to disclose his orders. Finally he spoke with authority, "I want everyone out in the courtyard in formation." At their looks of confusion he bellowed once more, "I want formations now!"

The space churned with movement until all had descended the steps. The courtyard he had just left filled with close to one thousand men standing in rows in full military gear.

He strode determinedly to the balcony to begin the worst night of his life.

The enormous group of well-trained men lined up and ready for orders brought a smile to Cyprianus' eyes. They prepared daily to be ready to take on the worst of the worst, from barbarian to insurgent. Their eyes showed pride and valor, dignity and strength. But tonight's mission was for cowards.

There would be no victory. The mission ahead of them this night would be remembered as a dark spot on the Roman character.

Placing his hand on the railing, he spoke to the troops, "Men, our king needs us," he paused, shut his eyes a moment and continued, "Just hours ago I was given notice that someone is trying to remove King Herod from the throne."

Hearing the whispers among the men, he allowed them a few seconds to breach protocol, "Yes, I received an edict from the King," he said, pulling the proclamation from the sack at his side and holding it in the air. "He has once again charged us with his protection." He could see the pride swelling throughout the ranks. Unfortunately, he felt none of that emotion.

"For the King," one man yelled from the ranks.

Many of the other men echoed the thought.

The leaders on horseback turned and barked out orders which brought the army back in control.

Palm upward towards the men, Cyprianus continued, "We will be victorious! Men, we will be victorious, but our mission is very different than what we have been given before."

A decorated rider on horseback rode through the entrance to the pavilion as Cyprianus continued.

"We have fought in all areas of the kingdom against many well-trained and equipped armies."

The rider found Alexandrus on horseback at the edge of the formation and came alongside him, whispered something in his ear and was permitted entrance into the Citadel.

"Unfortunately, this task will not occur in the same way the others have. Tonight we have a mission to complete within our own country, not very far from here." Hearing a commotion behind him he looked to find Alexandrus speaking to Dritus and then to Thorius.

"Men, we will be fighting an upcoming threat. It may seem insignificant now, but should prove to save our nation in the future."

Alexandrus ascended the stairs and approached Cyprianus from behind and waited standing at attention next to the military leader.

Cyprianus, halfhearted about his next words turned to the man quickly "What is it?" Cyprianus asked with irritation.

Removing his helmet he lowered his head, "Sir, I am very sorry, but I thought you would want to know immediately. Sir, there has been a break from the palace, the prisoner has broken free."

"There was only one prisoner, and I placed her in there myself. She was only this high," he whispered, making a low gesture with his arm, "Explain!"

"What I was told," the soldier said nervously, "was that the King's prophet was involved."

"Aurius? At the palace?"

"Yes, Aurius brought two soldiers with him. He placed them in the prison along with her, but after he left they broke out."

"Who were the two soldiers?"

"Sir, no one seems to know who they were"

"Those must be the two others Aurius was speaking of." Cyprianus murmured to himself. Looking Alexandrus in the eyes he spoke quietly, "The King will have our heads if that prisoner is not found."

"Yes Sir, I know."

Turning to look at the men standing in ranks below he considered his options. Was it more important he kill the babies in Bethlehem, or find the direct threat to the King's security? Knowing he had not accomplished his original orders, and that the palace and his King were in peril, he decided to scrap the Bethlehem mission for the evening.

This possibility of an infant Jewish king couldn't be a threat for years, he reasoned. *I have plenty of time to complete that mission if the King deems it necessary in the future. Maybe there is a God after all,* he considered.

Breathing for the first time in a full sun cycle, he announced to the troops, "I have just been made aware of a raid that occurred at Herod's palace. A highly prized prisoner has been abducted by what appears to be insurgents dressed as soldiers."

Angry murmuring broke out among the troops.

"Only defenders of Rome wear our uniform!"

The men cheered.

"Find these men. But do not touch a hair on their heads until you bring them to me. These men must be questioned first. Do you understand?"

Cries of "Audiremus!" sizzled through the camp, as the men shouted that they had heard and thus would obey.

"Alpha and Beta divisions, you will head to the Herodium and defend it from any potential threat. Leaders, you will determine what you can from the situation at the palace and return the information to me."

Pointing at the last two divisions he ordered, "Gamma, you will divide out and work your way through Jerusalem." The leader nodded.

"Delta division, you will be with me. I think I know where they are heading. Alexandrus, get your men ready, we leave in 10 minutes," the leader responded with a slap to his chest.

Before dismissing the troops he spoke once more, "If you find them, you will not harm them. You will bring them to me. I will mete out justice as it is demanded. Is that understood?"

"Yes Sir, Commander!" the men yelled.

"I expect it be done for Rome and Caesar!" he shouted enthusiastically.

"For Rome and Caesar!" the men responded in kind.

Cyprianus turned to enter the Citadel even as he heard the various leaders barking orders to their troops.

Knowing he should have finished off Aurius of Antioch when he had the chance, the leader knew he had to find the dangerous prophet before the prophet found the King, or this might be his last mission. This time he would complete the job.

The large doors of the fortification slammed behind him.

The desert flew beneath the horses' feet as they carried the two 21st century men and the two 1st century women toward Bethlehem. All but Keren marveled at the spectacular light show displayed before them, feeling new strength within them as they drew closer to the focal point of the brilliance. In spite of the extra load, the horses seemed also to have gained stamina and speed from the spectacular event.

Breaching the gap between the steeds with her voice, Keren asked Aaliyah where they were headed.

"The town called a House of Bread!" shouted Aaliyah in Hebrew. Hearing her words behind him Todd's eyes lit up with new understanding.

"Hudson!" he called over the swooping and rushing sounds around him, "You know in Hebrew, the name for Bethlehem means House of Bread?"

"You mean, like a bakery?"

"Well, yes! That means Jesus is called the Bread of Life, and he was born in a town called The Bakery," he quipped with new joy.

"God certainly plans things ahead – and with a great sense of humor, right?" Hudson smiled into the wind. These back-to-back missions weighed heavily on him most of the time, but – at moments such as these – he knew what a rare blessing it really was to be here, now, for this experience.

The sky grew brighter. Luminosities streaked across the heavens at a rate of hundreds per second, occasionally coming close to the riders and causing one or the other of the horses to flinch and break its stride.

Hudson yelled back at Todd, "Do you think the horses can see the lights?"

Answering with a smile, "I'd say so. They seem just as focused on the event up ahead as we do. Oddly enough, they don't seem to be anymore frightened of it than we are!"

"Well, Professor, are these lights what I think they are?"

"I believe they are, man. We are living the life, seeing something that only a few on earth have ever seen," he paused wishing he had a classroom right now. "Daniel saw some, Abraham did too." Aaliyah grabbed tighter as a radiant beam soared past, just inches from her, nearly scaring her from the horse.

Holding the reigns with one hand and patting her hands on his chest with the other he continued, "Lot saw two, and so did Mary just a few months ago. I bet some shepherds are hearing from them right now."

Hudson laughed out loud, "So we're seeing angels," he grinned, hardly believing what he said.

"Hey, you stole my thunder," Todd laughed. Everyone but Keren was feeling giddy with the sheer joy of the occasion in the air. "Yes, these are the angels of heaven anticipating the arrival of Jesus. At the bottom of that fountain of light I'll bet we find Mary and Jesus.

It says in Psalm 96 that all of creation rejoices. I think the horses are just as excited to get there as we are."

"They haven't slowed their progress a bit since we left. It's as if they are gaining strength with every step they take toward our Savior," the agent replied, noting Keren's hold tightening behind him.

The men looked forward, and Aaliyah peeked around Todd to observe the overflowing source of the glow ahead, rising from a small spot on the other side of the city they were about to enter.

The inverted cascade came to a point where it touched the earth, but plumed into a radiant fountain, spraying in all directions of the heavens. The higher it rose, the more three-dimensional it became. The travelers found that rays darted in and out of the stream as well as up and down through it. So many heavenly creations beamed into the night sky that the dark desert looked more like midday.

An irresistible exuberance overcame the three Christ-followers. First Hudson began to sing a version of "Amazing Grace," followed by Todd chanting like the angels around the throne of grace "Blessed be the Lord God Almighty, Who was and is and is to come." Simultaneously, Aaliyah sang a beautifully soft song in Hebrew, tears flowing down her face.

From the backs of their swift-moving horses, the three worshiped as if in the most beautiful cathedral on earth. And as they continued their praise, the lights within the plume began to throb and short waves of pressure pulsed in time with the visual effect. Over the next several minutes the rhythm became very ordered and the pressure impressions became so strong that the riders ceased their worship and stopped their horses.

Dismounting on a small ridge approximately one half mile from Bethlehem, they looked down at the town and the fountain on the other side of the city. With Keren wondering why they stopped and looking at the others, Todd, Hudson, and Aaliyah spontaneously went to their knees at the same time, tears of effervescent joyfulness spilling down their faces.

Keren eased off her horse as well, but backed away from them in an attempt to gain a perspective she somehow was missing.

As Hudson, Todd, and Aaliyah watched, the pulsations became stronger and the waves so intense that the three had trouble holding their ground. Todd grabbed Aaliyah and Hudson, pulling them to him as they waited for a sign of the event.

As they huddled there on the desert floor full of awe-filled worship, the ground rumbled beneath them, and an indefinable explosion of life blew the three to their faces. Full of confusion and now fear, Keren felt nothing the others did.

The woman saw their hair and clothing blowing in the wind, yet felt no gust. She could see the panic and wonder in their eyes, but witnessed nothing to elicit their response. Keren surveyed the area and found everything as it had always been. Nothing appeared to be out of the ordinary, yet even the horses showed signs of excitement. Out of distress, she began to pray to the God of heaven.

Within seconds, a pressure wave not unlike one from a nuclear bomb shattered the air around them, seeming to rush in all directions at once. Hudson knew the wave was so forceful that it would circle the globe before running out of steam.

Once the surge had passed, the three slowly looked at each other and tried to stand. Each glanced at the other to find their faces nearly white and glowing. What most people would have thought of as a radiation burn, the three laughed and cried knowing they had experienced the glory of the Lord.

Hugging, crying, praying and singing, the three danced for their God.

Keren continued to pray for a moment before she pulled at Aaliyah, who was in the middle of a Hebrew chant, "What is happening? What are you seeing?"

Giggling and laughing she announced, "We just experienced the birth of our Savior!" she cried.

"The Savior? What do you mean?" Keren asked haltingly. The last few moments had frightened her, and she was no longer certain she wanted the answer to her question.

With the men on their knees, Aaliyah took the next few minutes to explain that the prophecies concerning the Messiah were being fulfilled tonight in the baby born as Jesus. Keren nodded in acknowledgement of the prophecies foretelling the coming of the Messiah, and listened with curiosity as Aaliyah told her of his future work as a grown man and his coming death on the cross.

In detail she explained what she herself had learned only days ago. How the long-held sacrificial system was to be replaced by this Savior. How he would lay down his life for his people and only through the shedding of his blood was there forgiveness of sin and eternal life with God. Question after question Aaliyah answered from the scriptures as Keren seemed to suddenly remember everything she had learned from childhood.

After several minutes Keren seemed to grasp what had happened and asked why she couldn't see the light or feel the waves that Aaliyah had just explained seeing. For the first time the younger woman was silent and beckoned to Todd for help.

Speaking in Greek he answered both of them with his opinion of what was occurring, "You cannot see the most beautiful site ever created because you do not yet accept what Jesus came to offer you - forgiveness."

Eyes brightening, Aaliyah agreed with a quick head bobble.

Continuing his thought, "If you accept Christ as your Savior and Lord, you too will be able to see what we see. But, Keren, you also will be able to have a life beyond compare and will spend eternity with God the Father," he said, pointing toward the heavens.

Hudson walked over.

Keren shook her head and began to cry, "Why would God want me? I am not the kind of woman who deserves forgiveness such as this. I have no hope now. The man I love has left me, my family has banished me. The King will throw me from the palace when he finds that Aurius is gone and I am pregnant." She tried to wipe the tears with her garment, but finally pressed the cloth to her eyes as her shoulders began to quake with sorrow.

Todd bent his head to catch her eyes as he lifted her chin and smiled, "Well, all of that can change right now. If you accept Christ as your Savior, you will know that you are loved and cared for. God will see you as clean and pure because of the blood Jesus will sacrifice on your behalf."

Aaliyah hugged Keren, "It will not matter what your past was. All that will matter is the future God has for you."

Todd watched Aaliyah trying to persuade her mother to accept Christ. Unexpected tears ran down his own cheeks knowing the loss she had gone through, yet God in his grace might be giving back.

Watching the three conversing in a language he didn't understand, Hudson realized they were trying to tell Keren about Christ and explain to her how she might believe in him as her Savior. He prayed that God would guide their words.

Keren backed away thinking through what Aaliyah and Todd were telling her. She trembled and shook at what she had heard. It seemed so impossible. Could God really love humanity enough to come as a Man, as His only Son? More importantly, did God love her enough to save her? She fell to her knees.

Aaliyah kneeled next to Keren and Todd followed dropping to the ground beside her. The professor knew nothing to do other than quote scriptures that wouldn't be written for close to sixty years and be authored by a man named Paul who wasn't most likely born yet. He laughed at the conundrum.

"Do you believe that in just around thirty-three years, Jesus will die to pay for your sin and mine, and that God will raise him back to life – conquering death and giving you eternal life with him?

Do you believe in your heart that God will, well, that he will raise Christ up from the dead? And do you acknowledge that Jesus is Lord?"

With Aaliyah hugging Keren and staring at Todd, the woman raised her head and nodded in affirmation. "Yes, I believe God will raise him from the dead. He has done that often enough in our history when he wanted to. And, yes, I want Jesus to rule my life – as my Lord."

"Hudson, come down here," Todd said to his friend in English. Turning his face back to Keren he nodded, "Let's pray."

The four huddled in a group on the ground and closed their eyes as the professor led the 1st century woman through a prayer of salvation. Each knew the privilege it was to see a new creation in Christ, but to witness it on the day of Jesus' birth turned this beautiful moment into a historically unprecedented conversion filled with the appropriate joy of the day. Each would cherish this time for all of eternity.

As Todd said amen, Aaliyah hugged the woman tightly and Keren slowly opened her eyes to a new world. Immediately the blackened sky filled with unimaginable color and light. Everything the others had seen now filled her vision. Trying to stand, she raised herself only a moment before she was driven to her knees in awe and praise. Tears of happiness now flooded her eyes, and she joined Aaliyah in singing the soft song she had heard earlier as they had been riding. The song was one her mother had taught to Keren, and she knew today that she would teach it to her own child when it was born.

Hudson and Todd helped both women to their feet after a while and began to embrace the new sister in Christ. When Todd released Keren from his happy welcome, Aaliyah gripped him by the shoulder, turned his face toward hers with her palm and lifted her lips to his. Wrapping his arms around her in return he deepened the kiss and she held him closer still. After several seconds, Aaliyah slowly drew herself away from him just enough to look him in the eyes, "Thank you Todd, for my mother." Her Hebrew flowed perfectly, and he melted at her compliment.

With a smile on his face he pulled away in delight, "If I had known that was all it took to get a kiss, I would have found your mom earlier." His laugh was a bit unsteady, and it made her even happier.

"Because of this, she will not follow the same path, and I might have a mother to raise me." She wrapped her arms around his neck and kissed him again quickly.

All the stories Todd had heard about first kisses and true love were right. Fireworks exploded in his mind with the knowledge that this woman he held, he would hold forever as his own. He finished the kiss and whispered into her ear as he held her close, "I love you, Aaliyah."

"I love you too, Todd," she answered hugging him tightly.

Hudson broke the moment unceremoniously, "Do you hear that?"

Everyone became quiet and Keren turned to face the direction of the sound.

Not wanting to release Aaliyah, Todd answered with her still lightly in his arms, "Yeah, I hear it." Todd asked Aaliyah in Hebrew if she could hear the sound.

"It sounds like singing," she answered, asking her mother about the new experience.

Keren agreed that it sounded like singing, but unlike any kind of music they had ever heard before. No melody really, but rhythmic and beautiful – heavenly singing.

"The angels are praising God," Todd smiled.

"I have never heard a sound more beautiful. It doesn't sound like any music I have ever heard, but it is perfect."

"Hey Hudson, the lights have stopped moving, and are all staying in one position."

The men walked forward toward the edge of the formation and saw the city totally asleep with the largest event ever taking place just a mile away. The women held each other in a moment of perfect peace and let them men talk a moment.

"How can they not know what has happened?" Hudson asked. "They are right next door and are oblivious to the fact that the world is different."

"Hudson, it's the same in our time. Christ has come, and yet no one really acknowledges it. If it weren't for this experience, we might be in the same situation," Todd responded.

"Yeah, I guess that would be me before all of this," the agent lamented.

A familiar voice interrupted, "I don't want crash the party, but I still have a mission to complete."

Hudson and Todd and the two women were instantly pulled from the beauty of the heavens to the ugliness of the world.

"John," Hudson moaned, "What are you doing here?" Hudson took in a quick breath as he saw the Senator move quickly to the left and hold a knife to Aaliyah's throat.

Todd instinctively ran at the Senator.

"You come any closer, and I will kill her. I swear I will," the man said making an indention on Aaliyah's neck with the weapon.

Todd stopped in his tracks. "Senator, you can't do this. Do you not see what has happened tonight? Don't you see the lights in the sky?"

"I have no idea why you are talking about lights, other than that one really bright star, of course."

Keren, who initially was filled with joy at the sight of Aurius, was now in terror at what she saw him preparing to do.

"Aurius, where have you been?" she nearly cried as she walked toward him, "My love, what are you doing?"

Speaking with her in Greek, he groaned, "Keren, why do you have to be here?"

"Aurius, I had nowhere else to go. Without you, they would banish me from the palace. I, I," She hesitated to tell him of their happy news in this situation, "These people saved me," she finally spoke, gesturing to the group.

Seeing Aaliyah so close to Keren and John, Todd saw the resemblance. If the Senator knew he was threatening his daughter would he continue with his task? Knowing the story would be too unbelievable and difficult to explain, he sighed instead, "Senator, let her go. This can't lead to anything good."

"I will have my revenge. I lost my family, and tonight I will have them back," Hughes cried. Tears formed in his eyes as he held the woman he did not know as his daughter in a death grip.

"This will bring you nothing back," Hudson answered, not knowing how to proceed.

"Aurius, let her go," Keren pleaded.

"After my mission is complete, everything will be fine. I cannot have these men trying to stop me," the Senator said attempting to be somewhat warm with the woman he loved.

Staring at Todd and Hudson his words were defiant, "Men, you will start walking, and we will follow you to the manger site. I know you know exactly where it is, so this will not take much time. If you try anything to prevent my success, I'll kill your partner and your love."

"If you hurt her, I'll kill you myself," Todd growled.

"You get me to Jesus, and she will be released, now move," Hughes said without hesitation.

The irony of the situation tormented both men. The greatest gift of all and the One in whom their faith rested lay newly born, yet they knew he was still Sovereign. As each one's faith was put to the test they realized there was nothing to do but pray, and all five started down the hill toward Bethlehem.

Cyprianus entered the officer's section of the Citadel totally exhausted. Having been up for what seemed countless hours, the General walked over to a basin and washed his face.

"I should have killed Aurius when I had the chance," he said to himself. "If I had gutted him there, he would not be this thorn in my side now."

Standing and stretching he found a mug on a table and poured himself some wine. "If he gets back to the King, I will be the one gutted." He took a draught of the wine and sat a moment.

Irritated with his muddled thoughts he tore a hunk of bread from a loaf in a nearby basket and took a bite. As he chewed he thought through how he could rectify the problem at hand. The seasoned military commander knew the men would follow his lead. There was no doubt in his mind the leaders had no love for the faux prophet and, given the chance, would remove the man who had embarrassed their commander in front of the King.

Yet, the only person the King trusted at this point was Aurius.

Pulling his sword from its sheath, the man began making circles in the air, attempting to loosen tight and tired muscles.

He lowered the sword and spoke out loud, "It is obvious Aurius entered the palace on false pretenses with two men appearing as soldiers." Cyprianus remembered the palace guards saying he had entered without fear as he talked his way past them.

"He could have somehow alerted the palace guards if he had truly been captured himself, yet he did not. Why?"

Feeling his shoulders loosening up, he began to work his legs, lunging with his sword toward an invisible foe.

"Maybe he knows the men who were coming after him?" he said as if a light came on in his head. He made a piercing motion as the sword cut the air.

Standing straight again and feeling more awake, he put the sword back in its sheath.

"What if Aurius was the enemy all along?" he asked trying to work the problem out in his head. Cyprianus always knew the prophet had ulterior motives and could see through his façade in a way the King never could, but it wasn't until now that he began to put it together.

He remembered that day before the King, when Aurius had told of a threefold threat and it all seemed to culminate with the birth of a new king. That was the whole reason for the King's edict and the destruction of the babies in Bethlehem.

"What if Aurius was always after that baby? Perhaps those men who came after him somehow were out to stop him."

It seemed to make sense enough in his head.

"The only reason they would risk entering the palace would be to free the woman I captured earlier, yet somehow everything got mixed up and Aurius locked them up."

Feeling new life and energy, the General grew hot with anger. "From the beginning the King was being used. This was never about protecting Herod but killing a child who may be the future Deliverer of Israel."

Cyprianus left the quarters and entered the long hall leading to the main entrance. "I may never know who the child really is or what he will become, but I can protect him and remove a threat to both myself and the throne of Herod in the process."

Opening the large doors to the Citadel, the General looked down from the staircase to find Alexandrus standing at the ready.

Commanding from the top step, "Are the men ready, Alexandrus?"

"Yes, General!" the man answered with confidence.

Walking down the staircase, the General was revived. His mission had radically changed from the cowardly work he had been assigned not many hours ago. Rather than kill defenseless children, he would eliminate a true risk to the King and possibly protect an innocent child.

Feeling strong and redeemed, he mounted the fresh horse waiting for him and looked at the men.

He spoke to Alexandrus, "I want to start ahead of the men, follow me when the night watch changes."

"To Bethlehem!" he yelled in the direction of the men behind him as he sped out through the gate with the troops looking on.

—

Hudson and Todd led the group to the outskirts of Bethlehem. Knowing John was the only one to not see the plume of light to the northwest, Hudson took them initially to the southeast of town.

Seeing the streets filled with animals tied to posts and even some travelers sleeping in alleys next to houses, Hudson asked Todd, "Is this settlement normally this busy?"

Todd smiled, "You know what's happening. Do you remember the second chapter of Luke?"

Looking up and trying to remember the first few verses, "In those days, Caesar Augustus issued a decree…"

The professor continued with him, "…that a census should be taken of the entire Roman world."

"It's amazing that it's so accurate. Everyone had to go to their own town and register, and that's why Mary and Joseph are here."

"Precisely, my dear Watson," replied Todd also amazed at the accuracy of the Biblical account. "Normally this little city is just about ten to fifteen houses and nothing else." Gesturing around he explained, "In our time a church called the Church of the Nativity covers this spot. Even though it is a big church, it is still a single building and most believe it would take up the area of this town." Looking around, "I would say they're pretty close. The town is a little bigger than the church is, or I guess will be, but it's close."

John spoke up from behind, "Enough of the history lesson Professor Myers, get me to the manger site."

Todd looked back to find the Senator holding Aaliyah by the upper arm with one hand and his other stuffed in his tunic holding a dagger. Keren was walking next to him tightly grabbing him by the arm.

"Senator, the Bible doesn't give us longitude and latitude for this thing. We're doing our best. We're going to methodically walk the streets until we find the site." He stopped in the middle of the rocky road and turned toward the faux prophet, "If I find one scratch on her, I will personally kill you. Do you understand?"

"You may kill me, my new friend, but I will not be the first to go," he said yanking the young woman in front of him in clarification. "Turn around and keep moving."

"Come on, buddy, let's go," Hudson said grabbing his partner by the arm.

After turning him back around and keeping him moving they continued on their fake perimeter search for the baby Jesus.

Feeling the rough clay walls of the flat-roofed buildings, Hudson started conversing with Hughes.

"So, John, how did you get out of jail?"

"What do you mean? What jail?" he asked impatiently.

"In our time," the agent quickly responded. "Todd and I were told you would be taken to jail. We left the Oval Office with the President saying he was going to put you in a hole so deep, even light couldn't get down there."

With a chuckle he smiled wanly, "That didn't quite happen."

"The President never was going to put you in jail, was he?" Todd joined in.

"Let's say, we wanted the same end, just for different reasons."

"We know that you're out for vengeance. Your wife and daughter were killed doing missionary work, and so if Jesus is removed, they never would have been on that mission. I think I understand your motive," Hudson continued. "I understand, but there is no real logic to it."

"Yeah, if you remove Jesus, the entire world will be different," Todd added.

"That's the point, keep moving," the Senator growled.

"I don't think you get it, John. You're right in that, without Jesus there won't be the church and all of the good and sadly enough bad it has done throughout the ages," he said, counting off on his hands. "No crusades. There won't be the renaissance which was a departure from the ways of the church. Many of the cults which consider themselves to be based on Christianity and have caused so much pain won't be formed.

There won't also be a reformation. No real art. No real science. No real education. No Christopher Columbus heading out with what he thought was a call from God to find a new world. No Puritans wanting to leave England to freely worship. The list goes on and on. You can look this stuff up. It's been well-documented how Jesus affected all of these things for the better."

Turning a corner and starting back another direction the lesson continued.

"Without Christ we won't have the ethical and moral system that Jesus brought. Women will be treated poorly in nearly every culture around the globe. Value of life will never be lifted up, so babies will be left for dead when unwanted, children exploited. All of the evil of the world would have nothing to stop it.

People will be without hope or direction. Without Jesus there won't be an Easter, or Christmas where the world stops and thinks about others."

He looked over his shoulder, "John, who's to say that you'll even be here without Jesus? The entire world will be different. Who is to say your parents met, or their parents, or that, generations back, your ancestors were even born? Do you know what you're trying to do? Have you really thought it through?"

"Without my family, I don't want to live and thus it won't matter," Hughes said flatly.

Hudson took over, "We think we know your motives, but why would the President be in on your work?"

With a smile on his face, "This never really was my work."

"What does that mean?" both men asked.

"Just that. When the President initially found out about the project, and he found out very early, he had secondary plans for the machine."

"Why would he want to kill Jesus?" Todd questioned.

"Let's say, that without that moral and ethical code you were talking about earlier, he could do things and motivate people through their own desires in a way he couldn't if they held to a code of right and wrong."

"I think I get it," Hudson said looking at Todd. "A person following what he thinks is right will sacrifice himself for the better good. However, a person motivated by greed can be bribed into anything."

"Something like that," John affirmed.

"This has to do with absolute power. He wants control of the people." Speaking to the professor, he continued, "Look at the many dictatorial regimes. They have total control of the people because they have censured out Christianity and only allow the religions that support their leadership structure."

"You're right," the professor said counting on his fingers, "China, North Korea, countries in South America, and Russia for all intents and purposes. Without eternal hope, the people are more willing to work to follow their leader.

You would think with this kind of power and technology, he would have a plan more extravagant than the one in all the movies: power."

Hudson took over the conversation, "So the President wants to turn the U.S. into a dictatorship?"

Laughing out loud, he quipped, "Agent Blackwell, who says he wants to stop there?"

Having worked their way through most of the small city, the men got quiet. After several minutes and passing several more houses, Hudson spoke up, "So he wants to control the world?"

"Sure, with the kind of power he has, he can make just about anything happen." Stopping in the street, John added, "I've enjoyed this little tour of the first century cesspool that is Bethlehem, but I'm tired of walking. Where's Jesus?"

Keren spoke to Aurius in Greek, "Aurius, you must let Aaliyah go. She is frightened. Look at her! She is innocent and has done nothing to hurt you." For her part, Aaliyah had silent tears on her cheeks.

Looking down at the woman who glowed up at him with compassion, he answered her, "Keren, when they take me to Jesus, I will let her go."

"Why do you want to see Jesus?" Keren asked innocently. "If you will let her go, I will take you to Jesus."

Aaliyah spoke out, "Keren, no, you can't tell him."

"My love, ignore whatever she is saying and trust me. Where is Jesus?"

Having worked their way to the north end of town, Keren pointed to the west, "Do you not see it?"

"See what?"

"All of the lights in the skies. They are angels celebrating the birth of the Savior." With a smile of joy she asked, "Do you not see them?"

"I do not know what you are speaking of."

"How can you not see them? The entire night sky is heralding his coming." In her joy at the sight it took a moment for her to realize why he could not see it. Aurius was not a believer. "My love, you do not believe in Jesus, do you?"

"I believe, just show me the direction."

"Aurius, you need to give your heart to Jesus. He will release you from all of your inner strife." Placing her hand on his heart, she said, "You have a dark spot that only Jesus can light."

"Keren, just tell me where to find Jesus."

Horse hooves were heard just a few streets to the south.

"Why do you want to find him?" she asked innocently.

"I just want to find him," he ground out.

"Why?"

"I want my family back. He took my family, and I want them back," he blurted.

Understanding he has gone through great loss, "Oh, my love, I am so sorry for what might have happened, but we love you," she said touching his face.

Hudson heard footfalls from a position behind them.

"What do you mean 'we'?" he asked a bit off guard.

Backing away and into the low light of a burning lamp in a window, Keren placed her hands over her middle. "Aurius, I am pregnant with your child. It is the two of us who love you."

Aurius stood there speechless.

"With this child, we will start a new family. Whatever it is you lost, Jesus is giving it back."

At that, a large figure jumped at Aurius from between the houses dropping him and Aaliyah to the ground. Todd ran over and pulled her from the earth, lifting and holding her tightly.

Hudson pulled his sword and went after the man causing the altercation.

Within seconds, Aurius yelled out, "Cyprianus!"

With his sword to the prophet's neck, he announced "Now, it's time to end this."

Knowing what he said, Todd yelled at him in Greek, "No, you cannot kill him. We must have him."

With Hudson in an offensive position, Cyprianus pulled Aurius from the ground.

Keren yelled, "Cyprianus, please let him go. He is not a threat!"

With the sword still at the man's throat, Cyprianus demanded answers, "Who are you?"

Doing his best to answer, Todd spoke calmly. "We are not a threat," he said slowly, "we have come a long way to find him, and we need to take him back to our land for trial."

"Why are you dressed as Roman soldiers?" he queried.

"No one was hurt. We are only borrowing these uniforms to more easily take this prisoner from your country before he does more damage."

With Aaliyah holding on to him tightly, Todd continued, "We mean you no harm and will take care of John, I mean Aurius, if you let us."

Thinking through what he had heard, he replied, "In a few minutes my regiment will be here, but until that point, I want to see this baby he was so determined to kill."

Hudson was tired of being in the dark, "What's going on here, Todd? What's the problem with this guy?"

After bringing him up to speed while Cyprianus looked on in confusion at the unusual language, Hudson smiled, "Well, if that's all we can do, then let's take him to Jesus."

At that, Hudson turned and walked toward the light that was illuminating the night. He grinned as he led these people from various times, walks of life and ethnicities to see the true Light, the One that would be called Immanuel, or God With Us – One who would become the Light of the world.

Hudson turned toward the outskirts of the city, surrender etched in his drawn features. He hadn't really slept in days, and hunger gnawed him from the inside, competing with his aching limbs. All of his training told him to protect the timeline; to keep these people away from such a delicate scene as the birth of his Savior.

Just last week, he'd learned that obedience and trust go hand in hand. But the zealous desire to defend his Lord until his death warred with the truth that the same Lord was speaking to his heart. He need not be afraid. God is not mocked. Taking these enemies to the manger scene was the right thing to do, and with heavy steps, he continued his march.

Behind him, Todd comforted Aaliyah who held onto him tightly. But seeing the direction they were now headed the professor spoke, "Hey, man, you aren't really taking these crazy people to Jesus are you?"

"Yep," he answered curtly.

"That doesn't sound like the best idea." He shrugged off Aaliyah gently and grabbing Hudson by the shoulder, halting his progress, "We can't take them to the manger."

Hudson knocked his hand off, "We can, and we will," he retorted and started forward again. "It's the only answer."

Still stopped in his tracks, Todd glared at his back. He heard Cyprianus coming up close behind, leading Aurius at sword point. "Why is it the answer?"

Hudson stopped and turned around, "Because I know what we are supposed to do. I won't try to explain it because we've been through too much in the last few weeks to try to understand anything that happens. I just know that we can't control this any longer. Besides, we don't have the ability to stop an army, and from what he says," pointing to Cyprianus, "one is coming.

We can't stop Presidents, Kings, edicts, armies, soldiers, villains, and most importantly, God's will, so let's not try. Jesus is going to be born. That soldier can't stop it," he said, gesturing again toward the general, "That moron can't stop it," he spat toward Hughes, "Obviously we can't stop it by some arbitrary mistake we might make. So I'm taking everyone right to the action."

Irritated that they spoke a language foreign to him, Cyprianus shouted in Greek, "What are you discussing? Why are we heading out into the dark? I was told the baby was in Bethlehem."

Looking back at the general, Todd tried to explain, "We are discussing whether you are worthy to witness what we are leading you to. My friend is weary of fighting, and so am I. So do not fear, we are indeed taking you to the baby Aurius was going to kill."

"If this is a trick, I will kill your prophet, the moment I detect it," Cyprianus gritted through his teeth.

Todd smirked. Evidently, the seasoned warrior didn't know the threat really wasn't a bartering chip. He couldn't help but snort at the thought, "Our word is good. We will take you to the child."

Sword still in his back, Aurius marched forward in a kind of daze with Keren on his arm. It had only been a couple minutes since her announcement, and he finally found words to express his jumble of thoughts.

"You are pregnant?" Aurius asked gently of the woman at his side.

"Yes, Aurius, I am," she replied with a slight smile.

He next words came out haltingly, "You are sure it is mine?" he asked not wanting to impugn her reputation but needing to know the truth.

Understanding his meaning, the beautiful woman was not fazed by his comment. Touching his face, she spoke quietly, "Since I was given to you, I have been only yours. I would rather have taken my life than be with anyone else ever again." Palm cupped over the tiny swell at her middle she continued with joy, "Our child has been with us for three months now."

Stopping his forward motion, he felt the sword dig into his back. But still he bent to feel the bump that was his child. "Oh Keren, how could I be so blessed, after all I have done?"

She hugged him in spite of Cyprianus' scowl. "Did you hear me earlier? The Lord is giving back everything you lost. I know you will always miss your first family, but together we can be a family as well."

"Enough of this! Move," Cyprianus growled.

"Keren, we may be too far gone to ever be redeemed," Aurius whispered. He slumped a bit seeing his life in the light of this new reality.

"My love, God can pull us out from any hole we have put ourselves in. We must just trust him," Keren whispered back with a glow of confidence.

As the group continued to walk toward the source of the energy they had seen for the last several days, the lights began to take form and the pressure waves subsided. Up to this point, they had been miles away from the manger scene, and it was as if they were seeing comets in the sky. Now that they were less than a half a mile out, the lights grew in size and intensity and took on characteristics.

Each of the four Christ followers heard the singing become more pronounced and unified. It was like nothing they had ever heard but beautiful beyond description. The professor thought he heard instruments but knew the music had to come from the singing of the angels. The cumulative sound made a perfect symphony before God.

As they got closer, the movement of the lights around them became purer and more distinct. Activity above appeared to be quickened in a delighted dance of the angels, heralding to the world the birth of the Savior. Still, those closer to the earth and nearer the holy family stood quiet and worshipful in their places.

The beings closest to the small group allowed them to gape open-mouthed as they walked toward the culmination of lights in the distance. They could almost make out distinct traits in each one as they passed. The angels did not look like men, but they bore a strong resemblance to them yet were twice the size of a man.

These creations had no wings but appeared to be wearing a silky robe – at least that is what the travelers would have called it. The robe seemed to drop five feet below where their feet would be. The sleeves on the robe draped low as those who weren't traveling the skies had their hands outstretched in a form of praise.

Exhaustion slipped away from Hudson as new strength surged through him with every step. Todd lifted an arm around Aaliyah who smiled in return. And Keren beamed up at Aurius, watching him trying to decipher the miracle he saw on their faces. Cyprianus saw Aurius' confusion mirrored his own and felt an unwelcome kinship with the man he planned to kill.

They passed beings close by on occasion and noted how they stood at attention with heads bowed and faces radiant enough to burn one's eyes were it physical iridescence. The closer they came to the rocky formation ahead, the more accustomed to the sight they became.

The Senator saw nothing but rocks and darkness, but he knew something life-changing was ahead and slowed his pace, growing more nervous with each footfall. Years of self-service and deceit confronted him as he tried to avert his eyes from the knowledge that Jesus was alive and that he came to save souls. To save him. As the sword pressed into his spine he realized that he walked not to avoid the death behind him, but to understand the life before him.

Todd gripped Aaliyah's arm, wanting to talk through his new understanding of God and scripture, sin and redemption. His mind spun with new appreciation and knowledge of scripture. Suddenly, he recognized the place they walked as holy ground. With each step, he felt the need to lower himself, knowing this was a place for learning and not for teaching or preaching.

Hudson had seen pictures of angels in Bible School who looked like body builders wearing Roman soldier uniforms with large white wings. Amused at the comparison to these majestic yet unassuming creatures, he traveled past several more of them before he saw they had individual faces – more subtle than humans, but each distinct.

The creatures had hair of differing lengths and coloring. Even though they possessed a white-gold glow about them, he could make out unique eye colors and heard a different voice timbre from each. These entities were not copies of an original, but each created and formed as an individual.

Aaliyah started to mimic the song-like sound she heard from the angels. Todd knew she could not possibly know the song, yet her melody matched theirs perfectly. The realization came to him that while each of us is unique, all can match the beautiful song of praise that is pleasing to God. He bowed his head a moment in silent thanks for the gift of his true love as they moved forward.

Keren walked along beside Aurius whispering the visions she was seeing in his ear. She knew he could not see them because of his unbelief, so she prayed deeply in her heart as she did her best to make the reality of God's world apparent to him. He began to shake as she held him, so she tightened her grip and continued in prayer to her new-found Lord.

The general had also been around long enough to read people. He believed these four were definitely not acting. Aurius' lack of insight proved it. The man could lie better than anyone he had ever seen. Yes, they were experiencing a life-changing event, and he was left in the cold. He wondered again as to the reason behind it all.

Just hours before, he had heard the woman now walking ahead of him crying and praising to a God, speaking of visions in the heavens. He knew she wasn't delirious then or now. He grunted and pushed the prisoner forward.

Three quarters of a mile outside Bethlehem, Hudson suddenly disappeared from the group, entering the dark without a trace.

Everyone stopped and Todd spoke first in English, "Where did he go?" Knowing only John could understand him, he asked Aaliyah in Hebrew.

She answered, "He just melted into the blackness."

Todd looked to the left and the right and noticed that the wall of light created by the angelic beings was in an arc around a rocky outcropping just a thousand feet ahead.

"Stay here," he said, as he ran to the spot where Hudson last stood and then also disappeared.

Cyprianus was not a mystical man but knew there was more than magic going on. Maybe there was a God, and maybe they were on some type of holy ground. He stood nervously, suddenly feeling as insecure as a child.

When Todd reappeared, he found Hudson smiling next to him. "What do you think?"

The professor was amazed, "The angels' radiance is blocking out anything going on within the perimeter of the manger. I can see everything out," he said looking out at their entourage standing nervously just 100 feet beyond the barrier, "yet they can't see us. Why is that?"

"I'd say, they're giving Mary and Joseph some privacy," Hudson said.

Looking forward, Todd queried, "Where's the manger?"

"I'd guess it's beyond this mound here in front of us," he pointed at the circle of angelic covering. "That would be about the center of the sphere. Probably down in the valley."

"So what do we do?" Todd asked nervously.

"Hey, you're the scholar. I'd think you would have an answer for people about to see the Savior as a baby."

They laughed for the first time in a long while, but the immensity of their situation brought sobriety quickly. Thousands of years in the future they had followed Christ all of their lives. Now upon them had been bestowed the blessing of the beautiful scene of God entering the world as a baby – to one day conquer sin.

Todd took a deep breath and spoke, "Let me go get everyone."

Hudson nodded.

As the professor walked back through the barrier of light, he reappeared before the people. Aaliyah ran up to him and kissed him on the cheek in joy.

With a smile he turned toward the rest, "Come everyone, we are almost there." With a gesture, he turned with Aaliyah and disappeared through the barrier.

In the farthest position, Cyprianus saw that he could prevent the other two from entering. After only a moment's hesitation he came to understand his own need to finish this trek into the spiritual realm.

"Let us go," he pointed with his sword before sheathing it.

The prophet got to the spot where the others had disappeared and stopped. Looking at Keren he trembled, "I do not think I can go. I do not want to see what is ahead."

She encouraged him with a smile, "You must. You have been planning for this moment for a long time, and it is time to face the Savior."

Tears ran down his face as he and Keren walked through the barrier into the pitch black night. After their eyes adjusted to the light, they saw the other three up ahead. Cyprianus followed closely behind.

"Let's go, we're almost there," Hudson gestured in front.

Anticipation filled the air. Knowing they would soon see Him caused their hearts to rejoice. Although for Aurius and Cyprianus the feeling was not as comforting.

Aurius' rejection of God had set his life on a course for vengeance, while Cyprianus simply ignored him and lived for the day – hoping to die strong in battle. Each man knew that in a few minutes he would be confronted with the reality of the Living God. Neither denied any longer, but instead feared his own reaction to the Truth.

Cyprianus now walked alongside Aurius, each unaware of the other and lost in his own reflective thoughts.

Hudson, Todd and Aaliyah came to the edge of the mound first and looked down into the valley. Nestled several hundred feet before them, a small cave glowed with a tiny fire. Unlike the Sunday School pictures where a rough-hewn fence surrounded a small wooden building, this was a natural rock feature in the countryside near Bethlehem.

Small dirt embankments hemmed in the area in front of the cave, intending to corral the goats now sleeping in the valley below.

Inside the cave, they could see a man comforting a woman who held a newborn child. The firelight reflected the awe and relief on their happy faces as they warmed themselves in the fire's glow.

Not wanting to enter the scene, the small group on the hillside stopped, sitting on the ground in wonder.

When Aurius came to the edge of the mound an instant later, he took in the sight for himself and dropped to his knees. The place before him was not beautiful. The rocky formations were rough and sharp. The hills surrounding the cave were not picturesque and the ground was barren, dusty and dry, yet his heart knew it as the most divinely beautiful sight ever viewed by human eyes. Overcome with emotion, he bent his head and cried.

Keren placed her hand on his back to comfort him as Cyprianus stared at the scene from behind her.

"What am I seeing?" the general asked quietly.

Hearing his question, Todd came to his side. "You are witnessing the salvation for mankind."

"In those people down there? Kings are born in palaces not in an unprotected hillside," he retorted questioningly.

"If you are speaking about how man works, then you would be right. But God does not work like man. He chose to send his Son to earth as a poor commoner."

It was then that God, in his omnipresence, came and whispered the right words to both Keren and Todd as each laid out the plan of salvation in a time before the Spirit had come into the world or salvation had been secured through the cross. Todd smiled at the power and confidence he would have after this, knowing how God's plan has never failed in the past and will be fulfilled in the future – as if He has already been there, but is still with us now, and was with us in the past.

Keren whispered to Aurius, "My love, do you see how much God loves you? He is sending the Messiah, so that you can have life with him.

Our God is redeeming you and me. He has offered me a new life - with him and with you. He has given us a child and a hope and a future."

His face bent to the ground and she whispered over his shoulder, "You can have a new life. I know you have lost those you love, but you can have a family again, and live in peace. Do you want to choose to trust Christ as your Savior?" Aurius still trembled in silence. So she looked at the scene below and worshiped.

"Cyprianus, all you need to do is trust. Admit to God that you need him, and Christ will redeem your life," Todd spoke to the man who stared mutely into the night.

The general looked out at the glow of the fire below, "Could those Jewish peasants really have given birth to the Savior of mankind?"

Aaliyah turned toward him and took his hand, "Yes, they did. That Baby will grow to be a Man who will sacrifice Himself on our behalf. Do you want to spend eternity at peace with God?"

Aurius spoke quietly to Keren, "I have been so wrong. How could I have ever thought of killing the Savior? Lord, please forgive me," he said quietly through tears.

Pulling him from the ground, Keren whispered, "Look up."

Slowing straightening, he opened his eyes and immediately fell back at what they presented. "What is this? Where did all of these lights or beings or angels come from?"

"They have been here all along," she answered.

Unable to control himself any longer, Aurius outstretched his hands in praise. Looking up, he saw what looked like the eye of a hurricane of light spilling into the atmosphere. Everything was beautiful and quiet in the center, and Jesus was protected by legions of heavenly creatures.

Scanning the shaft of light back down, he made out thousands of individual beings all focused on worshiping the newborn King. His ears took in the music, and he felt the movements of the air around him as he praised along with them.

Behind him, Todd asked Cyprianus once again, "Do you want to trust God to redeem you from the death that separates you from Him?"

The general's eyes pierced through Todd. The professor could almost see his thoughts, the same thoughts he'd seen in countless others who did not hear God's call or choose to follow. This was a question Cyprianus had to wrestle with on his own.

"Everyone," the general said with focus, awakening them to the reality of their situation. "You only have a few minutes before an army of soldiers will be in Bethlehem. If they make it that far before you leave, you will be caught."

Hudson looked on not sure what was being said.

"I will give you time to get away and ensure my men do not head your direction. This Baby will be protected, at least tonight."

"What's he saying?" Hudson asked Todd.

"Please leave now. I never found you. Now escape before the sun comes up," Cyprianus, looked at the soft orange glimmer of morning on the horizon. "Please go. Quickly," he said in a way that made everyone move.

Todd pulled Hudson away from the edge. Seeing John had been transformed, they knew he would no longer be a problem.

Todd and Aaliyah led the group down the hill, arm in arm with a true peace about them. Keren held onto John and he held her head to his chest. But Cyprianus still stood motionless with his focus on the manger.

Hudson followed them, amazed. Again, the Lord had seen them through an impossible mission. He had come through time to stop a man bent on changing the world and now that man had accepted Jesus – the person he originally wanted to kill. They had found Aaliyah's mother and changed her fate, met a Roman general wrestling with the decision of a lifetime, and were now free to head back to the sphere and go home. Could God work it out any better?

But then Hudson stood motionless. The cold emptiness of fear rising in his throat.

Todd looked back, "Hudson, let's get out of here. The soldiers will be here soon."

He looked up and exhaled, defeat once again mingling with exhaustion, "We can't leave. The sphere is broken."

"I forgot," Todd said. "How are we going to fix it?"

"What do you mean, fix it? The sapphire lens is broken," Hudson responded in frustration.

Everyone else turned to watch the exchange only Aurius could understand.

"It shattered. There's no fixing it. We need another one," he placed his hands on his hips.

"Does it have to be polished smooth? We can never make that happen with 1st century technology."

Hudson started to pace, "No, huh-uh. It doesn't need to be polished. We just need the stone. Once the laser heats up, it will check for the proper magnification. If it doesn't find it, the machine heats the stone to alter its shape until the proper amplification is reached."

"So we just need any old sapphire?" Todd said, feeling better.

"Yes. The reactor in the sphere heats up causing the vehicle to glow. Once that happens, the laser is magnified through the lens. That magnified beam causes a small rip in space which allows the vehicle to travel. At least that's how Dr. Keith tried to explain it to me.

Diamonds were his first choice, but the larger ones were cost prohibitive. Sapphires are next on the *Mohs* hardness scale."

"I guess they aren't quite hard enough, because the one we had cracked."

Senator Hughes approached the two. "What's the problem?"

Todd cleared his throat, "We need a sapphire."

"What? For the machine? I thought the thing ran on diamonds."

"You weren't quite as 'in the know' as you thought you were," Hudson laughed sarcastically. "No, Dr. Keith switched to sapphires. The vehicle's broken, and we need a large sapphire to fix it."

Aaliyah and Keren wandered over and asked Aurius to explain. In Greek, he detailed that they needed a sapphire to help their 'wagon' get home. The women had never heard the word 'sapphire' before and looked to Todd for an explanation.

Todd tried to rack his brain, "What was it called, what was it called?"

"What are you asking?" Hudson questioned.

"The word sapphire may not have been used around here. During these times they might have called it something else. "Lapis lazuli, yeah that's it, lapis lazuli!"

Keren immediately spoke out, "I know of this stone. Herod has many."

Afraid of her answer, Todd asked her, "Where?"

"The King has an excess of the blue rocks in his palaces."

Hudson knew the answer was bad news, "She didn't say that the King has some did she?"

"Of course, anything else would be too easy," Todd laughed. "You're beginning to speak Greek very well."

"Yeah, the immersion method seems to be working for me," Hudson's eyes rolled involuntarily.

"The priests also have some." Keren interjected.

Jumping in, Aurius took over, "What priests Keren?"

"The priests for the temple Saturn. He is believed to be the god of the sky. Isn't that funny?" She smiled at Aaliyah, still a mother unaware of her daughter. "Only Jesus is the God of the sky and everything else." They embraced, still aglow with the events of the night.

Todd stared at the women, amazed at how much the ladies looked alike. Regaining his focus he redirected the conversation "I agree with you Keren. Jesus is God and there is no other. What about where we can find the blue rock?"

"Yes, Keren, what about Saturn?" Senator Hughes asked.

"He is a minor god, but there is a temple to him for the Romans on the east side of Jerusalem. I have been told the inside is covered in the blue stone. There is some on the walls and on bowls and everywhere. They acquire it from lands in the east."

"Hudson, it looks like we can find some sapphire, and it isn't very far from here. What do you think about breaking into a Roman temple for our next trick?"

Looking up he noticed the morning sun rising steadily over the horizon, "We better hurry before everyone comes for noon services, if they do that kind of thing."

"I don't think they have noon services, but I know what you mean."

"Let's get back to our horses, and then Keren can lead us there," Hudson said.

"Keren, can you get us to the temple?"

She gripped Aaliyah's hand and smiled, "Of course."

Hudson saw her smile, "I'll take her words to be a yes. Let's go west to Jerusalem."

—

Cyprianus took several minutes of contemplation before he left the mound site. He went through the words of the man who explained the destiny of the baby in the manger and looked back. Could that child, now lying in a bundle of hay be the God of the universe? Why would a great God want his son to lie in the feeding-box, when even the general's child had a bed and warm blankets? Why would he allow him to rest with common animals and be chased by armies? It just didn't make sense.

In the east the sun began to brighten the trunks of the trees, causing light to blend with shadow in so many shades of the dawn. He sighed heavily – his time was up. Wanting to ensure his troops got nowhere near this area; he hurried back to Bethlehem and found his horse. The philosophizing would have to wait for another day.

Trotting through the awakening town, Cyprianus found his men awaiting him on the outskirts. Alexandrus arrived and greeted the general.

"General Sir, we are prepared to carry out your orders," he slapped his chest.

"Commander, I have already been house to house and have found nothing."

"Sir, I thought you believed the escaped prisoners to be here." Alexandrus frowned.

"Do not question me."

"Yes sir."

"From what I heard, they were here but have left. I was told they headed west, and that is where we need to go."

"Sir, there are already men in Jerusalem. Should we not search this area, possibly heading east?" Alexandrus asked in confusion.

"No, we head west, if we have a chance of finding them, it will be toward Jerusalem."

"Yes sir."

"Quickly search this area, and I am heading off toward Jerusalem."

Alexandrus saluted and organized his men into a house to house and street to street search. Seeing the busyness of the military, Cyprianus left to the west.

—

It took a while for the travelers to find their horses. Once they did, they mounted up quickly and sped toward Jerusalem.

Jerusalem, Jewish city though it was, had many pagan temples within its borders, most of them relegated to the outskirts of the city – a fact that encouraged Hudson and Todd in their current exhausted state.

With John and Keren on one horse and Todd and Aaliyah on another, the agent yelled over at the professor, "What do you think we will get into when we get to the temple?"

"I believe it should be a pretty easy job. From what I remember, the Roman god Saturn is the Greek god Kronos. Kronos is known as the god of time and the harvest and often represented with a scythe. Frequently, you see sculptures of him holding a baby."

"Why would he do that?" Hudson asked trying to not out-pace the other horses carrying two riders.

"The people would implore Saturn to continue time so they would offer him the most precious things they had – generally their own children. Upon receiving the babies, he would supposedly devour them."

"Wow, what a nice guy."

"It was just less than 100 years ago in this time," pointing down, "that the state of Rome outlawed the sacrificing of children to Saturn. So, yeah, he's a bad guy."

Hudson looked over at the professor.

"In fact, he's often thought of as one of the worst of the gods. During times of peril or famine, some of the most influential families would sacrifice their children often numbering in the hundreds. There are cults who, even in our time, still worship him, often the satanic type."

"Do you think we'll be in a mess or will find a large force to go up against?"

"No, he's worshiped at certain times of the year and this isn't one of them. We should be able to get in and out pretty quickly."

"I hope you're right. I pray your creepy story isn't a foreshadowing of things to come."

"Me too."

The group journeyed for another fifteen minutes before they started to see the city. Being less than a mile square, the ancient walled city was reported to hold up to 35,000 inhabitants which meant even though the travelers were still a mile out, and it was just past daybreak, many people were up and active. Slaves were traveling to work sites. Business owners were bringing out their wares. Children were already playing while others milked goats or slaughtered animals. Trying to get in and out of the ancient metropolis without being noticed would not be an option.

Slowing their horses to a trot as they began encountering pull carts and walkers, Hudson yelled back at Hughes, "John, get Keren up here."

Bringing his horse up alongside, he asked, "What is it?"

"You are in the lead, have Keren get us to the temple."

The senator spoke with Keren, and she pointed toward the south. His horse sped off in that direction with the others in tow.

Another ten minutes of riding and the group had rounded the south end of the main walls of Jerusalem. Entering the Dung Gate, they dismounted and left their horses in a corral hoping to see them again very soon.

Everyone straightened their various outfits and looked at each other hoping to be as inconspicuous as possible. Senator Hughes was a wanted outlaw and his garish clothing representing the political elite would be easy to spot. Aaliyah was part Jew dressed as a Roman. Todd and Hudson were costumed as Roman soldiers.

It would take very little to blow their cover.

Of the group, only Keren had the opportunity to walk away without question. Everyone tried to move with purpose. Todd took the lead with Keren, and Hudson rounding out the group at the back.

Beginning their walk, they passed the Pool of Siloam. Todd was once again amazed to have been given the opportunity to see Jerusalem at the time of Jesus' birth and death. He knew he had many books to write in the future, so he engraved every sight, sound, and smell into his memory.

Keren spoke quietly to the professor, "The temple is in the Lower City, not far from here."

Aaliyah jumped in, "The Lower City – that is where I lived."

Her mother asked, "Where do you live now?"

Instantly Aaliyah was taken aback without knowledge of how to answer.

Her man jumped in with a crooked smile, "She is now with me, and we are relocating to another country."

The woman smiled back at the odd answer. "Are you to be married?"

Todd looked at Aaliyah then back at Keren, "Uh, yes. I think so." He looked at Aaliyah, "I would love to have her as my wife, if she will take me as her husband."

The young woman stared at him with tears in her eyes, "Yes, oh yes Todd, I would love to be your wife." Her face glowed a dozen shades of joy, and she hugged him right in the middle of the busy and bustling street.

Many looked on because of the awkward level of affection that was being given to a Roman officer, but knew better than to question or interfere, and so went back to their work with a shake of the head.

"What's going on here?" Hudson asked.

"It looks like I just asked Aaliyah to marry me."

"Right here, right now. You couldn't wait until we got somewhere a little more appropriate. You had to ask her here in front of the slaughter house and the goat pen."

Laughing at Aaliyah still hugging on him he answered back, "There was a certain ambiance about it."

Keren smiled and grabbed the young woman by the hand. "I am so excited for you. You will be very happy."

"Okay, people, I know this is a very special moment, but we need to get on with the task at hand," Hudson said trying to get everyone moving.

"Yeah, you're right, Hudson. I would have loved to have asked Aaliyah at a better time – and perhaps one day soon I will – but now, we need to go."

Keren smiled at Aaliyah who beamed with pride and excitement, "Come, it is this way."

After passing through several streets filled with houses and tradesman, they saw the building dedicated to the god Saturn. It was a simple white limestone structure in the shape of a square, twenty feet high by twenty feet wide. Two columns straddled each side of the one and only entry. No one seemed to be in or around the open structure.

"Evidently, Romans like quick and easy access to their god. One open door and no windows. What do you think?" Hudson asked Todd.

"It looks quiet."

"Let me go up and peek inside. Keep everyone here," the agent said as he headed toward the building.

It took only a few seconds for him to get to the entrance, scan inside and get back.

"Everything is covered in blue. There are decorations on the walls made out of sapphire and even miniature gods in the corners," he relayed to his partner.

"Great, let's get in there and get some."

Senator Hughes walked over and joined the conversation. "If everything we need is in there then why are we here talking?"

Pointing over to the door of the temple, Hudson said, "That's why we can't go in there."

A soldier appeared in the doorway, the men looked at Hudson.

With his hands on his hips, "There are four more in there just like him." The agent sighed for a second, "It feels like a Roman soldier convention."

"Why, on earth, would they be in there today of all days?" Todd stuttered.

"Yeah, I don't know. But they're in there, and we need them gone."

"Can we cause a diversion of some kind?" Hughes asked.

Hudson exhaled and looked at him. "Hughes, you still want to kill Jesus?"

Answering back he turned his face to the ground, "Men, I was so wrong. I may never know why God took my wife and daughter, but he has given me a new start in Keren and our child." He tightened his grip on the woman beside him. "To answer your question, I was wrong and the Lord forgave me. Now I will do what I can to share Christ's story."

"Well, that's a good change," the professor added with a smile. "It doesn't help us with our current situation, but kind of lightens the mood," he said, slapping the senator on the back and causing a puff of dust. "You need a bath."

"We all need a bath," Hudson added. "John, what kind of diversion were you referring to?"

Speaking to Keren, he explained the plan, and she nodded in agreement.

"Hudson, give me a few minutes."

"What's he going to do?" Todd asked his partner.

"I think when you see the conflagration you'll know what to do," he smiled.

"Fire? Let's get out of the way so we aren't seen."

"Good idea," he affirmed.

Senator Hughes walked several streets over and found a pen of sheep filled with straw. Casing the area, he didn't see anyone around and so opened the rough-hewn fence allowing the dirty white puff balls to escape.

Entering the corral, he found the corner where a small rock circle sheltered the remaining embers of a fire. A handful of hay held to the flame ignited quickly and he tossed it into a large pile against the makeshift wall of the pen.

The mound of hay must have been intended for the animal's next meal, but once the senator was sure the pile would light, he left the corral and moved quietly through another street back to the area of the temple.

Seeing smoke a block over, Hudson whispered, "I think he was successful."

Looking in the direction of the smoke, Todd told Keren to go. She immediately ran to the doorway of the temple and yelled, "Pur! Pur!" *Fire! Fire!*

Pointing in the direction of the smoke the woman continued to scream when the leader on the front porch called the other soldiers out to investigate the problem.

A frantic Keren approached the Roman still standing near the temple.

"There's a fire over here! Would you please condescend to help us?" With a womanly look of despair on her face, her lithe body led him away from the temple until she saw Aurius appear from behind a building to her right. Standing back she allowed the soldier to go ahead of her while she doubled back to the limestone structure.

When the last soldier turned the corner heading into the smoke, Todd and Hudson ran from around the building they were hiding behind and into the temple. Passing through the large limestone entry, they found a square room with nothing more than granite walls and an altar at the front.

The walls were very simple and had a star made of rough sapphire on one and a mosaic of the god Saturn on the other. At the front were several Corinthian columns holding a granite slab. An urn currently burning with incense and several miniature statues rested upon it.

Each statue was approximately one foot in height and showed the demi-god in different poses – him holding a sickle and another with him holding the sun.

The time travelers looked at each other and with the same idea smiled, "Will this work?" Todd asked.

"I think this will do just fine, and we can cause a little disruption in Saturn worship at the same time," Hudson laughed.

With almost choreographed movement, the men each picked up a statue, banged it on the side of the granite slab about the position of its neck and broke the sapphire heads from them.

"That felt good," Todd smiled.

Feeling the weight in his hand and tossing it up and down he agreed, "I think the sphere can heat this piece into a nice lens. But we'll take them both just in case."

The professor picked up the head in his hands and held it before his face.

"Alas, poor Yorick! I knew him, Horatio, a fellow of infinite jest, of most excellent fancy. He hath bore me on his back a thousand times, and now how abhorred in my imagination it is."

"Hamlet is good, but I think a little Julius Caesar would work better here, 'He is a dreamer, let us leave him!' So can we go now?"

"Hey, you're not leaving me."

"If you want to stay and finish your play, there may be some soldiers who'd enjoy it, but I've got to get home."

"Me too," the professor added.

They started for the exit.

Todd finished the banter, "When did you study Shakespeare?"

"Do you think I just sit around watching shoot-em-up movies?"

"Well, yeah, actually, I do."

Both men laughed as they ran from the door.

Putting the sapphire heads into their satchels, they found the other three travelers in a group in the middle of the street along with other onlookers watching the soldiers help put out the blaze. Still active, but under containment, the fire had taken over the fence and adjacent building. People were running in all directions looking for buckets and water with which to douse the flame.

Smoke began filling the streets as Hudson caught up to the group. "It's time to get out of here."

Aurius relayed the words in Greek, not that the women needed a translation.

Passing through narrow streets with people and animals running in every direction slowed their progress, but they methodically continued until they were stopped by a soldier on horseback.

"Men, help with the fire," Dritus commanded to the apparent soldiers before him running the wrong direction.

Trying to act as if they didn't see him, Todd and Hudson continued on.

"Soldiers, help with the fire," The commander barked, trying to turn his large steed toward them in the small street.

The group didn't stop their forward progress.

"Soldiers, stop your motion now," Dritus pulled his sword.

Todd and Hudson knew there was nothing they could do but face the man threatening them.

Seeing the group, he spotted Aurius from their encounter at the Citadel just a day earlier. He noticed they were with two women, and then remembered that two men dressed as Roman soldiers were also with the prophet. These five had brought this entire operation on them.

Seeing the recollection in the Dritus' eyes, Todd ran behind his horse avoiding the ancient steel blade as the soldier sliced at him. Hudson drew the man's attention as the professor slapped the back of the animal as hard as he could.

Instantly, the horse reared back on its hind legs throwing the large military leader to the ground. With the streets full of people running in all directions, the two men grabbed the dazed soldier and shoved him into a nearby window.

The few seconds were all they needed to run for their lives to the corral where they left their horses earlier.

Dritus was quickly up and back through the front door of the house when he spotted the direction they were heading. His horse had run several streets in the wrong direction, but he managed to find it quickly. Mounting it, he noticed the soldiers who were in the temple earlier.

"Get all of the men you can find and head for the Dung Gate. You are looking for two men impersonating Roman soldiers, two women and a politician. Do you understand?"

"Yes sir," the men agreed in unison.

He turned the animal and headed back toward the exit of the ancient city.

"Out of the way!" Dritus yelled with his sword in the air.

The streets filled with people helping with the fire cleared at his command, leaving a small opening for the massive steed to move.

He couldn't believe he had been so easily removed from his horse. His embarrassment would be the criminal's downfall.

The travelers, finally finding the exit where they left their horses, mounted up as the owner of the corral jogged over.

Yelling in Hebrew, he gestured to Todd and toward the horses.

"What does he want?" Hudson yelled.

"He wants payment."

Without prompting Aaliyah dismounted and began chattering disgustedly at the man. He let them go.

"What did she say?" the agent asked.

"She let him have it," Todd smiled. "She said that he didn't deserve payment for his lack of care of our animals. If he wanted to be paid, he would do a better job next time."

She grinned as Hudson started for the fence, finding Dritus blocking their exit.

"You will go no farther," the man called.

Hudson and Todd pulled their swords.

"You will move aside or this will be your last day." Todd spoke plainly.

Knowing the high ranking military leader most likely had soldiers running from every direction of Jerusalem to help him, Hudson guessed there wasn't much time. He pulled a water bucket from a fence post and threw it at the soldier. With just enough of a diversion he surged his horse past the man and pulled the neck of his armor from behind, dropping his own sword in the process.

Off balance Dritus gripped the reigns as his horse reared up.

Todd and Aaliyah surged forward. The professor pulled on the man's saddle from the other direction while Aaliyah kicked at the horse with her foot, irritating it further.

The professor continued to pull on the seasoned warrior from one side while Hudson grabbed his sword from the other with both arms ripping it from his tight grip. The agent threw the weapon to the ground and leaped on the man causing both to fall to the earth in a heap below Todd's animal.

Wrestling on the ground, the men punched and grabbed hoping to get the upper hand until Hudson found Dritus' sword. The reflection of the morning sun had glinted off it into his eyes, revealing its location behind a water container. Extracting himself from Dritus' grip he ran into the light and grabbed it. Before the soldier knew what had happened, Hudson had pointed it at the man who immediately knew he had no other recourse.

Todd speaking from his horse to the soldier with his arms up, "We do not want to hurt you, we just want to leave."

Hudson kept the sword pointed at the irate military leader.

"Let us go, and no one will get hurt," the professor continued.

With a nod from the commander, he knew the answer was yes.

Hudson got back on his horse, sheathed Dritus' sword, and dropped his head in respect to the man doing his job.

All five riders pushed hard through the last few streets as Dritus once again found his horse and mounted it.

Turning the large animal around, he followed the other three horses to the exit.

With Hudson in the lead, they sped through the large arch exit and out into the slums that encompassed the expanse outside of the walls.

Dritus stopped his horse at the exit knowing he couldn't follow them on his own and watched the riders from his elevated position at the wall of the ancient city. He saw them speed away from the exit and through the side streets in and out of crowds. At several points they found a dead end, but quickly turned around to discover another avenue out of the maze that was the poverty area of Jerusalem.

The escaped prisoners eventually reached the edge of the inhabited area. After passing through several valleys, they made it to open land where the group accessed a road away from the city. At that they took a direct shot to the northeast.

The troops arrived at the gate and approached the commander who was quiet in thought.

"Sir, we are here and ready for your instructions," the young soldier said as his men filed in behind him.

"Find the rest of the regiment. Then have everyone appropriate horses." He continued to stare off into the distance until all he could see was the dust from the people who had gotten away from him just a few minutes earlier.

Finishing his statement, "We have to head back into the desert."

Knowing that was his last command, the young leader yelled a few instructions and the men ran off in all directions with the expectation to meet back at their current position within twenty minutes.

Dritus continued his stare, "We will meet again. Next time you will not get away."

He turned his horse and trotted back into the walled city. Finding the sword from the man who had just taken his, he got off of his animal and picked it up. Vengeance boiled within him.

Twirling the hilt in his hand, he sheathed it at his side. "I will give this sword back to him by way of his gut."

He remounted his animal, breathed a few deep breaths and rode quietly into the city.

Cyprianus' and Alexandrus' troops marched through the south entrance of Jerusalem to find an army prepared for battle. Several regiments had been assembled and all were on horseback; something that hardly ever happened.

"What is going on?" the General barked finding so many soldiers at the ready.

Dritus rode through the massive arch entrance to meet him, "Sir, the prisoner, prophet, men dressed as soldiers, and another woman were here."

Taken aback he exclaimed, "What do you mean, they were here?"

"Just that sir, they jumped me and left."

Getting off of his horse, he tried to make sense of what had happened. The people who had taken him to the manger were supposed to be heading east out of the area and instead did the very opposite. *Why would they go west to Jerusalem?* he thought. *They arrived from the east and should have headed east.*

The General wiped a hand over his eyes, "Tell me what happened."

Dritus lowered from his horse. "Sir, they started a fire as a diversion."

"A fire?" he said confused.

"Yes sir, they started a fire to apparently get my men out of the Saturnian temple."

"Why would they want you out of Saturn's temple?"

"We cannot make much sense of it either, but they did this." He motioned to one of his men to bring the broken statues forward. After handing them to the commander he said, "For some reason they desecrated the shrine."

Looking at the headless figures, "They broke their heads off?"

"Yes, that is all of the damage we could find. They then tried to leave town, but I recognized them and attempted to stop them."

Cyprianus looked flat-faced at the man.

"Well, sir, they got away. It was five against one."

"You mean, two men, two women, and an old man. Which way did they leave?" the General asked taking one of the figurines.

"Sir, they left to the northeast."

The General walked through the Dung Gate and looked out over the landscape of Israel. From the hilltop city of Jerusalem he was able to see past the Dead Sea. *Why would you force me into this?* he thought.

"Sir, I have prepared the men. We are ready to follow the traitors to the ends of the earth," Dritus announced. "The men have horses and water."

With reluctance he looked at the leader, "You have done well, Dritus. It is regretful that they got away, but you have prepared adequately. This will not show on your record."

"Thank you sir," the man said with his head toward the ground.

Cyprianus looked toward the horizon and lamented his situation. He had done everything he could to allow the travelers to leave without incident. Now they forced his position.

Knowing his hands were tied, he turned to address Dritus, "Prepare the men, we leave immediately."

"Yes sir." Turning, the commander mounted his horse and barked at the hundred riders, "We ride for Caesar." He lifted his sword into the air and led them through the arch toward the east.

Cyprianus saluted to the men as they departed, before mounting his horse.

With the memory of the stirring scene in the countryside and the words of his acquaintances still on his head he spoke out loud, "God, if you are there, I need you now." He looked to the bright noon sky, "It is time to show yourself, or those people who follow you so whole-heartedly will die."

Lowering his head, he kicked the steed, forcing it through the exit.

—

The travelers drove the horses hard for over an hour before they stopped in Jericho for a break. Being once again in a foreign 1st century town they tried to get their bearings and find a place to get something to eat. The sun was blazing high overhead and they would need a rest from the noonday heat.

After finding a woman baking bread in an outdoor oven, Aaliyah was able to trade her nice outer garment for several small loaves of bread, some dates and a large bowl of cooked lentils. They each anticipated the moment when they could eat and rest.

Knowing the horses could not make the next stretch of the trip without a full day's rest; they took their food and walked the animals to a nearby corral. Aurius traded one of Hudson's satchels, Todd's sword and the horses for three new horses. The animals were much older and the owner was more than happy to make the trade. Yet as the new owners looked at the animals that would likely be put down – hooves made into glue – in the 21st century, they knew they only had 10 miles to their final destination. At that point the horses would be free to live out their lives in peace, and more than likely the original owner would find and sell them again.

Before leaving the area the five weary people sat down in the corral and ate. They drank their fill of water meant for horses and just talked. For the first time in the mission there was nothing but anticipation of the future. They weren't chasing anyone, and no one raced at their heels.

The timeline for the most part was unhurt and each of them had grown in their walk with the Lord or for the first time truly understood who he was and what he had for them. There was a general overall peace among the five.

Todd gazed at his Aaliyah with excitement for the future. Knowing the woman at his side was now his fiancé; the world couldn't get much better. Just a week earlier he was the consummate bachelor, and now he had the most beautiful and kind woman to share his life with. He laughed out loud.

Aaliyah who only weeks earlier was living by herself, barely surviving, now had a future husband who loved her. She knew Todd would always be by her side to love and protect her. They would grow old together, raising a family who would follow the Lord. For all of this and more she had a deep sense of peace.

Aurius sat chewing on the bread, no longer feeling a deep-seated hatred. Instead his heart filled with peace and hope for the first time in a decade. With his new family sitting next to him, he hugged Keren. The Lord was good after all and did have his best at heart. He patted Keren's middle then sat back against the post and closed his eyes in prayer.

Keren watched him rest and knew he had given up that dark spot he had been carrying for so many years, and that it was now filled with the love of God. The former palace concubine who just a week earlier had no future, now had a loving fiancé and child on the way. The Lord had revealed himself to her in miraculous ways, and for that she would never know how to repay him for his goodness. She determined herself to share God's message to everyone with whom she had the opportunity. Possibly the woman could work her way back into her family's life and enlighten them on the Messiah, and how he had come to earth. The idea made her smile and she backed into Aurius as he put his arm around her.

Hudson was exhausted. Having not really rested in days and living on old bread and bits of goat jerky he found hanging outside of houses, he collapsed. He looked around and was amazed at how the Lord had provided the way, time and again.

His buddy Todd finding a wife in the 1st century was beyond his mind's capability to understand, but then to see the man they had chased through time now a devoted Christ-follower and marrying the mother of

Todd's future wife made him stop trying to think through the paradoxes. His attention went to how he missed his beautiful wife and children. He fell asleep thinking of how he would see them in just a few hours.

—

Dritus drove the soldiers hard and they stopped and regrouped a few miles north of Jericho in Machaerus. The soldier knew where the runaways were heading and could think of nothing more than making right the wrong that had occurred earlier.

In all of his years as a soldier, no one had gotten the best of him, and yet these men with obviously no military training made him look like a bumbling fool. The only thing redeeming about what had happened was that it didn't occur in front of his men. If it had he would most likely not have retained his rank and would be cleaning up after the horses right now. He would have his revenge.

Cyprianus allowed Dritus to lead the expedition which would have normally been his to command. He was sore, tired, and overflowing with thoughts. *Could the baby really be the Messiah?* he asked himself. The scene was so simple, yet everyone around was profoundly changed by the experience. They heard sounds, saw sights, felt the presence of beings and were filled with emotion. He had none of it.

It was imperative he get his thoughts back on the mission –the one he didn't want to complete.

"Sir, we must leave," Dritus spoke with conviction, waking him from his thoughts.

"We have only been here a few minutes," Cyprianus answered back.

"Yes, I know but we have no time to waste. We must catch up with the criminals."

"Dritus, you know these animals must rest," he pointed to the horses covered in sweat, "and the men could also use a break."

"We can push them a little harder. We can be ready any time."

Knowing Dritus desired some payback, he tried calming him. "We will catch up with them soon enough, but we cannot kill a hundred horses or hurt these men in the process. The cost is too great.

We will rest for several hours. Ensure all of the animals are fed and watered and that the men have something to eat." Looking up he finished his thought, "When the sun drops below its zenith we will start off again, and then will find the people we are searching for," Cyprianus finished flatly.

With reluctance the commander replied, "Yes sir," and walked off to find the necessary provisions.

Knowing Dritus was a caged lion, Cyprianus feared for the travelers if his leader ever found them. He walked his horse slowly to a trough and allowed it to drink.

—

Hudson took in the scene before him. Washington D.C. did not look as it had before. The monuments were still there, such as the Lincoln and the Washington. The Capital building hadn't changed and neither had the White House, but as he stood in the middle of the Mall, he saw statues that weren't there previously.

Looking around, the beauty that was the granite-covered buildings took on more of a Greek look. In fact, many of the edifices appeared to reflect the majesty of Rome in its day. Although the city had originally been designed in the Greco-Roman style to intimidate dignitaries from other countries the feel was no longer strong but dark.

Walking around, he looked down upon the reflecting pool in front of the Lincoln Memorial and noticed Greek statues lining both sides. From his perch at the Washington Monument he gazed toward the Capital to see new pools in place of the green where people would play soccer or baseball. Statues lined these as well.

Squinting into the sun, he took in the majesty of the Capitol and looked to the top of its dome. Something wasn't right. He walked a few feet closer and squinted his eyes tighter. The statue on top was different.

The statue called "Freedom" resembled a woman – twenty feet tall – with a sword and a helmet. The form looked familiar, but now it was a man.

His eyes dropped back to the Mall to find the other figures lining the pools. They were all of one person. He ran from the Washington Monument as fast as he could. His mind racing at what he was seeing. Recognition needled him with no satisfaction. More and more as he ran closer and closer, he found figures in varied poses and depicting various scenes.

Some were of the Roman type where the man was dressed in a toga as if addressing the senate. Many were of the man hunting and conquering one animal or another. Some were of the person in a suit standing strong and in command.

Even though he was out of breath, he still ran. Getting closer and closer the face on the figures began to come into view. It was definitely a person he had seen before. Something had happened. Something had changed, and he was the cause.

Finally making it to the base of the closest statue, he looked up and fell to his knees. "Why, oh God, why?" he yelled.

Looking around he saw the sky darken and began hearing words in his ears chanting, "You have failed. You never really had a chance in the first place. You have failed."

Over and over again came the phrase, "You have failed."

Hudson yelled out, "Stop! Stop it, I am only a man. Stop…"

Todd shook him from his slumber, "Hudson! Wake up. What's going on? Hudson!"

The agent jumped from his position, sweat dripping from his face and eyes wild with disillusionment as the other four watched in concern.

Still unsure of himself he shook his head to clear away the vision and voice, "What happened? What's going on?" he mumbled.

"You were yelling for something to stop. Did you have a bad dream?" Todd asked concerned for his weary partner.

"Yeah, must have. I'm just really tired. That's got to be what it is. How long have I been out?"

"I'd say several hours," Aurius added.

Still unsure of reality he finally recognized that the sun had dropped, making the time around four in the afternoon.

"We need to go. We need some light to fix the lens." With a warm smile, Hudson looked around, "Let's get home."

The group rose from the stall floor and gathered what was left of their things. They found their horses and walked them out. After ensuring the skins were full of water and they had the satchels containing the sapphire heads, Todd looked over at his partner. "You ready?"

Still waking from the dream that seemed more real than imaginary, Hudson answered unsteadily, "I don't know if I have a choice." Thinking a second, he answered honestly, "Todd, I'm ready to get back to my wife and kids."

"I bet you are." Looking off to the northeast, Todd declared "Well lead us, O Captain, my Captain."

With a smile, he acknowledged them all, "Friends, we have come a long way, but it's time for all of us to get home."

The people smiled, even the ladies who didn't know what was being said.

"Let's head out," he said. And with a hand forward he nudged his horse onward and led them from the city of Jericho. The next stop would be the sphere.

After a hard two-hour ride the travelers made it to the site of the sphere just as the sun behind them glowed the burnished orange of evening. Darkness would descend within the hour, so there wasn't time to waste repairing the damaged vehicle.

Hudson dismounted first from his tired horse and walked around the capsule. "Todd, would you run out a distance and check the area?"

"Sure," the professor replied as he and Aaliyah sped off to ensure their departure would be without incident.

John and Keren arrived at the location last and Keren pointed and began speaking uncontrollably, astonished at the giant pearl in the middle of the dessert.

Dropping from his horse, and helping the first century woman down, Senator Hughes, held her hand and sat on a rock next to the machine. Knowing he was about to offer information that may be difficult to comprehend, he prayed the explanation would not cause a division between the two. As praying was still new to him, he closed his eyes in an embarrassing moment and quickly uttered, "Please help me."

He took a few minutes and tried to explain what she was seeing beginning with his real identity. Detailing how his people had great understanding and the ability to travel through time proved easier than he thought with a woman still in the era of mythological belief. American cynicism would have been more difficult to overcome.

Next he reminded her of his mission, and how his own foolish selfishness had nearly cost him his life.

"Keren," he told her quietly, "I meant the travel to ancient Israel to be for evil, but God had plans for my good, for our good. I met you. I have a second chance in life. A new family and hope for the future."

Still holding Keren's hand he said, "Keren, I love you. I want to spend the rest of my life with you and with my child."

With a smile, she looked into his eyes, "I love you Aurius, and I will indeed spend the rest of my life with you."

"Keren, my name is John."

She was unfazed, "I love you, John."

They held each other and looked off into the sunset as Hudson made his last tweaks to the underside of the vehicle.

Todd and Aaliyah had arrived from their perimeter check when they both dismounted. "How does it look?"

As the agent pressed his hand onto the side of the machine, the top of the sphere began to rise with a pop and a hiss.

Keren looked over and John held her tightly to reassure her that everything was going to be alright.

"I'd say everything is fine. No one seems to have been here," he answered Todd.

Each man lifted the satchels containing the sapphire heads from their horses, they both walked back toward the vehicle.

Pulling his from the sack, he looked at Todd, "Do you have any great lines to quote before I see if this is going to work?"

"Nah, Shakespeare is about as good as it gets for holding a head in your hand and I've already used him," the professor laughed.

"Okay, just wanted to ensure that was all out of your system."

Tucking the head from the sack under his arm, Todd reaffirmed him on that point, "Don't worry, if anything comes to mind I still have one head left."

"Super, we'll look forward to it."

The levels of light in the sky dropped to a rosy-orange hue. Unable to see much of the horizon due to the hills surrounding them, they were amazed at the beauty of the desert and Israel as a whole.

With the temperatures lowering, Hudson wished for a hoodie instead of armor as he crawled under the machine, "There's an opening just over here, that if I can get to it I can place the new stone in it and everything should be fine," he strained. Stretching his farthest he released a pent-up breath, "I can't seem to get to the opening."

"What do you mean? You were able to take the lens out earlier," Todd reminded him.

Crawling out from under the machine and dusting himself off, he thought through that.

"Sure. The stone is placed in one place and after it is heated, it moves into position. That firing chamber is farther up within the mechanism, and I can't get to it."

"Can we lift it?" the professor said trying to find a place to grab on the rounded surface.

"I'd say that's our only chance."

Pulling everyone over, Hudson explained the situation. Once in place he added, "Just don't pull on the legs. They aren't meant to take any extra strain."

The five travelers pulled and pushed with all their might. After several tense moments, the machine broke from its position and they were eventually able to move the pearlescent orb a few feet away from the rock.

Hudson dropped back to the ground and worked his way under the vehicle. After he had disappeared except for his feet, he yelled out, "Hey what's that sound?"

"What sound?" Todd answered quickly.

Sticking his ear to the ground, he placed his hand on the rock below the machine for a moment.

"I hear and feel vibrations. What is it?" Moving another foot, he placed his hand on one of the struts of the sphere, "The machine is vibrating. Like a dull earthquake or something."

Scooting himself out from under the device, with the sapphire head in his hand, he wondered aloud, "Something's not right."

Everyone looked around and Todd went for his horse.

Aurius tried to run to the top of one of the mounds surrounding the vehicle so he could see what everyone now felt. Before he could make it to the edge, Dritus and Cyprianus rode up on horseback.

With his sword pulled, Dritus commanded, "Do not move another foot, Prophet. That goes for you also, *soldier*," he said sarcastically.

Todd dropped the reigns of his horse and walked back next to Aaliyah. John did the same with Keren.

With Cyprianus looking on, Dritus took control of the situation. "Well, it looks like everyone is here in one big happy group." Looking at Hudson's hand he exclaimed, "There is the evidence that puts you at the temple."

Feeling the vibrations getting stronger, Todd asked, "What do you want?"

With a smile, "I want you and your people dead." The vehicle finally caught his attention, "What is that?"

John jumped into the conversation, "It would take too long to explain."

Dritus shot back, "You prophet will be the first to die, and I will take this throne in the name of the King."

"That is no throne," John answered wryly, suddenly amused at the lack of knowledge in this place.

"You know that right now it is five to two, and we are equally matched in weaponry," Todd said calmly.

"You were lucky in Jerusalem. You will not be so lucky now."

Cyprianus looked on quietly.

"What you do not know is that there are 100 military riders just a half of a mile out surrounding this spot and closing in. Regiments worth of men will also be here within the hour," he announced, pointing in a circle.

The secondary commander let the information sink in a moment before continuing - watching each of the travelers look at one another.

"There is no overpowering me. There is no escaping, and finally there is no living beyond this day."

The General continued to allow Dritus to speak.

"My General," Dritus pointed to Cyprianus, "has had enough of you," he finished pointing to John. "And I have had enough of the rest of you. We will execute each of you right here and right now."

Hudson looked to Todd, "What is he saying?"

"Buddy, it looks like there isn't anything left for us to do. We are surrounded in all directions and he plans on just killing us here and now."

The women, for their part, each closed their eyes in prayer to the God of heaven and gripped the arms of the men they loved.

"Dritus, give me a few moments with these people."

Dritus glared at Cyprianus in shock at his breach of protocol, "Sir, they are our prisoners."

"I understand that," he spoke softly, "and they will pay for their crimes. Give me a few minutes. Go back and have the men prepare for our arrival." When Dritus did not move he barked, "You heard my orders!"

Dritus blinked twice before turning his horse to the west and galloping to meet his men.

The General dismounted from his horse. "Why did you go to Jerusalem? I thought you would be heading east, and I sent every troop west. I gave you time to get away."

Todd walked forward, "Our vehicle needed some supplies."

"You are not from this place, are you?" he asked pointing to the ground.

"No sir, we are not."

"Are you some type of gods from the heavens?" Cyprianus asked trying to make sense of the vehicle before him.

Answering him, John took over, "No Cyprianus, we are very much like you. And if you let us go, you will never see us again."

Walking forward, he spoke with his eyes to the ground, "I cannot do that. If I let you go, I will be executed for my indiscretion and dereliction of duties." Looking John in the eyes he made himself clear, "I have a wife and child and will not put them through that."

Glancing toward Todd, he added, "You know, I almost believed in your God. I was very close," putting his fingers together, "But I prayed your God would protect you and he has not. If he had, then I would not be taking you to your death."

The group watched as Hudson guessed what was being said.

"I truly wanted to believe in something beyond this," he gestured to the rocks around him before dropping his arm. "But your God is no different than those my people worship. Large temples with no power behind them."

"How do you know?" Todd interjected. "We are not dead yet. Our God tends to move at the very last minute, often to test our faith."

"Well, we need to go," he dismissed the conversation, walking back toward his horse. "Dritus is chomping at the bit, and if I do not bring you out very quickly he will come in with a regiment of soldiers."

"Hudson, we need to go," Todd whispered.

"What do you mean? I have no intention of going with him. I would rather die fighting than die at their hand."

With a calm voice he insisted, "Hudson, we need to go. I don't know why, but this is not about us anymore."

Thinking again he said, "I can jump in really quickly and run through a test cycle. It will level the area and give us time."

Seeing Cyprianus mounting his horse, and feeling a total peace Todd reaffirmed, "Hudson, this is not about us." Aaliyah looked on at her fiancé with peace and smiled.

"We need to follow Cyprianus."

John and Keren looked at each other and John said, "Hudson, Todd's right. I have a total peace about leaving with the General." Hugging his lady at his side, "We will die for our God if that is what he chooses."

The General turned his horse and headed toward the edge of a mound, "Are you coming?" He looked back at the group.

Hudson had fought and fought for the last week. He had struggled and clawed from one skirmish to the next barely making it, but suddenly he knew this situation would not end in a fight. At some point, man has done everything possible and all he can do is rely on his God and the plans he has.

Looking at the four friends standing around him, he knew that they were right and for some reason, God would be glorified in their sacrifice. The fear suddenly left him and he dropped the sapphire head on the dirt.

Straightening his garments he said with a smile, "Friends, it has been an honor."

Todd walked up and hugged the man he had met just over a week earlier. Today, it felt like they had been brothers for a lifetime. "It's been an honor and a privilege."

Aaliyah walked over and tugged the agent down by the neck. "Tank yuu."

Hudson smiled, a tear running down his check.

John walked over, "Hudson, I'm so sorry for what I've put you and Todd through. But you know, God has blessed me immensely in spite of it."

"John, I don't want to go to my death with anger in my heart. I forgive you for this and I'm glad Christ has called you to follow him."

The men hugged and Keren looked on.

Watching the scene, Aaliyah walked over to Keren and hugged her. Knowing she couldn't explain the connection they had, she just cried in her arms. The tears weren't because of their short future but because of her love for her mother and how blessed she felt to have seen her again. Now that her mother truly had peace and joy in her heart, even if all she had was just a few minutes left before the Romans took their lives, she knew Keren would leave this world with love and peace instead of fear and pain. To Aaliyah, it was all worth it. The women cried and comforted each other with smiles of joy.

"Well, are we ready to meet the Romans?" Hudson asked with a smile.

Todd answered, "You know, I would have thought of something better than that."

"What are you talking about?" the agent asked.

"You could have modified Nathan Hale's great quote and said something like, 'I regret that I only have one life to give for my God' or something like that."

"I'm not going to copy somebody else for my last great line," Hudson laughed. "Anyway, I thought that was pretty good."

The group started following Cyprianus' horse.

Todd thought for a second as he held Aaliyah, "I think we need a good Shakespeare quote."

"How about this," Hudson supplied, "'Cowards die many times before their deaths; the valiant never taste of death but once.'"

"Wow, now that really speaks."

Aurius added to the banter, "I believe that is from Julius Caesar."

"Very good, Senator," Hudson smiled.

"I wish I had more time, there are really a lot of good quotes from that play," Todd added.

The five walked together in a line behind Cyprianus' horse. But as they got closer to the edge of the mound, the banter stopped, and they garnered the courage to continue their trek and not run away. Knowing they were doing the right thing did not make the journey simple. It just gave it a purpose. If their God wanted them to die, they would do it and hope that he would receive glory in their sacrifice.

Rounding the hillside they were able to see the countryside before them. The sun had dropped and the horizon reflected a shimmering purple feathered with white clouds lined with gold.

The prisoners naturally took in a deep breath at the beauty before them. As they looked below the sky and focused on the valley they saw soldiers in every direction. Scanning the countryside, they saw more than a hundred men in military garb prepared for war.

Finally seeing Cyprianus' assessment was right and that there would be no escape, the travelers felt sick to their stomachs. Yet their resolve did not change.

Todd spoke without taking his eyes from the scene before him, "I pray God has a ram in the thicket somewhere. But even if he doesn't, it's all worth it." He gave Aaliyah one more hug as she looked up and assured him with her eyes.

Leading the group from the mound toward the valley, Hudson spoke quietly, "Sara, I'm so sorry. I never meant for you to be hurt. Please forgive me."

The travelers followed Cyprianus without complaint toward the sea of men before them.

They followed Cyprianus in silence for a quarter of a mile, each knew they were doing God's work. Even if he allowed them to go to their deaths, the pain would be short and the victory long.

Continuing their trek, they were guided toward a group of archers surrounding Dritus on horseback. A knot formed in Hudson's stomach as he knew they were heading for an old-fashioned firing squad.

Todd knew the General was grieved by the undertaking he had ahead. His shoulders drooped and he stared at the ground. A Roman soldier generally held some pride in displaying the prisoners he had apprehended. Cyprianus showed no arrogance. He rode his horse slowly, as if trying to extend the inevitable. Undeterred in his hope, the professor knew God was working on the man's heart and smiled.

Once they arrived at the long line of soldiers, Cyprianus stopped his horse, dismounted, and walked to Dritus. "What do you have planned?"

"Sir, we are to execute the prisoners," he said with pride. It was obvious from his demeanor that he had proudly been through this many times before.

Looking over the archers, he mentally squirmed. He saw Dritus' excitement, and wondered.

"Dritus, is this something that must be done now? It is getting late. We might want to perform this task in the morning."

Dismounting, he approached his General and spoke with as much respect as he could muster, "Cyprianus, what is wrong with you?"

Raising his eyes to the younger man's he cocked his head, knowing what the man's next words would be.

"This man Aurius has embarrassed you as long as he has been in the King's court. Am I not right?"

"Yes Dritus, you are right," he answered wearily.

"Did he not send us out into the desert? Did you not leave him for dead?"

"I did."

Dritus jabbed a finger in Aurius direction, "If he gets out of here, he will tell the King what you did, and you will be on the pointy end of those arrows."

Cyprianus just listened with half-lidded eyes.

"You caught that prisoner and then she escaped. That is a punishable offense on your part just by itself."

The General looked at Aaliyah.

"Those two men pretended to be Roman soldiers. That is a death sentence on its own."

"Yes, you are right."

Gesturing to Keren, "I am not sure why one of the King's concubines is here, but because of her affection for Aurius, and her connection to him she should receive the same fate."

Nodding, the General agreed.

Walking up to Todd and Hudson who stood in the center of the line of prisoners, the commander pulled his sword and pointed it at them, "And because of what they did to me in Jerusalem, I would personally like to make their death slow and painful." He put the blade to Hudson's throat. The muscles in his neck bulged as the effort to keep from killing the fake soldier strained his patience.

Lowering his blade with great control he scowled at the agent, "You think you are strong, do you not? Would you like an opportunity to go against me?"

Todd jumped into the conversation that was not meant to be interrupted, "I do not think he understands you."

Dritus changed his focus, "Who was speaking to you?" he growled.

With a smile he shrugged, "I am just trying to make you look a little better in front of your men. My friend here does not speak Greek, or Latin, or Hebrew…"

"What are you saying to him?" Hudson asked.

"I'm just telling him that you don't know what he's saying. Our friend here is trying to look tough, and I want to help him with the façade."

"Well, you're right about that. I'd guess he said something about me fighting him or dropping the armor and going mano-a-mano. Huh? Or something like that. But, no, I really didn't know what he said."

Todd patted his back matter-of-factly, "You know you are getting really good at interpreting body language. You were just about right on."

"If we were to ever come back here again, I think I might have these people figured out."

Dritus drew his sword back and began to thrust it into Todd's personal space when Cyprianus yelled, "No, Dritus! We will do this as a military execution and no other way."

The younger man looked over at them, "You know these people should be killed, and it is your duty to ensure it happens," he stalked back to his men.

Having a soldier take his horse, Cyprianus sauntered over to the prisoners and spoke quietly. "I have no choice in this. If I do not execute you, Dritus will relieve me from duty and will then make a sport of killing you one by one. The most humane thing I can do is to make this as quick and painless as possible."

Taking a deep breath, he sighed, "I do not believe you to be enemies of the state and you have enlightened me to new ideas I have never thought of before. I wish something would have happened to prove to me your God is truly the God of the universe. I would have willingly offered my life to him. But we are here, and I am forced to do something I do not want to do."

Dritus looked on from the line of five archers prepared to fulfill their duty. He knew something was not right about the civil conversation, but waited in respect for his General to finish.

Todd looked at Cyprianus, "We know you have a duty and are prepared for the fate the Lord has for us."

"You still speak of the Lord," the General said amazed. "You are here about to be executed and you speak of the Lord."

"Yes, General, if our Lord chooses to release us, he will do it – and nothing can stop him. But if he does not, then we will spend eternity with him starting today. Either way, we are well taken care of."

Aurius spoke up, "General, I am very sorry for the difficulty I have caused you and the commands you have had to follow on my account. I was very wrong and the Lord my God has made me aware of it." He dropped his eyes, "Please forgive me."

Face full of confusion, he backed up a step, "I just do not understand you people. There is no way out of this, and yet you seem so at peace."

Aaliyah spoke up, "General, thank you for your kindness to me upon my capture. I have prayed for you to find peace in God."

Standing in front of the line of prisoners, "I have a duty to perform. I pray your God will save you from it." After looking at each person in the face, he turned and walked back to Dritus.

"Commander, the duty is yours."

"Yes, General," he said with a smile. "Archers to the ready."

The soldiers standing at attention as far as their eyes could see watched as the archers took their mark.

With the sky turning from purple to black and the stars beginning to shine in the heavens, the travelers looked one last time at each other and smiled. They knew they had done their best and that their God was pleased with their work. Each person stood tall and closed their eyes in peace.

"Archers draw," Dritus commanded.

The men pulled arrows from their quivers and, after placing them in position, drew the bow back to full length.

"Archers aim," the men locked in their sites and waited for the command.

"Archers...archers," Dritus' voice broke.

Standing and waiting to meet their God, the five began to hear movement among the soldiers.

"Archers...uh," Dritus couldn't finish the sentence.

The mumbling became stronger and the prisoners could hear fear in the soldiers' voices. The babbling became louder and Hudson could hear weapons dropping to the ground.

"Hold your positions, men," Dritus yelled.

With his eyes still closed, the agent mumbled to Todd, "What's going on? I wish they would get on with it."

Obvious fear was in Dritus voice, "Men, hold your positions. Do not be afraid!"

Todd's eyes popped open at the odd command.

Blazing white assaulted his vision. He squinted through the tremendous light and called to the others, "Everyone, open your eyes!"

The prisoners fell to their knees.

"What's happening?" Hudson yelled seeing hills full of chariots ablaze with what appeared to be white fire lighting but not consuming the beings inside it.

Looking more closely they realize the same beings they had seen the previous night were now blazing with glory and surrounding the entire Roman army.

Seeing the brilliance of their light and the sheer strength of their presence, the prisoners felt no fear. Awe consumed them as they began to laugh with joy and relief.

The soldiers who hadn't run were cowering in fear on the ground. Even the great commander Dritus was on his knees with his hands up in a subservient position.

The professor laughed out loud, "It's just like 2 Kings chapter six, where Elisha was protected by an army of angels. Praise God, he has delivered us from the Romans!"

The rest of the travelers began holding one another, praying and praising God their Savior.

Cyprianus stood in awe of the site.

With the travelers on their knees facing west, they were not able to see the Commander of the Angels standing directly behind them. But once he began to speak they turned to an authority who took orders from God alone.

The presence said one word, "Leave." As he did, they looked back. They felt the ground thunder and saw the sky glow. The soldiers including Dritus ran off in all directions or mounted a horse to exit as quickly as possible. Only one of the opposing forces was left.

Cyprianus fell to his knees and began praying. With his face to the ground spilling tears of joy he cried over and over again, "Holy, holy, is the Lord God Almighty."

The travelers prayed and sang. They laughed and hugged, knowing their God had miraculously protected and defended them when he had no responsibility to do so. Each of their hearts was humbled and overjoyed at the God who saves.

After several minutes, the last of the Roman army had fled over the hills out of sight. The leader of the armies of heaven looked down upon the travelers.

"Your work here is done." This time the ground did not shake and the words were kind and soft. "It is time for you to leave."

At the completion of his sentence, he lifted his face and scanned the hills around them. The glowing riders, horses and chariots, aligned themselves to take a position facing the leader. Armor glowing, he pulled his sword from its sheath and pointed it heavenward. After looking up to the sky, he smiled at them once. Then, in the twinkling of an eye, he soared toward the stars, the army close behind him.

The disappearance only took a moment. And the travelers were left in a small vacuum, huddled together on the ground.

Just as quickly as they were gone, the sky turned clear and the stars shined with brilliance as they had never seen. Each went back to their knees and prayed again, thanking God for his love of them and sacrifice of his Son on their behalf.

It was several minutes before Todd and Hudson walked over to Cyprianus.

"Now do you believe and worship the God of heaven?" Todd asked with a smile.

Standing shakily from the ground he nodded, "Oh yes, my friend, I believe in the God of my wife, and I will follow him forever." He embraced them then, a new man. "Thank you so much for changing my life."

"We did not do it, Cyprianus. God chose to show himself to you. Thank God."

"Oh believe me, I will, and for the rest of my life," he smiled.

The three other travelers walked up to Cyprianus and hugged him.

The celebration lasted a while when Cyprianus finally spoke, "Let me take each of you back to my home. My wife would love to meet you, and you can tell her about Jesus."

Aaliyah smiled, "My friend, you can tell her yourself. But only tell her that the Messiah has been born in Bethlehem. Listen to her, and learn of God. Your changed life will be enough proof of what has happened here tonight."

"What will come of this?" Aurius asked. "How will the army explain this?"

With a smile, "I imagine it will be written off as an army that was very tired and began seeing things. There will be no way to explain it, so we will not try."

Todd asked, "What will come of Dritus?"

"I imagine he has already made up a story of how he executed his prisoners after his men ran off. He will somehow get a promotion from all of this."

Hudson had been listening to Todd bringing him up on the conversation when he asked his friend to relay a question, "Ask the General what will come of him and his command."

Cyprianus looked down at the ground and thought for a second. Seeing that the travelers were waiting for his answer he grinned, "The last place I want to be now is in the military. But I can think of no better position to tell God's story than in a place so against him. I will continue my work, just with Christ in my heart. Maybe I can become a better leader of men by following the God who protects like this."

"Cyprianus, you are a good man and will be a great compassionate leader," Aurius added.

"I know God has a plan for you right where you are. Honor him now in all things, and he will direct your steps," Todd encouraged him.

Finding his horse, the changed man mounted it, "Well friends, I would ask you where you are going, but I have a feeling I would not understand the answer. So I will just say - thank you." With his hand over his heart, "I mean it from my soul. Thank you."

The group bowed their heads out of respect.

"I will pray for you." Turning his horse toward the west, and looking over his shoulder, he shouted, "I will pray for you, please pray for me." The horse started down the mountain as he yelled back, "Goodbye my friends and farewell."

The group watched him ride off before they turned and marched back up the mountain.

"You think he's going to be alright?" Todd asked with concern over Cyprianus' military position and work with the King clouding his features.

"I don't think God would offer him the realm of influence he has to not allow him to use it," Hudson countered with his arm on his friend's shoulder.

When they arrived back at the sphere, the agent turned on the perimeter lighting. Keren jumped back with a shock, but Aurius was able to calm her as she viewed technology that would not be invented for another 1900 years.

Hudson found the sapphire head he had dropped earlier and made his way to the ground. Crawling under the vehicle, he was able to quickly drop the lump of rock into the canister designed to heat the rare crystalline structure. After ensuring everything else looked good underneath, he crawled out from the belly of the vehicle and made his way to the cockpit.

After looking over the console and scanning through several submenus, he started the process to re-form the lens.

"Everyone, get back," he waved his arm as he spoke.

Instantly, the belly of the vehicle began to glow red as the laser started the re-magnification process.

Keren hugged in close to Aurius as he looked on.

After several minutes and a few blinks and beeps of the console, Hudson looked up, "It looks like it worked," he smiled at Todd.

The professor nearly clapped, "So we aren't going to die in the first century? Is that what you're telling me?" He hugged Aaliyah. "I may get to do some more teaching and drive my beautiful red Dodge Charger again?"

"Remember, we left that thing at the airport. It's probably been impounded by now and sold to help pay for the debt on this project," Hudson laughed.

"You know what, they can have it." His eyes found his fiancé, "I have this beautiful woman here."

Giving one last look over the console, Hudson lowered himself back to the ground. "It's going to be real tight. Almost clown car tight, but I think we can make it for the few minutes it will take to get us back to the 21st century."

As Hudson said the last few words, John and Keren walked forward. "Hudson, we can't go."

"What do you mean?" Todd and Hudson said at the same time.

John looked away for a second.

"Hudson I can't go back. All I have there is jail time, but here I have a life and can help to spread the message of Christ. Keren doesn't need to go to the 21st century. The last thing they need is another 1st century person running around."

Hudson stood there looking at him stone-faced.

John placed his hand on the agent's shoulder, "I am a changed man. My days of vengeance and self-focus are over. I have a wife as soon as we get married and a child on the way. I will do well by them and by these people," gesturing toward Jerusalem.

Todd walked over, "Hudson, let's let him go. He's right. Once we get back, the President will have him, and he will never get out. I think he's a different man."

The agent scanned over John and Keren. He had come through time to apprehend a man bent on vengeance. He had chased him for days though Israel. How could he just let him go?

First, he smiled at Todd; then he looked back at John, "Okay John, you can stay. We have enough mess with Aaliyah now being a 21st century citizen. I guess it can't be any worse to have you become a 1st century one. Maybe you two switching positions will make the equation work out right." He shook the man's hand.

Todd relayed what was happening to Aaliyah, and tears rolled up in her eyes. She immediately ran over and cried on Keren's shoulder. Only Todd and Hudson knew the true reason for her emotion. They knew that she had lost her mother as a child. To find her again and offer her a new life through Christ had been a dream come true. To have her taken away again seemed too much for the young woman who had already been through so much.

Todd grieved for her as the two women grabbed and held onto each other tightly.

Aaliyah put her hands through her mother's hair, "Keren, I am very proud of you and love you. You need to know that I will always pray for you, and that you will always be a part of me." Tears ran down her cheeks, "You need to know how strong you are and how much worth you have. Please do not ever forget that you are loved by me, John, and most importantly our Lord God in heaven.

No matter what comes, you will be fine if you keep your eyes on Him. Do you understand?"

Keren answered, "Yes, my friend, I understand."

Putting her face to Keren's, she just held her. Eventually she pulled away and said, "Keren, I love you dearly." Feeling the bump of her belly, she laughed, "And please take care of this child."

The woman hugged her one last time, "I will."

At that, John walked with Keren back to two of the horses. After putting his love on one, he mounted the other. Holding Keren's reigns, he pulled the horse alongside his own.

With the two looking back at Hudson, Todd and Aaliyah, John smiled, "Thank you men for bringing my life into focus. Without you and your witness, I would have been lost. Thank you and good luck with what you find in the future."

Todd and Hudson glanced at each other, not sure of what his last words meant.

The two riders rode away to the backdrop of a million stars. They would travel on to a destination now clear for their own making as they followed the call of God and surrendered to his will.

Once they disappeared from view, Aaliyah began speaking a mile a minute.

"What is it, Aaliyah?" Todd asked.

She walked around with her eyes wide open.

"Are you alright?" the professor asked.

With the biggest smile she could muster, "Everything works out perfectly."

"What do you mean?"

"I have a whole life worth of memories filling my mind," she explained. Continuing to chatter about going here and there with her father and mother and playing this or that with her younger siblings, she rejoiced. "I see my childhood and the various places we lived. I have a little brother and another sister. Oh God, thank you," she cried and praised him again and again as she continued to share her story.

Todd tried his best to relay to Hudson everything she was saying.

"We traveled to Egypt. We lived in the East. We spent time in Jerusalem. My father, I mean John, was a designer and was sought for his wealth of new ideas all over the region."

"You have new memories?" Todd asked amazed.

"I have the old memories, but also a whole new set. It is like a new life was placed on top of the old one." Stopping her movement, "I have so much joy. My mother loved me and so did my father. I had a great childhood."

"I guess once the timeline changed, everything new that happened was added to her history, and therefore she has two childhoods," Hudson said trying to make sense of what had occurred.

Hugging Todd, "Thank you for my childhood," she said with a smile.

"It was not me. If anyone helped to make this happen it would be Hudson."

She whirled around and kissed the large man on the cheek.

"What was that for?" he said blushing.

"She is thanking you for changing her past," Todd answered.

He laughed, "It wasn't me. God had all of this worked out from the beginning. You ready to go? I have a wife and kids I'd like to get back to."

Aaliyah nodded and stepped close to the machine for the third ride of her life.

"It looks like we are ready to go, Hudson."

After taking his spot, Todd helped Aaliyah into her position on his lap. Then cinching the buckle around them both, Hudson took his spot and started working the console.

"Where are we going to put this thing down this time?" Todd asked with some concern for arriving in the Oval Office again.

"Yeah, I'm looking through that. It seems the main facility coordinates are not here. Cox Manufacturing, our dummy corporation, isn't listed as a possibility."

"Why would that be?" Todd queried.

"I don't know." Trying to think through the situation he checked other sites. "Obviously, they have removed the Oval Office."

"Well, that would make sense."

Hudson continued to look, "Many of the possibilities and all of the secondary return sites have disappeared from the list." Looking over at his friend, "I don't know where to go. We have to know exactly where to land or we might end up in a mountain somewhere or a mall."

From this console, it's as if this vehicle never existed."

"What are you going to do?"

"There is one spot that I memorized as a worse-case scenario." Beginning to manually input the coordinates including elevation, he sat back. "I know where this will take us now. Once we get back, we can then figure out what to do with the vehicle."

"Okay, I trust you, buddy," the professor affirmed.

He ensured the return dates, coordinates, and elevations were all correct, and then sat back.

"Are you ready?"

Todd and Aaliyah sat back and nodded.

Pulling the other sapphire head from his satchel, "Hudson, what should I do with this?"

With a laugh, "Put it on your mantle. It'll be a great conversation piece."

The men smiled and sat back.

Hudson pushed the area of the console to lower the top half of the sphere. Once it was in place he started the countdown sequence.

Instantly the internal lights kicked off and the dash lights began glowing. Everyone within the machine could feel it start to vibrate and could smell the now familiar odor of ozone.

With just a few seconds left, Hudson said a quiet prayer as the machine began to hum and vibrate. "Lord, please, take us home."

Agreeing, Todd said, "Amen."

With the sound becoming deafening they saw the last few seconds tick down on the console until they closed their eyes and felt a tingle in their bodies as electricity began to cover the sphere.

When they thought they could take the sensation no longer, it ended and the vehicle disappeared into the future. The three weary travelers were on their way home, and the countryside, that just seconds earlier was awash with light from the explosion of the temporal vehicle, returned to darkness as if none of the preceding days had ever occurred.

After the two-minute tumultuous ride, the sphere finally came to rest. The riders inhaled at last and blinked a few times, checking themselves. As the cabin lights popped on and the console flashed showing the correct time and day, Hudson pushed the button raising the canopy.

Steam entered the cabin. "Is everyone alright?"

Looking Aaliyah over, Todd answered him, "I think so."

Nothing but trees engulfed the sphere and a small rough-hewn building off to the left could be seen.

"Where are we?"

"We are at my cabin."

Stretching his long frame over the side and lowering himself to the ground Hudson stretched out his hand to help the young woman from the vehicle. After she was safely on the ground, he assisted his friend.

"Why are we at your cabin? And where is your cabin?" he asked.

Walking toward a 1980's Ford Bronco he stopped. A rough cedar-sided building stood to his left, "I couldn't find any place that was safe to land the sphere. I knew nothing would be around my cabin, so here we are," he smiled, gesturing around.

"Well, where is here?" The professor asked feeling the cold night air and hoping they weren't in Canada somewhere. He put his arms around Aaliyah who was still dressed in the thin cotton.

"Here is Virginia. We are about an hour outside of Washington."

The professor breathed a sigh of relief.

Hudson found the keys hidden under a rock near the woods and raised the hood. Once he disconnected the battery charger, he lowered the hood, opened the door and started the vehicle.

"Voila," he said with a smile as the exhaust pipes rumbled beneath him. "Come on everyone. I'm ready to get home. You can stay with Sara and me until things get settled. She'll love you guys as much as I do. Hop in."

"We're ready," Todd said after buckling Aaliyah.

Leaving the sphere in the open area next to the cabin, the Bronco rumbled down the rocky dirt road. They turned occasionally from street to street until the off-road vehicle found the main thoroughfare that would connect to the highway home.

Each person sat in silence looking out the window. Todd held Aaliyah and Hudson thought of his family as the machine drove a bit faster than the speed limit allowed.

Even though the trip took less than an hour it felt like a millennia to Hudson as he remembered how good it would be to be home and back to normal. The events of the last week had changed each of their lives forever. Just like any tapestry, it is the individual threads, though not beautiful on their own, which help to form a thing of splendor. The Lord had used the difficult, miraculous, and life-threatening events to help solidify their walk in him.

Each of them had seen God provide and protect. They had witnessed his love for mankind, his miracles at work, and the way he defends his own – all in a spectacular show of glory. None of them could ever walk with their Lord and Savior the same way again.

It would take time for them to really think through what they had experienced, but each knew they were better for it. Although at the moment, they were thinking of their loved ones and a nice warm bath.

The three travelers had journeyed through time and had come out no worse for the ware. Each smiled knowing the experience was behind them and the world was unchanged, as the large vehicle took them back to uneventful lives.

EPILOGUE

TUESDAY, LATE EVENING, APRIL 21

A knock sounded on the door to the personal residence. President Langley, not a man who liked to be bothered during his family time put on his robe and walked to the large mahogany door carved with ornate figures of America's past.

Allowing entrance into the residence, the President found one of his cabinet secretaries standing in the opening. "This had better be important for you to come this late."

"Yes sir," the man in his thirties demurred. Even though he held a generic cabinet position, his real responsibilities – and the reason he was paid so well under the table - were in the secret project known only to a few people. He offered the leader of the free world a piece of paper, "Read this, sir."

The President perused the document then lowered it to his side, "So they made it back?" he asked, looking the man in the eyes.

"Yes sir, they did."

"Where is it?" he asked flatly.

"Somewhere in the Virginia countryside, about an hour and a half from here."

"Well it looks like Hughes failed."

"I would say so," he answered without emotion.

Folding the paper and placing it in the pocket on his robe, the man smiled. "I believe we must take things into our own hands."

The popping and cracking of a fire in the hearth behind the President drew his attention for a moment.

"What would you have me do?"

"Initiate the Jefferson Protocol. We will have our desired end if the entire world has to come down around us." Thinking a second, he continued, "And it just might."

With a slight grin he answered, "Yes, sir."

The door closed out the warmth of the fire as the man in the dark suit walked the long hallway toward the exit of the White House.